PASSION'S FLAME

Amanda could have sworn it was the hand of fate that made her presence known to Tony where he stood by the garden's gate. Whatever it was, he came alive and smiled with pleasure, knowing she was there in the darkness. He rushed through, like an eager youth keeping his first tryst with his ladylove.

Words were not needed as he came to stand before her. It was as spontaneous and natural as breathing that they should find each other. And as Tony's muscled arms encased Amanda's petite body, she pressed close to him, feeling the warmth of his broad chest against her.

"Oh, Amanda . . ." he murmured softly. Then—like a man thirsting for water—he lowered his head to taste the pure sweetness of her lips. . . .

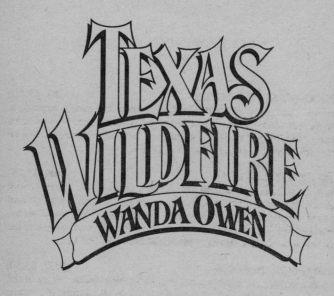

TEXAS WILDFIRE
WANDA OWEN

ZEBRA BOOKS
KENSINGTON PUBLISHING CORP.

ZEBRA BOOKS

are published by

KENSINGTON PUBLISHING CORP.
475 Park Avenue South
New York, N.Y. 10016

First printing: MARCH 1984

Printed in the United States of America

For my two darling daughters, Cherie and Sheila.

And always, my books are for Bob, my husband, and Leslie, my editor and friend.

I

A SUMMER MADNESS

ONE

Such a serene contentment washed over Jenny Kane as she sat in her garden courtyard. The spray from the fountain had a cooling effect on this hot summer day. With her head resting on the back of the wicker settee, she watched the varied lace patterns of the spraying water reflected against the background of the flourishing greenery and many blooming flowers. The aroma was divine.

This particular corner of her walled courtyard was her haven, her special place to relax. It was so quiet and peaceful here. Since it was a long time until the dinner hour, she cared not if she took a nap.

As she closed her eyes to sleep she couldn't remember being so completely happy as she was this day. It was so wonderful having Amanda home again. It made her realize just how much she'd missed her golden-haired daughter now that all her family was together within the walls of the sprawling old hacienda.

Suddenly, she heard her husband's voice roaring like thunder in the summer skies. "You come back here this minute, young lady!" he shouted in a rage.

"No! I won't hear another word on that subject,

Papa!" This was her daughter exploding with fury. Jenny moved to the doors to see Mark Kane's imposing figure standing in the doorway of his study and Amanda rushing down the highly polished hall defying her father's command she come back.

Amanda's head was held high and her gold curls tossed as she pranced angrily through the carved oak door giving it a furious slam as she left, and Mark looked like a thundercloud watching her go. Dear Lord, she tried to warn him about this very thing, Jenny mused. She knew instantly what he'd tried to discuss with her. She could not suppress a smile as she watched the two people so dear to her heart. Mark had to realize Amanda had a spitfire temper just like his, and that she was as stubborn and determined as he was.

The chubby Mexican housekeeper, Consuela, was also watching with amusement. Like Jenny, she secretly admired the little señorita's spirit. Señor Kane would not control her as he did the rest of the Circle K Ranch with his iron-fisted rules. Never! Consuela should know, for she and her husband, Juan, had been at the ranch before Amanda's birth or that of her brother, Jeff. Amanda had always been special to the Mexican couple and Juan had taught her to play the guitar like he had his own daughter, Chita. Consuela had taught her to dance.

Kane's twenty-year-old son was nothing like his bold, spunky sister, and Consuela suspected this galled Señor Kane. Even now standing there observing him with all that anger on his face, she could see admiration brighten his blue eyes.

Jenny, like Consuela, stood watching but saying

10

nothing to Mark. She let him stride angrily back into his study without uttering a word. Just hearing Amanda's remarks Jenny knew what her husband and David Lawson hoped for would not come to pass. Mark might as well forget it!

It had been tedious enough for her lovely daughter to adjust to the slower-paced, and, for her, inactive life around the ranch after living two years with Jenny's vivacious sister Lisa. The constant whirl of soirées and grand balls had impressed Amanda. While she felt a little sad about it, Jenny realized that Amanda would probably never be content at the Circle K again now that she'd tasted a different life in the city of New Orleans.

New Orleans had been Jenny's home and she had gladly left all the gaiety and sparkle of the city behind to be Mark's wife. Amanda had not that passion for this vast Texas land, or for a man, as yet.

Jenny mused that it had been Mark's decision to send her to New Orleans in the first place. That had merely been a step to remove Amanda from the clutches and attentions of the handsome son of Bianca Alvarado, Mario. Amanda, at fifteen, was a beautiful, blossoming figure of young womanhood. Mark had observed the two meeting while out riding on the range and that was enough to persuade him to send her away. Only a month ago, the same motives had prompted him to bring her back to the ranch after one of Lisa's letters had sent him into a fury at the dinner table. Boasting of Amanda's many conquests of young aristocratic French Creole gentlemen in their social circle, Lisa wrote with pride and delight of her niece. Mark exploded, "I'll not have one of those useless

11

French dandies for a son-in-law!" Before Jenny knew what was going on Jeff was on his way to New Orleans to escort his sister home.

This soft-spoken little lady with her gentle ways who adored her husband with all her heart saw trouble and torment ahead if he persisted in reining their free-spirited daughter too tight. It would never, never work!

Amanda was thinking the same thoughts as she prepared her horse, Prince, to go for a ride. The golden palomino seemed to sense his young mistress's mood and gave her a whinney, shaking his head up and down impatiently.

Amanda patted his lighter-colored mane lovingly and murmured, "You know, don't you Prince? You're as anxious as I am to be gone from here, aren't you?"

With the gear in place, Amanda hoisted herself up on the magnificent beast and gave him the nudge to go. And go they did, as wild as the wind. Her petite body seemed fused to the palomino as they swiftly galloped down the drive passing under the massive archway bearing the symbol of her father's brand, a circle with the letter K inside it.

Dressed in tight-fitting pants that molded every curve of her body and a sheer batiste blouse clinging temptingly to her full, rounded breasts as the breeze whipped against her, she looked glorious, and the sight of her and her golden hair blowing loose and free would have tempted the devil himself.

Although the man perched up on the high slope of ground astride his black stallion had merely paused at that spot to get his bearings of the countryside, he lingered to watch and admire the magnificent vision. She was the most beautiful sight he'd ever seen, and Tony Branigan vowed to find out who she was. He was equally impressed by the fine palomino she rode. The bright summer sun beaming down on her hair made it look like spun gold, and Tony thought she and the horse made a magnificent pair. He watched until they were out of sight and the grove of trees engulfed them, swallowing them up.

No longer restrained, Amanda rode down the slope into the valley feeling reckless and carefree, having no inkling that two pair of eyes were admiring her from different points in the rolling countryside. Both belonged to black-haired young men in their twenties with appreciating eye for beautiful women.

It was an unexpected delight for Mario Alvarado when he spied Amanda riding over in the distance as he returned from the range to talk to his foreman to check out how many of their herd had been taken the night before by the night raiders. He had been pleased to hear that night that the Rancho Rio had been spared. His hot-blooded Latin nature was as enflamed as it had been two years ago just seeing Amanda ride like some wild little creature. He would have her regardless of what Mark Kane said, he promised himself. His black eyes gleamed as he watched her go in the direction of the bend of the river. He knew her destination was that special cove she enjoyed swimming in. With a devilish smile on his handsome face he spurred his horse to pursue her.

Tony Branigan watched her, too. She was a vision of glorious beauty and excitement. It seemed the two golden beauties—she and her horse—were fused to-

13

gether. When he could see her no more he urged his black stallion, Picaro, to move on. Then he saw the other rider and halted up. The man was in hot pursuit of the girl and raw impulse urged Tony to follow. He reined Picaro around.

Mario had been right about her destination. As she arrived at the secluded spot she knew nothing of the commotion she'd ignited. By now, she was in a capricious mood and the argument with her father was forgotten completely. Shedding her clothing rapidly she plunged into the cool water of the river. It felt divine against her naked body. This was her own private paradise and she'd never heeded her father's demand that she not swim here just because Alvarado property lay across the river at this spot.

A million times she'd turned a deaf ear to his admonishing her. "You can't trust a damn Mex," he'd barked. She didn't share his opinion now and never had. A look of mischief played on her face at that minute thinking how hogtied he would be if she did marry Mario Alvarado. Mumbling to herself, she giggled, "Serve him right if I did!" Why, to be married to Derek Lawson would be almost like being married to her brother, Jeff!

She, like everyone in Gonzales County, knew her father's intense hate of Mexicans. Juan and Consuela Santos were the exceptions. She knew that his hatred stemmed from Mexican bandits having killed his parents right there on the Circle K.

Mario had watched her frolic and play like a child in the water. When she surged up tossing her long hair to and fro she looked like an exotic mermaid. With the tempting sight of her bare breasts meeting his eyes he

14

took a deep breath as wild, stimulating sensations shot through him.

"Amanda! It is me—Mario," he called out to her.

Amanda threw up her hand returning his greeting, at the same time checking herself to ascertain whether the water covered her breasts. Dear Lord, it set her to trembling to think such distance separated her from her clothing and that Mario Alvarado stood between. Every female around the surrounding countryside knew of his way with women. That Latin charm of his had won him a reputation by the time he was eighteen, and Amanda had not been fooled even at the age of fifteen as to why her father had wanted her away from the ranch and Mario's nearness.

He was so devastatingly good-looking that the sight of him standing there on the bank with his firm, muscled legs slightly apart and his hands on his hips smiling at her took her breath away. His hair was as black as the flat crowned hat on his head and the fine tailored black pants and shirt. She found herself slowly moving toward the bank with his black eyes urging her toward him as forcefully as a magnet.

She tried to sound casual as she requested that he turn around and walk a distance away if she was to get out of the water.

"Ah, but I was thinking of joining you," he teased.

"No, Mario!"

He had no intentions of doing that. Slowly, he turned and took a couple of steps away from the river's edge. "Your wishes are my command, *chiquita*. Only to please you is my wish. Come on out, for I give you my promise not to turn around even though it will take all my will power to resist." His eyes sparked like

15

black coals. It was true what he said but Mario was far too clever to anger her at this point.

Cautiously, she rose up out of the water with the sun reflecting against the droplets of water still on her nude body. Even though Tony Branigan had watched the interaction between the young girl in the water and the tall young man standing on the bank, he could not keep back a husky gasp of breath when she stood up boldy in the water looking like some Greek goddess in all her magnificent feminine glory . . . a feast to his eyes.

Thunderstruck by her beauty, he realized in the same instant that the man was his cousin Mario. He should have known it could only be Mario sniffing out a new female prey like the horny hound dog he'd been all his adult life.

Tony smiled smugly, thinking how irked Mario would be to know that he'd been rewarded the sight Mario was denied. Now as he stared at the two of them in a warm embrace and Mario giving her a kiss on the cheek, he was irked and envious. The sight of her had left him with an ache he'd not known for a long, long time. He, too, shared the hot-blooded Latin nature of his cousin. Like Mario, he'd taken his pleasure recklessly with the ladies. However, he'd not had the leisure time to indulge recently. Also, his rugged features could not begin to compare to Mario's. There was that streak bred in him by the Irishman, Terrance Branigan, that he'd have rather forgotten about.

He'd lived all his life using the name of Moreno, not Branigan. Now he was coming to Gonzales County, and he had been urged by his old friend U.S. Marshal Brett Flanigan not to use the esteemed name of Mo-

16

reno, his mother's family name. He saw the logic behind Brett's thinking and at the time the two had joked about the rhyming of Branigan and Flanigan, but now it rubbed him the wrong way with its bitter memories. He was Tony Moreno!

With a sudden, dramatic gesture the young lady's arm raised in the air and Tony saw her hand connect with Mario's fine-chiseled face. Tony chuckled, applauding the girl's courage, and watched intensely to see what took place next. Mario backed away and he broke into a laugh himself. Jauntily, he swaggered away, leaving the lovely girl standing there hands firmly placed on her finely curved hips.

More than ever he knew he must seek her out. She was not only breathtakingly beautiful but full of fire. Everything about her enchanted him.

The episode with Mario was not what Amanda had needed at all that afternoon. She flopped herself down on the ground mad at Papa, herself, and, last but not least, Mario Alvarado. How dare he slip his hand inside her blouse! No man had ever touched her there. None of the young French gentlemen at her aunt's soirées had ever ventured more than a fleeting kiss on the cheek in some secluded corner of the parlor or ballroom when a giant palm hid them from the view of the other guests.

What under God's green earth had brought out such boldness in Mario this afternoon? His arm around her and his first gentle kisses had pleasured her so that she'd yearned to linger there in his arms. Even when his hot, sensuous lips had trailed along her throat and the opening of her blouse, she'd not panicked. Then —oh, dear God, his hand eased within her blouse and

17

his touch had set off a flood within her. Like a liquid fire was searing her insides. She had never known such a titillating sensation before. She liked the feeling but it frightened her, for it was like jumping off a high cliff; she did not know what to expect.

Damn that Mario! He went away laughing at her and her naive innocence. He knew, damn him! He knew she'd never been touched there before. Dear Lord, she would have to be facing him in a few days at the gala fiesta Bianca Alvarado had invited them to attend for her daughter Maria's fifteenth birthday.

She tugged at the black leather boots, which were proving to be difficult to get on. However, once they were on and she was dressed she was in no hurry to return home. It mattered not that the sun was beginning to sink in the west, either. Her mood had suddenly turned reflective now with the incident with Mario. There was also the disagreement with her father, which bothered her, for there was no man she admired more than the powerful, masterful Mark Kane. Couldn't he see or understand that the man for her would have to be all the things that he was? She could never settle for anything less! Suddenly, it struck her like a bolt out of the blue how she would win the battle about Derek. Now, she was ready to go home feeling quite pleased with her cleverness. Mounting up on the palomino, she reined him homeward.

Some force like a magnet pulled her eyes over to the hill and there she saw a magnificent black stallion and a rider dressed all in black. The horse reared up and its rider flung up his black hat in a greeting gesture to her. They looked like a sculpture of fine black marble. When she turned back to look again they were gone,

18

and she wondered if she had imagined it all. She didn't want it to be a phantom she'd seen. She wanted him to exist.

His daughter's mercurial mood made Mark Kane curious as to what the little minx was up to now as they sat at the dinner table that evening. What was really going on behind that sweet angel face? If he had to guess he'd lay money on the fact that she'd met up with that damned Mario after hightailing it out of the house. He never assumed for one second that she'd changed her mind about their differences earlier. Not his Amanda!

It was good for Mark to see his sweet Jenny so happy and chattering away with their daughter, but at this minute he could have wrung her pretty neck for accepting that invitation to the fiesta. That was just flaunting their beautiful daughter in the presence of Mario. This was trouble, Mark considered. Mario was too good-looking and he knew it.

Throughout the years of their marriage, and for all of her easygoing ways, there were those times when Jenny put her dainty foot down on him. Oh, even his stubborn streak would not let him deny that Bianca Alvarado was a woman to be admired. She'd kept the Rancho Rio running and prospering after Miguel Alvarado's death. She was a hell of a woman! Her son Mario could not be Amanda's husband though, he firmly determined.

Mark's thoughts were replicated at that very moment by Bianca Alvarado's nephew Tony Branigan as he sat across the table admiring the dignified, stately-looking lady. He could see some resemblance between her and his mother, Theresa. While he'd worshipped his mother during her brief lifetime, he had detested his father. His cantankerous, silver-haired grandfather, Esteban Moreno, was the man he honored as his father. As far as Terry Branigan was concerned and if he still lived, he could rot in hell!

In that very authoritative air of hers Bianca was insisting he stay on for a visit. "Besides, Maria would be heartbroken if you don't help celebrate her birthday, Tonio." Her piercing black eyes darted down the length of the long dining table to where the lovely dark-haired girl sat smiling. Maria knew instinctively her mother would get her way, as she usually did.

"Please, Cousin Tony. You just have to." Maria's black eyes twinkled with a bit of the imp in her that Tony adored. She was as outgoing and friendly as the younger son, Miguel, was bashful and shy. Tony was quick to note the cool aloofness of his cousin Mario. He was very aware that young Miguel was intimidated by his older brother.

"For you, my little Maria, I will stay," Tony said, flashing her a broad smile. When he gave that crooked smile Maria thought her cousin devilishly handsome in his rugged sort of way.

"Wonderful! Oh, Mama, it will be the best birthday I've ever had, and you'll not be sorry, Cousin Tony."

"I'm sure it will be, my darling," Bianca laughed softly. No one would have guessed from the mask she wore the troubled thoughts running through her mind. Something troubled her son Mario, and she pondered what it was. He was almost to the point of being rude to Tonio, as she called him.

While his aunt might be at a loss about her son's aloofness toward Tony, Tony himself wasn't. He knew the resentment Mario felt toward him and the jealousy he felt about Grandpa Esteban's making him a partner in the Moreno silver mines in Mexico. Now, Esteban had given him the final say on the running on the huge ranch just outside the city of San Antonio, and all of this met with disapproval as far as Mario was concerned. In Mario's eyes, he was just poor relations—Terry Branigan's cast-off son! And Tony suspected that Mario's mood wasn't helped by the rejection by the beautiful blond-haired girl earlier in the day. A brutal blow to one with Mario's ego!

So when his aunt and Maria retired for the evening, Tony excused himself from the library and Mario's presence to seek some fresh night air out in his aunt's garden courtyard. Best to leave Mario to himself, Tony considered.

The night-blooming flowers wafted to his nose as he ambled down the stone path, and as he stared up at the starlit skies his thoughts turned to the beautiful girl. He imagined that she would have smelled as sweet if he were holding her close in his arms at that minute. Christ, he would have enjoyed that!

He could hardly fault Mario for stealing a kiss from those honey-sweet lips. He would have done the same thing. Recalling the harsh slap she gave Mario, he let out a chuckle. She was a little wildcat!

Some instinct deep inside him told him he would seek out this girl although he knew he didn't need that distraction at this time. As the whippoorwill over in the distance called to its mate, the girl seemed to call to

21

him. His thoughts of her were like a raging wildfire spreading and consuming him. Never had a woman had such an impact on him! Never had he hungered so for a woman he'd not even met.

TWO

Tony Branigan reined his black stallion, Picaro, toward the corrals where three of his aunt's *vaqueros* were milling around. About the same time he saw the smiling face of young Juanito rushing out of the barn to greet him. He had no idea of the hero worship swelling in the youth's chest simply because he'd given Juanito a few minutes of his time each morning the last few days since he'd been here at Rancho Rio.

Young Juanito swore Picaro, with his coat of rich black velvet, was the most magnificent horse he'd ever seen. "I'd like to own such an animal someday," he'd told Tony, his dark eyes gleaming.

Leaping down quickly, Tony led Picaro to the watering trough as Juanito met him there. Taking the red kerchief from his sweaty neck, he dipped it in the water to wipe his damp hair away from his face and smiled at the young Mexican. It was a steamy July day and the ride down to the river in hopes of seeing some sign of the beautiful golden-haired girl had proven futile for the second day in a row. Already she was proving to be a distraction he did not need. Hell, he didn't even know her name!

"Gonna be a hot one today, eh señor?" Juanito projected since it was still the morning hour.

"I think you're right, *amigo*," Tony grinned, unbuttoning his shirt and wiping the wet kerchief around his throat and downward over his tanned chest. Picaro cooled himself by taking some of the water before Juanito reined him away.

Tony would have found Juanito with his warm brown eyes impossible not to respond to. He was like a lovable pup, and there was a loneliness about the young lad that reminded him of himself before Grandpa Esteban had come into his life. Eager for someone to talk to and listen to him, Juanito had told him everything about himself and how he'd lived his entire life there on the Rancho Rio. His mother had died when he was just a tot and he looked upon the Señora Alvarado as some sort of saint.

Again, as on the last two days, the youth followed Tony around the barn, and Tony offered him one of his cheroots before hoisting himself up on the top railing of the fence to linger a while to talk. He asked him, "Now, I'm not keeping you from any chores, am I?" The last thing in the world he'd want to be guilty of was causing the kid to get a chewing out by the arrogant Mario. But Juanito assured him he had some time to talk and his face reflected the pleasure he felt that a man such as Señor Branigan liked his company.

While Tony had wasted the morning with his distracting thoughts about the beautiful girl and his jaunt down to the river had been futile, the next hour with Juanito was well spent. The lad was a fountain of information about the owner of the Big D Ranch, David Lawson, and about the wealthiest rancher in the county, Mark Kane. "Most think Señorita Kane is the most beautiful lady around, but not me."

"Oh—and who do you think is the most beautiful, Juanito?" Amusement played in Tony's silver-gray eyes.

"It is the girl named Chita I think is the most beautiful girl in the world," Juanito dramatically exclaimed, and he chuckled. Without any prodding from Tony, he told him that she was a servant girl at the Circle K Ranch.

"I see. She must be very beautiful, Juanito."

"Oh, si—she is that! It is true that Señorita Kane is very beautiful, too. Señor Alvarado certainly finds her so. I will still take Chita with her beautiful black hair. When that miserable Jeff Kane breaks her heart I will be there to comfort her."

"That is very noble of you, Juanito," Tony remarked. Juanito's chest swelled with pride and his devotion to Tony was heightened. Before they parted a little later, he quizzed Tony, "Which do you think is more beautiful, Señor Branigan, a blond-haired lady or a black-headed one?"

"Hhmmm? Oh, I don't know. Why do you ask?"

"Just curious. Señorita Kane is a blonde." The boy's comment answered the question that had been nagging at Tony the last few days. She had to be the lovely nude nymph he'd seen.

The days fell heavy on Amanda and the evenings were forever. Even certain objects in her room reminded her painfully of the grand times she was missing now not being back in New Orleans. There in the teakwood chest rested idly the exquisite pieces of jewelry her extravagant aunt had purchased for some particular gown she was to wear to some social event. There had to be a fortune lying there in the chest. The exquisite emeralds and diamonds were most expensive and the amethyst necklace and matched earrings were so beautiful with that glorious lavender gown hanging idle in her armoire. She could not deny she'd loved the pampering and spoiling. Always there was something to attend and new, interesting people to meet.

While she could not tell her parents how miserable she was, she knew she'd never settle for this kind of existence for the rest of her life. Lord, I'd rather be dead, she thought to herself.

Even her best friend, Mona Lawson, would not understand, because the only thing Mona ever yearned for in her whole life was being Jeff's bride.

She didn't like to think of herself as selfish and self-centered, but she'd tried so hard the last few days to make herself content around the hacienda. Because of the sultry heat she'd not even gone on her usual ride.

Sad to say nothing occupied her for long around the spacious hacienda. Her brother's company and his talk was about the land or cattle. However, she'd seen him sneak out of the hacienda at night, and she knew it was to the saloon in town he went, where he spent the hours carousing and playing cards. No doubt, he lost as he had in New Orleans during his brief stay there.

Tomorrow, she decided she would go to see Mona. It would be good to see her after all this time.

An unexpected shower of rain began to fall just as Amanda prepared to ride out of the barn on Prince. Disgruntled and dejected she turned the palomino around and led him back to the stall. It seemed to her as if Mother Nature herself was against her. So all she had to look forward to was a gray, gloomy day roaming aimlessly around the rooms of the hacienda.

A rustling sound up above in the hayloft drew her attention and she stood quietly to listen. It came again along with the soft moans of a woman's voice. This made Amanda more than curious.

"Oh, Jeff . . . *querido*," the voice moaned. Amanda knew that voice could only belong to one person. Her eyes flashed wide and her mouth gasped in shock. Her brother and Chita! Sweet Jesus, their father would kill him if he found out. Her brother was a fool to be so irresponsible with the daughter of Juan and Consuela. She stomped out of the barn, slamming the barn door with a mighty thrust. She hoped the loud noise might interrupt their little interlude up there in the loft and she cared not that they knew it was she down below.

Apparently, she had not succeeded, as she was to find out at dinner that evening. Her knowing eyes did not fail to see the lusty look in her brother's eyes as Chita swished around the table serving their meal. It was so obvious to Amanda sitting there, knowing what she now knew. Perhaps she should have a talk with Chita. Instead, she called Chita's attention to her, requesting another glass of wine be served to her. She was hardly prepared for her father's reprimand, which proved embarrassing.

"You've already had one, haven't you missy?"

"I have," she retorted, not hestitating to take a sip from her refilled glass. "But then I've been used to having wine daily. I did at Aunt Lisa's."

Mark's blue eyes glared down the table at her but Amanda glared back just as furiously. "You're not at Lisa's now, Amanda!"

Slowly, she pushed back in the chair but her eyes never left her father. "No, I'm not!" She marched from the room as her father demanded she return to the table. But she did not. Tears of frustration flowed down her cheeks as she climbed the stairs and rushed across the gallery to her room.

Kane sat at the table, slamming his napkin by the side of his plate. "Damn that girl!" More and more he was regretting the decision he'd made to let her go to Lisa's and that fancy Miss Barton's School for Young Ladies. She'd changed and changed in a way that didn't suit him at all.

Amanda yanked her clothes off in a fury, not caring if she tore the pretty sprigged muslin gown. With equal vigor she tore the cluster of pretty flowers from her hair. Off came the petticoats, which she threw into the gown lying there on the bed. Flinging herself across the bed, she allowed all the tears to free themselves until she felt drained and sleep came.

When she woke up a few hours later and looked over at the clock, she saw that there was a long night still ahead for her. She found herself to be famished and realized she'd eaten very little before her departure from the table. Getting up from the bed, she slipped into her robe and went downstairs barefooted.

At least her parents were retired for the night, and she found that to her liking as she proceeded down the steps. She knew Consuela would have left some of her pie there on the counter and other food in the cupboard. She would help herself to some of it and yes,

28

she *would* have a glass of wine, too. The belligerent streak in her really looked forward to that!

With a plate prepared for herself and a generous glass of wine poured she was walking through the semi-dark room to go back up the steps to her room when she heard a hissing noise. She stopped in her tracks.

"Pssss, out here, Mandy," the voice urged her. She looked toward the now opened doors of the patio to see the figure of her brother. Another man stood back behind him.

"Jeff? Lord, you could have scared me!" she chided him.

With the moonlight shining through the trees, she made a feast for the eyes of Derek Lawson ogling her as she moved on out through the doors. Every curve of her luscious body was silhouetted in the soft green satin robe by the light of the moon. That glorious spun-gold hair cascaded down over her slender shoulders, causing every raw male instinct to come alive in him. A salacious gleam came to his eyes, which Amanda could not see there in the dark. She did detect that her brother had been drinking as she stood close to him and recognized the man behind him. "Derek? Dear God, is that you?"

"Sure is, honey," he laughed, walking closer to give her a hug. "Lord God Almighty, you're prettier than ever!" He had to do battle with himself to keep from crushing her in his arms, wanting to bruise those beautiful lips with his kisses. The day would come when he would do just that, he promised himself. "Good to have you back, Amanda."

"It's good to be back, too," she replied, gravely

29

wondering if she meant that. She sank down in the wicker chair noticing the unusual look in Derek's eyes as they danced over her body. Dear Lord, they seemed to be devouring her!

Jeff broke the abrupt silence. "OOOh, Papa won't like you drinking that!" He chuckled and slurred his words leaving no doubt at all that he'd drunk quite a lot. Derek, too, smelled of liquor as he'd hugged her. What were those two hellions up to, she wondered.

"Shut up, Jeff! You're a fine one to talk, and besides, I'll do as I please." This brought forth a roar of laughter from both of them. She knew what they'd been up to that evening.

During the next half-hour as Amanda indulged in chatter with the two she found Derek to be different. Perhaps it was the liquor, but she saw a boldness there she'd not known before. While she could not define it, he seemed to lord it over her brother in a way she resented. The raw desire she saw in his eyes when he looked at her made her squirm, so that she was glad when he finally departed. While it was true that she'd seen desire in Mario's eyes, those eyes had said he wanted to make love to her, but Derek's eyes said something else.

She helped her swaying brother to his room before going to her own. For a while, she lay watching the moon through her window and pondered just what it was she had seen there in Derek's eyes that disturbed her so.

That same moon shining through Amanda's window invaded the small grove of pine trees where Derek Lawson sat perched atop his white stallion. In his dark solitude there in the late night hour he dreamed and envisioned his future. His and Amanda's.

The night was quiet, only the whispering breeze rustling through the tall pines. Nothing was going to deny him his dreams, for they had become an obsession with him. Nothing would stand between him and his ultimate goals, and at his side would be the beautiful Amanda. Seeing her tonight whetted his appetite to make it all happen sooner. He had to be the first to taste that sweet, virginal innocence. That was most important to him.

Finally, he reined the huge white horse out of the grove and toward the two-story white house he planned to be the master in soon.

Amanda greeted the bright sunshiny day with delight and eagerness to saddle up Prince and ride to the Big D. The sight of her riding up to his home pleased Derek's father as much. She was a gorgeous young lady, and it wasn't any wonder that every young buck in the county would desire to court her.

While in his eyes there was no one lovelier than his sweet little Mona with her black hair and black eyes, he could see that special bewitching quality about Amanda Kane that made her so striking to any man. Mona always reminded him of his beloved Carlotta when she was young. Even now, he could not bear to think of her dead and gone forever from him.

He stood by the corral and watched Amanda walk jauntily up the walk to his house and smiled broadly as he saw Mona dart out the door to embrace her. They'd been friends all their lives, and nothing could be more perfect than if Derek and she were to get married—as he and Mark had discussed several weeks ago.

Age had impressed on him more and more the tremendous burden of running the ranch. He'd found it easier and easier to give Derek the reins for months now. His son had taken them eagerly. Crazy as it might seem, David sometimes pondered if he'd not done so too greedily. That moment passed though, and David harshly chided himself for such thoughts.

The girls sat in Mona's sunroom surrounded by her pet project, her houseplants. Amanda teased her. "I see you've still got your green thumb."

"Yes, I always will, Amanda," Mona said, handing her friend a glass of lemonade Nina had served them. "Oh, I've missed you so."

Amanda confessed to missing her too, and at the same time she noted Mona's beautiful glossy hair tied back by a blue ribbon and her simple calico frock covered with a crisp white apron. She looked like a typical young rancher's wife—which was exactly what Mona wished to be. Mona chattered on, apologizing that she was sorry she had not made it over to see her, but Nina had been feeling poorly so she'd been helping out. She was anxious to know all about Amanda's many months in New Orleans, and her lovely onyx eyes grew wide as Amanda told her about all the grand balls and shops. Mona had never seen anything like the magnificent ships coming into a port city like New Orleans. Neither had Amanda until she had gone there.

"From all over the world they come, Mona. So many different people. It never gets dull." Amanda's eyes sparkled.

"You miss it, don't you?" Mona asked.

"Yes, and I don't know what I can do about it," Amanda confessed dejectedly.

"I know no other life, but then, Amanda, you were always different. It always took more to make you happy. You've been on the other side of the mountain now." Mona patted Amanda's hand with a look of understanding on her face. It made Amanda almost envy her friend, and it felt so good to have one person who could understand her. How glad she was that she had ridden over to see her this afternoon. It was consolation she needed, and it urged her to stay longer than she'd intended. When she did realize how late the hour was, she leaped up and exclaimed, "Lordy, I'm going to be after dark getting back. I gotta go!"

Mona rushed after her as Amanda ran for the front door. Mona called to her friend as she made it to the hitching post, "Amanda, you'll have to come with me to San Antonio to visit the Beckenridges. Think about it!" Mona shouted, hoping she had made Amanda hear her.

A nod of Amanda's head told her she had, and as she urged Prince into a swift gallop, she called back, "I will, Mona!"

Twilight was shrouding the hilly countryside and the most glorious shades of golds and purples lit up the western skies. Riding at a breakneck speed, she felt marvelous, and she credited it all to Mona. She was feeling more lighthearted and gay than she had in a long, long time. She would give some thought to going to San Antonio with Mona. It could prove to be great fun.

Tony Branigan sat on his black stallion atop the ridge and saw her with her golden hair blowing back wild and free. This time, nothing was going to keep him from meeting her. A force he could not deny or-

33

dained it, he decided, urging the black beast down the steep slope.

Amanda saw the rider descending the ridge over in the distance and her heart started to pound with wild excitement. She had not imagined the phantom rider the other day. This was the same man. She just knew it, and he had every intent of cutting off her path. A recklessness in her wanted him to. In fact, she even reined up slightly on Prince.

Even with the distance between them, Tony was aware of the palomino's slowed gait and he smiled. A daring, bold little creature she was!

This magnificent stranger all in black on his black steed coming toward her reminded her of a knight in fairy tales she'd read. His fine charger looking like black velvet caught her admiring eyes as he so sure-footedly came down into the valley closer and closer.

Suddenly and much to her disappointment, she saw "her knight" turn and start back up the slope of ground. She was shattered beyond words. In almost the same instant she knew why as she watched an approaching rider come from the direction of the Circle K. It was her brother, Jeff.

"Damn!" she muttered, spurring up Prince, for her illusion was gone with the wind now. She could have wrung her brother's neck, for he'd spoiled everything by coming upon the scene. Now, she'd never meet this mysterious stranger. In a few more minutes they would have come face to face with one another.

Poor Jeff received the blunt of her fury. "Lord, must I have an escort?" Amanda spit at him as he joined her.

"Wasn't my idea, sis. The old man sent me out to

hunt you. You should know how he feels about you riding after dark." He watched the tightening of her rosebud mouth and the flashing eyes turning almost deep purple. "Honey, you got to know that there is some truth to that. After all, there are drifters riding over the country who wouldn't give a damn that you're Mark Kane's daughter."

She said nothing but she realized it was true. Was that who her phantom rider was? She hardly thought so. No common drifter would own such a fine horse.

As they passed through the towering archway entrance with the circle and the K emblem at the top, Amanda inquired of her brother, "Jeff, are there any new families in the valley?"

"Not that I've heard of, sis. Why?"

"Oh, I just wondered. After all I've been gone for two years," she shrugged in an offhand manner. The wheels in her pretty head were working like crazy. Who, indeed, was that stranger up on the rise?

Jeff took Prince's reins and assured his bossy sister he would see to the proper care of her palomino, and she agreed to go on into the house.

Hoping to escape her irate father she chose to go in the kitchen door, only to bump into his granitelike form waiting and glaring down at her. Like an innocent child, she gave him her sweetest smile. "Oh, hi Papa! Sorry I'm late, but Mona and I just talked and talked. I gotta go wash up." She darted around him so swiftly that Mark had no time to admonish her. Besides, when the little imp smiled at him like that he was reminded of her as a small child—his little golden princess! She knew all too well, too, Mark Kane realized, that he adored her. God have mercy on any man who lost his heart over the little feisty filly, he mused, shaking his head.

He stood for a second to indulge himself in whimsy and smiled, forgetting for a moment that Consuela was in the kitchen. "CONSUELA! You may start serving dinner now!"

"Yes, Señor Kane," she replied, puttering around with her pots and trying desperately not to smile, for she had witnessed the young señorita work him so cleverly around her dainty little finger.

Mark Kane walked briskly out of the kitchen and Consuela breathed with relief, letting out the suppressed chuckle of laughter.

Amanda rushed on through the hall heaving a deep sigh of relief, patting herself on the back for her cleverness. Next time, and there would be a next time, nothing would prevent her meeting the mysterious stranger. Now, *that* was the type of man who haunted her dreams!

THREE

The two men rode tall in their saddles as the dawn broke over the Texas countryside. Both were robust, rugged individuals with faces tanned and weathered from time spent out on the range. Jake Farlow had served Mark Kane over the years as trail boss, foreman, and ranch hand, and the two shared a mutual respect for each other.

They were riding toward the south range of the Kane property to check out the herd grazing there after they'd shared a hearty breakfast and ample supply of Consuela's black coffee. To Mark, it was the most peaceful time of the day.

"When I think of the blood, sweat, and tears that's gone into this land, and to have these bastards come and help themselves to my cattle, I get so mad I can't sleep at night, Jake. I'm starting to fence with that barbed wire as soon as Slim gets it here."

"I'd be for doin' the same. Can't say as I can figure Mr. Lawson's not wantin' to fence yet," Jake remarked.

"Lawson can do what he wants, but let them try to cut mine down and we'll put a few bullets in some heads, eh?"

"Yes sir, that we will do. They can't be no worse than the Comanches and we've taken a few of them rascals, haven't we?"

"We did, along with a few Mexican bandits." Mark had one of his sudden impulses. "Got a hunch I want to check out, Jake. Think I'll leave you and mosey to the south tip over there."

Jake gave his boss a nod and pulled his reins to the left to part company with him. Mark Kane rode over toward the wooded area of pines. Looking back he saw Jake had already left the clearing to enter another part of the wooded area. He guided his mare slowly as though he was scrutinizing the grounds carefully. The area was ghostly quiet except for the calling of a mockingbird over in the distance. He breathed deep of the fresh morning air as he rode in and out around the trees. Somewhere over this way there was an old deserted shack.

Suddenly a deer leaped out in panic, rushing across the clearing to seek refuge elsewhere. Mark had to laugh as he relaxed the grip on his gun. At the same time, he praised his ability to draw his pistol fast. More than once that fast draw had saved his neck.

He rode on a few more yards before the sound of something in the underbrush echoed. Much to his regret, Mark found himself to be the perfect target, having let his guard down for a moment or two too long. An explosion broke through the air along with the acrid smell. The mare whinnied in panic and reared. Cursing his own stupidity, Kane felt himself falling to the ground with a stinging sensation in his shoulder and his blood already staining his faded blue shirt.

38

In the same minute that his body made a sharp impact with the ground, a stranger galloped up, leaped down from his horse and aimed his matched silverplated pistols. In swift succession they fired. The man's deep voice ordered, "Stay low!" Mark obliged him, as the earth exploded close to his leg.

Retreating hoofbeats sounded in the woods as the stranger's pistols fired again, and a sharp cry of pain told Mark his intended killer had been hit. He took notice that the man had moved to shield him from being a target. Stanching the blood flowing from his shoulder, he knew he had this man to thank for saving his life. "I owe you, mister," he mumbled in labored breath. Kane couldn't excuse his own carelessness.

Tony let out a flow of cuss words as he bent down to see how serious the wound was. Vexed that the gunman was getting away, he removed Mark's shirt. It was not a serious wound, he was glad to see. Now he wished he'd gone after the gunman.

"The name's Mark Kane. What's yours?" Mark asked, watching the capable hands working at his shirt. The man had the coldest damn eyes he'd ever seen. Something about the firm, set jaw told Mark this dude feared nothing and no one.

"Tony . . . Tony Branigan."

"Well, Tony Branigan, I owe few men in my life, but I do owe you a hell of alot. Don't recognize the name Branigan. You from around these parts?"

"No sir, I'm not," Tony replied, buttoning Kane's shirt. "Think you're up to riding?"

"Hell, yes! This ain't nothin' to an old bear like me," Mark barked gruffly. Tony saw the indignant look on the man's face. He was a prideful breed, Tony

39

realized. No wonder he'd sired such a beautiful, spirited daughter.

"Just asking to be sure. Never really doubted it for a minute, Mr. Kane. Here, let me give you a hand to your horse," Tony said, not daring to smile. Giving a whistle for Picaro to come to him, he helped Kane mount up.

Kane was not in so much pain that he didn't take notice of the fine black stallion that dutifully came to his master's command. He was a magnificent animal, with a coat as black as a raven's wing and as glossy and shining as black velvet.

"You got yourself one fine horse there, Branigan. Wouldn't mind trading you out of him." Mark gave out a chuckle.

"Ah, that would be like trading off a friend, sir. Picaro is my most precious possession," Tony admitted proudly.

"Like horses, do you?"

"More than just like . . . I admire a fine-bred horse." Tony moved over to mount up on Picaro after Kane sat into his saddle. He patted the long silky black mane. "Picaro is my very good friend."

It was a rare thing for Mark Kane to be so impressed by an individual as he found himself feeling about this young man . . . a stranger he'd not even known until a few minutes ago. His eyes warmed with affection for his horse as Amanda's did for her palomino, Kane thought to himself. She would appreciate this handsome fellow.

They rode together as far as the tall archway leading into the grounds of the Circle K. Mark talked to keep his mind off the nagging pain in his shoulder and Tony listened to his bragging about his land and cattle. It was not offensive though, for it was the way a man should feel. Tony admired the man's pride. He found Brett Flanigan's description of the cattle baron to be accurate. The U.S. marshal had given him a brief description of some of the more prominent families in Gonzales County before he'd left San Antonio.

"Come to work for me, Branigan," Mark requested as they prepared to go their separate ways. Tony's cool demeanor cracked for a moment. He had not expected this.

"I've got a loose end or two to take care of. Could I let you know in a few days?"

"Good enough for me. Hey, you saved my hind and I won't forget it. See you, young man," Mark smiled as he urged the mare through the archway.

"Glad I happened along, sir," Tony replied, riding off in another direction. It was only after he'd gone a few miles that it dawned on him that Kane had not questioned why he'd been on his property. Had Kane discovered what he had there on the southern boundary?

The dauntless Kane walked into the hacienda as though nothing had happened, seeking out Consuela's assistance instead of Jenny's. She would fuss over him too much.

"I'll tell her later, Consuela. No reason to upset her, eh?" Mark suggested. Consuela gave him an understanding nod. It was not the first time she'd joined in league with him to shelter the señora from concern and worry. It was time like this that Consuela saw him as a gentle soul and not a hard-hearted tyrant. "It will be

41

out little secret, señor," she assured him.

Amanda stood in front of the full-length mirror taking one last look at herself before joining the family downstairs. For the first time since she'd left New Orleans she had somewhere to wear one of the many fancy gowns hanging so in her armoire. The multi-flounced white organdy seemed to be the perfect choice for the Alvarados' fiesta, which was starting late in the afternoon and continuing into the evening.

At first she'd put on the pearl necklace to match the pearl earrings, but she hastily removed it. With all the little pink rosettes scattered around the low-cut neckline, it seemed too much.

With that one stubborn wisp finally subdued, she left her room to go downstairs. Halfway down the steps, she heard voices coming from the parlor.

She stood for a minute to admire her handsome brother in his deep blue coat and matching pants, and the sight of her mother in her gray silk made her wish there were more occasions she could dress up in her finery. With the clean line of her neck, and earrings on her ears she looked as lovely as Aunt Lisa. Her father was still a very handsome man. His deep gray coat and lighter gray pants were molded perfectly to his stout, robust body. Such a tower of strength he represented standing there a couple of inches over six foot tall. It was obvious from her mother's vexed tone of voice that Mark Kane had been still grumbling about having to attend the fiesta.

"I'll not listen to another word, Mark. You're like a silly child. Bianca Alvarado wasn't the one who pulled the trigger that killed your parents. It's time you let go of that hate you've harbored so long and buried it once and for all!"

Amanda's father rarely received such venom from his petite wife and Amanda stood smiling and applauding her. It was at that minute that Jeff turned to see his beautiful sister standing there and let out a low, long whistle of approval.

"Lord, look at Amanda!" Everyone did, with a sigh of admiration from Jenny and a disapproving look from her father at the low neckline. He dared not comment about it with Jeff and Jenny raving so about how lovely she was. Even he had to admit secretly that she was a ravishing sight to behold. This was what troubled Kane!

Instead, he urged his family to be on their way. Loaded into the buggy, the Kane family traveled toward the Rancho Rio with the Lawson buggy coming along a couple of miles behind them.

Her father's quiet, thoughtful manner was of no concern to the excited, happy Mona as their buggy rolled along. All she could think about was seeing and being with Jeff Kane. But all David Lawson could speculate about this late afternoon was why Derek had suddenly decided not to accompany them to the fiesta, especially when he must have known Amanda was going to be there. He'd decided he'd never understand his complex moody son. He seemed to be more difficult as time went by.

When they arrived at the Alvarados' gate, Amanda and her mother went ahead as Jeff waited to greet Mona and her father. Mark excused himself to talk to one of his rancher friends just arriving. So Amanda and her mother entered the courtyard alone without Jeff or Mark. Carrying their gift for the young Maria, they were observed by Bianca Alvarado, who left the cluster of her guests to greet them. Mario had seen the ladies arrive. In fact, he'd made a point of watching for Amanda's arrival. In his rush to get to Amanda's side he collided with his mother.

"My son, control yourself," Bianca gently chided him. "However, I can't blame you. She is gorgeous." Speaking softly and smiling up at him, she took his arm to meet the ladies. Knowing her hot-blooded Mario so well, she feared the dangerous situation such a tempting young lady could create. She wanted no harm coming Mario's way.

With greetings said, Mario played the gallant caballero, taking Amanda's arm to escort her over to the refreshment table. Always the gracious hostess, Bianca led Jenny over to some of her guests who had arrived earlier and were congratulating Maria. Sitting over by the fountain, the excited Maria was a little awestruck by all the attention coming her way. Jenny and Bianca were a study in startling contrasts. Bianca was tall and willowy with a dark loveliness. Jenny's jet black hair and complexion were as dark as Bianca's, but she was tiny and fragile looking. Both were very attractive ladies.

Over at the far side of the long veranda another man watched the newly arrived guests with interest. He leaned against the wall with his booted foot propped up on a huge urn holding a massive blooming plant. Tony Branigan's gray eyes were aimed in the direction of Amanda strolling along with Mario. She looked like a golden princess right out of an old fairy tale book in her snowy white gown. His jaw tightened and tensed as he ogled that ostentatious peacock, Mario, strutting

44

along amid the festive splendor of his aunt's garden.

Tony felt no urge to move around among the guests like his gregarious cousin, and he'd hardly arrived prepared to attend any festive occasion with the clothes he'd brought. His white ruffled shirt was borrowed from Mario and young Maria had insisted that he wear the pretty scarlet silk scarf at his neck. Only the black pants he had on were his own. To stay there in the background satisfied him just fine. The longer his cold gray eyes watched Amanda the more he wanted to satisfy the urge to sock Mario's smiling face.

Tony did not realize that his sun-bronzed face and muscled male figure had attracted the eyes of some of the young daughters of the ranchers attending the fiesta. He was so bewitched by the golden-haired Amanda that he didn't notice the other girls parading by the veranda, giggling and chattering in hopes of catching his eye. Even the approach of Mark Kane wasn't noticed by him until Kane's deep, husky voice exclaimed, "Branigan! Tony Branigan, what a pleasant surprise!"

"Hello, Mr. Kane. Nice to see you again," Tony said, accepting his firm handshake. With a vigorous pat on Tony's back, Mark invited him to join him. "Besides, I want you to meet my dear wife, Jenny."

Jenny stood with David Lawson and she turned to see her husband and the young man striding up. "I wondered where you were, Mark." She wondered who this young man was, too.

"Been talking to this young man, Jenny. Meet Tony Branigan, Jenny, and this is David Lawson, Tony." Mark stood there with his approval of the young man written on his face for both of them to

45

see. Jenny had heard how this gentleman had saved Mark's life.

"Nice to meet you, Mr. Branigan," Jenny greeted him, as did David Lawson. But David wondered just who he was and why he'd been included at the Alvarado gathering.

"My pleasure, Mrs. Kane, and you, too, Mr. Lawson. I can see where your daughter gets all her beauty now, Mrs. Kane."

"You know our daughter, Mr. Branigan?" Jenny questioned the young man whose piercing eyes locked into hers. There was a rugged arrogance about him that reminded her of Mark when he was younger, although they looked nothing alike.

"No, ma'am but I've seen her," Tony informed her.

"I see." Jenny matched his bold stare with one of her own as if they understood one another without any more words being said. Jenny's perceptive senses told her that Tony Branigan was attracted to her Amanda.

"Well, speaking of Amanda—where is she, Jenny?" Mark's searching blue eyes went over the crowd before coming back to Jenny. Shrugging her shoulders, she commented casually, "She could be anywhere, dear. Don't worry about Amanda." She knew exactly where Amanda was and with whom.

Damn it, he did worry about her! Especially with Mario sniffing at her heels. Mark fumed. The last sight he'd had of her she was holding Mario's arm and laughing. The intimate way they were looking at one another was enough to gall Kane raw.

Mario had every intention of making the most of the evening, biding his time and playing it patient until the start of the dancing. He had been the perfect gentleman, giving Amanda his full attention, even though a number of the pretty girls had flaunted themselves at him. He found a secluded place for the two of them to eat and saw to her glass of wine's being filled. Amanda didn't mind at all that her time was being monopolized by Mario. In fact, she was glad that Derek Lawson had not attended the affair and pushed his attentions on her. Even though she'd acted disappointed when Mona and Jeff had paused for a moment of conversation to tell her that Derek was ill. "Poor Derek, what a terrible time to get ill and miss all the fun," Amanda had lamented. The truth was she had not missed him at all.

"You lie beautifully, *chiquita*," Mario whispered in her ear as Mona and Jeff strolled on their way. His warm lips brushed the side of her cheek and she could not deny the stirring within her. The bold gesture was observed across the garden by Tony, causing him such distraction that he did not hear what Kane was saying to him.

Mark Kane was forced to repeat the question again. "Branigan, when am I going to have an answer from you on my proposition?"

"Sorry, sir. The music starting—I didn't hear what you said," Tony stammered, willing his eyes to turn away from the far end of the garden.

"Working for me—my hired gun?"

With Kane's question prodding at him and his eyes sighting Amanda still with Mario, a voice he realized was his own told Kane he could be there tomorrow.

"Tomorrow!" They shook hands on their gentlemen's agreement and Mark Kane, exhibiting his pleasure, broke into a broad smile. "Tomorrow it is!"

A soft, eager voice broke through the air, insisting, "Come on, Cousin Tony—come on and dance the first dance with me!" The excited Maria in her lovely yellow gown was tugging on his arm. She was such a pretty little thing!

Tony noticed the questioning frown on Kane's face and realized that he did not know his relationship to the Alvarado family. Quickly he enlightened Mark Kane. "Yes, Mr. Kane I am the nephew of Señora Alvarado."

He had hired a member of the Alvarado family? For once in his life, Mark Kane was speechless, for he'd prided himself all his life on being able to size a man up. Now, he'd picked a damned Mex to hire for his gunman! A surly look creased his face, and Jenny controlled the laughter seeking to escape from her throat. Never had she been more grateful to be led away to dance, and she blessed David Lawson for inviting her to join him. Her beloved Mark could not have looked more stunned if someone had slapped him across the face. She was impressed by the young man Tony Branigan, and it was going to be interesting to her to see if Mark's overflowing praise of him suddenly vanished.

As she danced with her old friend, she saw Amanda dancing with Mario. They made a striking couple. Her daughter's golden loveliness and Mario's dark, sultry good looks were the center of attention of the other dancers, Jenny noted. Then she looked over at Tony dancing with his petite cousin, Maria, and she could see why Mark would never have associated him with being kin to the Alvarado family. His skin looked as though it was bronzed by the sun and those quicksilver gray eyes were not like the almost-black eyes of all the Alvarados. Only that raven-black hair of Tony Branigan's was shared by Mario and the rest of Bianca's children.

Amanda knew they were the best couple on the floor. Mario could have been a professional dancer as he guided her so expertly. Out of the corner of her eye she caught fast fleeting glances of her mother dancing with David Lawson and Mona paired with her brother, Jeff. What she wasn't aware of were the fast whirls Mario was giving her to avoid the prying eyes of his cousin. He didn't like for one minute the way Tony kept ogling the beautiful Amanda. He'd resented his mother's inviting him to remain at the ranch for a visit. Bad enough that he'd become Grandfather Esteban's favorite!

As soon as the music had stopped, Mario wasted no time getting Amanda away so he would not be forced to introduce her. Once he had guided her to a secluded spot, he urged her to sit down on one of the wooden benches. Feeling quite smug that he had her alone, he sat down beside her. *Madre de Dios*, it was then she chose to request something to drink, and Mario was forced to be gracious and oblige her.

Amanda had not wanted a drink at all. She had wanted a moment of solitude to look as long as she wished at the man she'd seen dancing with young Maria. Moments before she'd caught sight of him she'd felt his presence close at her back. His heat seemed to warm her. Then when their eyes had met in one fleeting second before Mario whirled her around and away, it was as though she had looked into those same eyes before, although she knew she'd never met this man. Yet he fascinated her, and suddenly she wanted to rid herself of Mario.

She moved away from the bench as soon as Mario's tall figure was out of sight. Through the cluster of oleander bushes laden with white, pungent blossoms she glided, careful to hold her gown close to her legs so it wouldn't get caught on the branches. When she'd reached the spot from which she hoped to view the pair, she heaved a deep sigh of disappointment because Maria was now alone and there was no man with her. A pout of disappointment came to her lips. She ambled aimlessly around the bushes, paying no attention to a young couple kissing back in the shadows in a corner by the stone wall enclosing the courtyard. She knew not that she was being stalked there in the night's darkness. Like some predatory cat, the man moved. Her snowy white gown made her easy to follow and he was as curious as a feline to know just what she was up to. When last he'd seen her she was with Mario. What had so suddenly separated them, he wondered? Whatever it was, it gave him the opportunity he'd sought for hours now and he determined to take advantage of it. The time was now!

The sound of the music wafted to her ears but in the still of the night another sound came to her. She turned sharply and instinctively started to run back in the same direction she'd just come from, or at least, so she thought. Her unexpected swift retreat took Tony completely by surprise. She came at him like a raging bull and slammed into his granitelike body. His arms went around her, enclosing her snug and tight. Looking down at her he realized just how petite she was. A smile creased his lips as he remarked, "Well, this is a

50

pleasant surprise, señorita!"

His bold, deep voice demanded her attention and his warm body made itself known to her as she tried to wiggle free. His dancing, darting eyes made her flush with embarrassment. "How dare you! Release me! Just what were you doing behind me anyway?"

He threw back his head, giving a deep, throaty laugh. "Now, I could ask what a beautiful girl like you is doing back here in the bushes."

"That's . . . that's none of your business, sir!" Her eyes flashed with fire. Tony found himself wanting to drown in them. He found himself fired to kiss those half-parted, pouting lips. "Now I could tell you the same thing, Señorita Kane."

The fact that he addressed her by her name made her stop wiggling to stare up at him. He did not allow her to ask how he happened to know who she was. Instead, he said, "Oh, may I introduce myself . . . Tony Branigan at your service."

"Well, please oblige me, Mr. Branigan and let me go!"

In a low, sensuous voice he murmured, as his head bent lower, "I don't want to let you go, *querida*. Not just yet!"

His lips captured hers in a long, lingering kiss. Amanda surprised herself as she yielded to his gentle persuasion. Her mouth was pliant even as his tongue prodded for entry and she found she wanted him to continue to kiss her in this way in which she'd never been kissed before. The pleasure was so overwhelming that it mattered not that he was a stranger. Her head was whirling with a giddy feeling with his heat now consuming her. Never had a man's arm holding her,

51

molding her to him, so stirred such maddening ecstasy.

She knew not the instant his hand left her waist to move upward to cover her pulsing breast, but his touch made her gasp with the strange, new sensations it stirred. Tony gazed down at her lovely face warm with passion and knew instinctively that he held an untouched virgin in his arms. For all her flirting, teasing ways, no man had ever had her. What he saw on her face was pleasure and fright of the unknown. His own frenzied desires had his head whirling as well, or he would have noted the trembling of her body. No wonder his cousin Mario was so eager to woo her. He had yet to force any woman against her will, nor would he. This little hellcat was a lily-white virgin!

He was satisfied that he'd lit the flame for those honey-sweet lips and her melting response told him so. In his twenty-five years he'd had his share of women, and now he'd sensed the moment her body had quit fighting and yielded. For now, it was enough.

The fury of their emotions had left them breathing heavily. He stood, content just to hold her and look at her. Amanda tried to figure out what was going on behind those silver-gray eyes. Why was he giving her that crooked grin and looking so smug? The romantic insanity was now replaced by resentment and contempt for the man's audacity. Who in the hell did this conceited bastard think he was dealing with? She was Amanda Kane. Didn't he know that?

With her arm free, she reared back and struck him a mighty blow. With his face stinging, Tony grabbed her roughly to him and kissed her until she felt like her lips were bruised. When he abruptly released her, she stumbled backwards.

"You damned little wildcat!" he muttered, devouring her with the coldest, cruelest eyes she'd ever seen.

"You . . . you no good bastard!" she spat back at him. She whirled to get away from him but his arm snaked out and caught her to him again. This time the kiss turned gentle before he released her once again. With an assured smirk on his face, he declared, "The next time you'll *ask* me to kiss you, Amanda Kane."

"You're crazy, Tony Branigan. That day will never come!" This time she yanked her skirt high so nothing would stop her fast departure. She ran toward the lights of the garden area with his laughter ringing in her ears. Only the oleander bushes heard his vow as he swore, "Oh, the day will come, *querida*." He knew he would tame her. Her sweet lips could deny it, but her sensuous body couldn't. She would be his woman!

FOUR

Amanda watched the two impressive figures walking jauntily along the corral fence. They were so completely engrossed in conversation that they'd not noticed her standing by the iron gate. She tapped her quirt with nervous impatience, determined to remain there until they moved on away from the barn where she was planning to go.

It would serve the arrogant Tony Branigan right if she told her father about his boldness in the Alvarado garden, she thought to herself as she watched them amble along puffing on their cheroots.

Dear Lord, she flushed just recalling the gunfighter's strong arms holding her and kissing her. The intimate way he'd touched her and the strange sensation his touch had stirred!

She was not aware of the close scrutiny she was giving him, memorizing the small, curly ringlets of his sideburns and the way his black hair curled around the collar of his shirt. The very defined arch of his dark brow gave him the look of a skeptic, as though he was judge and jury of everyone around him. The red kerchief around his neck was the only distracting color in his black garb. Even his boots and flat-crowned hat were black. The six-shooters hung low on his hips, seeming to sway in time to that cocky striding gait of his.

Suddenly, his quicksilver-gray eyes darted over to her direction and she could have sworn there was a smirk on his tanned face. Oh, she detested him! So darn sure of himself!

She moved away from the gate and the focus of Tony Branigan. Men! She was in a foul mood where any of them were concerned and this included her father and brother. When she thought of Jeff and his undivided attention to Mona yesterday, acting like the devoted suitor when she knew that only a few days ago he'd been in the hayloft with Chita, she got angry. And there was her father, who seemed to think it was his divine right to pick the husband she'd spend her life with. And while Mario Alvarado was great fun to be with, he'd make a horrible husband. Why he'd slip out on his bride on their wedding night to bed some pretty girl he'd spied on his wedding day!

Men! She kicked at the carpeted grass. The whole lot of them exasperated her this morning. Of all the men, she detested Tony Branigan the most. The gunfighter was the worst! Even the respected name of Kane had not intimidated him. At least it had not appeared to, or he'd surely not have taken the liberties he had in the Alvarado garden the night before.

His haunting name had even been the topic of conversation at their breakfast table. Dear Lord, he'd obviously impressed her mother, to judge from her comments. She talked about his nice personality and good manners. Her father bragged about his fast draw with pistols and urged Jeff to get him to give him some pointers. Amanda was happy to see that Jeff, at least, wasn't enamored with the conceited drifter.

She'd left the table to get away from their talk for it had been bad enough to be troubled by his damnable face in her dreams the night before. Lying there in her bed the dream had been all too real for her. Why, she could have lifted her hand and felt his face, it seemed. She remembered all too vividly the touch and feel of him.

As she left dining table and rushed down the hall, her spirits lifted and Branigan was forgotten for a while.

She breezed past Consuela giving her a warm kiss on the cheek, and Consuela broke into a broad smile. It warmed the housekeeper's heart when Amanda gave her a show of affection. Consuela knew she was in that sweet angel mood. What the Mexican woman could not know was how swiftly that mood would change as she got to the iron gate of the courtyard and caught sight again of Tony Branigan talking with her father. The two of them stood between her and where she wished to go. She was determined not to come face to face with Branigan—not this morning!

She welcomed the sight of Derek Lawson riding up the drive on that white Arabian of his. He had spotted her there by the gate and waved. He was obviously over whatever was ailing him the day before that had prevented him from attending the fiesta, Amanda concluded, watching him ride straight toward her. He'd not seen her father or Branigan standing over by the corrals, which pleased Amanda.

That was far from the truth, for the main purpose

for Derek's trip to the Kane ranch was in fact his curiosity about one Tony Branigan. David Lawson had returned home telling him about meeting the gunfighter at the fiesta. From what Derek could gather from his father, Kane put great store by the newcomer to Gonzales County. Derek could tell from the way his father was talking the night before that he would be following Kane's move. So like his father, Derek mused. Always he'd let Kane lead and he followed. Well, that time was coming to an end. *He* would follow no man. Instead, he would do the leading.

He smiled as he rode up on his fine white horse to find Amanda standing there by the gate, for she served his cause to perfection. He gave no hint of having seen the two men standing over by the fence. From what he'd been able to observe out of the corner of his eye he sensed that this guy gave no quarter to anyone, and he'd have to remember that, for no gunfighter, his father, or the powerful Mark Kane was going to stand in the way of his ultimate goal. He had a dream of being the most powerful man in Gonzales County. This dream had become an obsession with the young heir to the Big D Ranch, the second-biggest spread in the county. He was going to dethrone old Kane and marry his golden-haired daughter at the same time.

He reined the Arabian directly over to the gate wearing that gentle smile on his face that could have fooled the devil himself. Oh, old Nina had taught him to be a nice young gentleman with perfect manners. He knew exactly when to exhibit these admirable traits of the well-mannered clean-cut young rancher.

"Well, do I dare to hope you were just standing here waiting for me to arrive?" he teased Amanda leaping off the horse.

Because it suited her purpose, Amanda played the coquette and retorted, "Why, of course, and here you came on your white charger." She hoped that rascal Branigan had his eyes on her now. Maybe he'd realize he'd not had any effect on her!

She eagerly accepted Derek's invitation to go riding with him and took his arm to go over to the barn to get Prince. As they came up to her father and Branigan, her father introduced the two men.

It was mutual and instant dislike as the two measured each other. Tony's eyes were as cold as steel as he glared down at Lawson, who was a few inches shorter. Amanda stood with a smug smile on her face as she witnessed the scene. Tony's black brow seemed to arch even higher and she could feel the chill of his eyes as they darted in her direction. She felt exhilarated as she walked on to get Prince and rejoin Derek.

"You two enjoy yourselves," Mark called to the two young people preparing to depart. He was delighted that Amanda was acting so cordial toward Derek. Perhaps it was a possibility after all that she'd come to realize what a fine husband he'd make, he told himself. She certainly seemed in a lighthearted mood.

With Amanda sitting atop her palomino and Derek preparing to mount up on his Arabian, Tony grudgingly remarked, "Nice to meet you, Lawson."

"Yeah, same to you Branigan," Derek quipped in an offhanded manner. More warmly, he bid Kane goodbye before reining the Arabian around to Amanda's side.

If Mark Kane had any great expectations around his daughter's accepting Derek's invitation that afternoon, he would have been sadly disappointed with her rambling thoughts later that same day. She had returned convinced that a ride by herself would have been more stimulating. They'd cantered along at too slow a pace to suit Amanda or her fiery Prince. Derek was as bad as her father and brother with his boring conversation about land and cattle.

When her father had quizzed her at the dinner table she'd made the brief comment that it had been a nice ride and nothing more. Dear Lord, there was really nothing more to say, she mused silently. All too serious business talk to suit her.

One way or the other she had to convince her parents to allow her to go with Mona to San Antonio. The summer seemed to never be coming to an end. Remembering the summer day she'd left the Circle K and traveled with Uncle Armand and Aunt Lisa to New Orleans, she recalled how swiftly the seasons flowed by with all the parties and theater dates during those two exciting years. Actually, it seemed more like one very busy twelve months.

After dinner, she'd retired to her room wishing not to linger downstairs. But once in her room the book she picked up to read or the letter she tried to write didn't interest her. The miserable ticking of the clock even vexed her.

Strolling to the window, she saw her brother riding out into the night, probably to meet Derek so the two of them could enjoy themselves at the Red Garter drinking and carousing. Sweet Jesus, just because she was a girl she was doomed to be jailed at the hacienda. It might be proper, but it sure wasn't fair! Oh, if only *she* was a man, she lamented!

A light breeze flowed through her bedroom window and it felt marvelous, making the sheerness of her gown touch her flesh. The sweet-smelling honeysuckle wafted to her nose from the trellis below. The golden moon lit up the garden courtyard below. Obeying the impulse to stroll down there, she slipped into her satin robe to do just that. There could not possibly be anything wrong with taking a midnight stroll in one's own garden.

Nothing or no one was going to dent this surging, voracious zest to live, she vowed, tying the belt of her robe. She'd indulge herself to an extra glass of wine, too, if it suited her fancy.

She took the back stairs so not to encounter her father should he still be up working late in his study. Slipping quietly through the kitchen, she cautiously lifted a glass from the shelf and poured a glass of wine from the decanter on the tiled counter before going on out to the patio.

Somehow, there was no loneliness there in the dark walking by herself. She'd never thought of herself as a loner, but then maybe she was. God knew, she was different from the rest of her own family. She seemed to fit no particular pattern, as did most people she knew.

She'd made the full circle of the garden and came back to sit on the patio, setting the half-full glass of wine on the table next to her chair. She gave a soft giggle to herself. Perhaps she was a daydreamer, and life was not a bunch of daydreams. But sitting here now in the moonlit garden sipping on the wine she felt a serenity, and enjoyed the magic of the night around her. The flickering glow of fireflies across the way made it seem really magic. One sparking ember was not a fire-fly's miniature lantern, though. Tony stood back there by the gate watching her and puffing on his cheroot. He'd caught sight of her there in the moonlight as he'd returned a few moments earlier.

He'd trailed Jeff Kane tonight to the Red Garter Saloon in town and watched through the swinging front doors as he joined Derek Lawson and a couple of other men to go into a backroom of the dance hall. Only then did he enter the saloon. For the price of a few drinks for one of the floozy dance hall girls by the name of Pinky he'd had a couple of facts confirmed, so the trip had been worthwhile and informative.

She'd snuggled close pressing her voluptuous breasts to his chest as he'd put his arm around her and ordered her one drink after another. He gave her his undivided attention and Pinky found herself enjoying her work more than usual. "Honey, Pinky knows everything that goes on in this place. In answer to your question about the kid. He's a nice sort, but that other—well, he's bad medicine."

"Oh?"

"Yah, real bad, and a mean sonofabitch. None of us girls like him." Pinky was speaking of Derek Lawson. As she talked on and on, Tony realized he had himself a fountain of information. He played the role of the generous patron, keeping her busy talking and switching her drinks for his. He wanted nothing fogging his brain and he knew her drinks were most likely watered down and weak.

Suddenly her eyes darted toward the door and he felt her tense when a disheveled-looking Mexican came out of the backroom. Laying a generous contri-

61

bution on the counter bar beside her hand, Tony gave her a pat and told her, "Pinky, my pet—I've enjoyed your company and we'll do it again, eh?" Without further ado, he turned on his booted heels to go through the door feeling the piercing eyes of the Mexican on him all the way out.

He rode the two miles back to the Circle K Ranch mulling over all the things the frizzy-haired dame had told him. He found interesting the opinion of the girls at the dance hall about young Lawson. One could surmise he wasn't such a lovable chap, nor was he the well-mannered gentleman the Kane family thought him. He felt rather pleased with himself that he'd probably sized up Jeff Kane correctly as an easily influenced young man dominated by Derek Lawson.

All this was swept away when he started to climb the stairs to his quarters and spied Amanda strolling there in the courtyard. Like golden moonbeams her long flowing hair seemed to him, and her gossamer-sheer gown made her easy to follow in the darkness. What was disturbing her sleep this night, he wondered. She looked like a lovely goddess toasting the moon and the stars as she lifted the glass of wine to her lips. His male body came alive with yearning as he stood watching her there by the gate. He walked stealthily like some stalking animal, quietly and cautiously.

Amanda sensed his presence before she saw his huge figure ambling up the stone path. He'd obviously passed through the iron gate without making a sound —like a phantom. Her heart began to beat a little faster with a surge of wild excitement which she could not understand, but she gave no hint of it as she chided him. "Tony Branigan . . . you scared me! What are you doing slipping around here this time of night?"

He gave out a deep, throaty laugh, and she noticed how his silver-gray eyes seemed to gleam in the dark as they bored into her as he advanced closer. "I find it hard to believe that I scared you, Amanda. I doubt that you scare easily."

He stood in front of her now looking down at her as though he could read her thoughts. There was a primitive sensuousness about the man with the pistol swaying from his trim hips as he walked up. Everything about him cried out his male virility. Yet she found his face not the most handsome one she'd ever seen by far.

She found herself inviting him to join her in a glass of wine. A minute later as she poured it she asked herself why, when she'd tried to avoid his presence earlier. As they sat together on the wicker settee and drank the wine she forgot about that because she found him an interesting conversationalist. They could have been sitting in her aunt's parlor talking.

She was surprised to learn that he'd been to many cities, including New Orleans. He, like her, found the city a flamboyant, fascinating place. She'd also noticed that he'd complimented the wine as a very good Madeira, as though he knew his wines. All this made her curious as to just who this man really was. No mere drifting cowboy handy with his six-shooter. Never would she accept that story after she'd listened to him talk tonight.

"You've been quite a wanderer, Mr. Branigan," she remarked.

"You could say that, I suppose," Tony said, not offering to expand on the subject. His arm rested casually around the back of the settee and touched her shoulders. Amanda had not realized how she'd let down her defenses while enjoying his company.

What she was very much aware of was the warm thigh of his muscled leg touching her in only her sheer gown and robe.

"See the sharp lightning over in the southwest? Someone's getting a summer storm," Tony pointed out to her.

"Oh, yes, I see it." A gusting rush of breeze swept across the patio where they sat. Tony gave out a light laugh seeing that a tendril of her long hair was caught to the branch of the potted greenery next to the settee and he reached over to untangle it. His arm brushed the front of her. When his eyes darted to her face, he saw the anxious fluttering of her eyelashes and sudden intake of breath. He grinned, realizing he'd brushed the tips of her breasts without meaning to. He knew those luscious lips were wanting to be kissed. God knew, he wanted to! So he did, slowly and gently.

Her soft, almost naked body tantalized him and seemed to mold perfectly to his.

He turned her to fit the front of his firm, muscled body now turned on the settee. How perfect she fit to him! He could feel her heart beating wildly as her breasts pressed against his broad chest. The front of his shirt was unbuttoned and the fire of his flesh seared her bare body where it touched her.

"Tony!" she gave a soft moan. His overwhelming maleness made her feel as though she was drowning as he carried her like a swift river current with him. When his lips started burning a trail down her throat to capture the jutting tip of her breast, she gave into a minute of protest. Tony was like a man intoxicated, drunk with desire for the almost naked girl.

"No, Tony!" Her voice was more frantic and her knee pressed against his thighs making him release her and begin to regain his composure. Then he broke with her completely.

"You're an exasperating female, you know that?" he barked at her, straightening up in the seat.

"You—you seem to think you can take anything you want, Tony Branigan!" Her body trembled from the impact he'd had on her. "I—I didn't ask you to kiss me!"

"Damned if you couldn't have fooled me! I'd have sworn on a stack of bibles you did. I only take what's offered me, honey. I swear I thought you wanted me to kiss you," he said, a teasing grin on his face.

"Then you were wrong, Branigan!"

"No, I wasn't wrong, *chiquita*. Your lips tell the truth," he said, strolling away from her with the sound of the smashing wine glass echoing in his ear. It missed its target.

FIVE

Torrents of water rushed off the tiled roof of the hacienda as Consuela puttered around her kitchen. The rumbling thunder and flashing lightning made her jump convulsively with each new explosion. Her snickering daughter's finding amusement in her fear of the sharp lightning did not help her mood. But then, the young were not smart enough to be scared. Too loco, she grumbled to herself.

"Here, smart one—serve Señor Kane his coffee and you won't have time to make fun of your mama," Consuela ordered, flipping her bottom with the dishtowel.

"Mama!" Chita shrieked, feeling the sting of the dishtowel and jerking so that her upswept hairdo cascaded down. Little good all her primping would do now that this cloudburst was coming down over the countryside. She would be having no tryst with Jeff now!

Most of the Circle K hands remained inside the dry bunkhouse and were already engaged in a card game. Tony sat in the spacious dining room of the house with Mark Kane. All that lightning and thunder he'd watched late last night while he was with the beautiful Amanda had moved out of the southwest over them now.

As Chita swished around the long oak table serving the two men, she found herself forgetting about Jeff as her dark eyes took in the good-looking gunfighter with the cold gray eyes. He was a cool one, this man. *Mucho hombre!* It was obvious the señor put much store by what the man was telling him, although she was paying little attention to what was being said. She was too busy admiring his fine masculine qualities.

Back in the kitchen as she went about her regular morning chores, her thoughts did drift back to Jeff and the peculiar way he'd been acting. Perhaps he was about to announce to her his plans to wed the lovely Mona? It was not as if she had not prepared herself a hundred times for his words. She knew the terrible chance she was taking in giving her heart and body to the rancher's son. He could never, never marry her. There were times when she trembled at the thought that she could become pregnant. The young *vaqueros* over at the Rancho Rio who'd given her the eye did not do to her what the tall, lean son of Mark Kane did. She'd been in love with him since she was ten years old. It was about a year ago she'd finally caught his admiring eye, and nothing could have pleased her more.

The fierce summer storm was the last thing Amanda wished to wake up to. As she sat propped up against the pillows, she was tempted just to go back to sleep. She would have had it not been for Chita's soft rap on her door and her voice asking for entry.

"You ready for your coffee, señorita?"

"Yes, Chita, come on in," Amanda replied, sitting up straighter in her bed to receive the tray.

Jenny was passing down the hall as Chita went through the door of her daughter's room. She had given up nagging Amanda about having a good breakfast. Her habit of just coffee was too well established since living those two years with her sister Lisa. With Lisa, it was always coffee and croissants. Her vivacious sister enjoyed the lunches at the quaint tearooms around the city of New Orleans when she'd shopped the day away. Oh, Jenny could remember those days when they were young girls, before the time that the handsome young Mark Kane came into her life to steal her heart and take her to this wild, untamed country of Texas. Her sister Lisa had called her crazy, and perhaps she had had to be crazy in love to have considered it. There had been those moments when she'd pondered it. Her giant of a husband soon swept any misgivings away.

As she walked on down the stairs to join her husband at the breakfast table, she was a woman sure she'd made the right choice. She was content and happy.

She recognized the broad shoulders of Tony Branigan as she entered the room and he rose to greet her as she approached the table. With a nod to her husband, she bid Tony to please have his seat. Once again, she was quick to notice his certain charms, which set him a few steps above the average hired hands who graced their home and table. It was obvious to Jenny that the two had been engrossed in a serious conversation before she'd entered. Mark was quiet and thoughtful.

"I think I'll be on my way then, Mr. Kane. A good day to you, Mrs. Kane," Tony said, raising up from his chair to leave the table. Mark mumbled a goodbye, his mind obviously occupied with something.

"I like him, Mark," Jenny declared quite simply. The truth was she'd felt like that the minute she'd met him at the fiesta. There was a bold honesty in Tony that Jenny admired and she felt it had most likely left the same impression on Mark.

"Uhhh, yeah, I do too, Jenny dear," Mark remarked. Then he too excused himself and left the table.

Upstairs, Amanda had finished her coffee as Chita attended to the minor chores of straightening up the room. In a sudden impulse, she decided to share the many, many gowns she now owned with the Mexican girl. Never would she need even half of them here on the ranch. Perhaps one of the shawls with its soft wool.

Eyes wide with wonder and disbelief, Chita asked her, "Are you sure, señorita? This lovely pink one and the yellow one too?"

"Of course, I am sure Chita. Now you tell me how or when I shall ever wear all that stuff out, eh?" Amanda laughed. Chita giggled, shaking her head. It was true, Chita had to admit. In the armoire there was a gorgeous gown of every color in the rainbow ranging from blues to lavenders, pale yellows to golds, and the lovely white ones. More than a dozen, at least! The varied dainty slippers lined up to go with the gowns were almost as many.

"Did you wear things like this all the time in this place New Orleans, señorita?" Chita questioned anxiously.

"All the time. It wasn't like this godforsaken country. Now, please don't tell your mama what I said, Chita."

"Oh, no, ma'am, I won't, but could you tell me about it?"

With the two of them sitting cross-legged on the bed, Amanda told her all about the same places and sights she'd just told Mona about. Like Mona, Chita had lived the whole of her life in Gonzales County.

Chita sat enchanted by the tales Amanda told and she could imagine nothing being nicer than being in the shoes of Señorita Amanda Kane. Not only did she have the eye of the dashing, handsome Mario Alvarado, but Chita had heard the gossip about Derek Lawson's wishing to marry Señorita Kane.

She left the room her heart warmed by Amanda's generous gifts. Already she anticipated wearing the pale pink gown and the yellow one. The soft wool ecru shawl would certainly warm and comfort her on the cool winter nights.

The act of bringing a little joy into Chita's life pleased Amanda, and as she left her room to go downstairs her own spirits lifted. Poor Chita had few luxuries in life. Then Amanda saw Tony Branigan sitting at the dining room table with her mother and father and she stopped short in her tracks.

Sweet Jesus, one would take him for family the way he had practically moved in, she thought, observing the three of them. If only her father knew the audacity of the man she doubted he'd be sitting there at the table.

Hastily, she darted down the hallway as she saw

him getting out of the seat to leave. She wanted no glib remarks or those mocking gray eyes gazing on her this morning. Back at the far end of the hall she watched him stride out the front door with his hat in his hand, and from the back, with his black hair uncovered, she saw a resemblance between him and his cousin Mario. Never though, when she looked at his face.

When she heard the door slam and knew Tony had gone on out, she started to walk back down the hall toward the front of the hacienda. Her father came through the doorway heading toward his study across the hall. But his eyes were straight ahead and he took no notice of her as he went in and closed the door behind him.

The rains seemed to be putting a halt to all activities around the ranch this morning and Amanda decided to see what had her father so serious this morning. Without any hesitation, she opened the door and entered.

"Amanda, honey—you just get up?" Mark Kane turned from his desk and the papers he was shuffling through.

"A little while ago. This miserable weather seems to be confining everyone to the house this morning, even you." She smiled and strolled around the corner of the large oak desk cluttered with an assortment of papers. She had no doubt though that her father knew where everything was and he would have exploded with fury if Jenny had Consuela straighten it up nice and neat.

"Sit down a minute, honey, and talk to your old dad," Mark urged. "Besides, I'm glad you happened in, 'cause there's something I wanted to talk to you about anyway."

71

All Amanda could think of was that she'd subjected herself again to the arguments he'd already given her about the virtues of Derek Lawson. Why had she been so stupid!

Mark noted the slight frown on her pretty face. "Now, honey, I think you'll be pleased about what I'm going to say. At least, that's the impression your mom gave me." Amanda saw him smiling at her.

She relaxed slightly in the overstuffed leather chair in front of the massive desk. Her eyes were bright now with curiosity. "What is it, Dad? I don't know what you're talking about."

"The trip with Mona to see the Beckenridges. You may go if that is your wish. Mother tells me you'd like to." He saw immediately her pleased reaction and the gleaming radiance on her face made him glad that after Jenny's arguments the night before he'd agreed with her to allow Amanda the week's visit in San Antonio.

"Oh, thank you. I do wish to go. Mona and I could have such fun!"

Mark was pleased with himself for he wanted his daughter's happiness more than anything. Regardless that she thought him such a hard taskmaster—he did want that. Someday she'd realize just how much she meant to him, he reminded himself. "Well, then, you just go to your plans. I thought maybe that would put a bit of sunshine into this gloomy day for you."

When she practically leaped out of the chair and rushed around to give him a hug, he had no doubts about how much he'd pleased her. "Oh, I love you, Dad." She rushed out of his study. As Consuela would have said, she was that sweetest of angels in that moment. Mark Kane stood smiling to himself. She had been a refreshing distraction from the news Tony Branigan had laid on him earlier. Now he had to return to some serious thinking. At least, he'd had one brief break from the matters at hand.

The barn was dark as Tony made his way to Picaro's stall. As he'd run from the hacienda he had found the rains letting up. Old Slim had the wagons already hitched up ready to take out on the trip to Austin to pick up the first of many loads of barbed wire. Tony was glad Kane had agreed that a man should accompany him.

Something alerted his senses even before he heard that familiar accented voice hissing "Moreno!" He turned to see the disheveled Mexican back in the shadows. What had brought him here to the Circle K, Tony wondered?

"Pedro?" He sauntered back in the barn where his cohort was haunched down in the darkness.

"*Si*, I bring you an urgent message from Flanigan. He wants you to meet him tonight at the hotel in town. At eight, Moreno." The man named Pedro was already working his body through the loose plank of the side of the barn.

"Something happened, Pedro?" Tony quizzed anxiously. Pedro merely shook his head and gave Tony the hasty reply that Flanigan would tell him tonight. "I must get out of here!" He was gone, scampering across the ground with the speed of a fleeing jack rabbit, into the bush where Tony knew he'd left his horse.

This would be his first contact with Flanigan since he'd left his office in San Antonio several weeks ago.

He remembered that day well, and wondered again if he was a fool to take this time out of his life. But he owed Flanigan.

Hoisting himself up on the black stallion he rode out of the Circle K toward the south. Amanda stood at her bedroom window upstairs watching his departure, and now that the sun was breaking through the clouds she turned from the window to change her clothing for the snug pants and blouse, intending to ride to the Big D to convey her news to Mona.

The sandals were exchanged for her black leather boots and she took time to sit at her dressing table long enough to plait her thick hair into one long braid, securing the end with a ribbon.

She wasted no time in trying to find her mother once she had gone downstairs. She told Chita of her plans and rushed on to prepare Prince for the ride over to the Lawsons.

The palomino seemed as anxious as she was to be on their way. He pranced impatiently in the stall and Amanda laughed. "You're ready, eh boy? Well, just give me a minute." Her father was right about them, she mused. They were perfect for each other. The palomino was her most cherished possession.

She liked this feeling now engulfing her about her father, for their battles had not pleased her. As she thought about it now, he'd not mentioned Derek Lawson again and she'd not even had to use the little idea she'd conjured up in case he approached her once more about David Lawson's son. How perfectly everything seemed to be working out!

Already she was thinking about which of her gowns she would take to San Antonio and mentally matching up some of the exquisite pieces of jewelry. Oh, it would be so much fun to go to the parties and theater while they were there. There was that quaint cosmopolitan air about the city of San Antonio, even though it was not the port city of New Orleans with many ships coming in from all over the world.

The countryside had never seemed greener nor smelled sweeter to Amanda than it did now after the early morning rainshower. The lush, knee-high grass swayed with the gentle breeze to and fro and amid the sea of green there were splattered the blues and purples of the clusters of late-blooming cornflowers. When she was in such a mood, she could see the beauty of the land with the cattle grazing in the distance.

How peaceful it was now compared to how it must have been when her grandmother rode over these vast acres alongside her grandfather, always with the threat of being waylaid by wild Comanches. What a tranquil time they were now living in, compared to the bloodbath at the Alamo, when Mexicans had slaughtered Americans within those walls. Would the restraining barbed wire and the ending of the open range bring on another wave of bloodshed and violence, she wondered? Talk from the men on the ranches hinted at it; she knew from hearing bits and pieces of their conversations.

Over in the distance, Derek Lawson had observed the buckboard traveling down the dirt road with a couple of hands from the Circle K. It was the sight of the golden palomino with its rider coming into sight that brought a pleased look on his face. He was anticipating the possibilities if Amanda accompanied his sister to San Antonio. He could then take advantage of the absence of her overprotective father. The truth of the matter was that his hate for Mark Kane was almost as intense as it was for his father.

Suddenly Derek's fist clinched as he sighted the cocky caballero in his fancy garb going toward town. He detested the arrogant Mario and everything he stood for. Kane's distaste for Mexicans was nothing compared to Derek's venomous hatred of them. Oh, he'd kept it cleverly hidden in the depths of his soul so far. There had been many, many times lately when he was filled with contempt for his own sister, with her dark coloring and that glossy black hair like their mother's.

Amanda's blond loveliness enchanted and beguiled him, for her fairness suggested nothing Latin. It was, perhaps, Jeff's dark hair and eyes that had urged Derek to play the bully with him since the time they were small children. He had learned at a young age that it took little effort to intimidate Jeff Kane. It sickened Derek to the point of disgust to see what a scringing coward Jeff was. How different from his beautiful sister!

He reined his huge horse down the slope into the valley to meet with the racing palomino. Amanda saw him coming toward her and smiled. As they met and accommodated their pace one to the other, he greeted her. "Coming to see me, Amanda?" His mood seemed unusually lighthearted and gay. Amanda teased back playfully. "Don't be so conceited, Derek, because it is your sister I'm going to see. I've got marvelous news to tell her. Father just told me I can plan on going to San Antonio with her."

"That is good news, honey. It makes me especially

76

happy to hear I'll be escorting the two prettiest girls in Gonzales County." There was a different air about Derek that Amanda found appealing. He was more relaxed and casual, she thought, looking over at his finely chiseled face. He was a good-looking young man actually, and very ambitious.

In the next moment as he spoke his whole manner changed, as he told her how his father was not getting the itch to hire a gunman for the Big D, too. "Can't figure your pa hiring any kin of the Alvarado family."

"Lord, Derek—not you, too? There is nothing wrong with the Alvarados. They're gracious, refined people, and Bianca Alvarado is one of the nicest ladies around here. Smart, too!

He remarked without thinking, "Too clever for her own good, just maybe!"

Amanda laughed. "Oh, mercy! So you are another one of those men who think that all a woman is supposed to do is keep her home and have babies, eh?"

"It's a full-time job, I've heard," he laughed.

"I suppose so, if that's all a woman wants to settle for. For me, I intend to have more than that. Can't imagine anything more boring or dull right now."

"Then you don't want to be a rancher's wife, Amanda?" The expression on his face was one of hurt and disappointment. He'd have to change her thinking, he realized.

With that particular flippant air of hers, she tossed her blond braid over to the side of her shoulder as she shrugged her shoulders and retorted, "You could say that. I like life in the city much better. That's why I'm so excited about going to San Antonio in a few weeks."

Derek left her as they arrived in front of the white

frame two-story house to go on his way. She had given him some things to think about as he rode away. The little headstrong bitch just had to be taught who'd be boss once they were married. She'd be more challenge than that stubborn roan mare he'd conquered a couple of weeks ago, but conquer her he would!

The sun was still high in the sky when Amanda bid Mona goodbye an hour later to go home. It seemed the days were always the longest in the last weeks of August. She veered from the trail she'd taken coming over to the Big D to go by the way of the river, with the idea of a fast dip in her cove before going on to the ranch.

It was only after she had rid herself of all her clothing and leaped into the river that she heard the echo of splashing water. Someone was invading her private little cove and she resented the intrusion.

Tony was pleased with his afternoon's work. He had found a running iron he was certain the rustlers had been using to change the brand of the stolen cattle. He decided to give himself a treat in the river to cool his sweaty body. It had been a long, hot drive from the far point on the south boundary of the Circle K.

His alert ears had heard splashing water and he decided to see who was swimming downstream. He knew who he hoped it was over there. He recalled that golden vision of her nude body in the river and the memory stirred him powerfully.

When he saw that his wish had been granted, he dove under the water and surged upward as he got close to her. Slinging his wet hair back and forth, he greeted her. "Hello, *chiquita!*"

Amanda sprayed his face with water. "Damn you,

Tony Branigan! You scared me!"

Tony exploded into laughter. "Oh, I doubt that very much. Told you before that I don't think you scare easily. Nice and cool, isn't it?" He gave her a flashing pearly grin.

"Yes," she reluctantly agreed, her eyes going to his broad, bare shoulders. He was as nude as she was, and that fact made her nervous.

His eyes danced with mischief over her bare shoulders. It was as if he could read her secret thoughts. She could swear he thoroughly enjoyed irritating her. He was the devil's own!

As their bodies swayed with the currents of the river, their thighs touched, and the effect of it reflected in both of their eyes. A slow, easy smile came to his face as he reached over to remove a stray wisp of hair hiding those lovely eyes from him. The bright golden glow of the sun made the deep blue turn to dark amethyst. Jewels so beautiful, they were!

Suddenly, his muscled body tensed and the look on his face made her inquire what was the matter.

"Shhh, Be quiet!" he ordered, pulling her close to his chest. The sweet agony of her nakedness pressed to his was too much to endure. Was it just a clever ploy to have his way with her, she wondered?

Had Tony not sensed danger, he would have found this situation akin to a scene out of his wildest fantasy. But he was certain he'd heard voices, and he listened. His chin rested on the top of Amanda's head and his hands encased her tiny waist.

Christ, it was someone approaching! He could hear the footsteps of booted feet and they were coming this way. His mind was whirling for there was distance to

79

be covered for him to reach his holster and pistols over on the bank.

Amanda heard the sounds now, too, and for the first time she appreciated why her father had cautioned her. She couldn't control the trembling when she heard the male voice say, "Come on out, purty thing. We see that there gold hair, don't we Frank?" A laugh broke the air and stumbling footsteps edged closer.

"Oh, shit Mabry—let's git the hell out of here. That gal down there is Kane's daughter. Just saw that horse she rides over there. Come on!"

Through the low-hanging branches of a nearby tree Tony could see the two men.

"You ain't no fun at all no more, Frank," Mabry stammered, slurring his words.

"I ain't signin' my own death warrant, you sonofabitch!"

There was only one thing he could do, Tony figured, hoping the fallen tree trunk would hide his naked body as he crawled to the edge of the bank so he could make a daring lunge for his pistols. Whispering to Amanda what he was going to attempt, he started to slither over the ground. He didn't have time to worry about the shocking sight he was giving Amanda of his naked buttocks. The pebbles bit into his belly and knees as he worked tediously along the ground.

The one named Frank slid on the muddy bank. Disgruntled, the seat of his britches soaked to his hide, he cursed at his buddy. "Ifen ya' so hot for a piece of tail why didn't ya' take yourself one of them whores back in town? I say let's go, damn it!" He struggled to raise himself up.

The slight distraction was all Tony needed to make

80

the grab for his holster and draw his pistol. The two drunks found themselves looking into a pair of ruthless eyes as fierce as drawn steel daggers. Neither man wished to test Tony.

"Now carefully boys . . . throw your guns over here," Tony ordered them. When they complied with his order, he snapped at them again, "Now, do the same thing with your boots and pants."

Mabry did his bidding and Frank followed. "Can . . . can we go now?" Frank's voice cracked with fear watching the rage reflected on the gent's face.

"Tell you what I'm going to do with you two. I'll give you a five-minute start before I come after you. Let's just see how far you can get, eh?" Tony waved them off to mount their horses. Stumbling and falling over each other, the pair dashed for their horses to get away. Tony convulsed in laughter.

Amanda watched the whole episode still standing in the shallow water. So impressed was she with how Tony had handled the pair that she forgot about her nudity and called out to him, "You were marvelous, Tony!" An angelic smile graced her face.

He turned to smile at her. The excitement seemed to make her face glow with a beautiful radiance. "Thank you, little one." His eyes lingered so long that she was embarrassed and she snapped, "Will you please turn around so I can get out of this water before I become one big wrinkle?"

He turned around, but every fiber of his being ached to make love to her. It took every ounce of will power to deny himself the pleasure so close, so tantalizing.

SIX

Her pensive air whetted Tony's curiosity, and he was amazed that she gave him no fuss when he suggested that they sit there on the riverbank for a moment and let the sun dry her hair. After a moment of starting to give him a protest, she readily agreed when he pointed out, "Don't make a damn to me but I just thought you might not want to explain why your hair's wet." When she saw what he meant, he flippantly teased her. "Well, we finally agree about something." When he laughed, she thought it had a nice, deep sound.

The truth was as Amanda sat there in the sun with the gunfighter, she found herself dwelling in whimsy. He had been her knight in shining armor, coming to her rescue. With her deep blue eyes searching his tanned face, she asked him, "Who are you really, Tony?"

"Tony Branigan." He gave her a crooked grin. He got up and reached out his hand to lift her off the ground. "Come on, we better get back."

As they rode along he suggested in a most sincere tone. "You should be more careful, Amanda."

"Are you suggesting that I don't ride out alone?"

"I'm saying you should be more careful where you ride and where you disrobe," he teased, devilment in his gray eyes.

"Oh, you! You are the most impossible man, Tony Branigan. I'll swear you are."

"I'm not impossible at all. Merely trying to give you some wise advice. The next time I might not be around to save you."

"I don't need you!" She tossed her head, looking away from him. "What in the world do you think I did before you came along? Dear Lord, you are the most conceited man I've ever met! You're . . . you're not my keeper!"

He laughed and tipped his hat in a gallant gesture, for by now they were at the archway of the ranch. *"Adios, chiquita!"* He rode on toward the corral leaving her there to fume and mumble to herself about his highhanded ways.

Yet, the rest of the day and night in the secret part of her mind the image of him kept emerging—her knight in shining armor defending her innocence and honor.

In his quarters above the stables, Tony found the night weighing heavy on him as he, too, thought about the afternoon they had shared. He'd almost had to bite his tongue to keep from telling her his name was Tony Moreno, damn it! "Branigan" choked him, even to say it. Why in hades he'd not chosen something else as his alias . . . yet, he had not lied . . . not really. The fact remained that he had gone by Moreno so long that it seemed far more real to Tony than the label of Branigan.

Old Esteban Moreno was the only father figure in

his life and there was no traces of Terrance Branigan ever having been a part of his life. His memory of his early childhood was keen and vivid. The image of the mother he had adored was forever engraved in his mind . . . the beautiful Theresa, youngest daughter of Esteban and sister of Bianca Alvarado. She was two years younger than Bianca and had been far more beautiful, Tony thought. He found it hard to believe that the sweet-natured, lovely lady he'd known as his mother had ever been an impetuous, reckless girl, tossing aside everything in her young life to run off with the likes of a young Irish seaman. Yet Tony knew that his beloved grandfather had not lied. Fate decreed that he had to tell Tony the story.

What a toll she'd paid for that impulsiveness, he lamented! Humbled and penniless, Theresa had returned to the palacial hacienda with Tony to throw herself on the mercy of Esteban Moreno. Her untimely death when Tony was only six should not have been, except for the fact that her heart was broken.

Did the man Terrance Branigan still live? For almost five years she'd waited and hoped, Tony knew, that he'd come back into port on a ship like the one he'd sailed away on. First, she'd haunted the wharves in New Orleans and finally they'd caught a packet ship and sailed across the gulf into the port city of Corpus Christi. She'd been elated, Tony remembered, over a tip from a sailor she'd met that her "Terry" was in port at Corpus Christi. So they had journeyed in search of his father and Theresa's husband. The port and the city yielded no sign of the robust Irishman with his brown curly hair and laughing blue eyes. The futility of it all and no money left made Theresa's decision to go on to San Antonio simple and easy. It was all she had left for her and the small boy.

Even now, Tony could see old Esteban's black eyes that first night they'd arrived at his home. Like a warm liquid they'd moved over him as the dignified gentleman bent down to look him in the eyes and the two had measured each other.

Tony's firm, muscled body spanned the length of the bed he now lay on, but that night he could barely lock eyes with Esteban kneeling down. As young as he was, Tony saw love in the old man's eyes that night, and so it had been between the two of them ever since. Even when he'd received a firm paddling for an act of mischief during those growing up years or a harsh verbal reprimand for a naughty boyish prank, Tony knew the love was there.

What had brought forth all the bygone days tonight, he wondered? Flinging his long legs over the side of the bed, he walked over to the small cupboard and took a bottle of his favorite brandy from the shelf along with a glass. Pouring himself a generous serving and picking up his cheroot, he ambled outside his room to sit there on the top step in the darkness.

He took a sip of the brandy, savoring it and enjoying it to the fullest. Then he took a puff of the cheroot and its pungent odor hung over him. Life was a crazy set of circumstances, he mused. God knew what kind of haphazard existence would have been his lot in life had Terrance Branigan not deserted them. He would never have lived in a fine home or received the education afforded him by Esteban Moreno.

When he'd returned from Mexico some six months ago after his sojourn there at the Moreno mines, he'd thought his life was neatly arranged. His plans were to marry the very beautiful daughter of his grandfather's friend Francisco Gomez. There again, he could have sworn by all that was holy that he'd found the girl of his dreams in the lovely Magdalena Gomez with her sultry dark eyes. Looking back now in this reflective mood, he knew her sweet-faced look reminded him of the dark loveliness of his mother. Was that what had drawn his eyes to her when she'd first accompanied her father to Esteban's home for dinner about two years ago? Perhaps it might have been, for now he knew it was not a love to endure a lifetime.

Had his wily old reprobate of a grandfather picked the beautiful, gentle Magdalena for his bride? He wouldn't put it past him, for he'd started to nag him about taking a wife.

Tonight it was easy to cuss Brett Flanigan, but he was not really the culprit. The little blue-eyed, golden-haired wildcat was the cause of it all. He'd had the best of intentions in giving his services to the U.S. marshall, and then he'd planned to return to San Antonio to pick up his life.

Until Amanda, Magdalena had been the perfect picture of the wife to share the life he'd for himself planned at the ranch just outside San Antonio. She fit with ease into the Morenos' social circle, and Tony had been her constant escort for months. Always beautifully groomed in expensive gowns and jewels, she was admired everywhere they went for her grace and charm. She shared his great love of the ranch and enjoyed their rides around the hilly countryside outside of the city.

But dear God, she didn't cause this fever in his

blood like Amanda did! If it was foolish for a man to feel as he did about a girl who showed him contempt most of the time, he had to admit he was a fool. Yet he couldn't rid himself of the poison. Even worse, his craving for her became stronger every day.

The quandary he now found himself in concerned what to do about Magdalena. There was Esteban to consider. He would not be the cause of a broken friendship of two old friends like his grandfather and Francisco Gomez.

Which was more important . . . honor or honesty? Tonight he felt as he had when he had been a strapling youth. He yearned to have a serious talk with his wise old grandfather. He could imagine those piercing black eyes regarding him. He'd not like what Tony must tell him, but he would have to see the logic that a temporary hurt for a nice girl like Magdalena would be better than a lifetime of pain. Tony would never want to do that to any woman, remembering his own mother with her broken heart. Somehow, this thought made his guilt easier to bear. He sighed and put these thoughts aside, for the hands of the clock were signaling that it was time to go for his rendezvous with Brett Flanigan in town.

A guilty conscience was plaguing Jeff Kane and making his nights sleepless unless he drank himself into a stupor. His perfidy, which had started out so small that it seemed no more than a boyish prank, had grown into a maelstrom of wrongdoing . . . things that scared Jeff to the point of madness.

To steal a few head of cattle to cover his gambling debt many months ago had seemed like the simplest solution that night when he and Derek had been carousing at the Red Garter Saloon. How readily he'd bought Derek's simple suggestion. "Hell, one day the whole damn lot will be ours, Jeff," he'd pointed out. There was a grain of truth in his theory. Jeff could even admit to himself that he'd experienced a sense of gratification, having for once in his life outsmarted the clever Mark Kane who everyone respected. Perhaps it even gave vent to his years of resentment against his self-assured sister. Even during her absence, he could never seem to step into her vacant shoes where Kane was concerned. But now, he was scared . . . frightened as he'd never been before. He'd never bargained for any killing, or robbing from anyone other than his own father's herd of longhorns.

Derek Lawson had taken on the traits of a tyrant. Jeff had seen sides of his character that spoke of such evil that Jeff wanted to go running to his father for help, but he didn't dare. He was caught up in this web of destructive evil, and he knew not where to turn for help. Derek's threats rang in his ears as he tried to lay his head on his pillow at night, and sleep would not come until he blotted it out with many drinks of whiskey.

Now that Amanda was back home he'd been privy to Derek's ravings about her, and Jeff saw that he was obsessed with her. He knew, too, his sister's stubborn determination not to marry him. It frightened him to think of what lengths Derek would go to. In his own way, he loved his sister, and he admired her tremendously. He'd seen Derek's cruel treatment of women over the last two years. It sickened him, and thinking of something like that happening to his beautiful sister ignited a spark of courage in him as nothing else did, he'd discovered with amazement.

He'd seen Derek break the spirit of man and beast, but he'd never stand by meekly if he tried anything like that on his sister. The presence of the surreptitious Tony Branigan had put Derek in a foul mood. Those cunning gray eyes seemed to hold a secret, and yet they seemed to be all-knowing and aware of any mysteries you were harboring within you, Jeff thought to himself. The man gave him an eerie feeling at times. He knew his effect on Derek Lawson.

Sweet Jesus, how could one man have sired such completely different offspring! No one could have been sweeter and nicer than Mona Lawson. Perhaps that was why he restrained his desires with her and used Chita for his male hunger. He could not bring himself to tarnish Mona until they were married. With Chita, it was different, for she was only a Mexican servant girl. The irresponsible young Jeff Kane felt no concern that her heart might be broken or her life ruined. That he was using her sorely and as heartlessly as Derek Lawson was using him seemed to have escaped him.

As Jeff's drunken stupor delivered the peace he sought for the night, Tony Branigan left the Circle K for his meeting with Flanigan in the old hotel in Gonzales.

The U.S. marshall had to have something important to tell him to ride all the way to Gonzales County, Tony figured. He wondered if there had been a new development down at the border in Reynosa. He'd find out soon, for the lights of the small hamlet were right ahead. He spurred Picaro to go faster.

SEVEN

The lean, lanky hired hand came rushing out of the barn to get to the corral where one of Kane's best cowhands was breaking in a cantankerous mustang, full of fire. Bill Fisher didn't want to miss the show going on. The hollering and howls of the other hands told him it was beginning as he slammed against the barn doors so he could get perched on the top rail of the corral fence.

Flinging the doors apart, he was met by a woman's shriek. "Oh, My God Almighty, did . . . did I hurt you, Miss Amanda?" He stood frozen in his tracks looking at the wide-eyed girl. Had he clobbered the boss's daughter? Her face appeared unmarked.

Amanda gave an uneasy laugh, hoping to ease his embarrassment and concern. "It's all right. I'm just fine. A little close, though."

Bill heaved a deep sigh of relief. "Lordy, I'm sure sorry. I was just . . ." Amanda interrupted him before he could tell her where or what he was about. She gave out a lilting little laugh. "I know, Bill, and get on over there so you won't miss it. Slim might just get himself thrown this time."

"Doubt that, Miss Amanda. Old Slim could ride the devil himself," the red-faced Fisher called back to her, stumbling on a rock with his eyes on her.

Like the men, she enjoyed seeing the taming of the wild mustangs from time to time, and no one could top Slim Christy when it came to breaking in a mustang. She had to marvel at his talent, especially at his age. Her father put great store in Slim. He'd been with the Kanes the longest of any of the men. Someday, they both felt, the wild mustang would no longer roam wild and free across the Texas countryside. They became fewer and fewer all the time, like the buffalo.

This morning Amanda felt no urge to watch the scene at the corral. She was riding into Gonzales for some sewing notions and a list of items her mother needed. For her mother's sake and at her insistence, she'd reluctantly put on the divided skirt instead of her preferred tight pants. She hated the excess serge material of the dark green skirt that was far more restraining than the snug pants.

She had to admit though that she understood her mother's reasoning, for this was the time of the year that all the ranchers hired more hands. The autumn was here and roundup was just around the corner. She knew, too, that many hands drifted into town during the day, as well as at night, to play cards and drink whiskey at the dance hall saloon. Invariably, fights would break out. More than once Amanda had witnessed brawlers careening through the barroom doors, scuffling and tangling, fists flying wildly and the men tumbling and rolling in the dirt road in front of the entrance.

Had Mark Kane been at the hacienda and heard

91

Jenny suggest Amanda ride into town to get her sewing articles, he would have instantly forbid it. But he had left early to see how his men were coming along on stringing the new barbed wire. Amanda had overheard her mother and Consuela talking about the long day he was planning with no break at noontime. In fact, baskets of food were going out on a wagon for the workers.

Jenny was occupied with her thoughts about Mark. She knew the importance of this day and what the act of putting up barbed wire represented in the county. Mark was declaring this land his, setting up definite boundaries.

Amanda took no notice of Tony Branigan down at the far end of the barn when she mounted up on Prince and rode out of the barn. Tony's nose detected the sweet fragrance of her even before he turned from his conversation with Red Cassity. He wondered where the little minx was off to in such a hurry. Obviously she had put little stock in his warning. He got the impulsive urge to follow her, gave Cassity a hasty farewell, and leaped astride Picaro.

Amanda had just passed through the archway entrance when she heard the rider's approach. Turning back to look and see who it was, she saw the big black animal and knew it was Branigan. She dug into Prince's side but the smaller palomino couldn't outrun the long-striding Picaro. In a minute he'd covered the space and distance dividing them. Tony tipped his flat-crowned hat with a jaunty air and grinned. "Good morning, Amanda." He allowed his eyes to dance over her from the top of her head to the firm roundness of her hips fitted into the saddle. She sat on a horse damned well, he thought to himself. Her back was straight and erect, making the jutting points of her breasts press temptingly against the sheerness of the blouse. Tony could not conceal the lusty look in his eyes. That would have been like trying to stop breathing.

"Who asked you to follow me, Tony Branigan?" She turned away from him looking straight ahead with a displeased air on her face, which wasn't exactly a true reflection of her feelings.

"Your father," he lied.

"He's not even at the hacienda. In fact, he's been gone for hours."

"Those were his orders, *querida*. Like it or not."

"Don't call me *querida* and . . . and we'll just see about your orders to escort me. I'll see if Dad told you that!" she taunted him.

"I feel a deep concern for your safety and you wound me deeply. If you think I'd not lay down my life for you then you just don't know the depth of my feelings," Tony dramatically declared. She resented even more his trying to play her like a child. Oh, he was a smooth-tongued scoundrel, but, as crazy as it might seem, she could picture him so clearly entertaining the fawning ladies in her aunt's lavish parlor. His small talk would charm the ladies and his appearance, dressed as he'd been at Bianca's fiesta, would impress them, as well. There was a rugged handsomeness about him. Without her realizing it, an amused twinkle came to her eyes, which Tony noticed.

What had brought that gleam of mischief, he wondered? What trick was she now plotting to let loose on him?

As she turned to meet his staring eyes the full impact of her radiant face greeted him and he was afire with desire. The sun shining down on her hair made it look like pure gold, and purple gemstones could not have been lovelier than those eyes. She was an enchantress!

When she addressed him her mercurial mood had changed the tone of her voice. "Tell me, Branigan—how did you come up with the name of your horse?"

Dear God, she never ceased to amaze him and surprise him! He explained to her that the black stallion was determined to test his will and it had been a matter of deciding who was to be the boss. "Picaro means rascal, and he was just that. As you can see for yourself, I was the winner, but it wasn't easy." He didn't like being a loser, she suspected.

Although she didn't say it, it was obvious he loved the magnificent animal as much as she adored Prince. For a fleeting second, she stared as boldly at him as he had earlier at her. Giving a mischievous laugh, she quipped, "I think I shall call *you* Picaro. God knows, you are a rascal."

He found himself laughing with her and once again they seemed to have forgotten their fighting and conflicts. Once again, Tony was convinced that with a girl like Amanda life could never be dull. He'd never know what to expect.

They both were surprised to see that they were entering Gonzales's one main street. Their lighthearted camaraderie had made the two miles seem like nothing.

They dismounted in front of the one merchantile store, belonging to Harold and Martha Anderson.

They'd known Amanda all her life. The plump Martha waddled from the back of the store as Amanda entered with the tall, good-looking stranger, who took Martha's eye immediately.

"Well, mercy me! Amanda, honey—how good to see you! If you aren't the prettiest thing. Look here, Harold, who's come to see us!" Martha's eyes stole a fast darting glance to the young man at her side. Her curiosity was whetted to know who he was.

"Nice to see you, Mrs. Anderson, and you too, Mr. Anderson." Amanda quickly introduced them to Tony, very aware of Martha's curiosity.

Harold Anderson quickly stated, "Well, you're working for the best outfit in the county when you're Kane's man, I can assure you."

Tony readily agreed with the merchant. Amanda watched the pair's instant acceptance of the gunfighter and wondered at Branigan's rare quality that enthralled people. Dear Lord, even her own mother and father numbered among the group.

She turned swiftly on her booted heels and wandered down the rows of counters holding a hodgepodge of various goods. Finally, Martha tore herself away to inquire of Amanda what she could get for her. Tony ambled around, helping himself to one of the tempting apples piled in one of the wooden barrels. After the third time of ramming into one of the hanging lanterns that dangled from the ceiling, he strided over to Amanda and in a formal manner excused himself. He told her he would meet her out by the hitching post.

Amanda raised a skeptical brow at his manner but decided to play his little game. "That will be just fine,

Mr. Branigan. I won't be long . . . maybe fifteen minutes." He gave her a nod and left. No sooner was he gone than Martha was singing his praises.

Amanda merely gave her a soft grunt and continued to roam around the store, where the Andersons wasted not one foot of the space. She was now in the back of the store with the sewing things that Consuela had asked for. Dozens of bolts of muslins and cotton materials stood on the shelves. Many odors came to her nose from the many jars of spices and herbs and mingled with the leather, tobacco, and dyes of the blankets and rugs.

Thirty minutes had passed. Her purchases were not bulky so she had placed them in the saddlebags. Amanda sat on the wooden bench tapping her boot heel impatiently, becoming more vexed with each passing minute.

When Tony finally sauntered through the swinging saloon door of the Red Garter Saloon with a frizzy-haired blonde hanging on his arm reluctant to let go, Amanda muttered a disgusted hiss. "Oh, I should have known!"

When he came across the street and had the audacity to ask, "Well, are you ready?" she could have murdered him for certain! Men! They were all the same.

Instead, she refused to answer him and mounted Prince without saying a word, slapping his hand sharply when he tried to assist her. She didn't want his touch on her.

"Sorry I made you wait," he said going on over to leap up on Picaro. She was riled good at him and he knew it.

"I hadn't waited. I just came out of the store."

She lied and he knew it for he'd seen her sitting on the bench while he was listening to Pinky's whispering in his ear. But it had been well worth it! She could have cooled her heels for an hour if it had taken that long for him to hear what he'd found out.

He was to discover out just how irate she was when a whirling cloud of dust was left behind as she spurred the palomino into a fast gallop, leaving him back in the distance. He let her have her way for a while. How easily the two of them had lied today. They were more alike than he'd realized. As perplexing as it was at times, he admired that stubborn pride. The willful little witch fascinated him.

He spurred Picaro into action. Now it was time he caught up with her and overtook her. He, too, had pride, and no little slip of a girl was going to outdo him. He'd tame her if it took the rest of his life to do it!

God knew, he'd be the first to admit that she was headstrong and spoiled, but that lively spirit of hers tantalized and challenged him. It was the thing that set her apart from any woman Tony had ever known before.

What Amanda Kane would come to realize, though, was that he was a stubborn man when it came to getting what he wanted. And he wanted the golden-haired girl with her perwinkle-blue eyes for his own.

EIGHT

The incident down by the riverbank had impressed Amanda more than she realized. She had always had a vivid imagination and the picture she conjured up in her mind about what could have happened that day if he had not been there to protect her from the two drunk drifters set her to trembling. There in the water naked, she would have been at the mercy of those two and just the idea of the horrible things they could have done to her was enough to make her cringe when she thought about it.

Subconsciously, this must have been on her mind as she rode Prince a few days later and veered away from her favorite spot on the shaded river bend. But for that, she would not have met Mario riding the border of the Alvarado properties.

He galloped up to meet her with that usual devastating charm, making her realize she was within a mile of the Alvarado hacienda. On his way to seek out his foreman, Lorenzo, which would take him to the border of their land with the Kane's, Mario was more than pleased at the pleasant treat of seeing Amanda again.

When he'd found her gone from the spot in the garden that night of the fiesta, he'd been crushed for a few minutes, until he was sought out by the luscious green-eyed Lucinda Evans, a neighboring rancher's young daughter. His slightly wounded male ego was quickly restored by the willing, eager girl, and the last few weeks they'd met several times and Mario had found her to enjoy a very healthy sexual appetite for a young, inexperienced miss, so overly protected.

Mario knew better than anyone that he was like a bee flitting from one lovely blossom to another. He could not conceive of any one woman's holding his attentions a whole lifetime. However, Amanda Kane had caught his eye when she was only twelve, a very mature twelve-year-old, and she'd continued to whet his appetite and his hunger to possess her. Perhaps it was because she'd always been a little remote and unattainable for an easy conquest. It was actually the summer she was fourteen, and just before she'd left to go to New Orleans, that he'd begun to have hopes of realizing that insatiable quest. He had made a promise to himself that he'd do it by the time she reached sweet sixteen, but Mark Kane had fouled up those plans. But Mario never pined long over any ladylove.

Like his mother, Bianca, Mario was clever and sly. He knew it would be foolhardy to play his usual games with Amanda Kane because Mark Kane would think nothing of shooting any man between the eyes if he played her false.

There was no woman Mario admired like he did his mother, and Amanda was the one woman who reminded him of her, with that spirited spunk and determination. He'd gone through his adolescent years resenting his mother's bossiness, her playing of the father role. That had long since passed though, for he could now appreciate how much burden his mother had carried after their father's untimely death.

Amanda watched him come closer and closer. He always struck such a fine figure in his expensively tailored clothes. It was no wonder the men around the countryside looked down their noses at Mario and his aristocratic airs.

She was always reminded of the fandango dancer she'd seen at the theater in New Orleans when she looked at Mario Alvarado, with his flair for the dramatic in his movements, and his animated chatter. Oh, he was a good tonic for a woman, she would certainly grant that. His flowing, flattering words were like music to one's ears—if you didn't allow yourself to be carried away. Like most females, she adored his flattery.

Today was no exception, he was the same exuberant Mario as he reined up and greeted her. She gave him a bright smile as she remembered their last meeting and how she'd deserted him there in the garden. He could have been peeved. Obviously, he wasn't.

"We are so close to the hacienda, why don't you ride with me over for some refreshments and see Mother? She'd love to see you, as would Maria."

"Why not!" Amanda flippantly replied. At least with Mario there was no mystery. He was certainly not like his cousin Tony Branigan, with his perplexing personality. Besides, she saw nothing out of order about visiting one's neighbors. So they rode toward the sprawling hacienda with its red-tiled roof in view now.

At the courtyard entrance, they reined up on their horses to the hitching rail and Mario leaped down to help Amanda dismount from Prince. "You were the most beautiful girl there at the party," he said. He let his fingers trail casually through her loose, free-flowing hair. "But I'd swear that today, with this lovely hair down, you are even more lovely."

Amanda smiled sweetly and was at the point of thanking him when the excited Maria came rushing out to meet them. As the youth Juanito came to take charge of the horses, the trio walked toward the front entrance of the house. Maria chattered like a magpie and Mario was tempted to wring her dainty little neck. He decided that he'd done the wrong thing by inviting Amanda to the house. Perhaps they should have gone for a ride around the countryside and had some privacy.

Once they were in the cool hallway, Mario urged his sister to announce Amanda's visit to their mother. "Please, *niña*, shut up and go get Mother!" Mario threw his hands up in exasperation and Amanda broke into a laugh.

Señora Alvarado entered the room a short time later, and when Amanda turned to see her she could not help thinking how striking this lovely lady was in her plain black gown adorned only with white lace cuffs and collar. She had marvelous features, which seemed to be enhanced by the blue-black hair pulled back from her face in one huge coil and the high Spanish comb tucked in place. How anyone could find this family of Spanish descent anything but refined and always gracious amazed Amanda. That included her own father. It could only be narrowminded prejudice.

101

Bianca invited her to sit down and ordered refreshments to be served. They were all ready to enjoy the cool lemonade when Mario was summoned to the hall by one of their *vaqueros*. With a disgruntled look on his handsome face, he excused himself. His mother gave a soft laugh. "I'm afraid my son is not too pleased."

"That's the way of a ranch, though. Always something coming up to need attention," Amanda remarked.

In the half-hour Amanda visited with Señora Alvarado the subject of her nephew Tony somehow managed to come up. Bianca inquired, "Is my nephew pleasing your father, Amanda?" That Mark Kane had hired him amazed her still.

"I would say father was very pleased with him, Señora Alvarado," Amanda replied. Her answer pleased Bianca.

Funny that she should happen to visit the Rancho Rio today, for Bianca had planned to send a message to Tony. He must be informed about the impending visit of Gomez and his daughter to the Rancho Rio.

It was only after Amanda Kane had departed and she sat at her desk writing the message she intended to send to him that she realized how much of their conversation had centered on her nephew. Señorita Kane had, indeed, asked many questions. Bianca smiled, finding it most interesting. A most amusing thought popped into her mind. She quickly pushed it aside, rationalizing that it was most unlikely. Or was it?

Long after the youth Juanito was summoned to deliver the message, Bianca sat in her room pondering this venture Tony had himself involved in that had brought him to Gonzales County and taken him away from his responsibilities at the huge ranch outside San Antonio, as well as at the Moreno mines in Mexico.

When Esteban had reached the age of seventy he'd turned the running of his vast estate over to Tony, and during the last few years her nephew had proven that he had an astute head for business. The ranch and the mines had prospered and grown. Yet the wise Bianca could well understand Mario's resentment about Tony's being his grandfather's favorite grandson. But she was fair enough to admit that Mario would not have been as capable of doing the job as Tony was.

Señora Alvarado's asking him to go to the Circle K had delighted Juanito, for there was the chance he would get to see Chita. His spirits soared as he rode toward the ranch at twilight time.

When Juanito had dutifully handed the message into Tony's hand and the two of them had spent some minutes in small talk, Tony noticed Juanito's eyes darting to and fro. Suddenly it dawned on him what the young lad was searching for . . . a sight of the servant girl, Chita. He smiled, remembering the first pretty girl who had set his heart to fluttering wildly.

"I think you might just find Chita, Juanito, if you walked over there by the flower garden. Before you rush away, though, I wish you to give my aunt this answer. Tell her I will come to see her tonight. By the way, it was good to see you again, *amigo*."

"And nice to see you again, Señor Branigan," Juanito said, already turning and stumbling over himself like a young, awkward colt. He wanted every precious minute he could have with the lovely Chita.

Tony strolled lazily to his quarters. His full concentration was on his aunt's message, and he speculated why Franciso Gomez would be coming to the Rancho Rio at this time.

Under no circumstances could they know he was here, and in no way could he have any encounter with Francisco, much less with Magdalena. Not now!

Most men would think him insane even to consider wanting to jilt the gorgeous, wealthy Magdalena. And Tony wasn't so crazy with this fever for Amanda that he'd forgotten the extent of Gomez's influence and power.

As it was most nights around the Kane bunkhouses, the hired hands got a card game going after supper, drinking whiskey to wash the dust out of their throats. The musician among them usually broke out his guitar or banjo to strum as a couple of the other men joined in to sing harmony. Sometimes Tony had joined in this camaraderie, but not tonight.

He rode out right after nightfall toward the Rancho Rio. Mark Kane observed his departure as he strolled in the garden feeling the need of some exercise after Consuela's meal. She had outdone herself tonight with that delicious roast and its rich brown juices. If he caught Jenny's head turned from him, he loved nothing better than dipping hunks of his biscuit in those juices. Dear Lord, it was good eating!

Many times, he'd thought about their different backgrounds. Jenny's family had lived on a much grander scale than his. Her father had been a successful businessman in New Orleans with a fine home and servants. Jenny and her sister Lisa had been the prettiest, most sought after young ladies of the city.

His family were people of the land—farmers. Life had never come easy and they had had no time for teas or soirées. Yet, somehow it had never caused any barriers between him and his Jenny. As it had been with him, it had been with her a matter of love at first sight.

It would have been his fondest wish that both his children would be so lucky in finding their mates. If Jeff had the good sense to marry Mona Lawson he would be that lucky. As far as Amanda was concerned, he had accepted long ago that it would take a special man to satisfy her. Although, he'd never admit it out loud, the last few weeks had brought about a change in his thinking. He was a man who rarely changed his mind but lately, he seemed to be doing a lot of it.

He didn't like questioning his own sound judgment as much as he'd been doing of late. Was he becoming affected by age, he wondered? He quickly shrugged that idea aside as unacceptable. It could not be true, for his strength was not waning. He could do as much and more than any man around these parts.

Privately, he was glad Amanda had bucked him about becoming engaged to Derek Lawson should he ask her. He'd not questioned her or Jenny about their relationship lately. Yet, there wasn't one iota of anything he could put his finger on to explain his sudden change of feeling about Derek. As often in life, time would tell.

He tossed the stub of his cheroot away and started to go back into the house when another set of hoof-steps drew his attention and he saw his son riding out and down the drive in front of the courtyard entrance. What in blue blazes were the young rascals up to tonight? First it had been Branigan, and now Jeff galloped off into the night. He ambled on into the hacienda, wanting only the comfort offered by his overstuffed chair and a couple of hours of reading before turning in for the night. Twenty years made a difference in a man's body and his stamina.

The grandfather's clock in the hall and entry way of Bianca's home struck the hour of ten when Tony left for the Circle K. She had found out no more than she had known before by the time he left. However, she had given him her promise that neither Gomez or his daughter would learn that Tony was playing the role of hired gun over at the Circle K Ranch. "I give you my word, Tonio," she vowed.

After her nephew left, she summoned Mario into her sitting room. She quieted his first attempts at protest with that authoritative air of hers. "We'll do this, Mario, because it is asked of us. You understand?"

"I can't say I understand, Mama, but I will abide by your wishes," Mario agreed begrudgingly.

"I appreciate that, Mario. Like you, I am in the dark myself, but I do trust Tonio, and he is family. I'm sure one day we will know. The matter of Magdalena Gomez and he is his business, but Francisco's goodwill is a family concern."

Mario nodded his head. Later as he left his mother to go to his room thoughts of the beautiful Magdalena visiting the Rancho Rio began to excite him. Tony's loss could be his gain. A brilliant idea was already seeding itself in his mind. A wicked smile creased his lips. Of course not, he mused, he'd never let it slip that Tony was but a few miles away. Let the little beauty think he'd taken off for parts unknown. A lady in distress always needed an understanding gentleman's shoulder to cry on. He'd be there to oblige her.

His romantic soul gave way to the wildest of fantasy. Who could say where the Gomez's visit to the Rancho Rio might lead, Mario delightfully mused.

The name of Gomez carried much weight in the city of San Antonio and in most of Texas. Should the whimsy hit him to apply his skill and education in the law someday in the future it would not hurt at all to have a father-in-law who was an influencial lawyer. His charm could be appreciated much more in the city than here at Rancho Rio. No, he would not utter a word about Tony Moreno's playing the game as gunfighter—Tony Branigan here in Gonzales County!

NINE

Tony rode out of the Rancho Rio into the moon-dappled countryside down the slope and crossed the river dividing his aunt's land from the Circle K. His aunt had eased any qualms he'd had when he had ridden over, but something else gnawed at him. As he rode along looking up every now and then at the dark sky, it seemed the eerie sight of the moon darting in and out behind the floating masses of clouds spoke of it—a danger lurking out there somewhere.

He could have been an apparition himself to someone watching him, as the huge black form of Picaro fused with the black of the night.

Eyes were observing him from over on a secluded rise of ground. A couple pair of eyes, to be exact. Their task completed and homeward bound now, the two riders had paused for one final minute of discussion before parting company.

One man's face distorted with a venom of hate and his hand caressed the pistol in its holster, itching to draw it and fire it. The other rider urged his partner, "I say we get the hell out of here."

"Wonder what that bastard's been up to?" he

mumbled, wondering whether Tony had been out snooping around where he shouldn't be. "He needs killing, I think!"

"It's obvious he's not been where we've been. He came from the direction of the Alvarado place."

Jeff Kane was anxious to get back to the ranch. The night had left him drained and he was in need of a drink to calm his nerves and shaking hands. He didn't even want to think about the scene that would take place when an angry Mark Kane inspected that cut barbed wire at dawn the next morning. Derek was scaring the hell out of him by now.

"I say we get out of here—now!" Jeff insisted.

"Will you shut your goddamn mouth? I'm going to see where that Mexican bastard is heading," Derek Lawson barked. "I'm going to be sure that he isn't going to meet up with Jake and the boys with those cattle. We sure as hell don't need that problem."

Jeff said no more for he knew it would do no good. Derek Lawson would remain frozen in that spot until he was ready to move on. Perhaps it was better that Branigan be away from the barn when he arrived back at the Circle K.

Tony reined the horse to the right and a small grove of trees. "Hold it, boy," he murmured softly to the spirited Picaro. He wanted a minute to search the darkness around him, which had seemed to be hanging like a shroud for the last few minutes.

He felt as though he was being stalked like an animal. Every bone in his body told him so and his flesh crawled with it. He sat atop his horse listening to the whistling breeze rush through the branches of the trees. His ears listened intensely for some sound and his eyes darted around over the open clearing of land he'd just ridden over, scanning the rise in the direction of the Lawson property and then back in the direction of the Circle K.

His hand slowly moved to the six shooter with that instinct that was so much part of him. It took only one split second to make all the difference in whether a man lived or died.

Suddenly, he strained to search the area up on the slope. Something foreign to the rest of the dark night had caught his attention. Something pale . . . almost white, he could have sworn. Then there was nothing, for the moon was now hiding behind a mass of heavy cloud.

Whatever it was it was enough for Tony to want to investigate it. He cautiously guided the horse out of the glade and edged along the clearing.

"The sonofabitch is heading this way. Well, he's going to get more than he's bargained for," Derek muttered. The pistol was now out of its resting place in the holster and drawn.

"Jesus Christ, Derek—are . . . are you crazy?" Jeff thought for one swift second Derek was tempted to move the barrel in his direction. Never had he seen such a look on his face. The panic he felt exploded in him to such a degree that without thinking about the possibility of Derek's shooting him in the back, Jeff jerked the reins of his mare. Riding like demons were chasing him, he didn't let up until he passed through the archway gate entrance, feeling secure at last in the haven of his home. Nothing could happen here, and Derek Lawson was taking aim on Branigan. Jeff wanted no part of that. His friend was a lunatic!

110

Tony's keen ears picked up the galloping hooves at once and he, in turn, put the spur to Picaro's side. His sudden advance as the moon came out from behind the cover of cloud made him the perfect target for Derek's aimed pistol. The night exploded with a sharp bang!

The hot, searing sting to the side of his head forced Tony to take cover behind a nearby tree. He was cussing himself, as Mark Kane had a few weeks ago when he'd allowed himself to be the victim of a gunman's bullet. Unlike Mark, however, Tony knew his gunman, because for the moment he had to hold up to mop the blood flowing in his eye, he saw the white horse galloping away in a speedy retreat. That Arabian was too unique to mistake.

It wasn't the wound that stopped him from giving chase to the bastard but something far more important. After his meeting with U.S. Marshall Brett Flanigan, he would not put Flanigan's months of digging in jeopardy to satisfy his ego. No, he'd wait most impatiently, but it would be taxing. He would settle with Lawson in good time, when it was right. Nevertheless, it galled him raw for Derek Lawson to think he'd won this time.

He made his way back to the ranch and put Picaro in his stall for the night. He knew by that time that his wound was minor. He thanked God Lawson wasn't an expert shot. Even though the wound was bleeding profusely, as was natural for a head wound, Tony took the time to satisfy his curiosity about Jeff's roan mare. It was as he'd suspected. As he walked out of the barn and to his quarters, he lamented sadly that it was a hell of a deal to have your own son stealing from you.

He couldn't figure the young idiot out. Jeff Kane had to be a fool!

Tending to his wound and pouring himself a stiff slug of whiskey, he sank down wearily on his bed and slowly removed his shirt, deep in thought. This job was tearing him apart, because his own emotions were far too involved—not only because of his feeling about Amanda, but Mark Kane, too. He'd come to have a deep respect for the cattle baron. His head ached with its own misery as he took a second glass of whiskey.

Christ, what a devastating blow all this was going to be to Kane's pride. His cattle empire was the largest in the state of Texas and it was being betrayed by his own son.

The liquor gave him a good night's sleep but the next morning his head felt like he'd been kicked by a mule and he took care to set the flat-crowned hat at a certain angle for comfort. He was not ready to meet with the roaring voice of Mark Kane ranting like an angry lion when he descended the steps of his quarters.

There in the gathered crowd of six ranch hands Kane stood and Tony assumed someone was catching holy hell. When he finally made his way down the steps and got to them he realized that was not the case.

"I'll kill the bastards! I swear it! They cut my wire last night, Branigan. Eight different places. The sons-ofbitches!" His face flushed red with his fury. "Did you see anyone while you were out last night, Branigan?"

His question took Tony by surprise, causing him to hesitate for a minute before answering. He stammered, "No . . . no, I didn't, Mr. Kane." He felt guilty as the devil. Those piercing blue eyes of Kane's were making him out to be a liar and he didn't like the feeling at all. But had he told the truth, it would have shattered the proud man standing before him.

Kane was a perceptive man and he wasn't exactly pleased or satisfied with the way his gunfighter had answered him. He didn't like feeling the way he did this morning. It would be a bitter pill to swallow to think he'd been so wrong about a guy like Tony Branigan. He'd seen enough to know that anything was possible. Branigan had an evasive air that bothered him.

As he was pondering what Branigan had been up to last night, he was also curious about his own son's nocturnal activities. He'd seen him ride out after supper and he knew when he'd returned. He wasn't courting David Lawson's pretty daughter, Mark Kane knew. So where was the young rascal going and what was he up to?

From the way he looked this morning at the breakfast table, Mark had concluded he'd had a bit of carousing at the Red Garter in Gonzales. He'd found it hard to keep from laughing, though, when his sweet, dear Jenny looked at the ashen face of their son and fretted that he was coming down with something. Dear Lord, she pampered the boy so. Boy, hell! He was a man in years and body and all he needed to do was start acting like one, Mark thought to himself.

Kane adored Jenny. She was everything and more that he'd ever asked in a wife but he did find fault in the way she excused and spoiled Jeff. He felt that she recognized her easygoing nature in him, while the headstrong Amanda was more like Mark.

When Kane left to go with the wagon and the men,

Tony felt something of a chill to the air, strange and new. It bothered him. Should he have told Kane about what had happened last night as he'd returned from the Rancho Rio? Deceiving Kane about what his real purpose in Gonzales County was was beginning to leave a foul taste in his mouth. He was at the point of confiding the truth to the rancher.

Tony's frustration was no more irritating than Mark's was as he rode toward the southern border of his land. He sure as hell needed the loyalty of his own men, and he was swimming in a sea of doubts and suspicions this morning.

The last days of the summer were placing a heavy burden on his shoulders. He was stubbornly determined to see that his barbed wire stayed up. The roundup and the taking of the cattle to market lay ahead of him. Only after that was done would life around the Circle K Ranch slow down.

He'd handpicked Branigan and his faith in himself would be shattered if he should be proven wrong. He prided himself that his forty-five years of living had taught him a few things about a man. As bothersome to him was the fact that he knew he'd given Branigan the chill earlier, and if he was innocent he'd not deserved that. Kane prided himself also on his fairness.

Tony rode along over the countryside deep in his own thoughts and something urged him back to the spot where he'd been ambushed by Lawson the night before. It was frustrating to go against his nature and not ease his itch to settle the score with the no good sonofabitch Lawson. Every fiber in him churned with the desire to ride over to the Big D Ranch. It would serve young Jeff right if he'd told Kane the truth. It

114

gnawed at him to think that his revenge had to be postponed. He knew Lawson's type, and he detested it.

It was a serene, peaceful countryside he rode through this morning. Over by the pine grove a white-tailed deer darted out to run across the clearing. Last night a shot had rung out just about where he halted now. But for the fact that Lawson was no expert with his pistol he could have been dead this bright, sunny morn. Damned if he could take that lightly!

He dismounted to sit on the ground and think. His mind was heavy with a lot of jumbled thoughts and mixed emotions. Long ago, he'd learned the hard way that a man couldn't mix business and pleasure, and, in spite of all of it, he had done it. A golden-haired angel kept getting in the way of his good judgment and he was helpless to stop it.

Sure as hell, her brother was involved in this thing, and when the end came, she'd end up hating him for arresting Jeff, Tony knew.

Perhaps it was family pride, but he felt certain that Mario wasn't involved, although he'd wondered about him in the beginning. Mario's only guilt was his insatiable ego with the ladies, Tony had concluded. That, at least, didn't make him a criminal.

What Tony couldn't figure was the insanity driving the wealthy ranchers' sons. The vast cattle empires would be theirs someday, given to them on a silver platter. It simply made no sense to Tony. No sense at all!

He reached in his pocket for one of his cheroots. There was no doubt in his mind that Jeff Kane had been a party to last night's episode out here, but neither was there any doubt who'd pulled the trigger of

115

the pistol aimed at him. So he now knew one thing for sure. Lawson wanted to be rid of him in the worst way.

A random thought came to mind about young Lawson as he sat deep in thought. Which plagued him the most, Tony wondered? Had Derek noticed the desire in his eyes for the beautiful Amanda, or did he worry about what he, Tony, might discover roaming around the countryside as Kane's hired gunfighter? Perhaps it was both!

Maybe he should find out—and he knew just how he could do that. He was rising up off the ground when he saw two riders approaching. As they drew nearer he recognized one as the old German Echert, and the other as his son, Franz. Their spread lay to the north of the Evans land, and they raised sheep instead of cattle in their hilly countryside. Tony wondered why they were coming all these miles out of their way to go into the town for their monthly supplies.

As they came up to where Tony stood by his horse, they greeted him. Old Hans Echert gave a curt nod of his head for he spoke little English. It was Franz in his guttural, German-accented voice who acted as spokesman. Tony found himself straining his ears even to understand the younger Franz, but he managed to make out that they'd come upon an injured man back on the trail on their way to town and he had requested that they seek help for him at the Circle K or the Big D Ranch.

Tony wasted no time leaping up on Picaro to be on the way in the direction Franz had indicated. He thanked the German farmers hastily and rode off.

The Echerts resumed their way back to the German settlement of New Braunfels, for it was there they

116

were heading and not toward the town of Gonzales as Tony had assumed when he saw them approaching.

Tony wondered as he galloped away from the pine grove if this was also the handiwork of Derek Lawson. If he was a gambling man, he'd have laid money on it.

TEN

When Mark Kane returned to his home after a long, tedious day of seeing that every foot of barbed wire was strung in place again and men were assigned to ride guard over the area that night to see that it remained intact, he was ready for a hearty meal, a shot of whiskey, and his bed. Instead, he was greeted with Branigan's news that one of his men had been shot and left for dead. It was the last straw, and Kane immediately declared his own war on the cutthroat outlaws.

"By all that's holy, I'll form my own goddamn vigilante band and waste no time calling in any sheriff or his deputies to string them up to the branch on a tree. Hell, let's face facts, Branigan—it's too vast. The sheriff would have to have three times the men he has to cover these three ranches alone."

What he said was true, Tony realized. He knew, too, that a vigilante group could mess everything up at this point. What Kane didn't realize was it could be his own son he could be putting a rope on to string up to a tree. Tony wasn't sure yet just how deeply or seriously Jeff was involved.

"I've got a hunch I'd like to try, Mr. Kane, but it's going to take a little more time, if you can gamble a while," Tony said.

Kane took a gulp of whiskey and poured Tony another shot in his glass. He puffed deeply on his cheroot, weighing his decision. Tony's relating to him that someone had taken a shot at him brought Mark up straight and wide-eyed in the overstuffed chair. He certainly wished no harm to come to the gunfighter—but it had lifted a tremendous load off the cattle baron's chest and eased any creeping doubts of Branigan's honesty.

"All right, Branigan—I'll play it your way for now. Hell, I'm getting old, I'm beginning to realize, 'cause I'm not going to even ask you what you got in mind. I'll tell you this one thing though—these bastards or one bastard knows these ranches and the countryside damn good—every path and trail."

Tight-lipped, Tony replied, "Yes sir, I agree." He got up, stretched his long legs and moved around the corner of the desk. It was best he took his leave before the conversation went any farther. He'd got the delay he needed from Kane.

He was almost out the study door when Kane's voice halted him. "Tony, I only ask one thing of you, and that is I want to be the first to know when you do find out. Wherever it leads, I want to know." There was an austere look on the older man's face.

"I'll tell you, Mr. Kane." He walked on out of the room. He could not promise that Kane would be the first to know. Mark Kane was a clever man, and Tony wondered just how much he did know already.

His rather sober mood was lightened when he saw

the swishing skirt of the sprigged muslin gown and the feisty filly wearing it. Bouncing golden curls bobbed up and down with each step she took as she rounded the base of the staircase starting to go up the steps.

He watched her and smiled. What would she say if she knew that he'd seen that shapely, nude body of hers. So far, he'd not flaunted that little fact to her. He'd let it remain his private secret. He'd memorized every sensuous curve his eyes had beheld that day at the river. That day he'd had no idea who she was or that he'd end up here at the Circle K Ranch working as a hired gun for her father. Life had to be crazy!

She was halfway up the stairway when she happened to glance down to see him standing at the base ogling her with that crooked grin on his face. "Good afternoon, Mr. Branigan."

"It *will* be now that I've seen you, *querida*," he said.

"Damn it, Branigan—I've . . . I've told you not to call me that."

He pursed his lips mockingly. "Oh, but you are."

"Branigan, you have a vivid imagination!"

"Oh, if you but knew. You see, we do agree on something. I'll make you a bet that you do, too."

She felt a flush coming to her cheeks, especially with his heated silvery eyes undressing her. Her flesh seemed to tingle and her heart pounded faster just looking down at his tanned face. Why did she permit this man to get so under her skin? Never would she understand it! Even though she searched for the answers she feared what they might be.

It was like some wild, primitive thing—these feelings she felt toward this presumptuous gunfighter. He

120

made her feel so weak to fight him, and she'd never felt weak in her life. He also made her feel like a child at times, and that irked her. He had a quality that completely shattered that self-assured, poised girl she'd thought herself to be when she'd returned from New Orleans.

Yet, later, as she sat on the floral-chintz-covered chair by the window of her bedroom and searched for answers to another problem confronting her—to which, as with her questions about Branigan, she feared the answers—it was Branigan himself she felt impelled to seek out to advise her. Sweet Jesus, her father wouldn't do. Certainly her dear, sweet mother didn't need the burden of concern and worry. To whom but Branigan could she confide this?

She had hoped when she'd come in from the dusty, grime-laden commissary and bathed, it would rid her of the gnawing concern about the episode with her brother. She had never seen Jeff explode in such a furious outburst of temper. Later, she'd questioned if it had been more like panic seizing him—like a scared child.

She'd even blamed it on the miserable heat of the day. Gonzales County was as hot in September as it was during August. Tempers did seem to flare more easily. Nothing really made sense, though, and she could not really hold the oppressive heat responsible. Once she'd bathed and dressed in her light cotton frock, she'd gone downstairs. This was when she'd encountered Tony. She had snapped at him when it was really Jeff she was so irritated with. He had really done nothing to rile her, she realized as she sat there now thinking about it.

Reflecting on those morning hours over at the commissary working side by side with Jeff, she recalled how smoothly they'd worked together, laughing and joking as they took the count of the sacks of grain and feed.

Then she'd gone to the far end of the building and was in the process of counting those last bins when Jeff came rushing back with his face ashen and almost distorted.

"Don't—you go on in, Amanda! I'll finish up." His voice cracked. She could tell he suddenly tried to calm himself, when he added, "It's so hot out here for you."

When she hesitated for a minute with her eyes wide from his sudden outburst, he urged impatiently, "Damn it, go on, Amanda!"

She didn't like the nudge he gave her or anything else about her older brother's attitude at that minute. As it had always been with the two of them she had the ability to outfox him, so she said nothing and left the building. As she gave him a parting smile and bounced out the door he'd had no inkling that Amanda wasn't going to let it go at that. She'd almost wished she hadn't been so curious, so she wouldn't be fretting now.

There was an old hole at the back of the building and she'd remembered it from their childhood days playing games around the grounds of the ranch. She slipped quietly around the corner of the frame building and peered in the old hole to watch her brother. What she saw heightened her curiosity that much more. Why would he be hiding money out there? He'd have no cause to hide it if it was honest money, would he? Wouldn't he keep it in his room?

She continued to watch until he placed it back in the hiding place. She stood up erect, realizing just how much lower that old hole was now compared to the time when they were kids. Then it had been eye level, but now she had had to bend in an awkward position to see through it.

She took another peek before going on over to the hacienda. Jeff had returned to the other side of the building to resume his work.

She couldn't know that Jeff had sat there making his final entries in the journal hating himself and his weakness. It never dawned on him that she would have thought about spying on him, but then he'd never anticipated this crazy thing with Derek would have gone this far, either.

Amanda strolled over to the bed, weary and weak from her foreboding thoughts about Jeff. Besides, the heaviness of the air made her feel lackadaisical. Even the animals out in the barnyard seemed affected by the weather. There was no hint of a breeze coming through her bedroom window.

Tony Branigan too found himself in a rather lazy mood. As he strode toward his quarters he saw old Juan Santos enjoying his siesta under the pecan tree. He was so sound asleep he didn't even hear Tony's heavy-booted footsteps passing by. With no qualm of conscience, Tony decided to go up for a short nap if it was possible there in his upstairs quarters. There was little breeze stirring and the birds gathered in the trees around the grounds seemed too lazy to fly around.

Amanda was as restless as the rolling masses of clouds rushing over the countryside from the southwest. She gave no thought to the fact that it had become dark outside as she changed into her snug pants and loose tunic blouse. The only thing consuming her suddenly was the idea of going for a ride on Prince and ridding herself of the tense feeling choking her so that a nap had been impossible. The longer she lay on the bed the more nervous she became. That was ridiculous, she'd decided. A ride on Prince was the only solution she could think of to give her release and peace of mind. As she darted toward the barn all she would have had to do was look at the warning signs in the sky to realize she was being foolhardy to go out in the open countryside. The tormenting storm within her that she was unable to calm actually frightened her. This preoccupation prevented her from heeding the gathering storm above her as she saddled Prince and rode out into the countryside.

II

AUTUMN'S GOLDEN HARVEST

ELEVEN

Tony Branigan could not logically explain to himself what urged him to leap up from his bed to look out the window. Sleep had escaped him after he'd stretched across the bed intending to take an afternoon nap. Yet as he glanced out the window he could have sworn he'd slept a few hours, for it looked like the afternoon had passed and twilight was shrouding the countryside. Surveying the skies more carefully, he noticed the eerie look of the sky. He didn't need anyone to tell him what was brewing in those ominous dark clouds. The ghostly quiet only confirmed his suspicions.

The fast galloping hooves of the golden palomino caught his attention immediately. Dear God, was she out of her mind going out with such a violent storm approaching?

Grabbing for his boots and yanking them on with all the haste he could muster, he rushed to get to the barn to get Picaro. Numerous whirlpools of dust swirled and rose as he made his way to the barn. Over in the distance the echo of roaring thunder could be heard and sharp flashing streaks of lightning trailed from the sky to the ground.

He had to urge the black stallion on out the barn door. Angrily muttering to himself, he agreed with Picaro that he had more sense than the crazy, irresponsible blonde he was going to rescue. He realized that his suggestion to her a few days ago that she'd need a keeper was a good one.

He'd seen her rein the palomino toward the south, of all directions. But by the time he and Picaro rode under the archway, he could barely make out the fading image of the palomino with its cream-colored tail and mane as the trees swallowed it up. She had left the pastureland behind and entered the wooded area.

Sprinkles of rain pelted Amanda's face as she reached the woods and the sharp streak of lightning broke across the sky causing Prince to jerk. She managed to keep him calm and under control. At least with the cover of the trees, she hoped to spare herself from getting drenched, because by now she knew there was no outracing the approaching storm to get back home. It did no good to call herself stupid now, but she knew she'd not been too clever. The signs had been there to see and feel all day had her mind not been so preoccupied.

A sudden crashing and snapping caught her ears as a huge dead branch high in one of the pines came thundering to the ground just in front of her. Her reaction wasn't fast enough this time to control the frightened, rearing Prince. Neither were her gloves dry, and her hold on the reins slipped. Helplessly, she felt herself slipping backwards and frantically grabbed to get the reins. With the impact of the ground and a sharp pain on her head, she felt herself drowning in a sea of blackness.

Picaro veered and weaved through the trees. Rain-drops moistened Tony's face as he cussed, seeing no sight of her at all. She had traveled farther ahead of him than he'd figured. He could not fathom any possible reason she'd do such a crazy thing. He had credited her with having more sense.

By now, his horse was nervous and reacting to those tremendous flashes of lightning and thunder. It was taking a strong, dominating hand to keep him in check. At least, one thing was in his favor—and Amanda's. Just before he'd ridden out of the clearing and into the edge of the woods, he'd watched for a second the path of those destructive funnel clouds going away from them. They would be spared that fury spawned by the devil himself. But the fierce edges of the wind, lightning, and cloudburst would still rain down on this part of the countryside.

He felt as though a heavy load had been lifted off his chest when his searching eyes caught sight of the pacing palomino. But his heart pounded wildly when he saw no rider.

He leaped off Picaro and rushed to the spot where Amanda lay, limp as a rag doll. He lifted her into his arms. "Thank God, you're all right," he whispered, even though Amanda did not hear him or the other rushing words of his concern and love.

Kneeling there on the ground with her cradled safely in his arms, he watched the awesome giant tentacle dip down and go up with those destructive, powerful winds sucking up in its vortex anything in its path. Its fury held him in a trance and he clutched Amanda closer before raising up to get to the shelter of an old shack he had noticed.

He found it difficult to handle both of the horses and Amanda because by now a deluge of rain was beginning to fall and galelike winds were upon them. Needles from the bending, swaying pines were raining down on them, as well.

By the time he got the two horses quartered inside the lean-to built onto the shack and Amanda laid on the old tick mattress on the dirty floor, the shack could have been a palace. It was dry inside, and the skies were solid now with clouds promising heavy rains. The shack had been less than fifty feet away.

He gathered up a couple of blankets to tuck around Amanda, for there was a sudden chill to the air now. That seemed crazy when only a short time ago it had been an ungodly sultry day. With planks broken from the side of the lean-to, he kindled up a fire in the dilapidated old stove.

The drapes of cobwebs and dirt mattered not to him as he surveyed the two rooms which for the moment provided a safe, dry haven for him and Amanda. Amazed, but pleased to find a supply of blankets lying around, he took a couple to the horses, hoping to add to their comfort.

It was only after he'd taken care of Amanda and the horses that he let himself dwell on tending to his own needs. As he'd just done to Amanda he stripped himself of his soaked clothing. He was glad she was still docile and weak from her sudden fall. Her only protest had been a soft moan of discomfort and a light fluttering of her eyelashes. She'd opened her eyes for only a second before closing them again.

He'd smiled, knowing there would be the devil to pay later when she found herself naked and knew he'd

130

undressed her. He'd worry about that later. At least for now, he was grateful to have her at his mercy!

It seemed Lady Luck was with him, for there was even a lantern which he'd held to examine her for any injuries. He tightened the blanket around her and held her to him until she finally quit trembling from the chill. Only then did he go to sit by the stove in one of the wooden chairs with a blanket around himself. While she slept he sat, thinking. This shack was equipped with too much. It was obvious to him now that he'd had time to think about it that someone had occupied it.

He heard her stir slightly and looked over to see her open her eyes, but she didn't speak. Instead, she snuggled up in the blanket only to turn over on her side. What a beautiful, bedraggled angel she was lying there!

A most pleasant idea hit him and he leaped up out of the chair to go to the lean-to, stumbling on the long blanket as he walked. With the flask in his hand, he returned to the chair by the stove. He made a vow right then and there to never be without a flask of brandy in his saddlebag from now on.

Never had a gulp of brandy tasted so good to him as he savored the heat of it traveling down his throat. He leaned back in his chair with his feet propped up on the other one feeling rather cozy and relaxed.

Amanda began to come out of her daze. She opened her eyes slowly to see her strange surroundings and Tony sitting in the dimly lit room with his bare chest and his torso wrapped in a blanket. The scratchy blanket made itself known against her soft skin and slowly her hands began to discover that every inch of her was

131

naked, causing her to shudder.

"BRANIGAN!" she shrieked suddenly, with a moan of agony following. Her head hurt so and her screaming stopped her short. More softly she inquired, "Branigan, wha . . . what the hell is going on?"

With that devil-may-care smile on his face, he dryly remarked, "Taking refuge from the storm you so stupidly rode out to meet, *chiquita.*"

"But . . . but wha . . ." she quickly pulled the falling blanket back over her bare breasts.

Yet with all her raving she would have had to be deaf not to hear the rushing water coming off the roof of the shack. She also remembered now that she'd taken the tumble from Prince and then—nothing.

When she looked up Tony stood before her like some fierce giant with his hand holding something. "Here, take a drink and shut up so I can tell you what happened."

"What is this?" That spirited fire was coming back into her eyes again.

"Brandy. Keep the chill from you." He sat down on the mattress. "By the way, how are you feeling?"

"Miserable and cold." She twisted slightly, just enough to remove her legs from touching the side of his body. His nearness was disturbing to her, knowing as she did that he, too, was nude. She'd seen their clothing hanging across the back of one of the chairs near the stove to dry.

"Don't know what in the hell was going on in that pretty head of yours, Amanda Kane, but that's why we ended up here," he informed her, without cracking a hint of a smile.

"What was going on is none of your business. I just want to get home," she curtly answered him.

"Well, little one, what you want and what you get are two different things. So until the rains let up and until our clothes are dry you're stuck here with me. Here, take a swig."

She obeyed him and then she turned her eyes toward him looking like an innocent, wistful child. "I'm hungry, Tony."

He laughed lightly, reached over and kissed her on the top of her head. Getting up from the mattress, he declared. "Then you shall eat, señorita."

She watched him move away, holding the blanket up so his big feet wouldn't get tangled. She heard the cracking of wood and the slamming of metal. "What are you doing, Branigan?"

"Ask me no questions and I'll tell you no lies, my sweet one. Just wait and see, eh?"

She did, using the time to run her fingers through her hair and giving it gentle shakes in an effort to dry it. To her delight, when she reached out and felt her sheer tunic it was dry, and it was sweet relief to be able to rid herself of the scratchy blanket. She sat with it still enclosing her body below the waist.

Time had no meaning to either of them as the evening went on. Amanda began to find it amusing that she was marooned here in the shack with Tony. The scandal of it even intrigued that reckless part of her. Poor Tony was not so lucky in being able to rid himself of his blanket, for his heavier work clothes did not dry so fast.

They ate the meager meal he provided and Amanda exclaimed, "You are a surprising man, Tony."

He wore a look of hurt on his face and sighed, "Ah, *chiquita*—why could you not have said 'amazing,' or perhaps 'delightful'?"

They both laughed, finding themselves caught up in a crazy sort of gaiety from the ridiculous dilemma fate had placed them in. The flask of brandy was practically gone by now and its effect had swept away any hostility from Amanda by the time they'd finished eating. Tony's black coffee was sheer ambrosia, Amanda swore to him.

"Ambrosia is the nectar of the gods," he murmured, his voice warm with passion. Her bewitching beauty held him in a trance as his gray eyes adored her in the dim light of the room. So isolated and alone with her, he forgot about everything outside this small world that had been theirs alone for the last few hours.

Slowly, he moved to take her half-parted lips in a kiss. Amanda sensed his yearning and it became her yearning too to be kissed. Sitting there with his broad chest bared and his dark hair tousled, he was a most sensuous male animal, and her pulse beat like a drum with the stirring he created in her.

"Kiss me back, Amanda *mia*. Kiss me, too," he huskily urged, his mouth moving slowly over hers. Lips and tongues touched and caressed with a liquid heat. Tony felt himself swell with overwhelming desire as she willingly melted to his body. With one swift movement he flung away the restraining blanket to take her lovingly in his arms and press her back on the mattress. His hands searched under the sheer tunic blouse until he found the rounded breast, which fit his cupped hand with perfection. His finger moved to circle the hardened tip and he sensed her deep intake of breath. Dear God, she felt wonderful there in his arms, as though she was made just for his loving. His slightly accented voice began to whisper in her ear his words of love in Spanish. There was no turning back now. Come what may, he had to have her, if only this once in his life. He had to taste the sweet nectar of this golden goddess he held in his arms.

His body covered her with his heat as they lay there on the mattress. His thighs pinned hers and his chest pressed against her throbbing breasts. The wildfire he'd ignited on her lips spread and burned through the whole length of her body.

When he raised to look upon her passion-warm face, she moaned his name softly, as if asking him to come back to her. The thought of being the instrument of even a moment of pain for her hurt him, but it had to be, for she was a virgin. There was no doubt of that in Tony's mind. Feeling the delightful fever of her body, he deemed the time to be right, for he was heady with throbbing passion.

"*Querida*, I will be as easy as possible. Just go with me . . . trust me, little one." His lips loved her until she arched in sweet agony for his taking. He made that thrust that caused her to gasp as his lips tried to soothe her.

More than anything now he had to bring back that peak of pleasure he knew she was sharing with him, and he moved slowly and surely to do just that.

When he felt her body undulate with ecstasy in time with him, it pleased him. "Dear God, you're marvelous!" Now that he'd tamed her he sought to brand her to be forever his and his alone.

It mattered not at all to Amanda what his station in

135

life was. Gunfighter or drifter! All she knew was they were soaring and whirling to the loftiest heights—far beyond her wildest imaginings. She wanted to go to this faraway land with him. Together they soared!

Later, they slept encircled in each other's arms, wonderfully exhausted and sated.

With the dawn's light and the rays of sunshine invading the small window on the east side of the shack, Amanda was the first to open her eyes. For a minute, she was disoriented. Had she dreamed the night before or had it all happened?

With the light of dawn came reality. There was no dimly lit room and no romantic air about the filthy mattress and the naked man there by her side with his muscled arm across her belly. She lay for a moment staring at the ceiling. Nothing was the same now! She felt ashamed just remembering the way she'd allowed herself to be conquered. Her fierce Kane pride reared its head with indignation.

Only the fact that she wanted no part of Tony Branigan or to have to come face to face with him urged her to move his arm off of her. Otherwise, she would have leaped off that filthy thing she'd slept on—and made love on the night before.

Everything about the night before filled her with abhorrence now. With the utmost caution she managed to remove his arm and raise up from the mattress. Once she was dressed, she tiptoed out to the lean-to and led Prince several yards away from the shack before mounting up and galloping away. Only after she'd left the wooded area behind and ridden into the pastureland did she heave a deep sigh of relief.

The absence of her soft warm body on the mattress

136

beside him made Tony rouse up suddenly. As he rubbed his eyes he realized his surroundings were hardly the heavenly place they had seemed the night before. Christ, this was the way it had looked to her, too. If only he'd told her what was in his heart last night! If only he'd convinced her it was love, not lust!

He leaped up off the dirty mattress. Without Amanda, the magic was gone, and he was just as eager to be gone himself! Somehow, he'd make that magic happen again, for she was a fever in his blood now.

TWELVE

Once he mounted up on Picaro and reined the black horse out of the lean-to and through the woods toward the clearing, all he could think of was how Amanda must despise him now. There in the daylight everything had lost the romantic luster of the night before. Perhaps there would never be another such night for them. If only he'd told her the things in his heart last night, it would have turned out differently.

He gave the nudge for Picaro to move faster feeling the need for some hot coffee to wet his throat and clear his head. As he reached the top of the rolling knoll he spotted her and the palomino just approaching the archway. By her side was his cousin, Mario riding his dapple gray mare.

Christ, the last thing he wanted right then was an encounter with Mario! He pulled up on the reins to see if they went through the archway together or if Mario departed without entering. Tony watched the two as they talked for a moment before Amanda moved on toward the grounds bidding Mario farewell. He then urged Picaro on only to find, much to his displeasure, that Mario must have spotted him across the distance.

Like it or not, Mario was riding over to greet him. He rode up to Tony with a broad smile and his hand thrown up in the air. "*Amigo!* If you've been one of those out searching for the beautiful Amanda, you can relax."

Only then did it dawn on Tony that a search party must have been out looking for Mark's missing daughter. He mumbled a halfhearted reply to his cousin. "Ahhhhh, yes. I've been out." Let Mario assume whatever he wished.

"You look like hell, *amigo*." Mario gave a light chuckle. "Truth of it is she obviously fared better than you did. I just left her, and, no doubt, she is now in the hacienda, all safe and cozy."

Tony stammered out some answer like "good" or "fine." Even with his mind foggy he surmised she'd made some feasible story about getting lost in the storm. No mention of him, though. Well, he'd let her tell whatever story she wished. He could play her game. "You find her, Mario?"

"Oh no, I was just riding by to see the damage from the storm when she came riding across the clearing. I knew the hour was far too early for the lovely Amanda to be out."

Mario's words were not registering, for Tony's thoughts were only about Amanda. She could not wait to be away from him, nor did she wish to face him this morning. Obviously, he'd been fooled that she was as happy and content as she'd seemed as she slept in his arms with her soft body snuggled close to his. "Guess I am beat, Mario. Think I better be on my way, eh?"

"Sure . . . sure, I understand, cousin."

"Give my regards to Aunt Bianca, Maria, and Miguel." Tony urged Picaro on and Mario turned to ride away.

As he rode through the curved archway and moved on to pass the gate leading into the walled courtyard he saw the gathering of the Kane family with Amanda the center of their attention. She was obviously telling her concocted story to her parents. For one fleeting minute her eyes darted in his direction and he didn't have to be told she despised him. It was there for that one brief moment for him to see before she turned her back on him, unable even to look any longer in his direction.

He rode on toward the cookhouse for the coffee he needed so much. From there he went to his quarters to change his clothes. His fury mounted with each passing minute. The day would come when that pert little nose of hers wouldn't turn up at him.

Whether she liked it or not, he had tamed her last night. She could lie to herself or to him, but she'd purred like a kitten. He'd branded her, too! Let her try to forget what had happened. Let her try to lie in some other man's arms and his face would haunt her. He ambled over to the cupboard and poured himself a generous drink of liquor. Damn her, he'd haunt her good! By the time he'd downed a second drink he was feeling much better.

Amanda had given her concerned parents her hastily concocted story, which seemed to satisfy them, and then excused herself to go to her room to rest. But the warm bath and light breakfast did little to relax her. That cold, cruel stare Tony had given her as he rode by caused goose pimples to run up and down her spine. She couldn't stand it and had to turn away from those glaring gray eyes. Sweet Jesus, she'd be glad to be away from here and Branigan!

For the next few days she carefully searched out her path before going into any particular place around the ranch, for fear of encountering him. Tony was as hell-bent that he wouldn't come face to face with her. He rode out early and came in late. He had refused Mark's invitation for dinner the evening before with some feeble excuse.

His searing flame had burned deeper than he could know. She lay in the bed at night with the big harvest moon shining through her window, and the happenings up there in the old shack were all too vivid. Those sensations he'd awakened would not be swept away like a gentle breeze rushing over her. She recalled his sensuous lips kissing her and her hunger for more. What gave him, of all men, such bewitching power over her? If the occasion arose again would she resist him? She didn't know, damn it!

Tony's sleep was haunted like hers. He cussed himself for being twenty kinds of a fool. Up to four months ago, he'd not known the little minx existed, and even now he had an exquisite beauty awaiting him back in San Antonio. Amanda Kane was just one woman, so why was he allowing such torment to plague him so?

The days following the violent storm and their night up at the old shack took their toll on more than just the countryside with its uprooted trees and devastated and splintered outbuildings. Oblivious to the other's turmoil, Amanda and Tony floundered alone in their own private hells. All their reasoning and logic didn't blend peacefully with the feelings in their hearts.

Stubborn pride and vanity made them deny themselves the truth, and so the price was paid by both for their folly.

It was the most glorious autumn day and Amanda had been counting the minutes until Derek came at the appointed hour to take her over to the Big D Ranch, from where, at an ungodly hour, they would start the trek to San Antonio the next morning.

She felt such exuberance it was hard to hide her overwhelming desire to be away from the Circle K. Jenny had seen it in her eyes at dinner the night before. Mark had, too, but would not allow himself to confess it. He was still feeling relief that she'd escaped hurt in the violent storm and returned safely after that long, harrowing night. It had been enough for him to see her riding through that archway. A smothering, heavy weight had been instantly lifted off his broad chest. His "little princess" was alive and home.

The whole episode had brought an enlightenment to the hard-nosed rancher, which he promised himself to remember. While he loved this land with all his heart, he loved his family more. That night his stolen cattle and his newly installed barbed wire meant nothing as he paced and worried about one missing daughter.

As the last few days had passed, he'd been in such high spirits he'd given no thought to Branigan's absences around the ranch and at his dining table.

The evening before had been almost like a festive occasion, with Jeff teasing Amanda about flirting with too many of those handsome young soldiers stationed at the nearby fort. Amanda had playfully taunted him, "Oh, it's not me you're worrying about. You're

142

just afraid someone will steal your girl away from you, Jeff." Amanda could almost feel the chill and fire of Chita's dark eyes as she served their dinner. Amanda had pointedly retorted to her brother in such a way. It wasn't to hurt the Mexican servant girl, but more to wise her up that her affair with Jeff could only be fruitless.

Amanda's acid tongue had done its damage, as Jeff found out when he looked up from his plate into Chita's prodding eyes. His mood suddenly turned moody and quiet. He should have known better, for Amanda's quick wit always surpassed him.

Jenny rattled on with a list of numerous things her daughter might buy for her while she and Mona visited the shops. As a last minute caution, she couldn't resist inquiring, "You sure you put in everything you'll need, honey?"

"I'm sure, Mother. I went over my list this afternoon. I wanted to make sure myself." Amanda had not felt so light in spirits for the longest time. She'd not even had a scowl from her father when she'd taken a second glass of wine. While she'd been most curious about Branigan's not gracing their table once or twice during the week, as had been his habit since coming to the ranch to work, she would not have dared ask her father why. Luck had been with her throughout the week, for she'd not seen his tall, imposing figure anywhere.

She'd vowed to herself by the time she returned to the ranch to have all the haunting torments of Branigan exorcised. In San Antonio, she was going to dance the night away at parties, shop extravagantly, and flirt with any handsome gentleman who caught her eye.

143

She would rid herself of Tony Branigan's yoke!

Fate put one stumbling block in her way. For a week she'd been spared the sight of him, but on the afternoon she was departing, as she was standing at the gate bidding her parents farewell, he came riding by on his magnificent stallion. Dear Lord, she was glad it wasn't the moment her father was giving her one of his big bear hugs or he would have felt the tremor breaking within her.

Tony's tanned face grimaced with rage as he saw the group. Lawson stood waiting for Amanda to turn to be helped up into the buggy. That so-perfect manner of his galled Tony, for he knew there was another side to this seemingly gentle young rancher. Derek gave Tony a look of contempt as he tipped his hat and greeted the group. However, Tony took no time to pause and rode on by.

As he passed by he could have sworn Amanda's fragrance lingered with him, and he turned to take a final look at her there on the seat with Derek beside her. Her face was glowing, it seemed to him, and they were laughing. At that minute he could have wrung her pretty neck with little effort.

That night he saw no reason to turn down Mark's invitation to dine with them. Amanda was gone for a visit to San Antonio, so her tantalizing presence would not be tormenting him.

Only a few miles away at the Big D Ranch, Amanda sat at the Lawsons' table and David Lawson imagined what a pleasant sight it would be to see her sitting there permanently as Derek's young bride. She had a certain quality that enlivened any room she occupied, he thought to himself. Why, his son was like a different person tonight. His little Mona was giggling and so very happy. There could be no other reason but the enchanting magic of Amanda's gracing their midst.

"Your papa managing to keep his wire strung, Amanda?" he finally managed to get a word in.

"Yes, sir. In fact, he's more than pleased and swears that he's had no missing head for about a week. No one would ever convince him that it's not the wire."

"Most likely the men taking shifts guarding the south border, I'd say," Derek projected.

"You could be right, and Papa says if that's what it takes then he'll take on more men. You know him! No one is going to take too much from Papa without him fighting back." Amanda gave a light laugh. No one knew her parents better than the Lawsons.

All Derek could think about that evening as he sat looking at her beautiful face in the candlelight was the time he'd have in San Antonio with her alone. He would find a way to get her alone, for there were many places to go that were unfamiliar and not clustered with people who knew both of them. The imposing presence of Mark Kane would not trouble them. Neither would that annoying gunfighter Branigan be skulking around.

Derek was encouraged beyond belief for he could have sworn she'd been flirting with him as they traveled in the buggy over to the ranch and again tonight during dinner. Those pretty amethyst eyes sparkled so as she'd gaily talked to him when they'd been alone and he was tempted to crush her in his arms and kiss those rosebud lips. He had to fight the urge and play his waiting game, for it was not the right time—not this afternoon!

Soon the time would be right for many things and many changes, Derek told himself, as he gazed down at the head of the long dining table at his father occupying the ornate chair. That would be his, too, sooner than David Lawson anticipated.

He wondered how his mild-mannered, genteel father had managed to survive in this untamed countryside through all the years. He was not among the breed of Mark Kane and never had been. Nor was he the dashing, daring rancher Mario Alvarado's father had been.

He had only to look at his sister Mona to see the ghost of his mother, Carlotta. Even at the time of her death he'd wasted no tears on her, the slut. By then he'd found out the truth about his little sister, and his insidious hate for her was sparked.

It was obvious that his father had never suspected that Mona wasn't his own daughter. Could he have worshipped her so much then? Derek rather doubted it.

Stumbling onto his mother's old diary had told it all to Derek. In its pages he'd read all about the love affair she'd had with Miguel Alvarado. It was he who was Mona's father. What poetic justice it had been that they had both died within two years!

How often his devious mind had thought about the possibility of Mona's being attracted to and marrying Mario Alvarado, her half brother! That would never happen, Derek realized, for her heart belonged only to Jeff Kane.

Those sharing the table there in the Lawsons' dining room that night with Derek Lawson would have been shocked to know the vile evil brewing behind his clean-cut features and gentlemanly demeanor.

None of them would be lucky enough to be spared!

THIRTEEN

It was an impressive group that was gathered in the lavishly furnished parlor over at the Rancho Rio this lovely autumn evening. The most elegant of them all was Bianca Alvarado in her traditional black gown brightened by her string of pearls at her throat and her most cherished piece of jewelry, the pearl and diamond earrings. They held precious memories for her and she wore them on any special occasion. The strong-willed Bianca was determined to black out the bitterness she'd carried in private about her beloved Miguel. When he had presented her with the jewelry, she had not known about his unfaithful heart. That bitter blow had come later.

Looking around the room this evening at her lovely family, she was glad she'd found the courage to be strong enough to overcome the jolting revelations after Miguel's untimely death.

The younger Miguel was going to be as handsome as his older brother one of these days, and her little flower, Maria, was as pretty as the blossoms in her garden. Mario had never looked more strikingly handsome, as his dark eyes gleamed unusually brightly, for

he was stirred by the lovely sight of Magdalena Gomez.

Ah, she knew her eldest son so well she could read
his thoughts as she watched him from across the room.

At Mario's suggestion, the two got up to leave the
room and go for a stroll in the garden. The moonlit
night and Mario's hot Latin blood were enough for
Bianca to send up a silent prayer that her handsome
son would behave himself. His dark eyes darted over
at her as they went toward the patio and he seemed to
read the message in her eyes, giving her a devious
wink. She smiled, thinking what a rascal he was.
Shortly after they left, she and Francisco left too to retire to her study to conduct the legal business he'd
come to the Rancho Rio about.

As soon as they were gone, Maria rushed over to her
brother Miguel and giggled. "He looks like a fat frog
with that paunchy belly of his."

"Shhhh, Maria! He might hear you," Miguel ad-
monished his sister, turning his back on her to walk
aimlessly around the room.

"No, he won't! And he waddles like a duck when he
walks. How he ever had such a pretty daughter I'll
never know. He's . . . he's as ugly as that old bull,
Diablo."

"Maria . . . Maria, you are hopeless!" Miguel
sighed, picking up his guitar.

"I'm just truthful, Miguel," she declared, swishing
her skirt to and fro. She paid no attention to the fact
that her eighteen-year-old brother was trying to ignore
her and kept chattering away at him. "Oh, she had
Mario breathing hard."

"Maria! Where did you hear such talk?" Mortified

149

at his sister's boldness, he was once again amazed by the many things she seemed to know about. At fifteen he had not known all about life, not like Maria. He pondered her source, figuring it had to be the servant girl, Elena.

Eyes twinkling and a teasing grin on her pretty face, she swished her skirt and retorted, "Oh, I'll never tell!"

Once again, her more serious brother turned his attention to his guitar and began strumming a soft, romantic ballad. Miguel truly had the soul of the gentle poet and lived within his own private world. He had a personality completely different from Maria's or Mario's.

His music wafted out through the garden providing a perfect atmosphere for his older brother, who was completely taken by the gorgeous Señorita Gomez.

Magdalena was very impressed by the gallant *caballero* by her side, for he was an exciting, handsome man. The truth was she found him more good-looking than Tony. Actually, there had been times when Tony's manners frightened her, and had he not proposed marriage she would never have allowed him the liberties he'd so boldly taken with her. Being his *novia* made it ease her conscience. The fact that her father and Señor Moreno approved their forthcoming marriage had eased many restrictions, Magdalena knew, that her father would have insisted upon with any other young man.

Such grace and charm Mario had never seen before in a young lady. She moved like an agile black panther, almost gliding slowly down the flagstone path. He led her toward a bench where the bright, full harvest moon would shine down on them.

He chose his words with care, but at the same time he determined to let her know how lovely he thought she was. "My cousin has to be the most envied man in all of San Antonio, Señorita Gomez."

She smiled and her face was radiant. "Please—we are out here alone, so call me Magdalena. We don't need to be formal, do we?" she purred softly with a slight accent to her words. Mario was delighted at her sudden informality.

"Ah, I see we think alike. Wonderful! I sincerely do envy my cousin, Magdalena. I wish we might have met sooner."

"Now, don't tell me a handsome young man like you wouldn't have a sweetheart, Mario. That would be impossible," she laughed lightly.

"No particular one—honestly!"

"Ah, so you have an appetite for many, *si?*"

"I think most men do, until they find the one that is set apart from all the rest—and a man knows this is the one." It had not stopped his cousin Tony, though, from casting his eyes on Amanda Kane. It was rather reassuring to Mario to know he was not the only man who had a roving eye for the beautiful ladies. Tony was just as guilty.

When they did get onto the subject of his cousin, Magdalena did not hesitate to voice her disapproval of his strange ways. "He's like a roaming gypsy, coming and going at will. Perhaps Señor Moreno does not mind, but I fear I do not wish this from the marriage I enter. You see . . . and please forgive me, Mario, but I do not believe the old darling this time. I think he lies for his grandson. Tony had only a short time ago re-

151

turned from Mexico, and I can't believe he's returned so soon to the mines." Mario realized she was no empty-headed little señorita.

"Oh?" Mario was not above sweeping this beautiful señorita off her feet and away from his cousin if he thought he had the slightest hope of accomplishing it.

"Tony is a restless breed of man and . . . and I have some very grave doubts at times."

Mario fingered at the black vest trimmed in braid, feeling slightly flushed and heady sitting there in the dark with this gorgeous creature so close. The tone of her words gave him a flicker of hope that the beautiful Magdalena Gomez was not completely out of his reach.

Her next words convinced him and even encouraged him to test her when she inquired, "Are you a restless wanderer, Mario?" She gave him a most provocative smile.

"The answer to that is a definite no, Magdalena. I've never strayed off the Rancho Rio too much or for too long." He could see she was pleased and impressed. In fact, she seemed to be openly inviting him to kiss those beautiful lips, but he couldn't chance becoming too bold too soon, for he'd not missed that silent demand his mother's dark eyes had given him as he'd escorted her out to the garden.

"I can see that you are not the self-centered man your cousin is, Mario," she said. "He was not even thoughtful enough to come by the house to say good-bye, must less to inform me, his *novia*, where he was going." Her pretty mouth went into a pout.

Mario was all sympathy and understanding. "Oh, you poor darling! A woman—a rare jewel of beauty!

152

That is unforgivable!" In a most delicate move his arm went around the back of the bench. At the same time his devil-may-care nature was provoked by the humor of this situation. What a laugh Tony would have to know his *novia* was of the opinion that he, Mario, was a more settled gentleman!

"Oh, Mario, how can I ever thank you for being so kind. You see, I was so depressed when I arrived here. I didn't want to make this trip with Father, and now I know that would have been a horrible mistake. I would not have met you."

His mother's admonishments meant nothing at this moment. The lovely señorita was asking him to take her in his arms as she leaned ever so slightly toward him. Mario's passionate nature could not resist her invitation, so he took her into his arms and gave her a long, lingering kiss. He congratulated his cousin Tony for being a good teacher. Her kisses were hardly typical of the chaperoned, cloistered daughter of the usual wealthy Latin families. Oh, no, this little lovely was well practiced and knew how to return a man's kisses.

He heaved a deep sigh, moaning, "Oh, Magdalena—you are marvelous!" I wish . . ." He crushed her to him again, not finishing the words he had started to say. When he finally released her, she looked up at him with an expression of reserve on her face. "I want to see you again, Magdalena. You know what I mean?"

A sudden shyness seemingly swept over her and she nodded her head. "I know, Mario, and I want the same thing."

The conversation went no further, nor did Mario's amorous attentions, for they were interrupted by the imp Maria.

Tony's name seemed to be the popular topic of conversation that night at the Rancho Rio. After Señor Gomez and Señora Alvarado finished the details of their paperwork and business in her study, Francisco accepted Bianca's offer of another glass of the fine French brandy. She was a very intelligent woman, and this the lawyer admired. He found her a pleasure to do business with, not like so many of the widows in San Antonio with whom he dealt most of the time. She had that dignity and finesse he'd tried to instill in Magdalena. Her tutoring had been left to him and his sister, Margarita, since his wife's death. He had been almost forty-five when Magdalena was born, so it had not been easy for him to deal with a young daughter.

Now they sat talking together like the old friends they were, but Francisco's mind was on other things while he idly engaged in light conversation. While he had the greatest respect for her father, Esteban Moreno, he pondered with some grave misgivings allowing his grandson Tony to court his daughter. At the time it had seemed perfect—the union of Esteban's grandson and Magdalena.

This evening he'd admired the handsome Mario with approving eyes. His charm and good manners were impeccable, and his elegant, fine attire was far more impressive than Tony Moreno's sometimes casual, rugged style. He'd appear around San Antonio at times looking like some renegade, Francisco considered, much to his chagrin. Francisco was a fastidious man about his person, as well as his home. It was a point that had always pricked him sorely, but old

Esteban had always joked it away when Francisco had lightly hinted about it once or twice.

Finally, when the conversation lulled, Francisco mentioned Tony to Bianca. "The young man seems to be very, very irresponsible Bianca, but your father has only the greatest praise for him. I will say that he works as hard as any peon, but this thing this time has disturbed my daughter. You understand my concern?"

"Oh, I can, indeed, Francisco, but I'm certain Antonio will have some very just reason for his absence. The young are a most impatient lot. I know," she laughed.

"Oh, I understand that tender part of Esteban's heart, and may I say, I find you the most understanding of women. Your fine son Mario has to be, too. He is a fine-looking gentleman, Bianca. I compliment you on your fine family."

The shrewd Señora Alvarado found his compliments very nice, but she also knew they were not given wholly without some reason. Francisco Gomez had been an acquaintance for many, many years. It was not as if their friendship had been brief, so she questioned his pointed innuendos. She did not have to ponder too long to figure out that he was disenchanted with her nephew.

Life was a comedy at times, she thought to herself an hour later after they'd both retired to their private quarters. While she sat at her dressing table letting down the long coil of her hair to give it the nightly brushing, she found it interesting that Francisco did not seem perturbed that his daughter lingered there in the dark garden with her son. She thought about Antonio, too. Right or wrong, she could not find it in her

155

heart to resent the fine young man. She was not a greedy woman, and she knew that Mario's wealth from his father's estate would equal Antonio's. Too much wealth was not always best.

As far as her nephew Tony and Magdalena, she did not see the two of them sharing each other's lives now that she'd spent a part of the evening with the lovely girl. As crazy and unlikely as it might seem, Bianca thought that the lively, golden-haired Amanda would complement her rebel of a nephew to perfection. She recalled something about the girl the day she came to call at the Rancho Rio that had ignited that idea.

Tony would be as unacceptable to Mark Kane as a son-in-law as her Mario had been, though. But then Bianca knew that children did not always follow the plans of their parents. Perhaps this new generation was smarter, after all, than her generation had been.

The heartbreaking disaster of her own marriage was certainly proof of that, she sadly recalled. After Miguel had died she'd mourned his loss for all those many months. She had loved that man so completely and devotedly that the shattering discovery of his unfaithfulness with Carlotta Lawson almost destroyed her. Her family never realized the depths of despair she had drowned in for a few weeks after she'd found Carlotta's handwritten messages among Miguel's papers in his desk.

His unexpected death had struck like a bolt of lightning. The virile Miguel had had no time to destroy the evidence of his little affair. Never had the lovely señora thought to care for another man—and there had been those who had tried to court her during the years. Instead, her time and energies had been spent

156

on her children and the Rancho Rio. Carlotta's own husband had numbered among the men who'd come to the Rancho Rio after his wife's death. Rather ironic that the two had followed one another in departing from this world. First Miguel, and then Carlotta!

Unlike Derek Lawson's findings in his mother's old journals, Bianca's discovery included nothing about the lovely little Mona's being Miguel's child. However, she'd speculated on that possibility. Many times, she'd been grateful that Mario's attention had never turned toward the Lawson girl. She'd been spared that ordeal. What could she have said? *Dios*, she could not linger on that horrible thought without flinching!

Instead her lovely face with its classic features broke into a cool smile as she stared into the massive gold-gilded mirror above her dressing table, and her quick, cunning mind considered what the lawyer had been slyly hinting about downstairs earlier. Francisco would not find it objectionable if her Mario paid court to his Magdalena.

Cocking her head to one side and raising a fine arched black brow, Bianca could envision the two as far more compatible and harmonious than Tony and Magdalena.

FOURTEEN

Amanda greeted the sight of the white frame house on the old Mission Road with the anticipated pleasure of a warm, refreshing bath to rid herself of the dirt and dust of the long day's drive.

Sally and Sam Beckenridge rushed down the steps to welcome their caravan as it pulled up in front. Sally was one of those pleasant, friendly souls who made you feel at home the minute you entered her door. Her husband was as gracious. Although it had been a few years since Amanda had seen them, she recognized them at once. The last few years had been kind to both of them. Neither had changed at all.

"Mercy, what a pretty picture you are, honey," Sally exclaimed giving her a warm hug as they walked up the path to the house. "Good to see you again, child."

Sam chuckled. "Amanda, I'll never forget the last time Mark and Jenny brought you to our house you had the cutest little straw bonnet and pigtails hangin' down—remember Sally?"

Sally laughed and nodded. "Lord a' mercy, you was about ten or eleven. Now it hasn't been that long since we've seen Mona here." The four of them moved up on the porch. Derek had rejoined the three Lawson men, so they could join up with the hands herding the mustangs out to their destination.

As Derek started to gallop off on his horse, Sally called back to him in that motherly way of hers for him to be sure and get himself back in time for supper.

Laughing, Derek assured her, "Oh, you can bet on that, Mrs. Beckenridge. Wouldn't miss it for the world."

Sally laughed, telling Amanda and Mona how he'd stuffed himself so with her squirrel and dumplings the last time he'd graced their table. "Love to see someone relish their food like that Derek."

With each step she took Amanda could see the dust lifting from her skirt and she wondered if Mona's throat was as raw as hers was. Sally seemed to be a mind reader, Amanda was to realize once they were in the house. There were cool refreshments awaiting their pleasure. The minute they'd drained their glasses Sally urged, "Come on, children. Let's get you up to your rooms where some nice refreshing baths will revive you, eh?"

"That sounds wonderful to me, Mrs. Beckenridge," Mona exclaimed with Amanda chiming in her approval.

At the top of the stairs, Sally showed the girls to their respective rooms directly across the hall from each other. "Now, I'll sent Carmella up to help the two of you. 'Fraid you'll have to share her services, though. As you know, Mona, we don't keep as many servants around as we used to." Sally excused herself to get the servant girl.

159

An hour later, Amanda was lying across the bed feeling delightfully clean and relaxed. She found herself more than content just to lie there and stare out the window at the swaying branches of a giant palm tree just outside her window. A most exotic smell of something blooming down below had a very intoxicating odor that Amanda liked but didn't recognize. She'd have to find out from Sally what the flowers were, knowing her mother's great joy in blooming plants.

She let herself give way to complete relaxation. It was going to be nice to be here for a while in San Antonio and away from the Circle K Ranch. Here there would be no threat of Tony Branigan skulking around some corner and she would be free of his imposing presence. On second thought, could she be absolutely sure of it? When she'd finally felt so smug about not running into him for over a week after that night up in the old shack, it seemed she could not be gone from the Circle K without that final sight of him the day she left.

The look on his face had stayed with her during the whole drive over to the Big D. Even when she tried desperately to be pleasant to Derek, he was there haunting her. Yes, she'd even go so far as to admit to herself that she flirted outrageously with Derek. And Derek had bought her ostentatious exhibition, she'd realized.

Well, to hell with Tony Branigan! He wasn't here and she planned to enjoy herself to the fullest. In fact, she would rid herself of him whatever it took to accomplish the feat. These were her last thoughts before sleep came.

The sun had set and the grounds of the Beckenridge

estate were showered with twilight time when Amanda rose up from the bed to glance out the window. A soft rap on her door announced the arrival of the young Mexican girl sent to assist her in dressing.

Shyly, she entered the room to ask Amanda if she could help her in any way. "My name is Carmella, señorita."

Amanda thanked her for pressing the blue gown she'd chosen before resting. It was a simple frock with dainty puffed sleeves with a delicate lace trim in a snowy white. She decided to wear no necklace, only her pearls on her ears. The lines of the gown were basic, with the slightest hint of a subdued bustle at the back. The neckline was not as low-cut as on her fancier gowns. The scoop of the lines gave only the slightest clue of cleavage. It was edged with the same dainty lace as the sleeves.

When Carmella said she was to style Señorita Lawson's hair, Amanda said that she could do it herself. Tonight she planned a casual style. It was an easy hairdo that Chita had shown her, but Amanda liked it. She sat at the dressing table going through the same motions she'd watched Chita do and was delighted when she achieved the same effect.

She got the teasing curls at her temples exactly the way she wanted them. The two sides were pulled up to the top, making a crown of three big curls. The back hung down in soft, natural wavy curls. She preened at herself in the mirror. "There! Perfect!" With that final approval of her reflection she bounced out of the room to cross the polished hallway to go to Mona's room.

A few minutes later the two girls decended the stairway, presenting a glorious picture of loveliness in their blue and yellow. Sally Beckenridge thought each of them was beautiful in her own individual way.

"My, look at our two pretty girls," Sam declared, coming out of their spacious parlor to greet them. To him they remained the children of his two old buddies David and Mark. He had found it hard to believe when Sally had pointed out to him that they were both the marrying age.

"Good evening, Mr. Beckenridge," Mona greeted him.

In turn, Amanda greeted her host and Mrs. Beckenridge, who had come up behind her husband. In the background, she saw Derek standing by the fireplace dressed in a coat of deep blue and gray dress pants. He was quite handsome and elegant looking standing there with a glass of wine in his hand. He had made it back in time to enjoy Sally's feast, as he'd promised.

Now Amanda saw Carmella moving around the parlor carrying a tray. She seemed to serve the Beckenridges in many ways and it was obvious that the house was staffed with few servants. She was not prepared to see the other man seated on the floral settee, though, and when he leaped up to stand, Amanda admired his lean attractive uniformed figure and good-looking face.

Who was he, Amanda wondered? Whoever he was his presence was making the evening more interesting for her—at least, until she got the idea that the Beckenridges were possibly matchmaking for Mona.

"Girls, let me present my nephew, Steve Beckenridge. He just arrived yesterday. Got transferred from back East. A lucky break for us," Sam said, leading

Amanda and Mona across the room. "Steve, this is Amanda Kane and Mona Lawson."

"Miss Lawson, a pleasure, and Miss Kane, it is nice to meet you." Captain Beckenridge bowed gallantly. His jade-green eyes surveyed each girl in turn. Amanda, being the bolder of the two, inspected him as carefully, as he gestured for them to have a seat there on the settee and saw to each of them having a glass of wine. Derek seethed within as the arrogant officer seemed to dominate the parlor.

His fury subsided when he escorted Amanda into the dining room for dinner and Steve took his sister's arm. Amanda felt certain that it was the Beckenridge's plan that their nephew and sweet little Mona would attract one another. She turned her attention for the most part to Derek during the scrumptious dinner.

Steve's intense attention directed toward Mona seemed to be embarrassing her, and Amanda found it amusing. Such a gap truly divided them now, she mused. What would her innocent dear friend think of her if she knew about that night in the old shack? While Amanda knew it was not true that there was any outward change in her, it had taken her days afterwards to finally accept it. She could have sworn it was not that way.

She just knew her folks would see it the morning she'd returned, and later, alone in her room, she'd checked every inch of her naked body and stared endlessly into the reflection in the mirror. Outwardly, she was the same.

Steve's eyes just happened to glance across the table to catch that moment that Amanda gazed wistfully at

163

the glowing candlelight. So thoughtful was she as she took lazy sips of the red wine—she was absolutely breathtaking, he thought, his gaze held to her as though he was hypnotized. There was nothing amethyst about her eyes this night, not to Steve's appraising eyes. He saw them as wood hyacinths or beautiful bluebells. They seemed to match her gorgeous blue gown to perfection. The simplicity of her frock made her seem even more elegant and grand.

Had the thought of courting or wooing Mona Lawson been there in his mind for one fleeting second earlier, it was now gone. It was Amanda he'd seek out, he quickly decided. However, he was more than aware of the sharp, stabbing glares coming in his direction from Mona's brother. So that was the way the wind blew, eh? Well, all was fair in love or war or so he'd been told. Derek Lawson did not worry Captain Beckenridge.

Whether it pleased her or not, Amanda had to admit secretly that she was now more perceptive to the male animal. She knew Steve Beckenridge was attracted to her. Oh, yes, Branigan had educated her. She'd have to give him that much. Neither could she deny that she found the deep green eyes devouring her with so much interest annoying. But perhaps he would be the one to make her forget Branigan.

Throughout the evening Derek rained his undivided attentions on her, and she tried to be gracious and kind. However, with Steve Beckenridge in the picture now she no longer wished to flirt with Derek as she had the last few days. By the end of her first evening at the Beckenridges she was plagued by a degree of guilt, especially as she and Mona climbed the stairs together. Dear Mona, she was surely blind to any male, except Jeff. But her soft voice was excited as she spoke of Steve. With a deep sigh of resignation, she remarked, "I guess I find most men pale beside Jeff."

Amanda wanted to scream out that she was too trusting, that Jeff didn't deserve such devotion. She wanted to tell Mona she should spread her wings a little before settling down for the rest of her life as anyone's wife. It would have done no good, though. At least, Amanda's qualms were eased where Mona was concerned, if she did decide to encourage Captain Beckenridge.

The next day Sally Beckenridge took them on a tour of the city and they had lunch at a quaint little tearoom. It reminded Amanda very much of the little sidewalk cafes of New Orleans, only this one was situated past the marketplace down by the river providing a divine setting for dining as they rested. Sally Beckenridge's capacity for walking amazed Amanda. She was tireless!

That evening Amanda and Mona both agreed that it was nice to retire early to their respective rooms. Derek did not return for dinner at the Beckenridges but remained out at the Jensen ranch to complete the deal on the horses they'd sold to Albert Jensen. So it was just Sally and Sam dining with them.

Amanda left her purchases where she'd laid them earlier with no interest in putting them away. However, in her mind she made the mental note that on their next jaunt she would get gifts for the men, as she'd already purchased small gifts for her mother, Consuela, and Chita. She wanted something for everyone back at the Circle K.

She lay on her bed for a full two hours, becoming disgusted that sleep would not come when she knew how weary and tired she was. Of all the stupid things to be occupying her mind—the gifts for the men. Father, Jeff, Juan Santos, and Branigan.

She sat up in bed, reprimanding herself harshly. Why had she included that cur? Was she daft in the head? Away from his overbearing, arrogant presence she should be able to dismiss him completely from her thoughts. A gift for him—never!

She rose from the bed, and, as she had as a small child, went over to the window to sit on the floor to stare up at the stars and the moon. To the heavens above and the gentle night breeze, she lamented, "Why, Branigan—why do you prove so blasted hard to be rid of?"

Where had the Amanda gone who always had control of herself and was always so sure of what she wanted? The blame for it all lay at Tony Branigan's feet. No other man had so stubbornly stuck to her that she couldn't easily shrug him aside. Not until Branigan!

No, not until Branigan had the memories of a man lingered and tormented her, and she resented it. His strong arms holding her close to his broad chest blotting out the rest of the world had made her feel as though they were the only two people in the world.

Those lips of his—so sensuous and demanding—had the magic to make her yield when she was determined to deny him. What was so darn different about him and the way he kissed her? Lord, she didn't know, but when his lips captured hers she never wanted him to stop.

The heat of his virile male body and those hands that touched the most private parts of her had stirred a kind of madness in her, making a searing liquid heat surge through her just remembering it. When the pulsing essence of him had filled her, such wild, wonderful ecstasy had erupted in her that she had been unable to restrain the moans of pleasure. Such rapture she'd never known—not until Tony Branigan came along.

He'd spoiled her for any other man, and for that she damned and cussed him. He was the devil's own with his magic. He was a fever in her blood, and she couldn't seem to rid herself of it.

The next few days the welcome attentions of Steve Beckenridge helped. The household was all aflutter about the big dance that was being held at the Armory, and Amanda got caught in the frenzy. She chose which gown she'd wear from among the ones she had brought. It had to be the lovely lavender one.

Utter frustration had engulfed the captain during the last couple of days, for it seemed hopeless that he could manage even a few moments with the beautiful Amanda without an audience. He'd already accepted his role as the sweet Mona's escort. With the most arrogant air Derek Lawson had let it be known that he was Amanda's escort for the evening. Captain Beckenridge disliked Lawson after their second encounter, and that had nothing to do with his interest in Amanda Kane. He'd seen that kind of look in men's eyes before.

By the day of the dance he'd accepted the fact that her visit was swiftly coming to an end and that she

167

would be leaving San Antonio and he'd not been allowed so much as a pleasant stroll alone with her. It had been the two girls he'd escorted around the town when he was fortunate enough to be rid of Derek Lawson's overbearing presence.

He decided that she was well worth making another try for during the afternoon while his aunt was busy supervising the decorating at the Armory. He knew his uncle was out on his ranch a few miles from San Antonio. Maybe this could be his lucky day—if Lawson wasn't hanging around the house. It was certainly worth a try.

He rode his fine stallion down Mission Road toward his aunt's two-story white frame house and prayed fortune would smile on him. It did.

Amanda happened to be the one to open the door to his knock. "Why, Captain Beckenridge—how—how nice to see you! I hope you've not been standing here too long. It seems the servants did not hear."

He made an impressive figure standing there in his uniform and headgear, a very attractive smile on his face. He almost held his breath, hoping against hope no one would suddenly make an appearance as he entered the hallway as she ushered him in.

He was almost tempted to turn down her offer of a cup of coffee, but he was also at a loss as to what to say was his reason for the visit. Amanda made it easy for him, though. "I was too excited about tonight to take a rest as Mona is so wise to do," she smiled.

His green eyes twinkled brightly as he commented, "I figured you right. I just knew you probably liked to dance."

"Now how did you know that?" she teased.

168

"Nothing really you can particularly put your finger on. Maybe the way you move, I guess," he wanted to bite his tongue fearing he'd been too forward.

She eased his concern by flippantly retorting, "Why I take that as a compliment, captain."

"Steve—please!" He gave her a broad smile. For a man past his thirtieth birthday he felt as nervous as a schoolboy sitting there alone with this enchanting beauty. To the men under his command he could be so stern and imposing, but now he felt like jelly inside. He felt unsure of himself and awkward.

"All right, it shall be Amanda and Steve from this moment on. Tell me, Steve—did you like it back in the East?" She knew he yearned to kiss her from the look in his eyes.

"I have to say I really did. In fact, since I've been back here I'm finding the heat a problem to adjust to, after all the time back there." His eyes couldn't resist traveling over the delightful curves of her simple floral-patterned frock while he tried to carry on their pleasant conversation. He caught himself lingering too long on the soft mounds of her breasts and quickly darted his eyes to her face.

When he was finally urged by the time to take his leave, he remarked, "I'm putting my bid in right now for a dance, Amanda."

"You have it, Steve." They stood by the front door unaware that they were being observed by a figure lingering at the end of the hallway. His entry had been at the rear of the house and the downstairs had been so ghostly quiet that their voices had carried as he'd started down the hall to go to his room.

"That I could have been your escort would have

169

been my desire, Amanda." Steve's green eyes were warm with sincerity as he confessed this to her. "Perhaps I could have the pleasure sometime in the future?"

Amanda could not help being flattered by his honest confession and admission of his attraction to her. Her time here in the city was drawing to a close and she mentioned this to him.

"I wasn't just speaking of this particular visit, Amanda. I know the circumstances and the element of time might prevent it, but there is the future ahead."

"Then the answer is yes, Steve—you may," she declared. Her reply infuriated the man listening in the background. He shared one thing with Steve Beckenridge and that was that desperate desire to get Amanda alone before she left San Antonio. His mood and his temper were black. Overhearing what he just had made him aware that he must keep her to himself tonight at the dance. He was her escort and he planned to make her know it!

In fact, the presence of Steve Beckenridge and his roving eyes made it more imperative to Derek that he leave San Antonio sooner now that his deal was completed. It also meant that he must carry forth his plans back in Gonzales County without further ado. Too many damned stumbling blocks were being thrust in his way. Branigan was an unexpected one he'd not counted on. Derek cussed the fact that his bullet had missed so miserably that night. He blamed that yellow belly coward Jeff and the distraction of his suddenly hightailing it away for his poor aim that night. The next time it would be different.

Now this cocky army captain sought to woo Amanda—even to the extent of asking if he might call on her sometime at the Circle K Ranch. She, flirt that she was, had openly and eagerly invited him to do so. The night ahead had to be used to his advantage, Derek promised himself standing there watching the two.

Three hours later the Beckenridges led their group through the doors of the Armory, where the tireless Sally had spent the afternoon decorating the place with flowers and bright and colorful stringing garlands. Yet she was as refreshed and gay as the girls and the ladies half her age.

She'd returned to the house early enough to have a hasty bath, change into her best gown and redo her rumpled hairdo. Amanda found her to be an amazing lady, and during her brief stay she'd come to adore her and Sam.

Sam looked fine, striding proudly along by her side, as Steve ambled along with Mona, who looked breathtakingly lovely in her snowy white frock with a single strand of pearls at her throat. Derek guided Amanda toward the milling crowd already gathered. It seemed to him as if every eye in the room was looking at her.

Her lavender gown was admired by each lady she encountered as they began to mingle with the guests. Amanda had also worn her cherished amethyst jewelry. Her glorious hair was pulled away from her face in a most flattering fashion exhibiting the earrings on her dainty ears. The clustered long curls fell down her back swaying to and fro as she glided around the room with Derek at her side.

"I shall not let you out of my sight tonight, Amanda. You put every woman here to shame. In fact, it is a sin for a girl to be as beautiful as you, I

171

think sometimes," Derek murmured softly, trying not to show how much he resented every man they passed ogling her boldly.

"Now, Derek," she teased, hoping for the life of her he wasn't serious. Hang it, if he was going to monopolize every minute of her time.

When they partook of the refreshments and the musicians marched up to the platform to begin to play, Derek immediately led her to the floor. But she could hardly conceal her amusement or delight when Sam claimed her for the second dance.

Three gentlemen followed in quick succession after Sam, each asking her to be his partner. Amanda swirled with her partners enjoying herself more than she had in a long, long time.

After five continual numbers of dancing, she was more than ready to join Mona seated over by one of the little tables by the far wall. But a gentle tap on her arm made her halt with the gentleman who was her partner at the time.

"Please excuse me, Mr. Dixon, but I believe I have this next dance coming up with Miss Kane," the male voice said and Amanda saw the uniformed figure of Steve standing there at her side.

Breathlessly she went from her present partner's arms to Steve's. They moved to the open door where the pleasing gust of air caressed her face and she gave a deep sigh. "Oh, Lord—that feels good! Do you mind if we sit this one out and catch the next one?"

"Not at all! Come on, I know a perfect spot." He hastily urged her out the side door for he was certain Lawson's eagle eyes were observing them.

The echo of the music playing inside followed them

as they scurried down the steps to the grounds and around the corner of the building. "Where are you taking me, Steve?" she giggled lightheartedly.

"You'll see," he laughed, a boyish grin on his face. They moved to a small cluster of trees where a gazebo stood. "Here!"

"I didn't even know it was back here," Amanda confessed remembering she'd passed this way many times since coming to San Antonio.

"I know. It doesn't show from the road or the grounds." He urged her to sit down. "Nice, isn't it?"

Amanda nodded, knowing from the look on the captain's face that he'd purposely brought her here for more than a breath of fresh air. While Branigan was the last person in the world her thoughts wanted to dwell on tonight, she couldn't stop them, for he had taught her about men.

She broke into nervous chatter more or less to conceal her own anticipation of what it would be like if Steve did take her in his arms and kiss her. In a way, she desperately wanted him to. What better way to wash Tony away, once and for all.

"You're a beautiful woman, Amanda," he said softly. Giving a light hint of a laugh, he added, " 'Course, I know you've already heard that a million times and I'm . . . well, I'm not a man with a silver tongue. Guess you could say I find it hard to put what I feel into words."

Amanda squirmed on the bench. She knew what he was leading up to. Damn, why didn't he just take her in his arms and kiss her without ceremony! She would have preferred it.

This usually very composed army officer had never

felt so unsure of himself. He repeated himself about how lovely he thought she looked tonight.

"You're going to make me have a swelled head, Steve Beckenridge." She gave a soft laugh, feeling his arm slip around her bare shoulders. Dear Lord, for a thirty-year-old bachelor he was a bashful one, she mused with a sudden impatience.

He moved near and stammering with uncertainty, he said, "I . . . I want to kiss you, Amanda." Almost irritated, she urged, "Then do it, Steve, and quit talking about it!" She pressed herself closer, and he leaned over to give her a kiss. It was an eager, hungry kiss, and her soft, sensuous lips responded in a way that surprised Steve for one brief moment. The rapture of holding her luscious body close to his swept aside any thoughts he might have had about her obvious experience and performance.

All he could say was, "Dear God, Amanda. Oh, Amanda!" Anything Amanda might have wildly anticipated happening with Steve Beckenridge—like bells ringing or a star falling from the sky—didn't. No blazing flame engulfed her body. The truth was she was left wanting.

Derek was standing in the shadows watching the entire fiasco with his fists clenched and the satanic desire to beat the captain's face to a pulp. Tossing his cheroot to the ground he marched toward the gazebo.

FIFTEEN

Under different circumstances Amanda would have reacted violently to Derek Lawson's interruption of the scene at the gazebo. As it was, she had confessed to herself much later in her bedroom long after the dance was over and they'd returned to the Beckenridge house, she had desired release from Steve's arms and his lips.

As nice as he was and as much as she'd given herself up to the moment of anticipated ecstasy, it had been lacking. She had sat up straight in the bed and could have sworn she saw that despicable, taunting face of Tony's. She could almost hear him saying, "Told you so, *chiquita*. Told you you were mine!"

Muttering to the night around her, she had spit out, "No, I'm not, Tony Branigan. Damn you!" But even so, she could not deny that Steve's fine figure in his uniform and his good-looking face with those green eyes had not titillated her like those cold gray ones of Tony's. His male body had not stimulated her as it had pressed against her. Whatever that bewitching magic was that Tony had that made her lips want to hungrily cling to his forever and ever had been miss-

175

ing.

Was she damned forever by this disciple of the devil? No miracle had been forthcoming, and her trip to San Antonio had not made the tormenting memory of Branigan lessen.

Since the night of the dance Steve Beckenridge had not come around to his aunt's and Amanda wondered if they had found it rather odd. Had the reserved captain been embarrassed about Derek's finding them in the intimate setting of the gazebo? Recalling his quiet, thoughtful manner as they'd left the Armory that night, she'd wondered about it.

The day before they were to leave for home she'd readily accepted Derek's invitation to accompany him out to the Jensen ranch. It was a lovely afternoon and Derek had promised that on the way they'd stop by the marketplace.

Surprisingly, she found herself having a marvelous time after they'd wandered among the booths of the vendors. He bought her a bouquet of daisies and a trinket gift for their housekeeper, Nina. He laughed after buying a large woven basket for Mona, explaining that it ought to be big enough for gathering her flowers back at the ranch. This Derek appealed to her very much.

Amanda bought some silk scarves and a colorful serape and a sombrero for Juan. From an old Mexican man with a wizened face she bought a pair of sandals and a carving out of wood of a fine stallion reared up on its hind legs.

They lunched in one of the quaint little tearooms nearby before reining the buggy toward the outskirts of the city. They'd held hands along the way and

Derek had, in a teasing manner, planted a light, gentle kiss on her cheek. She warmed to him in a way that surprised her and pleased Derek.

She was perfection, he mused, turning to look at her from time to time by his side in the buggy as the high-stepping bay trotted jauntily along the dirt road. He kept her mood light and gay by recalling times in the past that had mingled their lives together from the time they were tots.

He totally surprised her when he declared with absolute sincerity, "Oh, I have great plans, Amanda, for my life and my future. I don't plan to bury myself at the Big D."

With eyes wide and mouth gaping, she finally admitted, "Really? That surprises me, Derek!"

"Hell, no! Just because a man's a wealthy cattle baron doesn't mean he has to live every day on his ranch. There's all kinds of places to go to and things to see, if a man has the means to do it. I plan to have the means."

Amanda's eyes glowed bright with interest. "You mean like traveling to Europe and faraway places?"

"Why not? What's to stop you? There's always foremen and trail bosses to be hired." His clever approach was working.

"Why not, indeed! I must say you've surprised me this afternoon, Derek. In fact, I'm sitting here completely amazed. I had no idea of this wanderlust in you." In the wink of an eye she found herself suddenly changing her opinion about young Lawson.

"Actually, you've never given yourself a chance to really get to know me, Amanda—not in the way I wish you to," he smiled, flashing his pearly white teeth. It

177

was a rather nice smile, Amanda thought, and she had to admit that perhaps she had not. Because he had just always been around throughout all the years of her life, she'd not found him as interesting as men like Mario, Branigan, Beckenridge, or the young Frenchmen in New Orleans. During their growing-up years, the Alvarado children had not mingled with the Kanes and the Lawsons.

"What are you trying to say to me, Derek? How—what—I'm not sure I understand what you're getting at," she prodded. Derek masked his feelings well, and she knew all too well what he was talking about. He pulled the buggy over to the side of the road and reined up on the bay.

He removed his hat and ran his fingers through his sandy hair. "I happen to know what our two fathers have discussed about the two of us and I resent it, as you must. I want no one picking my bride for me. I'll do that, Amanda. No one is going to rule my life, you understand?"

Oh, how she could relate to that! If Derek could have known the points he'd won with those last words, he would have been jubilant. "I certainly do, because I feel the same way."

"Well, I'm glad to hear that, because I do care for you very much, as you know, but neither of them will take credit for anything that happens between you and me. Maybe I was wrong to say anything to you." His eyes came to rest in his lap.

She reached over to take his hand. "No, I'm glad you did. I think it good you did—really!"

Slowly, his eyes raised and he brought her hand to his lips, whispering against it, "Good! 'Cause I do

178

care very much." Taking her hand he spread her arms out and urged them around his neck letting his mouth find hers. She made no effort to refuse the kiss he sought. His lips were pleasing and warm and they urged her to return his kiss. She stayed with him as the kiss lingered, finding it more stimulating that Steve's clumsy efforts.

As he grew bolder, letting his tongue prod for entry, and was not denied, his spirits leaped. But for one fleeting second he was appalled, too. His sister would have been mortified, he thought, but not Amanda. Could someone already have been in her honeypot— that private place that was to be his and his alone?

Now he wished that it was night instead of afternoon, with the ranch just around the bend of the road where some rider could be coming by any second. His ever strong will took command. He released her reluctantly but was more than pleased that she had responded and his idea had worked. That little play on traveling to exotic places had met with her approval. Next time, he'd take her, possess her completely as he'd planned for so long.

He looked at her with desire written over his good-looking face as he ran his fingers through his sandy hair to remove it from his forehead. "God, you are something, Amanda honey!" She straightened up in the seat beside him and smiled as a rider came out of the Jensen property.

Derek considered himself smart not to have pursued his efforts any further and he flung the reins for the bay to move on. He let his other arm snake out to pull Amanda closer to his side and they rode into the Jensens' gate with this newfound intimacy. Amanda found herself completely baffled by the cozy warmth flooding her with Derek Lawson's nearness. Derek smiled, pleased as his fantasy visions paraded before him. She was yielding to his charms as he wished.

Later, after his business was finished, they rode back toward the city of San Antonio with the sun setting in the west and an aura of romance binding them as their buggy came to the fork in the road. Abruptly, the romantic glow was gone for Amanda and she straightened up in the seat. A rider atop a black horse galloped down in the opposite direction.

It was impossible, she told herself. Her eyes had to be playing tricks on her. Were her daylight hours to be haunted as well as her nights by Tony Branigan?

Had this man taken possession of more than just her body that stormy night in that old deserted shack? Had he as completely taken possession of her soul? God forbid that it was so! But she knew the rider was Tony Branigan.

As he rode along at twilight Tony was aware of some brief, but strange feeling swooping down on him with such intensity that he was tempted to pull up on the reins. As Picaro galloped swiftly down the dirt road Tony glanced back a couple of times. All he saw over in the distance was a buggy going in the opposite direction.

He was hell bent to get a few miles farther before nightfall. Tomorrow he'd make it back to the Circle K Ranch as he'd promised Mr. Kane. He was bone-tired, and after seventy-two hours with less than five hours of sleep he was looking forward to camping down by the river for the night.

This unexpected jaunt to San Antonio had been prompted by a message from Esteban, one that urged him to request a few days off from the Circle K. Kane's permission was granted and Tony had galloped to San Antonio as fast as Picaro would carry him. The fine Arabian he'd negotiated for almost a year ago had finally arrived from England from the Featherstone Farms. Esteban would not release the vast sum until it had Tony's final approval. So he had gone directly to the Moreno ranch, Casa del Plata, even before going to the fine old mansion in San Antonio. His efforts had been rewarded the minute his eyes gazed on the mare, Shalimar. She was a beauty! A perfect mate for Sultan!

The mare was proud and spirited as she pranced around the corral. Holding her head and tail high, she came by the fence where Tony stood admiring her. A true queen she was, and she knew it. What fine colts she'd produce for him, he thought, continuing to observe her.

Over at the hitching post, Picaro gave out a whinny voicing his jealousy of Tony's attention to the new mare—or perhaps his approval of her, too.

By the time he left the ranch to journey into the city Tony was more than assured that she was worth every cent of the price. By the time he had a bath, a scrumptious meal and several glasses of Esteban's best wine he had to give way to the exhaustion of his body.

It was the next morning while they had breakfast that Tony and his grandfather had their chance to talk. Old Esteban had seen the weariness of his grandson the night before. Come morning he would talk with Antonio.

181

"You know you're not exactly a popular subject with Francisco, don't you my son?" the white-haired gentleman pointedly quizzed Tony.

"I can imagine, sir. At least now you know why I've been gone and what I've been doing. I regret that I had to leave here with such sketchy details for you. At the time we, at least, had Aunt Bianca to play middleman. Otherwise, I could not have been alerted to Shalimar's arrival."

Nodding his head with understanding, Señor Moreno gave him that generous ready smile. "And so am I, Antonio. I have missed you very much. So you will soon be returning to San Antonio?"

"Very soon now, Grandfather. A few weeks here before I join Pedro down to the south." Tony paused in his eating with a faraway look in his eyes. He sat thoughtfully with his hands clasped together, his long, slender fingers rubbing back and forth as he mused silently.

"You are going to have a lot of explaining to do to one very impatient señorita, if I know anything about women, Antonio," Esteban projected with a sly grin on his still handsome face.

"That is another thing we must speak about, Grandfather. I can't marry Magdalena."

Esteban choked and gasped. His eyes turned that shade of black denoting extreme delight or violent fury Tony recognized as he had throughout the years his grandfather had raised him. "What are you saying to me, Antonio Moreno?"

"I apologize, Grandfather, for blurting it out like that, but I don't apologize for what I've said. I will have more finesse and be more diplomatic dealing

182

with the matter, I assure you. But it would be unfair to Magdalena most of all, for my heart could never belong to her. Another has it," Tony confessed. "I didn't plan it so. In fact, I sincerely thought at the time I cared for Magdalena."

"I see." Esteban gave a long sigh.

"I hope you can understand, for I would never do anything to destroy the friendship between you and Francisco. But what a horrible fate it would be for Magdalena to never have my love. I could not do that to her."

Esteban had to respect his grandson for that, but he was shattered by his revelation, nevertheless. "This young woman is back in Gonzales County?"

"Yes, Grandfather."

Esteban reached over to pat his grandson's hand to show his faith in him as he had so many times in the past. "You are right, of course Antonio—it—it would not be right to marry Magdalena under these circumstances."

Tony raised himself from his chair and embraced the elderly gentleman. His deep voice was soft as he spoke, and old Esteban's heart could not have been hard or harsh against the young man if he'd tried. "Oh, Grandfather—remember when I was little and you were describing to me what a wildfire was? It spread and burned out of control, you said to me. That is this feeling within me for this girl. She is a fever in my blood."

"Ah, that fever—yes!" Esteban could appreciate what his grandson was speaking about. His seventy-odd years of living had not dulled vivid memories of a time past when he was a virile young man and the

183

wild, savage fever had engulfed him.

He was also clever enough not to argue with Tony, for it would have been futile. The wildfire was a thing that had to be quenched!

He credited Tony that he was man enough to come to him and tell him. He patted himself on the back for having instilled a code of morals in his grandson. Esteban did not hold with the old custom that brides should be picked or grooms chosen. Terribly unfair! It had made for much misery in peoples' lives.

Esteban's fine aristocratic features were soft and mellow when Tony released his arms from the elderly gentleman's shoulders. He sank back down in the fine-carved oak chair with its rich, deep blue velvet cushion. "You do see what I mean, and you understand, don't you? I want that, Grandfather—more than you know."

"Oh, I do, and with the most delightful memories, Antonio. In fact, I could almost envy you. One time around in this old world isn't enough. Ah, I'll tell you, Antonio, I'd like to live it all over again," he chuckled, giving Tony a wink of mischief. But what about Francisco Gomez?

SIXTEEN

Mark Kane was elated at the sight of the black stallion galloping through the archway with its weary rider. The two men didn't linger long in greeting one another. But Mark was pleased as he walked away, and Tony sought his bed for some sleep. Branigan had kept his word as he'd promised, and that meant a lot to Kane. While he was curious about the young man's request, he respected his arrogant assumption that Kane must accept him on faith and trust. Even now, he'd offered no explanation to Mark. He couldn't fault him for that, for he was that kind of man, too.

The truth of the matter was he'd not needed Tony's services anyway. The countryside had been unusually peaceful and the roundup was running so smoothly Kane was amazed. It had been the same over at the Big D, Mark found when he paid a visit to his old friend David Lawson. The two of them had joked about the pleasingly uneventful days just past.

"Hell, maybe it's the calm before a storm," Kane jested with his friend. "Just seems funny that it should so suddenly stop. Guess I shouldn't question it. Maybe the bastards moved on to some other county."

David laughed and turned the conversation to their children.

"I've missed my little Mona," David confessed.

Mark laughed. "I know a young man who's missed her too, I think." He spoke of Jeff and his moping around the hacienda the last several evenings instead of his usual nightly absence after the dinner hour.

That spurred David to bring up the subject of Derek and Amanda. His praise of Mark's daughter flowed generously and he mentioned that this visit to San Antonio might just prove to be the thing to bring the two young people together.

"Why, Mark—we might just be hearing an announcement when they get back tomorrow or the next day." David gave a broad grin.

Perhaps his old friend did not note the forced smile he gave him, and Mark hoped not as he rode back toward the Circle K, but the idea of the marriage did not appeal to him as it once had. When his thinking had changed he couldn't say, but this autumn day the match didn't exactly taste as sweet to him. After all, he reasoned, Amanda was only coming up for her eighteenth birthday, and Jenny wouldn't mind at all having her daughter under their roof for another year or two.

During that ride back to the Circle K many thoughts crossed his mind. The truth of the matter was with the winter months coming on and the roundup time over he'd be letting the extra hired hands go as he always did. His hired gunman's services would not be needed, either. As quiet and calm as it had been lately, he would be hard put to justify the price of his salary now.

He could have sworn Jenny had been baiting him the other night after the dinner hour when Branigan had left after sharing the evening with them. She had asked for how much longer he would be hiring the gunfighter and he hadn't given her an exact answer. He rather suspected his wife, like him, had formed a genuine liking for the impressive young man.

Once or twice Jenny had mentioned how pleasant it had been for him to join them for dinner since Amanda was away. They had both found him rather tight-lipped about his past and his family, but the inscrutable gunfighter could not hide certain qualities that appealed to Jenny and Mark. For all his cleverness, Tony had revealed his brilliant mind and shrewd business head when they'd spoken of ranches and cattle. While he hadn't mentioned his background in engineering, he could not hide his intelligence.

It went beyond the point now with Mark Kane of just pride that he'd picked a damned good hired hand or that Branigan had saved his life and he owed him, but he dared not voice his idea even to Jenny.

No one had the capacity to wound his male ego like Amanda Kane, and Derek Lawson was ready to slap her lovely face by the time they reached the Beckenridge house at dusk. The sudden chill she put on him with that mercurial air of hers had him befuddled. The temperamental little bitch was testing him sorely. The whole time away from the ranch had yielded him nothing more than a few kisses and now he was left tormented, an ache in his groin. The time was over when he'd play his well-rehearsed role of the nice, mild-mannered gentleman. To hell with her and han-

187

dling her with a silken touch! She obviously warmed to the rugged gunfighter and so she would to him. She'd get no more consideration than any whore.

When they left San Antonio the next morning just as the sun was rising in the east, he dwelled on his vile, evil plans for the future and didn't share in the girls' idle chatter as they rolled away from the city.

The venom within his tormented soul would have shocked and startled the lighthearted misses with him. They were so busy discussing the trip and their purchased gifts for the folks back at the ranches, that they took little notice of Derek. Mona was used to her brother's long periods of cold reserve and thought nothing about it. Amanda surprised herself by her eagerness to get back to the Circle K.

The night before as she'd packed her bags before retiring she'd suddenly found herself caught up in the same anticipation she had had about leaving home to come to San Antonio. It had been a marvelous time she'd remember always. She had strolled about the glorious grounds of the old San Jose Mission built many years ago by the Indians, as the padres had explained. She had stood by the walls of the Alamo imagining the bloodbath taking place there forty years ago, and goose pimples had run over her body.

It had a startling effect on her, which she did not understand. There was a certain pride within her now that had not been there before she'd come to San Antonio about the country she'd lived in and the countryside she'd heard her father boast and brag about all her life. She now understood that certain twinkle in his bright blue eyes.

On that late autumn day as they returned and

Derek's buggy pulled toward the archway with the circle and the K she experienced a sense of pride she hadn't had when she'd left home.

For one fleeting moment, she mused silently about how her father might know her better than she knew herself. Darned if she planned to admit it though—not yet!

She knew Derek had not been too pleased about bringing her on over to the Circle K when they'd pulled up at the Big D's hitching post earlier.

"I'll just be going on home, if you don't mind Derek," she'd insisted, since it was only a little after four in the afternoon. There was more than enough time for him to get her there before dark. Home was where she wanted to be.

Her deep blue eyes pleaded in a way that was hard for him to deny graciously, especially with Mona being helped out of the buggy by Mr. Lawson.

She really had an itch to see that Branigan, he muttered under his breath. Well, there would be no more delays or disruptions now that they had returned!

As his sister walked arm in arm with their father after saying their farewells to Amanda, Derek jerked the reins angrily and yelled, "Get up!"

Amanda darted her eyes swiftly in his direction, and it took no stretch of the imagination to know he was disgruntled that he had to drive her on home. She shrugged her shoulders, thinking he acted like a spoiled child about not getting his way. Derek had always been that way, even as a child when they had romped and played in the fields around the ranches. Let him pout! She couldn't care less, for the burning desire just to get to the Circle K engulfed her. Pri-

189

vately, she had to confess her urgency surprised her.

After Amanda was left at the hacienda with her family smothering her in hugs and kisses, happy for her return home, Derek tore out of the Circle K at a reckless speed that Mark Kane noted. He surmised young Lawson's temper was riled and he had grave doubts that David's anticipated hopes had come to pass. Personally, he was rather glad it had turned out as it had.

Amanda was too busy chattering with her mother to give Derek much of a goodbye and thanks for getting her home. When the family shared a brief spell of talking before Amanda went upstairs to rest and have a bath, Mark noted with the utmost pleasure that his daughter was genuinely glad to be home. Nothing could have delighted him more. He was glad he'd not denied her this trip into San Antonio. Jenny, bless her heart, had been right!

Amanda acted so gay and happy, and Mark Kane thought she had never looked lovelier. It was very clear to the rancher that his daughter was unperturbed by young Lawson's upset. Whatever had him so riled had certainly brought out a trait in him Kane that had not witnessed before and it certainly didn't enhance Mark's opinion of him.

With a capricious gleam in her eyes as Juan helped carry her filled wicker basket in along with the luggage, Amanda gave the order, "Now, no snooping until after dinner!"

As her parents exchanged smiles of delight about their daughter's return home, she breezily bounced up the stairs to rest and refresh herself before the dinner hour. "See you at dinner, Mama. You, too Dad." She gave them a lovely smile and vanished up the stairs, just as Jenny was about to inform her that Tony Branigan would also be dining with them that night.

Derek had pushed the bay unmercifully back to the Big D Ranch. It was only later he'd realize the image he'd presented of himself to Kane. But he tottered on the brink of madness now, with rages he couldn't control. That night David Lawson was too engrossed with Mona to notice the tenseness of his son. Only later did he become cognizant of Derek's fractious mood when he boasted of what he'd been up to while Derek had been gone. "I've been letting you handle too much. It's time I took more of the responsibility, son."

"Wha—what are you talking about?" Derek's eyes flashed and his fingers tensed on the dinner fork. What had the old fool done, he wondered? Christ, he had never counted on this sudden burst of vigor out of the old man.

"Got the first load of our barbed wire in and set the men to stringing it on the Kane border. Mark and I will join our efforts. Don't you see—his east border will be our west one?" he told his son proudly.

His reply was a hissed, "I see." Derek glared at his father who happened not to be looking up at the time for he was relishing the delicious food Nina had prepared for their homecoming. But Mona saw her brother's eyes and something in them made her tremble. She'd seen that look other times in their life. She knew that cruel streak in him. Once when her kitten scratched him he squeezed it around the neck until it died. He would kick their dog brutally for the slightest thing. Mona's gentle nature was repulsed at those times.

She started a nervous chatter about something just hoping to make that look disappear, but it didn't, and suddenly Derek took a hasty departure from the table. David Lawson put no importance on it, for he was thoroughly enjoying his daughter's sweet presence.

Even as Mona climbed the stairs to retire later she'd not been able to shrug aside the bad feeling nagging at her. She knew Derek was still out on one of his many nocturnal jaunts somewhere. She often wondered where her brother went and what he did until the early morning hours. Many times she heard the thudding of his boots dropping on the floor when he prepared to retire. It seemed he didn't not a care that he woke her up at that ungodly hour. There were times he seemed not to care for anyone's feelings but his own.

Everything in her said she should love him. After all, he was her brother. But the last few years he had not been easy to love. It was the completely different personality of Jeff that endeared him so to her.

There were times she'd caught Derek staring at her in the strangest way, and she'd though she saw hate there in his blue eyes.

SEVENTEEN

She was a tormenting enchantress standing there on the stairs. Sweet Jesus, she bewitched him like a sorceress casting a spell on him! He felt a lump come into his throat and a burning, searing ache in his groin. Even his dark brown pants felt tight, and he fidgeted. His brown leather vest felt too warm suddenly. Christ, he had not known she was back, or he'd not have accepted the dinner invitation tonight!

Tony felt a wave of embarrassment, hoping he hadn't been obvious to Amanda's parents sitting there by him. He need not have worried, for Jenny and Mark had both heard her light footsteps coming down and turned to see how lovely she looked in her simple black flowered frock with its dainty puffed sleeves trimmed in white lace. Her spun-gold hair framed her face, hanging loose and casual, unadorned except for the tiny white blossom she'd tucked at one side from the bouquet Chita had placed in her room earlier.

Tony was no more prepared for this development than she was when she turned at the base of the stairway to be met with the sight of his firm, muscled body molded into the brown pants and leather vest. His penetrating gray eyes stabbed right into her soft flesh, feeling like a silver flame. Her stomach seemed queasy. She felt her lips quiver. Dear Lord, she prayed she wasn't giving herself away. Why did he have to look so darn handsome? She could almost feel those sensuous lips on her mouth as they'd been that night. The truth of the matter was she felt a sudden urge to rush into his arms, fling her arms around his neck, and let her fingers stroll with lazy motions through the curling black hair nestled over the collar of his cream-colored shirt.

Instead, she swayed up to the group. "Good evening everyone. What a surprise to see you, Mr. Branigan!"

"Oh, honey—Mr. Branigan has been our guest often since you've been gone. I might add, a most pleasant, entertaining one, too," her mother declared sweetly.

All the time her mother was speaking Tony stood with that crooked smile on his face, that black brow of his slightly raised and his eyes moving from the top of her head to her shoulders and downward.

"Oh, well, how nice," she remarked lamely, taking a seat next to her father.

Tony sat back down, striking a casual pose and crossing his long legs, and she noted that for once he was without those silver-plated pistols swinging on his hips. "Well, I have to say, your mother is a most gracious, dear lady to be so thoughtful about my eating right."

Oh, that silken-tongued rascal! He had completely beguiled her mother. Jenny's dark eyes were warm with admiration for the man sitting across from her.

"I was lonely without you, honey," Mark spoke up. "Amanda, I think you might not be so formal, and call him Tony—right Branigan?" Mark chuckled.

"Whatever Amanda wishes to call me, sir." His eyes taunted her as he spoke. She looked at her father with her sweetest smile. "All right." She was thinking of some choice name very suitable to label him with.

Tony was thinking how she looked as innocent as a child sitting there by her robust father, so tiny and petite. He knew, too, that he'd taken that part of her away, but he wanted to give her more than he'd robbed her of, for she was passion's woman if he'd ever seen one. He knew he must convince her before he left here that what they'd shared was a love to last a lifetime. That haughty, cool indifference could deny it all she wanted to, but he'd never accept it. God, the time was so short!

Consuela served the chilled white wine with their dinner of her special herbed chicken and fresh garden vegetables and home-baked bread. Of course, she'd not forgotten Amanda's favorite dessert—chocolate cake. All through the dinner Amanda could have sworn Tony was playing with her like a fencer with his epèe, so she parried back and forth with him.

By the time the dinner was over and the ladies retired to the parlor, leaving the men to enjoy their brandy and cheroots, Jenny's astute eyes had seen the strange forces being generated between her daughter and the gunfighter. She knew it was not her imagination. The two were attracted to each other.

When they were settled in the parlor, she requested that Amanda play her a tune on her guitar. Without thought, it was a pretty Spanish love ballad Juan had

195

taught her that Amanda chose to strum. She broke into singing just as Mark and Tony strode into the room.

When she came to the part in the song that said, "who will my lover be?" her eyes were drawn to Tony's, and what she saw in his silver-gray eyes told her what she already knew. Perhaps she was a wanton, but she did want him to make love to her again as he had in the old deserted shack. Those wild and wonderful sensations had remained with her. She could not erase them—and she'd tried with both Steve and Derek.

Once more, she knew she must touch, taste, and feel the heights of that rapture he seemed to stir in her. If but once again she must climb with him to those loftiest heights of pleasure. She must, or she felt she would just die! If there was a price to pay for her folly, then she would pay it.

Later, after Tony had left and her parents had retired to their room she indulged herself in another glass of wine before going to her room.

But she never got to the stairway, for a sudden impulse changed her mind and she went into the courtyard. She strolled toward her mother's favorite spot where the fountain stood. She could recall the advent of the fountain when she had been a small child. It was the one special luxury Jenny had requested of her husband. It brought her special memories of her home back in New Orleans, Jenny had told her daughter numerous times.

Like Jenny, Amanda found it pleasant to just sit and listen to the soft rippling sound of the spraying water falling into the small pool. Sitting there on the bench she could almost agree with her father's idea that the stars shine the brightest in the Texas skies. A million of them seemed to be up there this clear autumn night. The moon was a perfect ring, all golden and bright.

Sitting alone with only her thoughts for company she thought about that hour just before the little gathering had broken up. She'd finished her song and laid her guitar aside, and to attempt to shake off the strange, titillating effect of Tony's eyes as she'd sung, she had gone to the corner where she'd earlier left her wicker basket holding her gifts.

She'd given her mother the lace collar and cuffs and presented her father's gift to him. She left Jeff's pale blue scarf to give to him tomorrow, since he was absent from the family gathering tonight.

Carrying the Santos' gifts, she'd excused herself to go to the kitchen before Consuela left for her quarters.

When she'd returned to her parents sitting around the massive stone fireplace engrossed in their conversation with Tony Branigan, she saw that in her absence her father and the gunfighter were sharing a nightcap of brandy together.

There in the basket lay one more article—a silvery gray silk neck scarf. She remembered her purchase of it along with the blue one for Jeff. She picked it up and slowly ambled over to where Tony sat. "Here Mr. Branigan—Tony, I mean—this—this is for you."

His eyes twinkled with amusement as his hand took the scarf from her. He let his hand lightly caress hers and looked directly into her gemlike eyes. There was a heat that shot between the two of them; each could feel it.

Amanda moved back questioning herself. Had she really picked that scarf for him? It did remind her of his devastating silver eyes.

"Why, Amanda—how very nice of you to think of me while you were in San Antonio. Thank you very much," he said with the charm of a gallant. Damn him, she wanted to cry out that she wasn't thinking of him. A little voice inside her wouldn't allow her to deny it. Oh yes, you were, it silently chided her.

A primitive force as old as the ages called to Tony, for he knew even when he said goodnight to the Kanes and Amanda that he was too tormented this night for sleep. He tried dulling his senses and his feeling with his own favorite brand of brandy once he'd entered his quarters. He opened a new tin of his favorite cheroots and plucked out one of them.

He went back out into the night just walking aimlessly and kicking at the dirt with the toe of his leather boot. Whether it was conscious or subconscious, he found himself there by the black iron gate of the courtyard, staring up at the two story adobe and stone hacienda to the window belonging to Amanda's room. It was dark like the rest of the house. So she slept already.

Obviously he didn't ignite overwhelming stirrings in her and make her nights sleepless—as she did to him. Everything around the Circle K Ranch seem to be at rest, except him. No nightbirds were even calling out and only the rustling breeze whispering through the tall tree branches broke up the stillness of the late night hour.

Looking up at the starlit skies, he thought how it

was a night for lovers, and his being ached to be making love to the golden-haired girl up there in that room. There were moments when he found himself wishing that stormy night up in the hills had not happened, for then he'd not have known the sweet honey nectar of her lips or the passion fire of her yielding, soft body. No, damn it—had that night not happened he would not ache to caress her loveliness and smell the fragrant essence of her closeness.

Perhaps it was a sudden gust of breeze that carried the spray of water over toward the bench where Amanda sat lost in her daydreams that made her give forth a shriek of surprised delight. Someone with the heart of a romantic might have sworn it was the hand of fate that made her presence known to Tony standing there by the gate. Whatever it was he came alive and smiled with pleasure to know she was there in the garden's darkness, as if waiting for him to come to her. He did, rushing through the gate like an eager youth keeping his first tryst with his ladylove.

"Amanda?" His deep voice implored, not sure where she was in the walled courtyard.

"Tony? Tony, over here." She rose from the bench flinging her hand up, not thinking about the darkness making it impossible for him to see. She knew her voice was guiding him toward her as she heard his boots clicking as he walked over the flagstone path toward the fountain.

Words were not necessary as he came to stand in front of her, and she knew it as well as he did. It was spontaneous and natural as breathing that they came to one another. Tony's muscled arms encased her petite body and she pressed against him feeling the warmth of his broad chest against her breasts.

"Oh, Amanda *mia*," he murmured softly. Like a man thirsting for a drink of water, he was content to hold her for a moment before bending his head down so his lips could taste hers. Her response told him she was as wildly hungry for his kisses, for he could feel the deep intake of her breath when he paused for a moment to gaze upon her face.

As if in agony, she gave a soft moan. "Branigan— Branigan, I could hate you for what you do to me!" She writhed as if she was trying to fight this spell she found herself under.

"But you don't *chiquita*. No, you don't, and you and I both know it!" he whispered in her ear as his one hand held firm to the curve of her waist and his other hand covered her jutting breast.

"Oh, Tony! Tony!" she gasped. That heat of him moved like smothering lava from the tip of her breast where his hand played its magic to the pit of her stomach and downward.

"We can't fight it, Amanda. Damn, you know it," he declared in a husky voice. He didn't wait for her to answer him, but bent down and lifted her up in his arms. In hasty, striding steps he took her across the courtyard in the direction of his quarters over the stable.

"Tony?" she started to question their destination, but he quieted her with his kisses raining on her mouth as he covered the distance. He took the steps two at a time.

Her tiny body seemed like nothing in his powerful arms, and his masterful style was part of the spellbinding attraction she felt for him.

His booted foot kicked the door open, and only when he'd shut it the same way and stood at the foot of his bed did he release her. Again not a word was uttered as she lay there on the bed and he removed the leather vest and then his shirt.

He stood before her—a magnificent animal with his broad, bare chest. With abandoned care she gazed upon him. He smiled at the childlike look about her lying there with that golden mane all fanned out. "I adore you, *querida*. You fire me as no other woman has ever done." He bent down on the bed, leaning over her. Even his masculine smells had an intoxicating effect on her—the tobacco and the brandy mingled with the smell of leather.

With her half-parted lips still warm from his kisses, she purred, "Do I really, Tony—fire you?"

He flipped her over to unhook her gown. His thigh rubbed the side of her rounded hips. "You know you do, you little imp." Again he flipped her back over to face him. With her gown removed, he proceeded to remove everything that covered her and her golden nakedness was displayed to him. He let his eyes devour her for a moment before the urgency to remove his pants forced him to leave her side.

There was no initiating hurt or pain this time as there had been the night at the shack. He gave her only pleasure from the moment his body met with hers. His fine, muscled body with its strong, overpowering force guided her unhurriedly with him in the sensual pleasure he wanted her to know. She followed him with an eagerness that delighted and pleased him beyond his wildest imaginings. She was his woman of fire and passion, and no one would ever take her from him.

He brought her so completely alive with his touch and caress, soft and featherlike. He teased and taunted her, stirring the same fever in his blood as she had in his. Only then did he carry her with him to that new horizon they'd yet to reach. There, they soared and whirled in that ecstasy and rapture so sensuously sublime that when Tony made that final powerful thrust Amanda gasped with breathless exaltation.

She lay in his arms, not knowing the Spanish words of love he whispered to her. *"Mi vida, querida,"* his sleepy voice murmured before he fell into a deep sleep with her snuggled close to the curve of him lying by her side. Their sleep was sweet, they were completely content.

Neither knew that they'd been observed going to Tony's quarters. The minute Tony had carried Amanda through the door of his quarters, the lone rider perched on the hill reined his horse around. He knew now beyond any doubt that he would never realize one dream obsessing him. He took out his frustrations cruelly on the fine white Arabian steed.

A new obsession took hold in Derek's distorted mind at that early morning hour as he rode back to the Big D Ranch.

Never in his life had he hated someone as much as he did Tony Branigan!

He had been robbed of the one woman he desired. Now she was tarnished and soiled by the nephew of Bianca Moreno. In Derek's eyes that made her no more than a slut. Tony Branigan's whore!

EIGHTEEN

Amanda woke up with a start. The sun was shining through the window, blinding her. She turned to see the empty space beside her and the dented pillow where Tony's head had lain during those early morning hours. Christ, why had he not woken her up so she could have returned to the house before daylight?

"Oh! Oh, I'll swear I could kill him!" she muttered jumping up out of the bed. What a mess she was in! How in the world was she ever going to get across the distance between the stable and the house without anyone's seeing her now? She took a quick peek out the window to see if the hired hands were already milling around the barnyard and the corrals.

Hastily she reached for her garments trailing from the side of the bed around the corner to the foot where her gown lay. Mumbling a string of cusswords equal to any the cowhands would use, her eyes flashing with fire, she struggled into her underthings. "Oh, you'll pay for this, Branigan! I'll swear it!"

It took forever, it seemed, to get the back of her gown hooked. When she finally accomplished the chore she searched the top of the chest and through some of the drawers in hopes of finding a comb or brush. None could be found.

Lord, sure as God made little green apples Chita would be coming to her room with the coffee and find her gone. That didn't bother her as much as running into her father or mother. And there was Consuela stuck in the kitchen at this time of the morning.

She smoothed and tucked her rumpled hair as best she could. Her mind was busy with what lie she could conjure up should she be unfortunate enough to meet up with one of them. She stood for a moment at the door, reluctant to open it. That impetuous streak in her came to life. She went through the door and kept telling herself it wasn't the end of the world if she was seen. What did she care if one of the men did see her?

It was only when she got to the ground that her legs began to tremble when she had to cover that open space to get to the hacienda. Front or back entrance—which should she attempt to enter? She decided on the back and slipping past the bulky Consuela, whom, she knew she could fly past like a flash of lightning.

She intended to rush or run the distance but her legs were like jelly. As she made her way and went through the gate, her confidence built. Abruptly she was halted in her tracks, unable to proceed. Her swishing skirt was caught on the grillwork of the iron gate. Impatient and irked, she yanked the skirt upward to release it only to discover she'd not put on her stockings. In her hurry to get dressed, she'd slipped on her slippers only and her stockings were still up in Branigan's room. Well, they'd have to stay there.

She had no time to linger on that as she moved in and around the bushes and shrubs toward the back entrance. Consuela had done her a favor by leaving the back door ajar, as she often did to rid her kitchen of the cooking odors. She slipped inside and took time to search out the spacious kitchen area. She only had to wait until she saw Consuela waddling with her food-laden tray through the arched doorway into the dining room to dart through and make for the back stairway. Lord, it had not been complicated at all! She'd fretted for nothing, she told herself.

As she walked down the hallway to her room, she heaved a deep sigh of relief. She'd made it!

Inside her room, she flung the covers from her bed, slipped out of her gown with the now torn hemline. She sat in only her underthings when Chita rapped on her door. "Come in, Chita."

Smug and satisfied with herself, she accepted the Mexican girl's tray. In her sweet angel's voice she told Chita, "I'll pick up my room this morning, Chita. You can run on."

Grateful for one less chore to do, Chita replied, *"Gracias, señorita.* Enjoy your breakfast." She went on her way.

Amanda sat up amid the mountain of pillows and bit into the flaky delicious biscuit lavishly spread with butter. Oh, it was Tony Branigan's ear she'd like to bite into for his thoughtlessness. He didn't give a darn about the embarrassment it could have caused her—but then, he'd got what he wanted last night. Pouring a second cup of coffee, her mind was clearing from the sleepy fog and she plotted what she could do to even the score and bedevil him.

But could she really fault him for what had happened last night? Her own recklessness and daring

205

had made her go out into the garden, for her body burned for his touch. She knew he might drift as quickly from her life as he'd so unexpectedly arrived in it.

She moved from her bed to set the tray over on a table and strolled over to her desk. Taking a casual glance out of the double windows looking out over the front of the house, she spotted Branigan walking along with Slim Christy. His deep baritone laughter wafted up to her windows. Slim must have told him something very amusing, she decided. They ambled by the courtyard gate. Just watching that self-assured gait of his reminded her of their shared intimacy.

He hadn't cared a whit about the embarrassment she could have endured. The selfish oaf! That should tell her just how much she meant to him. All he wanted from her was to satisfy that male lust for her body. His actions obviously told her that, so she was a fool to make more of it than what it was. She had fed his hearty sexual appetite. Last night, she'd hungered, too.

As she watched him and Slim move over toward the corral she took in the whole of his black attire, knowing so well after last night the body beneath the clothes. This time she felt less embarrassed as she thought of their intimacy, than she had after that night at the shack. She knew without looking in her full-length mirror that there would be no changes in her body. There was no call to stand nude and examine every inch of herself.

Yet there was a lingering tenderness in the places where his ardent lovemaking and touch had played her like an instrument. She remembered the fulfill-

206

ment of utter delight she'd felt as the man she now saw below had collapsed atop her in his last powerful thrust. A crazy sort of wonder prodded at her about why every bone in her tiny body was not broken. He was such a giant of a man. But as she recalled him standing before her nude with those muscles rippling, firm and hard, she recalled how trim his waist and his hips were. In fact, now that she recalled it, her Aunt Lisa had a statue of a magnificent Greek god with nothing but a fig leaf covering the front part of his maleness. It could have been Branigan, she mused.

She turned from the window as Slim and Tony disappeared into the barn. A simple little peasant-type blouse and full gathered floral skirt appealed to her this morning, and she went to the armoire to get one of the three that Consuela had stitched up for her since her return from New Orleans. She dressed and took a seat at her dressing table. With long, lazy strokes, she brushed her long hair and finally made one single large braid tying a ribbon on the end of it. With her feet slipped into sandals, she left her room to go downstairs.

Chita certainly had a long face, Amanda noted, as they met in the upstairs hall. She inquired of the girl, "Did your mother give you the gift I brought back for you, Chita? I forgot to ask you a while ago when you brought my breakfast."

"Oh, yes señorita, and I thank you," Chita politely remarked, but there was no feeling or exuberance, which Amanda found unlike Chita.

"Well, I thought the flowers would be so pretty in your dark hair. Guess you know I've always envied

207

you that gorgeous black hair. You and mother both," Amanda declared with flippant, lightheartedness.

Chita forced a smile to her lovely oval face. "Oh, señorita—you are the one to be envied." She slowly moved away leaving Amanda, who had no inkling of the implications of Chita's words or the burden troubling her soul. That dreaded moment Chita had known for so long would come had finally happened when Jeff had come to her and they had lain once more together. In a few more weeks the announcement of his marriage to Mona would be made—during the holiday season, he'd told her. It was his duty to tell her personally, he'd said, but what little consolation was that to her?

It had determined one thing as far as she was concerned, though. She encouraged at once the attentions of Diego Ramos over at the Rancho Rio. She needed a quick proposal of marriage now, and she was confident Diego would propose if she encouraged him. Nevertheless, her nerves were frayed with panic.

Amanda bounced into the kitchen to plant a kiss on Consuela's chubby cheek and got herself playfully swatted with the Mexican woman's dish towel. Chuckling, she told Amanda, "Juan wishes to tell you *gracias* for that grand sombero. He's strutting around like a rooster this morning, *señorita*. Wait until you see him."

"Well, good. I'm glad he likes it and glad it fits."

"Well, if his head gets much bigger, it won't. He's asking to get his tail feathers clipped," Consuela laughed.

"Ah, Consuela—you wouldn't do that," Amanda teased her and skipped on out of the kitchen. She knew she would find her mother in the comfortable little sitting room down the hallway from their parlor. She was not to be disappointed, for she found Jenny sitting there, quiet and thoughtful.

"Mama? Hello, now just what were you dreaming about?"

"Amanda—come—come on in. I've just had a delightful letter from Lisa. Here, you can read it for yourself. She and Armand are coming for the holidays."

"Really! I'm so excited!"

"They'll be here for the holidays and your eighteenth birthday. Can you believe it?" Jenny's dark eyes gleamed like black onyx with her delight and happiness.

Amanda read the letter and she found her mother's excitement rubbing off on her. What fun it would be to see her precious Aunt Lisa and dear Uncle Armand again! What life they'd add to the ranch for the holidays! Her letter stated that they just couldn't face the holidays minus Amanda this year. Lisa lamented how the late spring and summer months had dragged miserably by without Amanda's lively presence.

"Bless their dear hearts. I adore them," Amanda said, handing the letter back to her mother.

"It's obvious they adore you too, darling," Jenny smiled, putting the letter aside. "Mark hasn't read it yet. Poor man, he was feeling so encouraged these last few weeks and the roundup had been going so well, but he had to ride out early this morning with Jake. They found something in the waterhole and some of the cattle are sick. One or two are dead."

"Good Lord, wonder how that could be?"

"Only one way, Amanda. Someone put something in the pond." Jenny went on to tell her that theirs wasn't the only pond contaminated. The Rancho Rio's waterholes, at least a couple of them, had been doctored with some stuff that they couldn't identify. "Mark's sent one of the men into Austin with a sample. It was Mario who rode over at the crack of dawn this morning to talk to Mark and see if they'd hit ours too."

A rider had been dispatched to the Big D Ranch by Mark, and he'd returned with the news that the Lawsons had by some miracle been spared, Jenny told her daughter. Amanda was suddenly caught up in her own private musings and wondered if it had been this that had taken Tony from her side in the early morning hours.

Just as quickly she dismissed that idea. Dear Lord, was she trying to excuse his thoughtlessness and irresponsible behavior? No, the truth was he hadn't cared about how she'd get back to the hacienda and the room where she should have been sleeping that night. Don't play the fool, Amanda, the logical girl within screamed at her.

"How will they keep them away from that bad water, Mama?"

"Have to drive them to the north, honey. See to it no strays double back." Jenny blessed the fact that the long cattle drives of the old days were not necessary since the Texas Central Railroad had reached Austin five years ago.

When Amanda left her mother she knew it would not be the most pleasant of evenings around the Circle K that night. Both Amanda and her mother were due for a surprise, though, where Mark Kane was concerned. Instead of the raging, ranting lion they'd expected, he was unusually subdued and quiet and spoke not at all about the latest event. Jenny laid it to his being exhausted from the day he'd put in.

She noted the slump of his shoulders as they dined and watched his fingers run through his heavy mane of graying hair. Jenny had only to look at him to know he was troubled.

The only time his brow wrinkled in a frown was when he inquired of Jenny why Jeff wasn't gracing their table again tonight and Jenny had to confess she didn't know where her son had scurried off to this evening. "Maybe he's gone to see Mona, dear."

Kane gave a grunt of an answer, and shortly he excused himself to retire to his study. "Got some papers to look over, if you ladies will excuse me." He left.

Amanda wondered about Branigan's absence this evening, but she dared not question her father about it. With dinner over and Jenny content to pick up her needlepoint to occupy the rest of the evening, Amanda took a stroll out in the garden.

Her footsteps took her to the barn and to Prince's stall. Poor baby must be in need of an outing, and she would make a point of taking him out tomorrow.

A moan of pain interrupted her visit with Prince and she turned, startled, to listen. It was a man's voice, and she followed the sound to a far stall. A mop of tousled black hair met her eyes. The man's head was bent over his chest and for one fleeting minute she thought it was Tony. But by the time she entered the stall she saw it was Jeff.

"Dear God, Jeff—wha—what happened? Are you

211

drunk? She bent down and cradled his chin in the palm of her hand, lifting it up. Puffiness and swelling had already set in and blood, still damp and some of it dried, made him an awesome sight.

"Jeff!" She prodded at him, but he only mumbled and moaned. "I got to get you up to the house!" She leaped up to leave.

"No, Mandy!" he yelled with tremendous and painful effort. "NO!"

She hesitated, surveying him for a moment. "All right, then I'll clean you up and let you rest out here for a while. I'm—I'm going out to the trough and get this wet—all right?" She tore a part of her petticoat ruffle off and darted out.

Jeff leaned back against the wall and thanked God it was Amanda and not his old man who'd come upon him.

It took Amanda three trips of trotting back and forth to the watering trough before she cleansed her brother's battered face. Someone had taken a sadistic delight in battering Jeff's handsome face. Compassion swept over her as he sat there as helpless as a child allowing her to tend to him. She knew it hurt even though she tried to go as easy as possible.

"God, Jeff—you're a mess. Who—what sonofabitch did this to you? Some drunk at the Red Garter?"

His sharp-witted sister had solved his quandary for him. It was as good a tale as any, he decided. "Yeah, sis. It was a drunk at the dance hall. Guess I should have stayed at the ranch tonight."

No drunk had done it, nor had he even been in Gonzales during the evening.

Jeff could not absorb everything that had happened that evening. He'd lived out a nightmare and he knew he'd looked into the eyes of a madman who would like to have killed him. This man was supposedly his life-long friend.

NINETEEN

There had not been too much in his life, Jeff figured, that had pleased his father. For as long as he could remember he had strived so hard for Mark Kane's praise. He was one of those people, it seemed, who was always at the wrong place at the wrong time. Nothing came out the way he anticipated. But this early evening, his spirits were high, for he knew he had David Lawson's approval to ask Mona to marry him. As for Mona—he was always sure of his precious Mona and her undying love.

At dusk he'd ridden out of the Circle K to go over to the Lawsons and formally ask her to marry him. He'd even prided himself that he'd taken no drink of whiskey before leaving. David had insisted that he stay for dinner and he had. Afterwards, he and Mona had strolled in the twilight around the grounds and stood atop one of the rolling, grassy mounds back of the two story white house. She'd said yes to his proposal as he'd known all along she would. Theirs had always been an uncomplicated relationship. His easygoing nature and her gentle one blended in perfect harmony. Even as children, it had been so. The same had not been true, even back then, with Derek and Amanda.

Clever deceit and cunning wiles were just not Jeff Kane, and without the strong influence of Derek Lawson, Jeff would never have gone off on such a wild, reckless escapade as he found himself floundering in now. For all his weakness and the many months he'd allowed Derek to intimidate him with threats, he had now drawn the line for himself at certain of Derek's activities.

These last weeks of drinking heavily had not made him forget, and his hell was still there. But he'd come to realize something during those drunken stupors. At least, he wasn't the cold-hearted bastard Derek was. He did have a conscience, or he wouldn't feel so bad about what he'd done. That was consolation. Coward he might be, but a couple of times when he'd had just enough whiskey in him he'd had the guts to defy Lawson. This hadn't sat well with Lawson.

Derek's fits of fury chilled Jeff to the core of his being, especially when he spoke with such an intense dislike of his family. That urged Jeff to protect sweet little Mona from that unknown fear he felt overwhelming him.

He'd been pleased that Derek had not been on the premises during his visit during the evening. When he'd finally bid his bride-to-be good evening and ridden toward the Circle K, he was at more peace with himself than he'd been for many, many months. They'd be married this winter they'd decided. The announcement would be made in November. She'd live at the Circle K as his wife, and Derek's poison couldn't touch her then, Jeff mused.

These were the happy thoughts occupying him

when that white Arabian with Derek atop him came rushing out of the grove of pines as he trotted homeward.

"Hey, Jeffie—buddy—hold up!" he called out in that insolent tone Jeff had begun to resent more and more. Derek reined the huge white horse up beside Jeff's roan. "Don't have to ask where you've been or what you've been up to. Want to know what I've been up to lately?" That self-important air didn't impress Jeff as it once had.

"Guess that's your affair, Derek." He gave the roan enough rein to continue on in a slow trot.

Even the air around them seemed to suddenly grow thick with tension and Jeff didn't have to turn to know that Derek was glaring at him with displeasure.

"In a hurry, Jeff old boy?" Derek smirked in that manner of his that had become more and more pronounced in the last few months. Best he mollify him rather than spark that temper that was always ready to explode, Jeff considered. "I was on my way home. Got to get an early start tomorrow on a job for the old man."

"Come on . . . Over here by the creek. I gotta take a leak anyway." He veered the horse over by the creek, dismounted and began to relieve himself.

Jeff followed him, tying the roan to a sapling and sitting down on the ground. He picked up some small pebbles and played idly with them. Derek joined him fastening up the front of his pants. He lit up a cheroot and leaned up against the trunk of an aged oak tree. "Had a nice evening with little Mona, eh?"

The light of the moon revealed the cynical look on his face. There were no cowardly thoughts going

216

through Jeff's mind at that moment. He sat there wishing he could knock the hell out of the arrogant bastard. He'd seemingly spit his own sister's name as though it was foul to his taste, and Jeff resented that.

"It was more than nice, Derek. I asked your sister to marry me. We'll make it official at Thanksgiving."

"Well, well, well. Now isn't that wonderful." Derek flopped down on the ground and put his arm around Jeff's shoulder. "Guess as a good friend I should enlighten the groom-to-be about a few little things. Guess I'd be remiss if I didn't tell my old buddy the genealogy of his bride-to-be, eh?"

Jeff shrugged away his arm and stared at Derek. "You drunk, Derek? Hell, there nothing about Mona I don't know. Goddamn, we've known each other all our lives!"

Derek reared up and swaggered, swelling with the rude awakening he was going to lay on Jeff. "You don't know for shit! You want me to tell you who you're really marrying, eh? Well, grab this my friend—you're marrying Miguel Alvarado's bastard, not David Lawson's daughter." He broke into a rage of wild laughter, bending over double. "Yes sir, a damned Mex!"

"CHRIST!" Jeff knew he was a man driven by crazy obsessions, but this was too much. "You're a damn lunatic! You're lying!"

Derek continued to laugh and shake his head. "Nope. My whore mother, Carlotta, and Miguel spawned the little bitch." To hear Mona called a bitch was too much for Jeff to take and he sprung off the ground like a bolt of lightning and lunged for Derek with no thought to the fact that his thin, reedlike build

217

was no match for the husky Derek or that he had never indulged himself in fighting like his friend. So it was no match but a massacre, with Jeff the easy loser.

Long after Derek had gone on his way, Jeff roused himself up and managed to mount up on the roan and make it to the ranch and the barn where Amanda had found him.

His bond of love for his sister had never been greater than it was as she so tenderly tended to his wounds. An hour later he found the strength, with her support, to make it to his room. Never had he felt hate so intensely as he did for Derek Lawson. He swore whatever the cost to himself he'd prevent the vileness and evil of Derek from touching Mona, or his sister.

He drank deeply from the flask he'd had Amanda retrieve from his saddlebag before they'd left the barn to come into the hacienda. Tomorrow, he'd turn over a new leaf. Never again would Derek Lawson bully him—even if he had to kill him in the process!

In those hours just before the dawning of the new day Jeff lay on his bed, eased by the whiskey, and reflected on Derek's cruel words. Had he only meant to wound and hurt, as he so often did? Had he merely pulled this ridiculous tale out of his evil mind? Could it possibly be that his lovely Mona was, indeed, the daughter of the aristocratic Miguel Alvarado, husband of Bianca? This was madness, absolute insanity!

Amanda was utterly exhausted by the time she reached her room and got undressed. She could not forget the face of her poor brother, and there was never a time in her life that she'd felt so sorry for him. That pathetic look of helplessness as she went about cleaning and tending to his face would be marked in her memory for a long time. He was like a small child instead of her older brother.

Maybe he'd keep himself out of that cheap dance hall with its gambling, drunks, and whores. To a rough and rugged guy like Branigan, this would never happen, but Jeff was a gentle sort. Perhaps it was why he was always displeasing their father.

Mark Kane should have had a son like Tony. That would have pleased him, Amanda knew. Oh, yes, there was that link of camaraderie those two could share that Jeff would never quite measure up to.

She tossed for the longest time and finally exhaustion made her sleep.

When Tony finally climbed the stairs to his quarters after the long, exhausting day and entered the room the first thing he noticed was the lingering essence of Amanda and the unmade bed with the sheet dragging half on the floor. But for the sharp rapping fist of old Slim on his door, Tony would have got to hold her in his arms and make love to her again before they'd parted, he reflected thoughtfully.

It wasn't the way he'd planned it for her to wake up and find him gone. This time he didn't want a repeat of the night at the shack. He wanted more than anything to let her know the depth of his feelings, especially now, with his departure so near.

He'd not caught one glimpse of her all day, but then it had been a busy one and he felt it as he sank down on the bed. It was then his eyes saw the little clump of something on the floor and picking it up, he smiled. Amanda's stockings!

Ah, they were soft, too. As soft as her lovely thighs as they'd encircled him the night before. Christ, it had been a glorious night! What was it about her that set her so apart from any other woman he'd ever known or had in his bed? He couldn't put her in a slot—he'd tried. Any one particular thing about her didn't account for the magic of the bewitchment. Even the golden fire of her passion in his bed was not the whole of it. He didn't know, and perhaps he never would, but it was there. Dear God, how it was there!

He stretched out weary and tired under the sheets and heaved a deep, heavy sigh feeling the sweet comfort of the bed. It had been a long, busy day. Only then did any impact register about the forgotten stockings Amanda had left behind in his room. A lady just didn't forget to put on her stockings before slipping into her shoes unless she was in a hell of a hurry or upset.

The little wildcat would surely greet him when next they met with the chill of the winter wind. He bet she had slept until the sun was high in the sky and had the devil's own time slipping back over to the hacienda.

Oh, she'd pretend to be a little ice maiden with him. The little minx! He'd thaw her out, though. He'd done it before and he'd do it again, he consoled himself. There was nothing to be done tonight anyway, and he wouldn't have the energy to try.

However, the next day or two left Tony beginning to wonder about his ability to thaw her. The little imp was avoiding him, he knew, and he never caught her alone without someone around. He itched to turn her over his lap and paddle that tempting behind a couple of times when he caught that taunting, devious look in her eyes. She was certainly hell bent on trying his patience and the days were growing short now before he was to leave. It looked like it was going to take the Harvest party Jenny Kane was having to ever get her alone in the dark to drum some sense into her pretty head.

The news that disturbed Tony the most was the conversation he'd had with Slim and learning about the Kanes' relatives coming in for the holidays. Tony remembered her fondness for New Orleans and he damned sure didn't want to lose her now and have her running back to New Orleans with them when they went home.

Once this thing was done for Flanigan, he'd take her anywhere her heart desired to go. Hell, he was a wealthy man. They'd honeymoon for months all over the Continent. Honeymoon? Marriage? Dear God, he'd never ever approached the subject with her!

He could have courted her properly but for this crazy business for Flanigan. Ironically though, if it had not been for this mission for the marshal he'd never have met her at all. So perhaps he owed Brett Flanigan, after all.

There was no one he respected more than Flanigan except for his grandfather. He'd found himself drawn to Slim Christy more than the other Kane men because he reminded him of the marshal. As Slim called it, they did a lot of "chewin' the fat." Slim's comments had been most interesting when Branigan had brought up the subject of Jeff's messed-up face.

"Hell, I was there that night, Branigan. Weren't no durn fight there that night," the rawboned cowhand declared, giving a generous spit of the tobacco juices.

221

"Ain't goin' to say anything to Mark, though. That's between him and his boy. Fact was—it was dull as a doornail in town that night. Me, Jake, Ed Johnson, and a cowpoke from the Big D were about the only ones there. Young Jeff got that there beatin' somewhere else."

"So you're saying Jeff lied?"

"That I am. Most likely the young stud mighta been caught messin' around with some pretty little rancher's wife, you know?" Slim chuckled. "Whoever did it was out to teach him a lesson. That's sure obvious."

If Slim had been talking about his cousin Mario Tony could have bought that, but not Jeff Kane. However, he would not try to change Slim's opinion. Let him think that.

"Being the son of a wealthy rancher, I guess Jeff, as well as Lawson's son, don't have no trouble where the young ladies are concerned," Tony baited him.

Slim scratched his head. "Reckon not. Been here a few years, like you know. From all I've always heard Jeff's been sweet on Miss Mona. Neither one of them young pups are like their pas." He bent closer to Tony, adding, "Truth is I always considered David Lawson a fine, good man, but as far as his son is concerned I think he's an asshole!"

"How come, Slim?"

"Couldn't tell you if my life depended on it. Call it a gut feelin', I guess."

A spark lit up in Tony's slate-gray eyes. He and old Slim shared mutual feeling about Derek Lawson. He was a dangerous man!

222

TWENTY

For over twelve weeks now, Tony had covered many acres of the vast Kane Ranch with its rolling hills and lush valleys. His favorite spot was the wooded area of pines flourishing not far from where the Guadalupe River flowed and Sandy Creek emptied into it.

The waters were clear as crystal this morning as he paused for Picaro to quench his thirst after their ride from the Circle K. There'd been no recent rain to muddy up the stream and he could see the multitude of minnows swimming aimlessly in the shallow water.

He felt no rush to return to the ranch and took a moment to enjoy the beauty of the autumn day by flopping on the ground. He stretched out and leaned back against the trunk, cocking his flat-crowned hat slightly down over his forehead to shade his eyes from the bright midday sun.

Proof was what he needed and that he didn't have yet. He knew who'd tried to shoot him and he had no doubt that it could have been Derek who tried to ambush Kane that first day they met. He had figured out why Kane had been shot after he'd stumbled onto the branding iron when he'd come to the Circle K to work for Kane. Mark Kane had been shot because he had got too near the spot where the outlaws had been changing the brands of the cattle before herding them south toward the border. Panic had made Kane the target. But he felt that that wasn't the real motivation for someone trying to shoot Kane, and that the contaminating of the Kane and Alvarado watering holes could not be that obviously explained.

While he didn't have the evidence he needed, Tony suspected he was dealing with a sadistic megalomanic, who had no qualms of conscience about anything or anyone as long as it got him what he wanted. That kind of man was the worst and the most destructive. He felt that Jeff Kane had probably received a sample of this cruelness after what old Slim had told him. If he could gain Jeff's confidence he would try to help him. Although he had no great love for Jeff, he did for Amanda and Mark.

Only one thing would deter him from going through with this mission for Flanigan. He'd blow it all to hell before he'd allow Lawson's poison and filth to touch the beautiful lady he loved more than life itself.

Earlier, he'd watched her ride off toward the Big D and an awful lump had come into his throat. Something had been going on between the brother and sister before she mounted up on Prince. Jeff had deposited some sort of message in her hand and they'd seemed to chat in a serious manner. He'd continued to watch as Jeff flung his hat to the ground, dismayed and disgruntled. He had kicked at the earth as though he was mad at the world.

Tony had felt a moment of pity for young Kane as he ambled toward the barn with a downcast look on his face. What was he brooding so about, the gun-fighter wondered? It had probably not been too easy for Jeff to be going through his life expected to fill the big boots of Mark Kane.

Jeff's dismay, which Tony had witnessed, had come from the sudden realization that Amanda would discover he'd been to the Big D Ranch that night and not in town. He was going to have to answer a million prying questions from Amanda the minute she returned from the Big D and seeing Mona. Knowing his sister, she'd not let the matter lie once Mona told her about his visit that night he had asked Mona to marry him.

However, once Tony mounted up on Picaro and rode to that shady cluster of pines he spent his energies on more complex matters. His hat slouched down over his face and his broad shoulders pressed back against the trunk of the tree. He felt very lazy and lifeless not wanting to move from the cozy spot. He even dosed off.

A tall figure ambled out of the edge of the woods with a shotgun resting against his shoulder. Tony's fast draw made him walk cautiously and yell out at him, "Hey, *amigo!*"

Tony jerked up to see his cousin Mario striding up with a broad smile on his face. "Mario, what are you up to?"

"A little quail hunting. Don't give me away to Señor Kane, though. Guess I roamed a little farther than I realized and crossed the creek up the way. That is when I spotted Picaro and knew you were somewhere nearby."

Tony motioned him to come on over. "I'll not say a word."

"Good, the bounty hasn't been worth getting shot over."

Tony pushed his hat back on his head, giving a light chuckle. "Doing any good? Nothing like a dinner of quail."

"A few, but not enough for the way Maria devours them. I caution her if she doesn't calm her appetite she'll end up being as big as Josie." He propped his shotgun up against the trunk of the tree and took a seat by Tony.

"How is your mother and the family?"

"Fine. 'Course Mother is not too happy about losing so many head of cattle to the poisoned water," Mario informed him. "Weird the Lawsons were omitted, don't you think Tony?"

"Yeah, I guess," Tony replied, offering his cousin one of his cheroots.

"I found it so. I am of the opinion that running a *ranchero* always has its problems, though. This morning one of our men came up missing and of course Mother is troubled about that. It's old Ramos's son Diego and he's worried silly. 'Course you know how everyone at Rancho Rio comes to her. Mother is their savior."

Tony shrugged his shoulders. "Oh, he'll probably show up. He's that young man that Maria was admiring so much, I believe, wasn't he? The great horseman, I think she boasted to me."

"He is, and a good worker, too. Guess that's what has Mother just a little concerned. It isn't like him at all."

"Maybe some pretty little señorita has caught his eye and he's taken himself a little holiday, eh?" Tony

226

gave his cousin a wink, having no idea he'd jokingly hit upon the truth.

"You could be right. Diego seems to catch the ladies' eyes. Maria's had a crush on him for the last two years. Speaking of the ladies fair, how is the fair Amanda?" Mario inquired. "I heard she'd been away in San Antonio." Tony's handsome cousin had his motives for quizzing him. Mario suspected the attraction there and he heartily welcomed it. Since meeting the sultry Magdalena, he was anxious to pursue her, and Tony's absence from her life opened the door for him to try to woo her. Mario's impulsive nature would not stay idle.

"She is fine, I guess. I've been too busy to keep up with the spoiled daughter of Mark Kane, Mario," Tony lied, displaying a matter-of-fact look on his tanned face. However, Mario wasn't so thoroughly convinced that his cousin was kept all that busy. He was hardly breaking his back at work this morning, it would appear.

He taunted Tony, "Ah, cousin—with a girl like Amanda around I would find it hard to work at all. Remember, *amigo*, we have the same Moreno blood flowing in our veins and we're both decendants of one Esteban, who, I understand, was the dashing *caballero*." Mario rose up from the ground and started over to mount up on his fine horse. The two exchanged smiles and Tony suddenly realized Mario was a more likable guy than he'd sometimes credited him with being. Mario's private thoughts were similar.

Mounted up on the huge beast, he called down to Tony still sitting there on the ground, "You know, Tony, when you think upon it we have the right to

227

hold our heads as high and proud as anyone around here. That old rascal Esteban drilled it into me years ago that his great-great-grandmother was one of the fifteen families sent from the Canary Islands by the king of Spain—remember? I know you've heard it, too." He boasted, "We are the true barons here."

"Yes, I've heard it." For the first time, Tony felt Mario's acceptance of him and it made him feel good. "You're right, Mario. I'd never thought about it before." He gave his cousin a broad smile, genuinely liking him.

The two cousins bid each other farewell. Tony urged himself to return the ranch, and on the way there he once again felt a deep relief that Mario's faults did not include anything more serious than chasing the ladies.

Speaking of ladies, he reminded himself that he must make a point of returning to its owner the pair of stockings folded in a tight little knot in his pocket. He grinned, anticipating her face when he handed them to her. What he did not anticipate and what took him by stunned surprise was the stinging slap her dainty hand gave him a half-hour later when they met at the corner of the barn after having arrived back at the ranch within minutes of one another.

He'd noted that she seemed like she was in a hurry, bent on getting to the hacienda at once when he'd called out to her. He'd rushed up to her with the stockings in his hand. He grinned impishly. "I think these belong to you." His smile had been friendly, but Amanda took it as a smirk. When she saw what he held in his hand she exploded, for her day had not been that pleasant and she was not in the mood for his devilment.

When her eyes darted down swiftly to see the stockings, reminding her of that night, she slammed his mocking face with her mightiest blow. Tony could almost feel his strong, muscled body rocking. "What the holy . . ."

Amanda had already whirled around and started on. She heard the deep voice of Branigan calling, "You damned little wildcat!" He strode with giant steps to catch up to her, not caring that Kane or any of his men might be seeing him. His huge hand grabbed her by the shoulders causing her to shriek, "Damn you, Branigan—take your hand off me!"

"What was that for, eh?" His gray eyes burned with their own pride and fury. "What was that slap about?"

"Because I felt like it!" She wiggled trying to break his hold on her, which was unforgivable torment and she probably knew it. Undaunted, he took his other hand and put it on her other shoulder and turned her exactly the way he wanted her to firmly kiss her half-parted lips. She gasped at his boldness here in view of everyone. Releasing her roughly, he muttered, "Well, I did that because I *felt like it!*"

As she turned in a huff, he gave her a swift, sharp swat on her rear. She turned, but didn't stop. "I hate you, Branigan!" All the time she kept marching toward the courtyard gate with his irritating laughter ringing in her ears. How dare he do that? Was he crazy as a loon?

As she marched through the gate, she grumbled, "Oh, I'm going to kill him someday!" Had she known that Jenny had seen the whole spisode and had been laughing at them she would not have believed it. The truth of the matter was Jenny Kane found it all very amusing and in her heart she knew this man was the one who was going to conquer her restless daughter. That dominating streak would intrigue her daughter, and that kiss spoke of tender gentleness tempering all that ruggedness. She suspected he held the key to her daughter's heart.

She said not a word to Amanda as she marched on past her in her secluded spot in the garden. But the amused smile remained on Jenny's lovely face as she watched her daughter enter the door. To herself she mused silently, Ah Amanda, maybe you don't know it yet, but he is the man for you.

She had some grave misgivings, though, that her beloved Mark would accept him as their son-in-law.

But he should not really object, Jenny rationalized, as she began to cut more chrysanthemums for her dinner centerpiece. Tony was a lot like the Mark Kane her young girl's heart had fallen in love with. If anything, he possessed more grace and good manners. Ah, but how different it was when a man measured his daughter's suitor!

As she walked back into the house, her thoughts turned from her own daugher to Consuela. If only she could think of something to ease the pain of her devoted housekeeper. She would not have thought Chita could have pulled such a foolish trick as to run away. Did one ever really know what was going on in one's children's minds?

Poor Juan was now out and had been all day since dawn's first light when they'd discovered Chita's message lying on her pillow. Obviously, she had left during the night. Why, only yesterday morning she'd been going around the hacienda tending to her regular daily chores as usual, and Jenny would never have imagined her to be plotting such a foolhardy stunt.

Jenny felt deep concern for Juan and Consuela and what this could do to them. The girl was young and if she got herself in trouble it would be her burden to bear. God forbid, it was not fair or right that her two dear parents pay for a stupid girl's mistakes. It was enough in this world that a person paid for his own mistakes, without paying for his offspring's too.

Jenny loved the Santos as though they were family and she sent up her prayers for them many times that day.

TWENTY-ONE

The odor of beeswax and lemon permeated the hall-way and the dark furniture gleamed with a glossy, high-polished shine. Jenny had Mark and Jeff move the massive pieces around to make more space in the center of her parlor floor for the Harvest party.

Lord, she wished a dozen times the invitations had not already been sent out and accepted by most. Otherwise, she would have cancelled it. Poor Consuela was trying to carry out her many chores, but under duress. Amanda was being a real little trooper trying to help out with the many tedious tasks that would have been Chita's duties.

It was a monumental task to put the shindig together, but Jenny had never minded it before. For the last few days Jenny had watched her daughter work diligently and as hard as any servant. She better never hear it said around her that Amanda was spoiled and pampered. A free spirit she was, but she wasn't too proud to work. Her daughter did what suited her, caring not if it always met with others' approval. Jenny found it most admirable.

Some of Kane's men were very good musicians and

each evening that week they put in sessions of playing together on their guitars, fiddles and banjos. Hammers and saws were put to work to build a platform floor for dancing outside as long as weather was permitting.

"Oh, I'll just die if it rains, Mama," Amanda had declared.

"Nothing we could do about that, honey. We'll just have to keep our fingers crossed on that and pray." Jenny would not project trouble of that sort. That side of her nature, Mark swore, kept her from acquiring wrinkles as he had. Jenny merely laughed at him about that. However, her mirror did show her a rather smooth face for a lady of forty.

With another busy morning behind them and lunch finished, Jenny suggested to Amanda that they deserved a slow, lazy afternoon for a change. "We have some time to play now, shall we say," Jenny told her as they relaxed on the little patio just outside the dining room.

Consuela came through the open dining room door to step out on the patio and announce Bianca Alvarado. Jenny was delighted to have her neighbor paying one of her rare visits to the Circle K.

Jenny left Amanda there on the patio to greet Señora Alvarado in the parlor. After the ladies had greeted each other and Jenny had taken a seat she realized Bianca's visit was no casual afternoon call. She seemed concerned that the servant lady might be coming in and out and politely turned down Jenny's offer of some refreshments.

"I know you've probably sensed that this is something more than a social call. The Mexican lady—is

233

she Consuela?"

"Why yes, Bianca—she is." Already Jenny's mind was racing ahead with projections. Dear God, don't let them have found Chita dead, Jenny lamented, fearing the worst.

"I should probably have spoken to her but I thought it best I talk to you first. Her daughter Chita is at our ranch, Jenny. I only learned of it this morning, although we have received the word of her running away. I want you and Señor Kane to know this, so there will not be hard feelings. You do understand this, don't you Jenny?"

"Why, of course I do."

"The reason I felt I should come. The young people won't, and they are scared silly. You see, Chita married one of our *vaqueros*. But I assure you, Jenny, Diego Ramos is a fine young man. However, I don't approve of how they went about it. I have given them use of one of the cottages on my land, for I must tell you, Jenny, that the marriage was consummated before they returned to the Rancho Rio, so what could I do? I felt rather sorry for the two of them. Chita seems to be a sweet girl."

"Oh, Lord!" Jenny was so surprised it was all she could say.

"I know! That was why I thought I should talk to you first. I know Chita is only fifteen or sixteen and I had no idea how the Santos would take it. I would have insisted that she return to the Circle K had they not confessed to me that they are, in truth, man and wife."

Jenny not only understood, but completely agreed with Bianca. Consuela and Juan would have to accept what had happened and Chita's decision would have to be lived with now. "I think you've done the only thing you could do and I, for the Santos, thank you. I don't have to tell you we love the family very much."

"Well, Jenny—she could have picked a far worse young man. He is a hard worker and honest. He seems to adore his young bride. Do any of us dare ask more than that for our children? If we do, does it make it happen?" Bianca smiled, feeling a heavy weight had been lifted off her chest. Jenny Kane had made it so much easier than she'd anticipated. Her fretting and worry had been for nothing.

"Should we both tell Consuela? I think she may be so relieved to know her daughter is safe and close by that the shock of the marriage will go softer," Jenny smiled, and Bianca nodded with approval.

They did just that and Consuela's reaction was much as Jenny had said it would be. By the time the Mexican housekeeper rose from the chair to excuse herself and find her husband the look on her face was rather serene after her long days and nights of worry. Jenny could almost have cried for her beloved Consuela, knowing how she would have felt if it were Amanda.

"I thank you with all my heart for your kindness and thoughtfulness, Señora Alvarado. I'll be forever in your debt," Consuela declared, fidgeting with her apron. Her dark eyes gleamed with a hint of tears.

"Come to the Rancho Rio anytime you wish, Señora Santos. Everything will be just fine." Bianca patted Consuela's hand to assure her and relieve any apprehensions she might have had.

Let no one say a foul word ever against Bianca Alvarado, Jenny Kane vowed silently. She was a gracious, queenly lady with a heart of gold. That included Mark Kane, too.

The two ladies said their goodbyes and Jenny walked to the entrance with her neighbor. They paused for a moment on the veranda before Bianca started on down the flagstone walk. "This day has meant much to me, Jenny," she said. "I just wanted you to know how I felt before leaving."

Jenny understood the words she had not spoken and she felt the same way. She told Bianca so, and the two gave each other a warm embrace before parting.

Amanda eagerly volunteered to accompany the gift-laden buckboard over to the Rancho Rio. It was to be Juan and Consuela's way of giving their blessing to the newlyweds. Of course, Jenny was more than generous with her own offerings that accompanied the Santos' gifts to their daughter and her groom, Diego.

With her black felt flat-crowned hat jauntily set to the side of her head, Amanda gave a final tug on her black twill divided skirt and slipped into the matching vest to be on her way.

The wagon was ready and awaiting her out by the barn and one of the ranch hands would drive her. With a quick farewell to her mother and Consuela sitting at the end of the dining room table busily going over their plans and menus for the Harvest party only a few days away now, she was ready to rush back into the hallway when Jenny's voice called to her.

"Now, Amanda—don't forget to invite Chita and Diego to the party, honey."

She gave her mother a nod of the head. Consuela

added to be sure to tell Chita she loved her and was anxious to see her.

"Oh, I will, Consuela," she called back, turning swiftly on her high-polished black boots to be gone.

She scurried down the walk and through the gate to get to the barn. The wagon stood ready, but she saw no driver. In fact, the corral was completely deserted, with not one man in sight.

"Oh, for Christ's sake," she grumbled. She turned swiftly to return to the house when Jeff called to her and came out of the barn door. There had been a closeness between the two since the night she'd tended to his wounds and Amanda was glad. Bearing this in mind, she rushed up to meet him, thinking it would be nice for Jeff to accompany her to the Rancho Rio.

"Want to take me to the Alvarados' to deliver this stuff to the newlyweds, Jeff?" she asked, having no idea he'd refuse her in the next minute. When he said he couldn't, it irked her and she frowned.

"And why can't you? You don't look all that busy to me." She stood glaring up at him with her hands firmly clasped at her waist.

As Jeff started to stammer and fumble for a reason, a deep voice interrupted and as far as Jeff was concerned saved him. Tony ambled up to them. "I'll drive you, Amanda."

"Morning Branigan," Jeff greeted him. "I appreciate you stepping in for me." Jeff didn't wait around for Amanda to protest and hastily rushed away leaving her alone with the gunfighter.

Tony saw her frustration and noted the sigh she gave as Jeff retreated from them.

"Come on, then—let's—let's get going," Amanda

sighed, resigned that it was to be Tony taking her to the Rancho Rio.

He smiled, wondering why she fought him so hard. She didn't find his presence all that distasteful and he knew it. No, it was something else that frightened the golden-haired Amanda! He suspected it was her own feelings that scared her, which as yet she couldn't come to accept.

"Allow me, Amanda," he said, lifting her up and into the buckboard. As if she was as light as a feather he hoisted her up on the wooden seat and moved around in front of the team of horses to climb into the other side of the wagon. She watched him move finding it impossible not to be aware of his maleness and virility even though she tried to guard her thoughts. On the seat beside her, he adjusted his silver-plated pistols at his side before calling to the team, "Get up!" Off they went with their wagon bearing gifts and household items for Diego and Chita. Tony pushed his hat back on his head slightly at a cocky angle and broke into a whistle, letting his eyes dart over at Amanda's solemn face.

The stubborn little minx! He even adored this quality about her, though, and he wondered how many times he'd have to tame her before she would forever purr for him. Maybe a lifetime!

They arrived at the Rancho Rio and the first smiling face Tony saw was Juanito's. It quickly changed, though, when Tony asked directions to Diego Ramos's cottage. Only then did Tony remember the youth's declaration of his undying love for Chita. Poor Juanito, how low he must be feeling to have to accept that his love had married another!

"See you later, Juanito," Tony called out to the young Mexican.

Tony guided the wagon in the direction Juanito had instructed. Less than a mile away from the sprawling hacienda Chita stood in the doorway of a little house. Utterly surprised, but obviously pleased, she broke into a smile as she rushed on out to greet them.

The girls giggled and hugged one another like old friends, not like servant and mistress, Tony noticed as he stood there until they finally broke apart. Then he removed his hat and offered his congratulations. "I'll get this unloaded while you two visit, eh?"

"Your mother and father send their love and blessings, Chita, and so do all my family," Amanda told her. "So I won't forget it—you are invited to the Harvest Ball this Saturday. Mama told me to be sure to tell you."

"Oh, señorita—this—this is all so nice," Chita stammered, overcome by all the things Tony was already carrying into the small three room cottage.

When the last article was deposited on the floor of the front room, Tony was ready to accept the refreshing cup of coffee Chita had ready for him. He lit up a cheroot and sat down on the tiny porch and propped his foot against the wood column to rest.

The few additional pieces of furniture transformed the little cottage, which had had only the bare necessities of a bed, a table, and two chairs, along with a small stove. The closet had been pegs on the wall, so Chita welcomed the chest of drawers Jenny had sent. The lovely coverlet would certainly beautify the bed. The ladies' rocker would be a joy after only the straightback chair, but Diego's strong body would crush it into splinters, Chita thought to herself.

Having finished his coffee Tony called to Amanda, "Suppose I visit with my aunt for a while and I'll return for you in a half-hour so you and Chita can visit?"

"Yes, Tony—that would be nice," Amanda told him. He gave her a nod and went to the buckboard. It was a considerate gesture, she thought as she watched him turn the wagon around to head back up the dirt road to the hacienda.

Tony was considering how soft and almost harmonious she'd seemed as she'd agreed with him. She was an enigma that always challenged his curiosity.

He smiled, urging the team up to where he saw Juanito waiting there by the Alvarado corrals.

As he'd told her he would, Tony returned to Diego's cottage in a half-hour. Amanda emerged from the door with Chita following her and thanking her again for all the gifts.

"I would welcome a visit from you anytime, Señorita Kane. I will ask Diego about us coming to the party. Give my parents my love," she said. Amanda gave her a nod and joined Tony, feeling pleased that she'd come. Chita seemed happy and content in her new surroundings and home, and Amanda was glad.

Chita stood watching them until they faded in the distance and their wagon rolled along into the valley leaving the Rancho Rio behind.

Then, as she meandered back into the house to examine the boxes full of miscellaneous items, such a wave of contentment swept over her it was almost frightening. She loved this humble little house and she was growing to love the big oaf of a husband she'd married out of despair. Perhaps fate had had a hand in it and it was going to be a blessing she'd not expected.

She could hardly in reality consider him an oaf, for Diego was very nice-looking, only a little shy and awkward. Surprisingly for his huge size he was a gentle, considerate lover, and he worshipped her. So easily and eagerly he'd jumped at her bait—and she vowed she'd never allow him to be sorry he'd taken her as his bride. He'd never questioned her not being a virgin on their wedding night and she'd sighed with great relief. With that obstacle past, she would not fret about the weeks to come, because it was nothing for a baby to be a few weeks early. Who could say it wasn't Diego's baby she'd have in the springtime?

Only she would know that it was Jeff's baby she carried in her belly. His first would belong to her, not Mona Lawson. She smiled smugly, not a little satisfied about the promise of the days ahead.

She would go to the Harvest party and parade proudly with her husband Diego at her side. Let Jeff Kane see his dark, sultry eyes adoring her! Let him see the hot-blooded passion and desire in her Diego's hands holding her around the waist, as he held her whenever he was near her!

She laughed softly as she lay back on the floor with one of the bright-colored pillows cushioning her black thick hair. In her heart she thanked Jenny Kane for the touch of luxury the soft silk pillow provided. Just a little thing, this beautiful red silk pillow, but it brightened her cottage so, Chita thought.

TWENTY-TWO

She seemed so quiet and thoughtful as they rode for the first few minutes that Tony could not detect which Amanda was there beside him. Fumbling for something to say, he finally commented, "She seemed happy."

"Huh—oh yes, I'd say so." She kept looking ahead and down the dirt road. "Yes, Tony, I was glad to see her so content." Her words were expressionless and Tony knew her mind was a million miles away. Why, he couldn't say, but it bothered him.

"You all right, Amanda?" his deep voice spoke softly.

She turned to look at him with a puzzled expression on her face. "Why, Tony, you surprise me every now and then! Of course, I'm just fine." She gave a soft laugh, finding it amusing that the man sitting beside her would concern himself about her pensive mood. He could be sweet at times.

"I . . . I just thought maybe Chita said something that caused you concern. You were so quiet."

"Oh, Branigan I'm not always a chatterbox. I guess I was just getting serious for a while—which

I do get from time to time. I guess I was thinking how funny life is. I have always been rather close to Chita. We played together as kids and since I've been back we've talked a lot. I had no idea she was thinking about marriage or even knew a Diego Ramos."

He couldn't help a smile coming to his lips. She was so childishly cute he wanted to cuddle her. At a time like this she seemed vulnerable and it brought out a protective feeling in him.

She turned those amethyst-blue eyes on him and her voice was delightfully soft and mellow. "I question what love is."

"Do you, *chiquita?*" His gray eyes gleamed and he dare not offend her by being flip for she was earnestly sincere. "If you don't know now, I'll warrant you'll find out soon enough." Even though he'd promised himself to not tease her, his voice must have hinted at it.

"Now, Branigan, for once in your life don't be devious." It might be crazy for her, of all the people she knew, to choose Branigan to have this discussion with. Actually, she knew no one else to talk to about it.

Ever since she'd left Chita's little cottage she had been flooded with crazy ideas. Somehow her quick and clever mind had started putting the pieces of a crazy puzzle together. Yet it was rather ridiculous, too!

No, she'd best not mention it even to Branigan for he might just laugh at her. Instead, she tossed her pretty head haughtily and shrugged her shoulders. "You just might be wrong about me."

Before she knew what he was about, the buckboard pulled to the shoulder of the road and he laid the reins

243

down. His hands took her shoulders ever so gently and he pulled her over and lifted her bodily up to place her on his lap. Her eyes were wide and excited and he knew what she was thinking. She was right, for he did intend to kiss her and, truthfully, she wanted him to.

"Kiss me, Amanda!" His sensuous lips tempted her to obey.

"No!" She stared at this bold, impulsive man whose heat was already invading her.

His head moved slightly closer. His deep voice murmured barely above a whisper, "Kiss me, Amanda, as you and I both know you want to." The force, so overwhelming, urged her like a magnet to meet him halfway and their lips came together. Lips blended and moved one against the other, with a life of their own. Tony's one hand clasped her waist while his other hand cradled her head at the back.

She gave a soft moan of pleasure and she murmured his name softly, causing him to swell with satisfying delight. She was naive if she dared to deny she loved him, and the day had to come that she would confess it. He'd make her!

"*Querida*, never tell me you don't know about loving. You were born to love and be loved."

He cussed under his breath as his alert ears heard the pounding beat of hooves coming in their direction. His wild desires had to be denied. Reluctantly, his strong arms had to release her and he noted the questioning look on her face. It told him more than she realized. She had not wanted him to stop. God knows, he hadn't wanted to stop!

The unclinching pair had been observed by the approaching rider galloping toward them. It really didn't surprise him and it eased his conscience considerably about his feelings about Magdalena Gomez, for he had been right about his cousin and Amanda. Mario broke into a chuckle. This confirmed it.

He wore a broad smile as he halted up on his horse to bid the two of them good afternoon. "Good day to you two. You mean to tell me that I missed a visit you've paid to the Rancho Rio?" He flipped his hat back on his head as his dark eyes danced first at his cousin and then at Amanda.

"You did," Amanda volunteered, twisting nervously around on the seat. Like two kids with their hands caught in the cookie jar, she and Tony exchanged glances.

"Ah, I regret that, but Mother and Maria were nagging me to check out the freight office in town to see about the piano's arrival. But I went for nothing and I'm going home to face an angry Maria. Her patience is growing thin. She can be a handful."

Tony found Mario's sultry eyes lingering too long on Amanda to suit him and he hastily informed him of their purpose for going over to the Rancho Rio.

"Ah, yes—the newlyweds. An unexpected uniting. It rather serves to unite the Rancho Rio and the Circle K Ranches, doesn't it?"

"I hadn't thought about it, but you're right, Mario." Amanda lightheartedly laughed.

"Just shows how the most unlikely things can come to pass. Would you not say so, *amigo?*" His dark eyes twinkled with mischief as he poked a little fun at his solemn cousin. He could hardly blame Tony for being disgruntled about having his romantic interlude so abruptly interrupted. Christ, he would be just as furi-

245

ous as Tony looked right now!

Idly Tony replied, "Yeah, that's so, Mario. Listen, we've got to be on our way."

"See you Saturday night, Mario?"

"Of course, *chiquita!*" He set his horse into a trot knowing Tony was seething as he waved back at them.

"Get up," Tony called to the team. His jaw was set firmly and his teeth were clenched. He ached with a hunger gnawing at his gut and tried to tell himself to forget it. The chance to satisfy it had been shattered by Mario.

Amanda stole a fast glance in his direction and she saw the fury on his tanned face. Putting on her angel's face, she inquired of him as he had of her when they'd left the Rancho Rio earlier, "You all right, Branigan?"

The little imp! He could have swatted her bottom, for she knew he was irked and why. He was in no mood for her taunting or baiting.

He barked, "I'm fine! Just got things on my mind."

"Oh, I gathered that, Branigan," she remarked, giving him a provocative look.

Now, she was the tantalizing temptress creating the lustiest of thoughts and ideas in his head. But for the sight of the adobe stone hacienda, he would have not been able to deny himself. As it was, he planned to deposit her at the gate of the courtyard and seek release in the cool waters of the nearby river. His first impression about the golden-haired Amanda had proven so right—she was a devastating distraction!

Jenny could not have asked for a more glorious day that Saturday morning. It held such promise for the perfect weather for the evening entertainment in her spacious garden courtyard. She bubbled with delight, for no one could control or project what the weather would be when the invitations were sent out to all their friends and neighbors. So she always crossed her fingers and did a lot of praying.

It was so comforting to be able to have the long tables carried on out and set up ahead of time. This gave Jenny more time to rest and relax before her guests began to arrive.

It was a time when her usually domineering husband stayed meek, allowing Jenny to rule the roost. He confined his activities to the area where Juan Santos always took charge of the barbecuing out by the open pits. The huge sides of beef and pork were flavored with Juan's special seasoning of vinegar, pepper, and salt that was his secret. He swore even Consuela didn't know his recipe.

Jenny's first Harvest party had been for the men and their families of the Circle K Ranch, but over the years it had been extended to her close neighbors as they became her friends. The first mistress of this house had been Mark's grandmother and then his mother. During her reign, the house had been enlarged by three more rooms. Now the spacious hacienda consisted of twelve rooms.

The beautiful walled garden courtyard had been built especially for Jenny when she'd come to the Circle K as Mark's young bride. It was to Jenny Mark gave credit for the present splendor of the Circle K and its grounds. He never rode under that archway to go toward the house without swelling with pride about the love Jenny had put into their home.

This time last year Amanda hadn't been home. He figured it would be a livelier affair this year with his beautiful, vivacious Amanda around.

As the sun was setting in the west, wagons began to roll toward the Circle K Ranch. Some guests came on horseback. Jenny's garden took on a glow from all the colorful garlands and lanterns hung among the trees.

The Alvarado buggy carried Bianca and Maria. Mario rode by the buggy's side on his fine Thoroughbred. Miguel had remained at home with his sprained ankle propped up, disgruntled that he'd have his dinner served by tray. Maria's appearance in his room all dressed prettily in her yellow gown had only depressed him more.

Bianca Alvarado was gowned in black with a magnificent high-standing Spanish comb at the back of her hair made of mother-of-pearl. Pearls adorned her neck and ears and she looked especially elegant. Mario's expensive attire was new and had been purchased recently while he was in San Antonio to keep a secret tryst with the lovely Magdalena.

He sat on the dapple gray stallion knowing he looked magnificent in the black velvet vest lavishly trimmed with gold braid. He had always chosen to ignore those who considered him the peacock. He liked his elegant attire even though it was wasted out here on the ranch. The city life was more his style, he'd decided, especially since he'd met Magdalena. The truth was he'd made a few decisions over the last four weeks and if all went the way he intended, it could fall to the young Miguel to run the Rancho Rio.

Mario had no remaining qualms of conscience after the other day about moving in on his cousin's lady friend. He did intend to pay special attention to the Mario and Amanda this evening, though. He confessed to himself that he'd changed his opinion of his renegade cousin who fit neither the role of the Texan nor the Mexican. Tony was and always had been a loner, remote, and a little mysterious.

When they had been younger and the two of them had discussed the lovely señoritas, Tony's attitude had been that of a rather cold-hearted guy who merely sought to satisfy his male hunger from time to time. He acted different with Amanda Kane, though. The lovely Magdalena had given Mario the distinct impression that Tony was no devoted, amorous lover. Yet with Amanda, Mario was quick to note Tony's resentment if Mario ogled her too long. So tonight, Mario would observe what he could.

Coming from the opposite direction the Lawson buggy rolled along. Derek had realized that he had to try to smooth Jeff's ruffled feathers. He'd been foolhardy the night they fought, but Jeff was so dense he'd wrap him around his little finger as he always had.

Less than a mile behind the Lawson buggy, the Calhouns and Johnsons were traveling. Anticipating their guests' arrival the Kane household was a beehive of activity. Jenny and Mark stood ready to greet their rancher friends and Mark had himself a glass of bourbon and branch water. Jenny's bowl of sweet fruit punch did not satisfy his taste.

Amanda had decided on the lovely pale blue-green gown with its overlapping flounces that made up the skirt. Each flounce was bordered with dainty black lace. She wore a narrow black velvet ribbon choker at her throat. At the center was a miniature pin in enameled hues of green and blue. The bodice had a low scooped neckline with an off-the-shoulder effect. Narrow ruffling edged the neckline and the shoulder straps of the gown. She wore no earrings and her only piece of jewelry except for the choker was a ring that had been her Aunt Lisa's when she was a girl. It was an aquamarine set in filagree gold and she wore it on her little finger.

She certainly did miss Chita's expertise with her hair. The new girl filling in was a hard worker and eager, but she had no talent with hair so Amanda had to rely on herself. She tried a couple of different styles before deciding to pile it in an upsweep crown of curls, leaving a wispy curl by each ear. She pinned a black velvet bow centered with aqua flowers at the back of the curls. It proved to be most attractive. Around her wrist, she placed the cord of her fancy black lace fan. She put some jasmine scent behind her ears and at the cleavage of her breasts and felt she was now ready to join her parents downstairs. Her mood was as lighthearted and gay as her brother's was heavy with apprehension anticipating the sight of Derek Lawson.

It was to be Jeff's misfortune as he and Amanda descended the stairs together to sight Derek Lawson standing at the base. Amanda, sensing her brother's instant tenseness silently questioned this reaction. Why would his friend's presence displease Jeff so?

"Breathtaking! Amanda, you never looked more beautiful," Derek greeted her, looking quite the impeccable young gentleman. Each sandy hair was in place and his clean-shaven face broke into a pleasant smile. "Hi, Jeff." His blue eyes searched for some inkling of Jeff's attitude. That surge of gallantry on

Jeff's side that night had taken him by surprise and he was no longer so sure he could anticipate his moods.

Jeff gave him an offhanded hello, hastily inquiring about Mona.

"I think you'll find her and Dad talking with your folks," Derek told him, still concentrating on his face, which could have been a frozen mask. It rattled Derek's nerves slightly. It was a first for young Lawson and he didn't like not being in control.

Suddenly he and Amanda were alone and Jeff had swept on by him. He found himself hardly listening to her talk. She took his arm and they strolled on out into the garden making light conversation. "Come on, Derek let's get something cool to drink," she insisted. The Johnson's daughter stood over by the refreshment table entranced by the magnificent Mario Alvarado. Little Maria had Jeff and Mona laughing about something. Everyone seemed to be in a festive and gay mood there in Jenny's glorious garden courtyard. It was an ideal evening approaching, with the twilight caressing the grounds with hues of purple and rosy golds.

"I don't see your Dad, Derek. Didn't he come?" Amanda asked as they now began to stroll slowly and she greeted the guests.

"I think he's over there by the fountain talking with the señora." He referred to Bianca Alvarado.

"Oh, yes, I see him." She also saw her parents doing as they always did, moving in and around the crowd to greet each and every guest, and with the hired hands of the ranch and their families. It was Jenny's sweet way of showing the Kane family's appreciation for the hard year put in. It had endeared

Jenny to the men and their families of the Circle K in the same way Bianca was endeared to her *vaqueros*.

The festive air, lighthearted laughter, and the beginning sounds of the guitar playing caught Amanda's full attention and she took no notice of Derek's face as he glared with repulsion observing his father acting like a gushing schoolboy.

A pair of observing gray eyes were watching Derek Lawson stroll with Amanda, but Derek's eyes only saw his father. Tony had seen that kind of hate before in men's eyes and he knew it was dangerous and destructive. If what he thought was true, Derek Lawson was a powder keg ready to explode.

Amanda must have felt the intense glare of Tony's eyes in their direction. Something urged her to look over by the veranda, and there he stood, looking so handsome she felt a tremble in her stomach. His black hair was slicked down and groomed, all but that one unruly wave that would not be conquered. He wore her gray scarf at his throat and it matched the light pearl-gray shirt he had on. His light wool pants of deep blue were molded to that perfect male body of his, as all his pants seemed to be.

His frown mellowed into a broad grin when he saw her watching him. When her rosebud lips spread slightly to return his smile he felt himself flame instantly. Damn, she looked gorgeous! He did not remember ever seeing her in that particular color but she should wear it more often. It did things to her with that tawny-golden skin of hers. He hadn't really taken note of it before but her complexion was dark for one with such blond hair. It was a bewitching portrait she made.

He played with the glass of branch water and bourbon Mark had stuck in his hand saying he was sure Tony would prefer that to Jenny's soft punch. When the time came for him to leave the Circle K, and with a lot of soul searching put in, Tony had decided he was going to level with Mark Kane. He deserved to know and if, God forbid, something happened that he didn't make it back to the Circle K, he wanted Kane to know the truth.

Amanda found the solemn-looking Tony out of character. Now it was he who was being stared at by her. He seemed so adrift and alone in his serious mood that she was urged to comfort and console him. She wanted to be there by his side.

She could hardly believe it herself but she turned to Derek Lawson to excuse herself to go over to where Tony stood. Perhaps there was something brewing around the ranch that he was concerned about, for he had his matched pistols in place—and he *was* her father's hired gun.

Tony wondered if his eyes were deceiving him as he lowered the glass from his lips to see her briskly walking toward him. Each little flounce bounced to and fro with her determined steps. He was more pleased than he'd dare admit that for whatever reason she was coming to join him.

"Tony, you don't look like you're having a very good time. Something the matter?" Her eyes had to be the darnedest things as she stood there looking up at him now. As blue and as green as her gown they seemed to him. A day or two ago he'd have said purplish-blue.

In a confidential tone, he bent over to whisper in her

ear, "To tell the truth, there might be. Could—could we get ourselves a fresh drink and go somewhere so I could talk to you about it, *chiquita?*"

His rugged face cracked not a hint of a smile. She told him they could and let him lead her over to take two glasses of wine before they went over to a secluded corner of the garden.

Delightfully hidden by her mother's broad-leaved greenery, he urged her down on the bench. "Have some of your wine." She did as he urged, wondering what he was going to tell her. What new plague hovered over the ranch?

He took a sip of his, watching her lovely face. Christ, it was almost a sin for a girl to look so devilishly sensuous and desirable. He knew he had her guessing and pondering.

"I can't stand it any longer, Branigan. My curiosity is killing me." She set her glass on the bench, having gulped more than half of it.

"Neither can I, Amanda," his husky voice told her and he pulled her into his arms, kissing her urgently on the lips. He continued to kiss her as she tried to mumble a protest. As his heated lips kept urging her to join his pleasure she found herself weakening and enjoying it.

When he finally released her and sat grinning at her, she broke into a soft laugh, surprising him. "You are incorrigible!" Silently, she admired his ingenuity and cleverness.

"Where you're concerned, I am, and I didn't lie, *querida*. Something *was* wrong, for you were not with me. See, I am now cured and happy."

"Oh, Tony, you are crazy," she laughed gaily.

"About you, Amanda," he said, looking more serious and sincere.

For the life of her, she could not give this handsome man with his magnificent eyes some flippant answer as she had so often. Even his act of connivance had struck her as amusing. Her reckless heart could not deny that she found him the most exciting man she'd ever known.

She gave a dejected sigh. "Oh, Branigan!"

He could not read the secrets of her mind but he knew what was going on in his. "Amanda *mia*, you cannot tell me you do not feel as I do. I wouldn't believe you. Tell me, if you can."

His tanned hand held hers. He waited, letting his eyes dance over her face. "Damn it, Tony—you know I do. Right or wrong, I do," she murmured barely above a whisper. She knew it was a hopeless affair and one she'd most likely end up hurting for.

He took her slowly into his arms, his face warmed by the overwhelming passion surging in his body. "No, no, Amanda—there is nothing wrong with it, at all. It was meant to be and we've both known it from the moment our lips first touched and our bodies met. Is it not so, *chiquita?*"

She gave herself up to him and his ecstasy, as untamed and wild as hers. "It is so, Tony," she gasped, feeling his flames engulf her. "Oh, dear God, Tony!" He delighted in her eagerness for his touch and caress.

Rolling over on his back, he carried her with him, wanting her heat to cover him. Tonight he wanted her to make love to him. He wanted to be devoured by the woman of fire and passion. His voice was husky with desire as he murmured, "Make love to me, *chiquita*. God, you feel so so good." His muscled body gave a quiver of pleasure as he lifted her over him and placed her just so.

Amanda gave out a moan of delight as he did. His strong hands pressed her hips, urging her closer to him. She leaned back so his lips could capture the tip of her breast and when he did an exquisite heat shot through her, bringing another moan of delight. "Oh, God, Tony!"

"Yes, Amanda *mia* I know! You were made for me . . . me alone," he whispered as he released one tip and took the other jutting breast. This night he wanted no part left untouched or unloved. Every inch of that golden, satiny body must know him and the depth of his love for her.

His lips traveled down leaving a flaming trail wherever his tongue teased and taunted, and she arched, inviting and wanting him to not stop. Her fingers entwined through his thick mane of hair as she moaned his name over and over again. Such sweet agony he created she felt breathless!

Tony had not soared to such a high pinnacle before with any woman. Amanda's uninhibited, sensuous movements added to his joy beyond his wildest imagination. They moved together rhythmically. God, he felt as though he never wanted this golden moment to pass and reach that ultimate climax. Even with his strong, determined will he could not hold back the volcano ready to erupt.

Rolling her over on her back and covering her with his body, he murmured in her ear, "You're mine, *querida!* Dear God, this night makes it so!" He plunged himself into her as Amanda pressed his buttocks, wanting the full force of his power to fill her.

The fury of their explosive passions shook both of them beyond belief and they gave out moans of the rapture swallowing them up. Tony fell exhausted against her, raining kisses all over her face and whispering words of love in her ear.

Later, he held her in his arms with her damp cheek resting on the cluster of black chest hair as he removed the wisps of hair from her lovely face. He'd never believed it possible to be so completely bewitched by a woman as he was Amanda Kane. Forever, he could hold her like this. Her sweet body fit to his with such perfection. It was as though she was made for him. From the moment he'd first laid eyes on her he'd known it.

III

A COLD WINTER'S WIND

TWENTY-THREE

Many miles away from the Circle K Ranch on the outskirts of San Antonio two men were holding what could be their final meeting for many weeks to come. They were a most unlikely pair of comrades—U. S. Marshal Brett Flanigan and a mangy-looking character draped in a dirty serape and dust-covered sombrero. This renegade was worth every cent Flanigan paid him, and the marshal knew that at any time the old man could be killed for "ratting" on his *bandito* friends.

Brett couldn't even remember when he and old Tito's paths had first crossed and Tito had first started working on different jobs for him. He knew that men who performed the dangerous jobs that Tito did seldom lived to old age. He suspected that the bewhiskered man was aged more by the dissipated life he'd led than by the number of his years. It seemed to him he'd first approached Tito when he was in jail, having been arrested in connection with a stabbing down in a coastal town. That had to be about ten years ago.

Tito had arrived at their rendezvous point this evening after three days of hard trail riding from a point down by the Rio Grande. A small hamlet, Encino was the outlaws' final roadhouse before they took their stolen cattle across the river into Mexico. These ranches and corrals were given the name of roadhouses by the bandits when they used them to hold their stolen loot.

"Pedro doin' all right at Palita Blanco?" The marshal wanted to know because this operation depended on every one of the gang's roadhouses being struck in the order they'd so intricately planned.

"He is ready for the arrival of Moreno, his old 'bandit' *compadre*. They have bought his story. According to Pedro, it is here the gringo boss, as they call him, will arrive for the split of the take. Your deputies await the word in Reynosa and in Encino."

"You are priceless, Tito! You sure no one suspected anything while you were in Palita Blanco?"

"I would swear to it," Tito declared, sucking deep from the whiskey jug.

Brett Flanigan tried to assure himself that everything was going to run smoothly, but it was a hell of an operation and so many were involved in it. "Well, I guess it's about time I sent the word to Moreno over in Gonzales." He rose up from the chair, situated the holster to a comfortable position on his hips and strode toward the door of the cabin. "Get some rest, Tito. You've earned it, old friend." Brett noticed Tito's rheumy eyes were looking glazed from the whiskey and weariness. Flanigan went out the door and into the night.

Everything about the beady-eyed man reminded Derek Lawson of a creeping, crawling reptile, and any time he was forced to be around him he felt repulsed by Sid Thomas and his appointed bodyguard, Tulsa Jack Dawes. They made him feel contaminated with some dread disease, but he needed the likes of them to accomplish his goal. Soon he would be through with them and it would be good riddance.

The last of the stolen head of cattle were now on their way south to Palita Blanco, but he had come to the Red Garter tonight to give an order that he wished carried out at once. This time there could be no misses.

"We'll see to it, Lawson. Tulsa Jack'll get it done for you, won't you, Jack?" Sid said with that twisted smile on his face. A fierce, ugly scar along the side of his face gave him a grotesque look.

"My pleasure, Lawson," Tulsa Jack answered with a salacious look on his ugly face.

"All right—and right away." Derek hastily turned from the pair and made for the back door of Sid's back room. Before going out into the night, he repeated, "At once, Tulsa Jack!"

The outlaw gave him an insolent look. He didn't exactly care for the attitude of the young rancher.

"Said I would, didn't I Lawson?" Dawes's voice had a menacing tone that cautioned Derek to just leave. The crazy halfbreed wasn't one to trifle with. Derek knew a little about his past. He'd lived in Indian Territory before riding with a band of outlaws up into Kansas to rob and steal. However, Dawes was trigger-happy and he killed without compulsion. Derek was no fool!

It was good to walk out the back door of the Red Garter into the night air, fresh and free of the foul smells of the saloon. Derek on the white stallion galloped through the starless, black night toward the Big D Ranch with a feeling of elation swelling within him. The wheels were set in motion and nothing was going to stop him. He envisioned coming to the "end of that long tunnel," where he'd emerge the victor.

With Branigan dead and an unfortunate accident happening to David Lawson, he would rule the Big D. Mona's marriage to Jeff would take her away—she'd never posed any problems anyway to his well-laid plans. The fine old two story house at the Big D would be his and Amanda's home, and he would rule all the vast acres of the ranch and be the baron.

Jenny felt it had to have been the best Harvest Party ever—and part of the joy was having Amanda home again. Now, with that festive occasion behind her, she planned to turn her energies and efforts toward the approaching holidays and her sister coming from New Orleans.

Jenny was more than pleased lately about Amanda and her new attitude since she'd returned from San Antonio. She was delighted about the new calm that had settled around her. That exploding, reckless restlessness that had characterized her when she'd returned from New Orleans seemed to have been swept aside lately, Jenny thought. It was something both she and Mark had noticed.

Consuela, too, had mentioned to Jenny what a sweet Amanda had been the last week. When Amanda had grabbed her playfully around the waist and announced that she was going over to the Rancho Rio this morning to pay Chita a visit to cheer her up since she'd been sick it gladdened Consuela's heart. Life was good. Perhaps, it was the approach of the holidays.

"Well, I was so disappointed that Chita and Diego didn't get to come to the party," Amanda told the housekeeper.

"Yes, I was too, señorita, but that nice Señora Alvarado gave me the news that Diego told her Chita was feeling under the weather and he'd thought it best she not try to come. I'm glad my Chita has a thoughtful young man. You tell her hello for me, eh?"

"I will, Consuela," Amanda replied, spritely skipping out the kitchen door. The light chill to the air felt delightful and added to her zest to be atop Prince to ride wild as the wind over to the Rancho Rio.

Amanda wore a light twill jacket to break the nip of the cool late October day. She'd tied a bright kerchief around her head instead of the flat-crowned hat. Branigan watched her leave the barn and smiled, thinking she looked as darn seductive in those boyish, tight-molded black pants as she did in one of her alluring gowns. Her golden mass of hair piled out the back of her tied scarf blown askew by the gusting winds.

God, he wished it was all behind him, for the thought of leaving her tore him apart. He didn't relish the miserable idle weeks ahead of letting his face get covered with beard and doing practically nothing at the house with Esteban. His existence there would have to be that of a hermit. All the time she would be back here, and with a girl like Amanda anything could happen and usually did!

He figured she was heading for the Rancho Rio and

was tempted to leap on Picaro to follow her. Seeing her had made him forget that Slim and Jake were waiting for him to join them. It was that cracking voice of Christy's that distracted his eyes, reminding him of what his destination had been before the sight of Amanda befuddled his mind.

Since the night of the Harvest Party, it seemed they'd finally come to a point of understanding, a truce of sorts. Nothing could have pleased Tony more. Yet, he dared not count on anything for certain. He'd learned long ago that dreams could be shattered in the blink of an eye, so he took this sweet-tempered Amanda and enjoyed the moments they shared, knowing each new day brought his departure nearer. At least, they were not spitting and barking at one another.

She was different somehow, and he could not exactly say how, except that she no longer denied to him that he affected her as she did him. No longer did she fight the savage wanting of his love. He reminded himself, though, that neither had she confessed she loved him, as he had to her.

No one was more aware of the strange changes within her than Amanda herself. She'd come to terms with herself that she could not fight the force of her feelings for Tony Branigan. It was a quenchless thirst for him to make love to her. Regardless of his station in life, he had the capacity to stir this wild, insatiable desire that made her feel more alive than she'd ever felt before. And no other man she'd ever known had enflamed her so.

All she had to do was be near him and his heat and maleness overwhelmed her. His eyes, his touch, and even his deep, throaty laugh had a unique effect she'd never associated with any man she'd ever met or known before. Now, she could admit what she'd refused to confess to herself when she'd returned from her visit to San Antonio. Her eagerness to get home was on account of Branigan. She'd missed even his devilment during her absence.

The night of the Harvest Party when they'd made love she had been carried beyond caring about anything else and had yielded to him as never before. Afterwards, she had questioned whether all women felt such fulfillment and ecstasy. Since then, the glowing radiance seemed to reflect itself on her face for she'd never been more beautiful and her temper was mellowed by happiness and bliss.

Her visit to Diego and Chita's humble cottage left her spent and depressed. Even young Juanito, seeing her ride past him, knew something was wrong from the way she sat atop her fine palomino as she cantered by without her usual friendly greeting.

"Señorita Kane—may I inquire about Chita? Is—is she feeling better today?" His eager face looked at her and his anxious concern was written there for her to see.

Halting up on Prince, she said, "Oh, Juanito. please forgive me. My mind was occupied. What did you say?" Juanito repeated himself.

"Oh, yes—yes, she is better. Up in a few days, I think." She gave the youth a wan smile and nudged Prince to go on.

Christ, why couldn't it have happened when she wasn't there, and then she wouldn't have had to know about it! A tearful Chita had known it was coming to

267

this for days, she'd told Amanda. The two of them were now bound to share the secret that up to today only Chita had carried in her heart. The severe cramps had been what had urged her to take to her bed and not attend the party. And then this morning, during Amanda's visit, the gushing flow hit as Chita poured them coffee.

Embarrassed, the mortified Chita protested as Amanda helped her. As Chita lay across the bed dissolving in tears while Amanda folded a clean cloth for a pad and took the blood-soaked pad to destroy, she knew that the unusual clot meant that she had lost Jeff's child.

In her misery, she'd moaned this loss, and then Amanda examined the cloth and gasped, "Chita—oh dear God, Chita! You—you were—oh Lord!"

Chita, with her eyes misted, nodded. "Oh, please, Señorita Kane—please tell no one. I'll be all right, and no one but me will have to suffer if only you'll keep my secret."

Amanda quieted her and prepared some tea. "It will be only our secret, Chita. I promise. You don't have to tell me, for I know—have known for some time about Jeff. Only one thing I *must* know, and tell me the truth. Did Jeff know?"

"No, he didn't. That last night we were together he told me he was asking Señorita Lawson to marry him soon and that was why I did what I did. I could not disgrace my mother and father." She burst into another flood of tears. "Oh, I just couldn't!"

"It will be all right, Chita. I'll help you. This, I promise. The Kanes owe you. Thank God, Diego loves you and this can be just a bad monthly period

268

like any woman has from time to time. It will be all right, Chita. Believe me!" Amanda felt really sorry for her. Even if Chita had not confided in her, it wasn't hard to figure it all out.

For the next two hours Amanda toiled away in Chita's little cottage as the two of them chatted back and forth like dear friends. It was Chita lying there on the bed and Amanda performing the chores like the servant. Chita vowed silently she'd never forget what the señorita had done for her that day.

By the time Amanda had a huge pot of beans cooking and a golden brown pile of cornbread cakes piled in a stack that she'd fried in deep fat instead of in Chita's small oven, her hair was falling over her face and she was damp with sweat.

Weary and brushing the meal from her sleeve, she gave Chita a weak smile. "Lord, I appreciate Consuela more! That's for sure." But when she finally took her leave from the cottage she was pleased with herself and felt good within.

Juanito rode near the edge of the wooded area and looked up to see the golden palomino leaving the Rancho Rio. He had to confess the señorita was as beautiful as Chita. He halted his horse and watched Amanda go down the dirt road. Then he spurred the horse on.

He rode toward the woods that adjoined the Kane property with the Alvarado lands. Falling leaves provided a most magnificent carpet of gold and red for the floor of the forest. The squirrels scampered around gathering nuts for their larder preparing for the cooler months ahead. But the nip to the air didn't seem to discourage the calling of the birds. Juanito abruptly gave the order to Pedro to halt. "Whoa, Pedro!"

There at the edge of the clearing was a stranger Juanito had never seen before and he moved his horse slowly and cautiously. The first thought coming to Juanito was that he was a lecher stalking the beautiful Amanda. So he veered in and out of the trees to watch the man. He was a mean-looking hombre, and Juanito knew he was not employed by the Rancho Rio or the Circle K. Of the Big D he could not be sure, but something told him he wasn't.

It suddenly dawned on Juanito that Amanda was not within the man's line of vision, for she was by now traveling around the bend in the dirt road. With closer scrutiny he saw the object of the man's eyes. The huge black stallion caught Juanito's eye, and he knew it was Branigan the man was watching like a hawk.

The man ambled his mount slowly and deliberately and no one had to tell the young Mexican that he meant to do harm to the Señor Branigan. Instinctively, Juanito sensed it. He watched, panic-stricken and feeling helpless.

The gleaming barrel of a pistol caught Juanito's eye as the man targeted in on the tall figure riding to meet up with Amanda atop her palomino. Tony was cutting across the open clearing, giving the man a simple, easy mark. Frantically, Juanito searched his mind about what he could do to help his friend Tony Branigan, and all he could think of was giving out a loud Comanche howl, for he was without any kind of weapon.

The woods resounded with the wild howl of Juanito's voice and Jack Dawes' arm jerked with the shock of the noise coming from his rear. He knew he'd

270

missed his target and turned swiftly to see what in the hell stalked him!

Juanito knew the danger he'd called to himself and kicked at Pedro wildly to take him away as fast as he could.

TWENTY-FOUR

When he saw that beautiful crown of golden curls slump and rest against the silken golden mane of the palomino, Tony died a million deaths before Picaro got him there beside her. Her beautiful eyes opened up for him to see she was alive and she hissed, "Sweet Jesus! Tony!" Her eyes were wide as if she was asking him if she was all right.

"*Amanda mia!*" was all he could say, cracking with the depth of emotion welling in him so furiously he felt he could hardly breathe. He knew a man could pray a dozen prayers in a brief moment's time for he had done so. He took hold of her reins and without asking he turned the palomino around to go back to the Rancho Rio. Blood stained her jacket and he would not chance the ride back to the Circle K until he knew the extent of her injury. His aunt's ranch was much nearer.

"Tony?"

"Shhhh, I'm going to tend to you, darling, before we go any farther. I won't have any fuss." She didn't give him any for she saw the small circle of blood staining her jacket.

Tony held her encircled in his arms, tenderly leading Prince's reins. She felt so precious to him, and he couldn't bring himself to think about the fact of what that bullet could have done to her had it been a vital spot. Even now, he knew it was a flesh wound and not serious. Amanda, too, was quiet and thoughtful, content to rest against Tony's strong, broad chest and feel safe in his protective arms. She was aware, though, of his heart pounding but she didn't realize the fury churning within him.

The sight of them riding up brought a flurry of attention from the three *vaqueros* roaming around the grounds. Mario was among them. He knew at once something was amiss. His cousin's face was as angry as a thundercloud and Amanda was riding in front of Tony instead of on her palomino.

He rushed up to them and took hold of her as Tony lifted her down to him and hastily leaped off the horse. "Let's get her inside so I can see to her wound, Mario. Some bastard took a shot at her or me. If it was me, he was a poor one."

"Caramba!" Mario gasped. "Come." Tony wasted no time and swept her up in his arms to stride quickly alongside Mario. They were met by a puzzled Bianca and an excited Maria.

Amanda was now more alert and was befuddled by all the attention of everyone hovering over her. Tony had her jacket removed and was examining the small wound while Bianca was ordering a servant to bring warm water and cloths from their kitchen.

Amanda looked up at Tony's face with all his concentration directed at her bare shoulder. "I don't understand, Tony, why someone would want to do this."

273

Perhaps, it was the trauma he'd undergone, but he forgot that there was an audience standing around and he leaned over, kissing her flushed cheek. "I don't think it was meant for you, *querida*."

His kiss and the term of endearment drew exchanged glances from his aunt, his cousin Maria, and a smiling Mario. He had been right about the two. They were, indeed, lovers. Wonder what Señor Kane would say to that? Bianca Alvarado was sharing her elder son's thoughts. She had only to look now at her nephew's tanned face to know what he'd just confirmed.

Neither of them seemed to care that anyone else in the room existed. It was Tony who washed the small wound after he'd taken the pan and clean folded cloths from the Mexican servant.

Bianca bent down to Amanda lying on the couch, allowing Tony to take charge. "What about a glass of wine, Amanda? Would that, perhaps, make you feel better?"

"Yes, thank you, Señora Alvarado. I would like one," Amanda told her. Bianca called to her servant who was leaving the room since her services seemed not to be needed.

Mario had moved over to take a seat in the overstuffed chair and Maria followed him to flop on the wide arm and chatter away in her brother's ear. Whatever it was she was whispering Mario nodded his head in agreement and his dark eyes ogled the couple with a twinkle of amusement.

He watched his cousin brush the golden tresses away from Amanda's face before he set about binding the grazed wound. Only then did he turn his attention to the others. "Could I trouble you for a glass of wine too, Aunt Bianca?" He'd handed Amanda her glass, situating her comfortably against a couple of the satin pillows there on the couch. He seemed oblivious to the revealing intimacy they'd all witnessed.

It only dawned on him an hour later, as he and Amanda mounted up on their horses outside the gate of the courtyard and Mario's look of mischief seemed to be teasing and taunting him as he called out, "Hey *amigo*, take care of your beautiful lady."

Amanda turned back to wave and give him a smile and Mario gave her a wink. Tony said nothing, only giving his cousin a crooked smile.

The rascal knew, Tony surmised. Well, it mattered not, for soon he planned to let the whole county know she was his. As they rode at an easy pace toward the Circle K Ranch he stole glances at her from time to time and she gave him that sweet smile each time, making his heart swell with love and his body flame with desire. He reached out his hand across the distance of the palomino and his black stallion. She took it, saying, "I owe you, Tony."

"Ah, *chiquita*—I will collect full payment. I am greedy where you're concerned." His gray eyes were soft with no hint of the cold ruthlessness Amanda had seen on numerous occasion.

She gave out a laugh telling Tony her spirit was returning and the shock of the afternoon drama was fading. But he'd not forgot one second of it, nor would she. That score would be settled by him pronto. This was the foreboding bothering him the most about the evil invading the Gonzales countryside. When it began to touch the Kane family members Tony knew that would be the test of how far he'd carry out his orders from Flanigan. It had reached the limit today by touching Amanda.

When they arrived back at the Circle K, Amanda insisted he come to the hacienda and help her explain to her folks just what had taken place. Too much had happened today—first to Chita and then to her. She was feeling the effects of it all now as they came to the gate of the walled garden.

Once inside with her father and in the parlor, Tony noticed the strained look on her face. As he had at the Rancho Rio, he took over and suggested, "Why don't you go on to your room, Amanda, and take some rest. I'll tell your parents everything that happened."

Like a docile child who needed no coaxing, she nodded and rose up, taking the Consuela's hand.

"Yes, honey—you—you go lie down until dinner," Jenny chimed in. She would have had to be blind not to see the protective, possessive manner of Tony with his eyes following Amanda up the steps and around the gallery to go to her room. How could she not appreciate his protective caring attitude for her daughter, she told herself. Mark too was cognizant of Tony's manner, and, surprisingly, he did not feel any resentment.

By the time Tony had related the details of the earlier hours Kane was flushed with ferocious fury. By the time Tony ended his tale, Kane jumped out of his chair, pounding his clenched fist into the open palm of his other hand. "Goddamn, the sonofabitch!" Blue fire lit in his eyes and he turned to Jenny, saying, "Dear, excuse us please. I need some man talk with Tony. Right now, I'm in no mood to guard my lan-

276

guage."

Jenny gave him no fuss, for she knew her volatile, hot-tempered husband well. He was more than upset. The full force of the Kane fury was upon him. So she left before Branigan got a chance to inform him that he was sure the bullet was intended for him and not Amanda.

When Jenny reached the hallway a frantic rap on the door drew her attention and she went to answer it. When she opened the door a young Mexican youth stood before her. "Señora Kane, I seek Señor Branigan. My name is Juanito."

"Come in—please," Jenny urged. "This way." She led the thin young lad back to the parlor where she had just left her husband and Branigan.

"Tony, there is a young man here to see you," she announced as they entered.

"Juanito, something wrong?" Tony noted the anxious look on his young friend's face.

"Come on in here, young man," Kane barked, impatient to get on with his conversation with Branigan.

"Yes, sir." Juanito was always awed by the sight of Señor Kane.

He went awkwardly in Tony's direction. "I have something to tell you, Señor Branigan, about the shooting. I saw the man who was trying to kill you. In a way, it is my fault that the shot hit Señorita Kane. I didn't mean for that to happen, though. His dark eyes went down to the floor.

"You saw the man, Juanito?" Tony came alive. "Who was it?"

"I never saw him before, señor. I watched him follow your path as you were riding across the meadow to meet up with the señorita an I saw him aim. I . . . I had no way to stop him so I gave out this wild yell to startle him and his arm must have jerked. I never meant to cause harm to your daughter, Señor Kane." His eyes misted. Tony put a consoling arm around the boy's shoulder. "You're quite a good man to have around, Juanito, and I owe you."

Juanito's dark eyes turned up to look at his friend. "Gracias, Señor Branigan."

"My daughter will be just fine, young man, and I agree with Branigan here. You are a brave one. That took a hell of a lot of guts to distract a man with a gun in his hand. Come on and sit down here and let's talk about this guy you saw." Kane motioned him over to one of the chairs.

Juanito broke into a broad smile. He felt honored and privileged to be asked to join such important men. "Oh, yes sir—I can tell you what he looks like. A mean-looking hombre he was!"

Jenny had been doing something she rarely did, but her eaves dropping had greatly relieved her concern that someone would have tried to kill her beautiful daughter. She went upstairs to look in on Amanda.

Downstairs, Juanito prepared to take his leave and return to the Rancho Rio. Tony and he exchanged a comradely farewell. The gunfighter knew he was indebted to the young Mexican for saving his life.

Mark sat in the parlor as the two walked to the front door. Branigan had been right in his assumption of the intentions of the gunman. When Tony returned to the room Kane's broad shoulders were slightly slumped, and he sat pensive, unaware his gunfighter had returned. It was now Tony's intention, since all this had

278

happened today, to have a talk with Kane. While they were alone he'd planned to confide in the cattle baron his true identity and why he'd come to Gonzales County early last summer.

In fact, he'd lain on his bed at night, staring at the ceiling and rehearsing how he would tell Kane. He'd tell him of his love for Amanda and of his ability to provide her with the comforts of life that she'd been accustomed to here on the Circle K Ranch. He'd tell him about his future plans for the fine old Moreno Ranch outside San Antonio. Oh, he'd envisioned his and Amanda's future together many times these last few weeks since coming to the decision that he and Magdalena could not possibly go through with their marriage plans.

Seeing Kane sitting there wearily when he walked back in from seeing Juanito to the door, Tony decided it was not the right time. So instead, he softened his deep voice as he announced himself. "Mr. Kane, I think I'll be going now."

"Huh . . . oh, sure Tony, and thanks for what you did for Amanda," Mark mumbled offhandedly. It convinced Tony that it was wise not to continue with any more talk this late afternoon. Enough had happened around the Circle K for one day.

He strode across the grounds in an unhurried way thinking about Juanito's description of the man who'd been hell bent to do him in. No way did that description fit Derek Lawson. So was it one of his Red Garter cohorts?

He knew where he would be going as soon as it was dark—to the Red Garter and the dance hall girl, Pinky.

TWENTY-FIVE

On Thanksgiving the Lawsons and the Kanes shared the day and the lavish mountain of good food spread on the long table in Jenny's dining room. Consuela had prepared a succulent ham with raisin sauce, and there was the golden-brown roasted turkey with the cornbread dressing that Mark liked. Yams, tender peas, and sweet juicy corn were served, along with cranberry sauce and spiced peaches. The housekeeper had baked an array of pies and cakes to suit everyone's particular taste. Jenny loved the pumpkin. Amanda's favorite was the peach. Jeff and Mark craved the perfection of Consuela's cherry pies.

The meal was served at six in the evening and as usual after the tremendous meal everyone became very lazy, filled to the brim with so much delicious food. But today excitement swelled the walls of the Kane hacienda during the evening hours when Jeff, with a boyish grin on his face, announced his and Mona's plans to marry.

While Amanda could not have been happier for her brother and her dear friend, she felt herself squirming under the constant looks in her direction from David

Lawson. She knew, or at least she thought, she could read his mind. He was hopeful that his son would be announcing the same news one day about her and him. It would never be, she wanted to scream at him. She found his constant smiling face ogling her offensive by the time she could excuse herself from the table. It wasn't that she genuinely didn't like him, but on this occasion his attitude irked her.

Tony was spending the day over at the Rancho Rio and she found herself missing him dreadfully. It would have been a much more pleasant day had he been by her side instead of Derek. She tried her darnedest to be gracious and nice to him. Actually, she couldn't fault Derek, for he couldn't have been more gentlemanly. He just wasn't Tony, a little voice kept sneaking in and saying. Face it, the voice silently urged, you love Tony Branigan, Amanda. Accept it, and enjoy whatever there is to find in the handsome devil's arms.

Mona floated on a soft white cloud soaring so high she needed no wine to stimulate her when Mark proposed a toast to the two young people.

By the time the evening came to an end, Jenny was alive with the plans for the late December wedding. Mark had declared the gift of a new home to be built there on the Circle K about two miles over from this house and David Lawson had said he would purchase all the furnishings. The lucky young couple were to be given what most work their lifetime to acquire.

The pleased smile on Derek's face was purely selfish for he was more than delighted about the prospects of being rid of his sister and having her away from the Big D Ranch.

David Lawson was glad his son seemed so pleased, for he was the first to admit that Derek had always been a selfish, self-centered person. He acted genuinely delighted and that meant a lot to his father.

As the grandfather clock struck ten, the elder Lawson rose from his chair declaring it had been a day to remember, thanked the Kanes for their hospitality, and suggested it was long past the time they should be going home.

Amanda smiled, trying to abort her deep sigh of relief. She was weary of the gathering and Derek's last-minute attempts to hold her hand. She wanted suddenly to be alone.

Tony had left the Circle K early that morning long before the arrival of the Lawson family. He chose not to encounter the group for many reasons, mainly Derek Lawson. While he'd always prided himself on his self control and strong will power, he could not be sure of his actions should they meet now.

He knew now after his noctural visit to the saloon in town that it was Derek's foul hand who'd played the death card by hiring the killer's services of one Tulsa Jack Dawes. He'd only had to describe the man Juanito had told him about for the girl Pinky to immediately exclaim, "Oh, that's Jack. Jack Dawes. Tulsa Jack—they call him that 'cause he comes from Indian Territory is the way I heard it."

He'd thanked her and given her amply padded rear a pat and tucked a coin in the bosom of her revealing garish gown adorned with limp, tired-looking feathers.

Pinkie's information made Tony's trigger finger itch with impatience. A showdown with Lawson was overdue. Knowing what he knew made him want to retch at the thought of a vermin like Lawson being near the woman he loved.

While it was always pleasant to be around his aunt and that pixie, Maria, he couldn't exactly say that he had enjoyed the day. Young Miguel was a congenial young man whom he always found eager to share his company. However, he was surprised when his aunt informed him that Mario had journeyed into San Antonio to spend the next three days there.

"It will be a pleasant surprise for father, I'm sure, to have Mario for a visit, especially with you gone, Tonio," she remarked as she poured him a glass of her favorite sherry.

After he'd visited with his aunt and taken a stroll in the woods with Miguel and Maria, they were all ready to return to the house to devour his aunt's delectable spread of food. Maria deposited the branches of gold and rust that she'd picked in a huge clay urn and the fallen pine cones in a dish of pottery.

It was only when Tony and Bianca were alone that he told her he would be leaving soon. She searched his face and asked, "Then will all this end for you, Tonio? I've had a bad feeling of late."

"It will be the end of my investigating here in Gonzales County, but it will not be the end of my job, Aunt Bianca."

"I see. You cannot tell me any more?" Her fine arched brow raised.

"I cannot tell you more at this time. Someday, I'll tell you everything," he smiled at her. Oh, he wanted very much to say how glad he was that his investigation had not led to the Rancho Rio, but he didn't.

Bianca knew that her son was not merely going to San Antonio to see Esteban. He was also calling on Magdalena, but she felt no disloyalty was being dealt Tony after she'd witnessed the tender scene between him and Amanda Kane. Tony could not love Magdalena. No man could look upon another when he was in love with one woman the way Tony was that day, she'd convinced herself. So she had no qualms about telling Tonio a half-truth.

However, what Bianca didn't know or dream in her wildest imaginings was the distance things had already gone between her son and the sultry Magdalena. His last visit had set the two of them to planning. This visit was to make their final plans to elope. Mario's three days in the city would be spent making the secret preparations for their marriage and extended honeymoon abroad. Magdalena had found in Mario everything she could never force upon Tony, and Mario had found the woman who fit him perfectly. Nothing was going to stop them now, conventional traditions, or family.

They were drugged by the amazing wild passion that had come so suddenly and unexpectedly into each of their lives. After Mario's second visit to the palacial Gomez home, Magdalena had sensed the unvoiced approval of her father. Trusting to fate that she was right she confessed to Francisco what they had planned.

"Please, Papa—for all concerned, act like you know nothing. It could preserve your friendship with Señor Moreno when it happens," Magdalena had pleaded one night a few weeks before Mario's return to the city.

"I promise," he had replied, seeing how shrewd his

lovely daughter was. For it was true that if they eloped and the marriage was consummated, he could hardly have it annulled just because she was promised to Antonio Moreno. Old Esteban could certainly not hold him responsible for an impetuous daughter. She was, indeed, a brilliant, sly fox.

The more Francisco reflected about it, the more Magdalena's decision pleased him. By the time Mario came to call he was greeted by an affable Señor Gomez.

The evening Mario was due to arrive back at the Rancho Rio, he and the lovely Magdalena were being married in a very simple ceremony, with only Señor Gomez in attendance. Francisco was already mapping out his son-in-law's future as his partner in his established law firm in the city as soon as the two young people returned from their European honeymoon. He was elated about Magdalena's choice of husband, for he could see Mario already in more favorable terms than he could ever have imagined the independent, headstrong Antonio. There had been a wild recklessness about Antonio he'd always questioned. In truth, he breathed a sigh of great relief.

The next morning he left San Antonio in his carriage with his driver to journey to the Rancho Rio to break the surprising news to Bianca. He didn't dread this visit as he did the one he would have to pay upon his return to the city to Esteban Moreno.

However, upon his arrival at the Rancho Rio and when he was waiting for Bianca's appearance, he was seized with a case of nerves. When she entered and saw him, her lovely face turned ashen and pale. She seemed to find it difficult to speak. "Is . . . is something wrong, Francisco? Has Mario been hurt?"

He rushed to her side, speaking hastily to quiet any fears she had. "Oh, dear Bianca . . . no! He is magnificent! He . . . our children were married, Bianca. I . . . I hope you will approve. Granted it was very irresponsible of them, I've calmed down and accepted it." Francisco kept patting her hands nervously. "You all right, my dear?"

Bianca quickly regained her composure with the welfare of Mario assured. His marriage to the lovely Magdalena came as no real shock to her, but she had to admit she'd not expected an elopement from the rascal.

"I am fine, Francisco—really!" She even gave him a smile, straightening up and throwing back her shoulders in that stately manner of hers. "Come, we'll have a glass of my finest Madeira."

What a remarkable lady she was, Francisco mused, as he followed her over to the fine rosewood sofa to sit down. After he'd eased himself down on the sofa, she walked on over to the teakwood liquor cabinet and took the cut crystal decanter to pour their drinks without summoning the servant.

"You know, Francisco I feel very good about this marriage of our children."

Señor Gomez's huge chest swelled with delight. "Ah, I do too, señora. I do too!"

As they drank the Madeira Francisco related the couples' plans and Bianca realized the many weeks Mario would be gone. "In that case, I guess I must get busy grooming Miguel to take over for Mario," she smiled. It would seem that things had a way of working out for the best for both her sons. Always, it had

286

been Miguel whose nature would adapt to a lifetime around the Rancho Rio. He loved the animals and the quiet of the countryside. It would come easy to Miguel to give his complete devotion and love to the Rancho Rio.

Later when she called Miguel into her sitting room to tell him of his brother's marriage and to express her desire that he take over his brother's duties, she had never seen such elation on her eighteen-year-old son's face. He stood there tall and proud.

He rushed to her and hugged her around the neck. "Oh, thank you Mother!" he said. Bianca could feel the excitement churning in her son, and she, too, swelled with satisfaction. It had been one of those gratifying moments in life Bianca knew she'd always remember. It was as if she'd given him the moon. Maria could wait until tomorrow to be told of her brother's marriage. As she fanned her waist-long hair comfortably on the silk pillows, she smiled, wondering what her little "imp" would say. Maria had always been her special blessing as her last child.

TWENTY-SIX

Amanda couldn't know the heaviness in Tony's heart as they rode that November day, but he was trying to be that devil-may-care rascal with the glib, silken tongue she was always telling him he was. How little she knew of him, he mused silently.

The word had come last night from Flanigan, urging him to get back to San Antonio as soon as he could get there. He knew the importance of everything's working like clockwork once the sequence of events began. Otherwise, the months of planning would not be successful. Flanigan was determined to get every one of the outlaws and smash the operation. He was dedicated to this project of eliminating the worst bunch of cattle rustlers ever to hit this part of Texas.

Amanda had been such a chatterbox she'd not noticed the black moods he'd drifted in and out of. She was elated over her aunt and uncle's coming for the Christmas holidays and her birthday. She tossed her head with an arrogant air and looked over at him. "You can't call me a child in a few days, thank goodness. Did you hear me, Branigan? I'll be eighteen, Tony Branigan," she playfully taunted him.

He broke into a laugh. "You'll always be an adorable child in some ways to me, *chiquita*. I find myself wanting to pamper you and in the next moment wanting to spank that cute little bottom."

"Tony, you are impossible! So why do I put up with you?" She laughed, tilting her head at a flirtatious angle. Deep golden waves made the perfect frame for her oval face. Her eyes gleamed so bright and alive. There was something else there in her eyes for him to see and it had been there for the last few weeks. It was love, and he knew it!

His lips were most sensuous, Amanda thought, when he gave her a certain smile with that oh-so-devilish look in those smoky gray eyes. "Don't you know yet? Haven't you really figured it all out, Amanda?"

"Sometimes, I think I know, and other times I get confused about everything and everybody."

"Don't you think everyone feels that way at times?"

"I . . . I guess so."

"Your shoulder seems to be just fine," he remarked, finding himself becoming far too serious for such a lovely last day. He wanted to keep it light and gay, for another such day would be weeks away.

"I should have had old Trinidad Riveria give me some of her potions. From what Chita says they perform miracles for her. She felt marvelous the next day after the old *curandera* stopped by. She doctors all the *vaqueros'* wives with her native herbs and plants in her role as doctor, nurse, or midwife, Chita says. I went over there right after the holiday, you know."

"I see. But no, I didn't know."

"Yes, I rode over after the Thanksgiving holiday

and I didn't stop in to pay my respects because she had company—a carriage was in front."

He was too absorbed with her to give any thought to the company Bianca might be having visit her. Amanda's busy lips held him far more intrigued and he reined Picaro closer so he could lean over to her. "Shut up long enough for me to kiss you," he murmured lustily. She complied willingly, meeting him halfway.

But for the cold chill of the season, he would have yearned to go to that cove in the river where he had first caught sight of his golden goddess. There on a blanket he would have poured out his heart and his love to her, enough to warm him through the dreary weeks ahead.

He'd already decided that he could not burden her with the truth—not yet. If he told her the truth as he planned to tell Mark Kane, then he would reveal the danger he faced as well. No, she could not know now!

"Amanda *mia* . . . Amanda *mia*, you are mine!" His eyes closed as he kissed her again longingly with the thought of leaving her tearing him apart.

"Tony, darling," she sighed, wanting to press herself against his firm male body, but unable to get that close atop their horses.

The flames tortured them both, but there was no place for the lovers to seek refuge from the rest of the world in the bright light of the afternoon. His voice was husky with desire as he asked her, "Come to me tonight! Will you, Amanda *mia*?"

She nodded, trembling with want. They spurred the two fine horses in the direction of the red-tiled roof of the hacienda.

She had expected he would part with her when they

arrived back by the barn, but he didn't. As he walked by her side up to the house, he told her of his need to talk to her father about a certain matter.

Only when they reached the base of the stairs and she started to mount the first step did he release his strong hand from hers. She returned his warm, intimate smile.

Tony found Mark in his study. It was the perfect cozy setting for the winter day, with the fire going in the small fireplace and Mark puffing on his cheroot, his booted foot cocked atop the edge of the desk.

With a rap on the facing of the open door to alert Kane of his presence, he said, "Sir, may I speak to you?"

"Sure thing. I'd enjoy some talk. Jenny is far too busy for me. That uppity sister of hers coming has put my good wife into a frenzy."

"May I?" Tony asked, indicating he'd like to shut the door.

"Now, that's a damned good idea, son. Want a little nip of brandy? I do!" Kane ambled over to the chest, opened the door to remove the Napoleon Brandy and two glasses. "Something wrong, Branigan?"

"No, sir . . . nothing's wrong. But it's time I set the record straight, sir." He sat down and took a sip of the brandy. "I must ask your patience with me and for you to understand I've got to go back some months, Mr. Kane."

Mark Kane frowned wondering if he was going to like what he was about to hear. He, too, took a sip of brandy.

"I am Tony Branigan, and I'm not. Now before you think me loco, let me explain. I am actually Tony

291

Moreno of San Antonio, the grandson of Esteban Moreno. You've known from the first that Bianca Alvarado was my aunt."

"Yes . . . yes, I knew that," Mark barked with impatience.

Tony explained about the name of Branigan and why he'd come to Gonzales County and the strange twist of fate that had put him on the scene the day he'd saved Mark's life. "Hired by you was perfect cover for me to check things."

"Damn and double damn!" was all Mark could say.

"I was snooping around that day for some clues. You see, the marshal suspected a connection somewhere in the vicinity of these three ranches. This thing covers one hell of an operation." Tony omitted places and names.

Kane had the need for another drink and offered one to Tony.

"I've told you this in confidence, the very strictest. There is a reason, sir. I must leave at once—in the morning at the latest. I—I've come to think a lot of you, sir, and I felt I could trust you. In a few months, you'll know the outcome, either from me or someone else."

"Tony, I . . . I don't know what to say other than I'm proud you feel as you do about me. I have to tell you the feeling is mutual, young man. You can never know how many times Jenny and I have tossed your name around. We both knew there was a hell of a lot more to you than any drifting gunslinger."

"Well, I appreciate that, and I plan to come back to the Circle K after this is all behind me to give you a firsthand report. There is another reason, too." Now *he* felt the need for a gulp of his brandy. "I love Amanda."

"I see." Mark measured his statement.

Tony stammered like a schoolboy asserting his ability to care for her in the custom she was used to and emphasizing his endless love for her. Stone-faced, Mark Kane wasn't making it easy.

The twinkle in Kane's blue eyes surprised pleased Tony. Mark gave a laugh. "Young man, do you think you can tame that headstrong filly?" Tony could not restrain a grin coming to his face, but he dared not answer him with honesty, not this time. Instead, he declared, "I can sure die trying, sir!"

Kane bellowed with laughter. "My God, if any man can, I'd wager it might just be you, Branigan, and I'll tell you, just between you and me, you've got my permission to try."

"Thank you, sir, and I have to insist that all this be kept from Amanda until I return. It's best, Mr. Kane."

"All right, Branigan . . . I'll abide by your wishes."

"It's necessary, Mr. Kane," Tony stressed. He fumbled in his pocket for something—one last matter to be taken care of before he left. He handed the small case to Mark, saying, "I will be gone by Amanda's birthday and I'd like to leave this with you to give to her."

Mark took it and nodded his head. "I'll give it to her. You don't think you could wait up just a few days for that, then?"

"No sir, I can't," Tony told him in a solemn tone.

"Would you have dinner with us tonight, Branigan?''

Tony did not want the torture of sitting across the dining table from Amanda without being able to touch her, so he declined graciously. He wanted only those moments when they could be completely alone with each other. To be opposite her with her bewitching loveliness taunting him would be an agony he'd not add to the torment he was already enduring.

"Mr. Kane, I'll leave now, and for a while I guess this will be farewell, too."

They gave one another a manly handshake and each looked deep into the other's eyes. There was a strange surge of feeling in Mark's chest even he couldn't explain to himself as he held this young man's strong, tanned hand. He found a tremendous lump coming into his throat when he finally muttered, "Take care, Tony."

Later as he sat back down at his desk he equated his concern to that of a father for his son. He realized the extensive depth of his feeling for the gunfighter. As quickly as he thought of him as "the gunfighter," he corrected himself. The young man was Tony Moreno, and while he didn't know Esteban Moreno personally, he'd certainly heard of the esteemed gentleman and the renowned family of the Morenos.

Yet he still found it hard to believe a young man with Tony's considerable wealth and prestige had taken on this job. He was an amazing individual, one to be greatly admired for his courage. He was Kane's kind of man, and by all that was holy, Mark had, indeed, pegged him right.

To the walls of his study Mark mumbled low, "Damn, I'm going to miss Branigan." Moreno was going to take a little getting used to, Kane mused.

He placed the small leather case in a corner of one of his desk drawers and left his study. The afternoon sun had faded and dusk shrouded the countryside. It seemed the nights came earlier now. He walked down the hall to the entrance of the hacienda, deciding to take a stroll before the dinner hour at seven. Never was there a more beautiful sight anywhere than the sun setting over the Circle K, regardless of the season.

The hues of purple blended into rosy red over on the horizon, looking as though they touched the earth. Even the winter months here in Gonzales County weren't as brutal as in Kansas, Mark thought recalling those days when he had driven cattle up there. This was God's country—out of all the places he'd traveled. His thoughts and prayers were going to be with young Branigan, who was going to rid his paradise of the devils trying to destroy and ruin it.

The red in the sky could mean rain, and a shower wouldn't hurt a thing, he reasoned. He turned to walk up on the high rise of ground giving a view into the valley below when he noticed a cloud of dust rising against the setting sun. A carriage moving at a moderate speed was rolling toward the ranch entrance. Could it be, he wondered? Sweet Jesus, Jenny wasn't expecting Lisa until tomorrow or the next day. How like that unpredictable Lisa to pull one of her little surprises!

More than once he'd thanked God that it had been the lovely black-haired Jenny he'd chosen over the other beauty, Lisa, that night so long ago in New Orleans when he was a randy young man out for an evening in the wild, wicked city of New Orleans back in

1854.

As he recalled that night, he could have so easily picked the other dark-haired lovely as the sisters had stood side by side at the Cotillion Balle. He'd been visiting one of his father's old friends and had gone along with the man's three sons to the gala event. After that night, he didn't leave the city until he'd wooed and won his sweet Jenny. The two of them had returned to Texas and Gonzales County together.

Mark put his memories aside to rush to greet his guests. The carriage had come to a halt and the long, lean frame of Armand Vega was emerging from it by the time Kane came up.

He called out to the French Creole gentleman who was his brother-in-law. For all his dignified reserve, Armand had always been warm and outgoing to Mark. He had to be a saint to put up with the flighty, frivolous Lisa.

"Mark, *mon ami*—it is good to see you," Armand greeted him, one hand extended to Lisa to help her down and his other hand brushing back his rumpled mane of almost snow-white hair. As Mark saw the smiling Lisa alight all he could think about was the tizzy Jenny would be in from their early arrival.

For no particular reason other than that the deep, rich shade of green was a flattering color for her and the fact that she wanted to be especially pretty when she kept her secret rendezvous with Tony, Amanda dressed in the long-sleeved gown for dinner.

She wore her hair loose and flowing with its natural soft waves. She was already thinking about how she would eat fast and excuse herself from the table to retire. A devious smile played on her face as she plotted how she'd slip out through the kitchen into the night to go to Branigan's quarters. Was she a shameless hussy to go on this nocturnal visit to her lover's room? Perhaps, but she could not have denied him, for it meant denying herself as well.

She'd accepted this savage infatuation for what it was a few weeks ago and there were no regrets. Only lately at night when sleep wouldn't come had that annoying little voice within her, always prodding or seeding doubts, nagged her. He'd never once mentioned marriage. He'd never mentioned—as a gallant suitor should—his intentions for the future. His words of love had been a mingling of Spanish words which she did not always understand with English ones—all about his desire for her, his wanting of her, or his need. Those could be the words of a man spoken to his mistress.

They were not thoughts she liked to dwell on too long, so she determined to pay no attention to that irritating voice.

Another voice came to her ears as she opened her bedroom door and there was no other person in the world it could have belonged to but her beloved Aunt Lisa. They had arrived!

She fairly flew down the stairs shrieking their names. Her Uncle Armand lifted her up, laughing as he whirled her around in his arms. He gave out that deep laugh of his, declaring, *"Ah, ma petite*—so good to see you again!"

Once he set her on the floor, she and her aunt clasped each other in a warm embrace. Jenny and Mark watched, seeing the love and warmth her aunt and uncle felt for their daughter.

Suddenly, Lisa turned Amanda loose as if she was inspecting her niece's looks and sighed, pleased at the beautiful sight of her. "*Mon chèr*, isn't she a sight to put your eyes out," she directed Armand to take notice as she gave Amanda a turn, making her whirl around. Amanda gave out a giggle.

"You can see now why I came home so spoiled, Mother," Amanda pointed out to her two adoring parents.

"Come, let us all go in to toast your arrival," Jenny urged the group toward the parlor. Lisa locked her arms with Jenny and Amanda with Armand and Mark trailing behind the ladies. "And where is our boy, Mark? Where is Jeff?" the dignified-looking French Creole inquired.

"Truth is, I'm not sure, Armand. Out on the range, or over at the neighboring ranch seeing his girl. We weren't expecting you for a few days yet."

Armand threw his head back and laughed, "Well you know my Lisa! Once she got her luggage ready, nothing could hold her back in New Orleans."

Mark nodded, thinking to himself that he knew her well enough to marvel that a man Armand's age kept up with his wife's vivacious sister. Well, she'd slow her pace here on the ranch and poor Armand just might get some rest. However, his brother-in-law looked fit as a fiddle, considering he was ten years older than Mark. As far as that thick head of white hair, Mark could not recall a time when it wasn't mostly white.

They joined the ladies chattering away like magpies. Amanda was raving about her aunt's traveling ensemble. Lisa smiled with delight, for her clothes were a passion she indulged herself in.

"*Chèrie*, you are ravishing! I wouldn't have believed it possible that you could have gotten any prettier than you were that day you left." That all-knowing eye of Lisa carefully surveyed her niece's divine sensuous curves, along with the look on her face. Was it the glow of a young lady in love, she found herself wondering. "Oh, Jenny, Jenny—it is going to be so wonderful to share the holiday with the people we love so." Her eyes, though, were scrutinizing her beautiful niece.

They had a toast and then a second one before Lisa and Armand were shown to their rooms to refresh themselves.

It was one night that dinner was not promptly served at seven, as was Mark Kane's rule. The hour was eight when Lisa and Armand came back down the stairway to join the assembly awaiting them. Amanda had found it amusing as she watched her father fret and fume as he paced the floor.

He made a point of informing Jenny. "This one night, Jenny! Only this one night! The Circle K will not suddenly change its routine."

"Yes, my darling," Jenny purred softly. "Tomorrow I will fill Lisa in on our routine so she can start her primping earlier to be downstairs." Secretly, she knew it wasn't too easy where Lisa was concerned, but she would try for Mark's sake.

One thing Jenny had no doubts about and that was that the next few weeks would be lively ones with her sister around the Circle K. However, Lisa's visit could prove very taxing to her husband. Mark Kane had never been a man to live by other's rules. Jenny expected to be right in the middle of the two of them, soothing rumpled feathers from time to time.

Suddenly, Amanda began to fidget with impatience as it dawned on her about the lateness of the hour. When she finally made her appearance at the top of the landing, Amanda heaved a sigh of relief at the sight of her elegantly gowned aunt descending the stairway. At last, they would be able to dine.

TWENTY-SEVEN

The lively talk, delicious dinner and the wine flowing generously made the evening fly swiftly by. Jeff arrived as they'd just finished dinner, having stayed at the Lawsons' to dine with his bride to be.

Tony had played cards with the guys after sharing supper with them. He'd tipped the bottle with Slim Christy before Slim took his leave to go on over to his house. Being a practical man, Tony accepted the fact that he might not see any of them again. Just as quickly, he swept such thoughts away to join in their cajoling and drinking there in the bunkhouse, making sure his chair was placed so his view of the walled garden gate was not blocked.

The little minx was beginning to try his patience by the time it was past ten. The four hands he sat with were hale and hardy drinkers and one slug after another was beginning to have its effect on him, so he bid them goodnight. The night air and a stroll around the grounds was needed to clear his head, he decided.

He grumbled to the dark about her lateness. Didn't she realize how precious the minutes were? Then he had to remind himself that she didn't know it was their last night for a long, long time.

With the arrival of the Kanes' guests late that afternoon perhaps she would not come. That thought riled him, knowing how fond Amanda was of that aunt of hers from New Orleans. When he was at the point of tossing aside the cheroot he been smoking and ambling on up to his quarters, he saw the downstairs suddenly going dark. Now maybe she would come to him.

Christ, he was tense tonight! His gut felt all in knots. He paced back and forth like a panther, awaiting some prey to come on the scene, but no small miss came rushing through the gate to his anxious arms. He was at the point of calling himself a fool, for he was acting like some lovesick schoolboy. Never in his whole twenty-five years had he acted so idiotic.

More than ever, as he paced in the darkness, he knew how vulnerable he'd become since he'd lost his heart to Amanda Kane. Once again, he turned on his booted heels to head for his quarters. The hell with her; he was getting weary and his throat was dry. The need for a drink might have to satisfy the void if Amanda wasn't going to fill his arms tonight.

The Vegas had been in their room less than a half-hour, but Lisa, as was her habit, was still dawdling at her dressing table taking down all the curls so perfectly placed atop her head. She'd told Céline, her little French maid, to go on to her quarters earlier.

She didn't know that Armand had not heard the last five or ten minutes of her conversation. She repeated herself. "Could you, Armand? I know I couldn't stand to live in this godforsaken place? Armand?" She turned to see her husband's eyes shut in sleep. "Poor dear."

She hoped this trip hadn't been too much for him, for she knew he'd not been feeling too well. He had been as eager as she had been to come, though, and so she didn't fault herself that it had been her prodding.

She rose from the stool and removed her sheer peach-colored peignoir, tossing it over on the chair. It seemed so dark outside the double windows. She was used to standing outside on the little balcony of their suite at home. She lingered there by the windows. Such vast darkness, she thought, no lights as on Saint Charles Street. She wondered how poor Jenny had ever found contentment all these years in this desolate countryside of Texas. I would surely have wilted away, she thought.

However, the same glorious golden moon up above was shining down across this Texas landscape as on their fine palacial home back in New Orleans. Perhaps it was its silvery rays that reflected on Amanda's spun-gold hair as she scampered like a deer out the gate and across the short distance to the stone carriage house or stable.

Lisa stood glued to the window, curious about what the little pixie was up to. Perhaps she now understood why Amanda was watching the time and almost jumped out of her skin each time the grandfather clock chimed after their dinner was finished. The little minx had a rendezvous to keep!

Her vivacious aunt smiled, her heart beating a little faster when she watched as Amanda went into the arms of a delightful-looking gent bouncing down the side steps of the building. It was obvious the man had been waiting for her niece. Yet he was minus his shirt, as though he might have been preparing to retire. Most interesting!

Lisa watched the two young people embrace most intimately. She could almost see the rippling muscles of his fine man's body with the bright moonbeams lighting them up as if the two of them were performers on the stage at one of the fine theaters in the city.

"Oh, la, la," she gasped, abruptly rushing to muzzle her voice so she wouldn't wake up Armand. Amanda did have herself a lover, and a most magnificent one from what she could observe. Well, that didn't surprise her at all, and now she was sure she had pinpointed the different loveliness of her niece. She was a woman now, and, Lisa imagined, a woman fulfilled. Who was he, she wondered? Now, she was going to find sleep hard to come by, and had her darling Armand not been so weary she would have been tempted to get in bed beside him and seek release from the flames of yearning and desire stirring her after watching the two young lovers.

Tony had been removing his clothing and was at the point of accepting the fact that Amanda was not coming to him when he happened to spot her dashing across the grounds toward his quarters. He didn't stop to put his shirt back on as he rushed out of the room and down the steps to meet her. So urgent was his need to feel that supple, soft body crushed in his arms, that he quickly dismissed his disgruntled feelings that she was so late getting out of the hacienda. All that mattered was that she had come.

Panting and out of breath, she gasped as he encircled her in his arms, lifting her up off the ground. "I thought I'd never get out of there!"

He pressed her even closer. "It doesn't matter now that I'm holding you, *Amanda mia*. God, I'm a starved man . . . so starved for you, *chiquita!*" His deep voice moaned as though he was in agony and his lips eagerly sought hers. She felt the heated power and force of him, leaving no doubt about his desire for her. It was wild and wonderful, for she felt giddy from the same need. "Oh, God, Tony. Tony!" she breathlessly sighed before he captured her lips again and hastily hoisted her up in his strong arms. Striding swiftly up the steps and through the door, he laid her down on his bed to love her one last time before he had to leave her.

His gray eyes devoured her as he spoke softly. "Love me tonight as if there was no tomorrow, *querida*. As if there was only just this one tonight." Beautiful, romantic words she didn't understand followed. But it didn't matter that she didn't, for the way he said them told her they were warm with passion. She was in such a heat of passion and savage yearning that he wanted to please her. With anxious, eager hands, he removed her clothing with his eyes adoring each lovely golden part of her he bared. She stared with as much boldness as they both drowned in each other's eyes. When there was nothing between them but flesh against flesh Amanda pleaded in a soft whisper, "Take me, *querido*."

She had never called him that endearing term before in his native language and it meant everything to him to hear her say it to him on this night of all nights. He drove himself into her with a mighty thrust, wanting to fill her as he'd never done before. In sensuous, undulating movements he brought her to peaks of pleasure that made her moan in delight.

Wanting to gaze upon that lovely face so flushed with flaming passion, he paused. "I never get enough of you. I never could," he huskily murmured, bending to catch the tip of one of her pulsing breasts in his mouth. He was causing sweet agony, but he wanted to affect her so. Tonight he must take her to such lofty heights that no other man could ever have what was meant for only him and him alone.

"Dear God, Tony . . . I shall die if you do . . ."

"No, *chiquita*, I won't let you," he interrupted, giving her the ecstasy she cried out for.

She felt her breath would surely not come in the next second, but it did. Oh, yes . . . yes . . . yes! The words were only felt, not spoken, for she felt herself consumed by the magnificence of this man. Surely this rapture could not be wrong. Something this wonderful had to be right, she found herself thinking amid this frenzy of ecstasy.

Everything about them seemed fused together. They were one body . . . one person as they moved and swayed round and round and higher and higher.

Tony felt himself reaching the limit, and as strong as his will power was he strained to last longer as he knew this night would have to last him so many long, lonely weeks.

"Mine, Amanda. Always, mine," he moaned as though it was a sacred vow that they both must keep after this night.

"Yes, Tony . . . I promise . . . always," she whispered. She felt the searing fire of his brand deep within her. A floodtide erupted he could no longer restrain and she arched to meet his powerful thrusting.

Slowly, she felt herself descending down and down

into that sublime calm, total exhaustion engulfing her. He, too, felt that sweet, sweet tiredness and sank down by her flushed body.

Quietly, they remained snuggled and curved to the other one's body to absorb the feeling of cherished closeness. Tony wanted never to leave the petite body fitted to his so perfectly.

It took the strongest will power Tony had ever exerted to make himself release her some thirty minutes later. Gay and chipper was hardly the way he felt, but he appeared so to Amanda when he teased, "Come on, little one, I won't be blamed this time for allowing you to sleep until dawn. Get your cute little butt out of my bed!"

"Tony Branigan . . . you're awful!"

He laughed. "We both are!" He could not allow her to stay there on the bed. "No, it is the last thing in the world I want, Amanda, but there is a houseful of people over there and it is best while everyone is sound asleep and it's still dark."

"I know. I'll have to be more careful, for Aunt Lisa is a light sleeper and she's one of these people who might be up until two or three 'cause she'll stay in bed until noon if the notion strikes her." She busily gathered up her clothes and began to dress.

A short time later Tony walked her as far as the courtyard gate, taking one more long, lingering kiss to keep him warm during the dreary nights stretching before him until he could return to her. The clock chimed two as Amanda tiptoed into her bedroom.

Much to his chagrin, Tony slept until seven. His plans had been to be away from the Circle K an hour or two earlier. But he encountered only the cook after

307

he loaded his meager possessions in his saddlebags. With a couple of cups of black coffee in him, he told the cook goodbye. "Take care, Pete." He strode outside to where Picaro stood awaiting him at the hitching post. He took no notice of the woman watching him.

Lisa Vega could not remember a time in her life when a man had held her so enthralled as this magnificent male did. She'd watched him amble out of the cookhouse with a lazy cat's gait. His trim physique seemed to be molded into his black garb. Just observing him, the perceptive Madame Vega didn't have to be told there was a cocky arrogance about the man. Even the way he wore his flat-crowned black felt hat exhibited that. She knew this had to be the man the darling Amanda had had her rendezvous with last night.

She moved toward where he now untied the reins of his huge stallion. The horse was as magnificent in its way as his master, Lisa thought, appreciating the blackest, glossiest coat she'd ever seen.

Only a few minutes earlier she had been fuming at herself for being up at this unheard of hour, but now she was glad. She wanted to meet this man . . . this paragon. He must be, if Amanda was meeting him in the dead of night. None of her young suitors had inspired her so much or so recklessly while she was in New Orleans.

Out of the corner of his eye Tony caught sight of the shade of mauve and a swishing skirt. A very petite, most attractive lady was coming his way. Tony knew instinctively this was the aunt Amanda had told him about in the most enthusiastic terms. Sisters or not, no one would mistake her for Jenny Kane. There was a provocative air about the way she walked, and as she came closer he saw the same look reflected in her eyes. This was a different type of woman!

"Good morning, monsieur," she greeted him with a flirtatious tilt of her dark head. Tony noted that dark hair was about all she did share with her sister Jenny.

"Good morning, ma'am." Anxious to be on his way, he encouraged, but he sensed he wasn't going to be allowed to get away so easily.

Lisa was never at a loss for words with strangers or anyone. "A marvelous beast you have there, Monsieur . . ."

"Branigan, ma'am. Tony Branigan," he shot back. Blast the woman! He wanted to be away before the ranch hands started moving around the ranch or the Kane family chanced out of the hacienda.

"I am Lisa Vega, Monsieur Branigan . . . sister of Jenny Kane." She found herself very intrigued with this strange young man and his cool gray eyes. They were devastating eyes, and Lisa found herself pondering the hooded moodiness she felt lingering in them.

"I . . . I thought you might be. Nice to meet you, ma'am," Tony said, striving to be gracious. He took off his hat and extended his hand to her hand offered to him.

In a gesture that surprised and delighted her, he gracefully brought her dainty hand up to his lips and kissed the fingers. "I must take my leave, Madame Vega. I hope you enjoy your visit here at the Circle K Ranch." He turned swiftly on his booted heel and mounted up on Picaro, waving farewell to Lisa Vega and the Circle K.

Gaping with wonder, she stood watching the pair gallop down the winding drive toward the towering archway and only when they disappeared from sight did she turn and walk toward the iron gate of the courtyard. He was like no other ranch hand she'd ever encountered on her visits to this untamed countryside—as she had labeled it since her first jaunt to Texas to see her older sister.

She was suddenly ready for her croissants and coffee. Then she remembered that here she'd have to settle for Consuela's biscuits and coffee. Those flaky, light biscuits weren't too bad, but they weren't croissants!

TWENTY-EIGHT

Jenny saw her sister sitting there and she couldn't believe it. Not Lisa, up and already having her breakfast! Was it the country air having some kind of intoxicating effect? The sister she remembered slept until noon, breakfasted in bed and finally got her eyes opened by one in the afternoon. She walked on into the room to greet Lisa and called out for Consuela to bring her coffee.

"Hope you slept well," Jenny smiled, sitting down at the table.

Although she smiled at Jenny, the always candid Lisa declared, "Well, I didn't, but that doesn't matter. I'll nap the afternoon away and catch up. Ah, Jenny, I rest nowhere like I do in my own bed."

The sisters laughed and Jenny recalled that never had Lisa been a person to adapt easily to new situations. Lisa could not have married anyone but a city dweller. There had been no adjustment for Lisa when she married. She had gone from their fine mansion of a home to the palacial home Armand had purchased for them. Their father had been a wealthy, influential man in the city of New Orleans, as was Lisa's hus-

311

band. While she adored her sister, Jenny felt Lisa had remained the frivolous belle she had been at sixteen.

Jenny could not help comparing the two of them this morning. God knows, neither was really the carefree, giddy belle of sixteen or eighteen! But there she sat in her simple sprigged muslin with her white-specked black hair in its neat double coil at the back of her head with the part down the middle. Lisa looked like a delicate pastel painting in her mauve gown edged with exquisite lace around the neck and sleeves. Wispy curls flattered her smooth face with its flawless complexion. Lisa's excesses in clothes and jewelry staggered the more conservative Jenny. Dear Lord, the huge diamond on her sister's finger looked so heavy and almost uncomfortable to Jenny. Her sister's other small hand was adorned with a sapphire and diamond ring that had to have cost Armand a small fortune.

"Oh, Jenny dear, I met the nice Monsieur Branigan this morning while I strolled the ground. *Mon Dieu*, he is a handsome devil!"

Jenny laughed. "Tony? Oh yes, he is very nice."

"Put him in a fine cut of clothes and in my parlor in New Orleans and he would have the ladies fawning over him in droves, I promise you," Lisa declared, giving her a wink.

"Oh, Lisa . . . you never change. You were born a coquette, and at eighty you'll be one."

Lisa gave out a lilting laugh. "I think you are probably right, Jenny. But I can swear to you that I never went to bed with any man but Armand."

"I can believe that, Lisa. I really can," Jenny told her and she could have sworn that Lisa seemed surprised by her older sister's remark.

With a wicked gleam in her dark eyes, Lisa jested, "I can tell you if I was of that mind your Tony Branigan would tempt me."

Amanda stood in the archway, muzzling her mouth to keep from giggling. Dear Lord, was there no end to Tony's conquests! Obviously Aunt Lisa had met him and was already spellbound by that strange magnetic force of his. Sweet Jesus, last night! Every inch of her pulsed still from the heat of their lovemaking. If only Aunt Lisa knew, she couldn't help thinking!

As quiet as she stood behind them, something alerted the two to her presence and they both turned at the same time. "Good morning, chèrie. Come here and give your Tante Lisa a big kiss," Lisa urged.

Amanda did as her aunt requested and then kissed her mother. Once again, Consuela was summoned from the kitchen and Jenny decided then and there that she was going to have to hire one of the tenants' wife or maybe a couple. Lisa could be a very demanding person and she was used to being waited on hand and foot.

Amanda didn't wait for Consuela but went through the door to help herself to coffee. Amid the flurry of chatter that went on through the day at the hacienda, Amanda had no time to seek out Tony or even dwell on thoughts of him. Her aunt kept both Amanda and Jenny entertained.

By afternoon, Jenny had to admit she was ready for a moment of solitude and peaceful quiet. Lisa's energy could be taxing and wearing hour after hour. Mark and Armand were absent for the whole day, not returning until four in the afternoon, and Jenny noted her brother-in-law's weary-looking face. She felt the need to caution Mark that Armand was not a man used to the outdoors. His days were spent behind a desk.

"Don't run him too much, Mark. He's not a robust, rugged man like you," Jenny cautioned him.

"I won't, Jenny. But perhaps I should tell you that I think Armand rather enjoyed the quiet and peace of riding with me around the ranch. You know, Lisa is exhausting at times. Maybe, Armand has reached a point in his life that he'd like to get off Lisa's constant whirling social sprees."

"Maybe you're right, darling," Jenny sided with him. She had welcomed her solitude after Lisa went upstairs to nap.

A day and a night had passed when Amanda began to question the absence of Tony Branigan. She determined to investigate his usual haunts around the ranch. It was at the corral that she happened upon Slim Christy and inquired of him, "Where is Branigan, Slim?"

Slim had always thought Amanda the prettiest little thing he'd ever laid eyes on, and, contrary to the general opinion that she was a spoiled brat, Slim didn't see her that way.

"Why, he left a couple of days ago, Miss Amanda," he told her in that matter-of-fact way of his. He noted that her pert little face looked like she'd been slapped.

"Left . . . for where?" Her eyes flashed almost purple and her head whirled.

"Left, Miss Amanda. You know . . . like all the extra hands do after roundup time and until the spring comes and Mr. Kane begins to need extra help agin."

"Oh!" She turned in a wild motion with her skirts and petticoats flying in the breeze as she dashed away. Slim stood, puzzled about the way she'd said, "oh," as if she was shocked, and the by crushed sort of look on her face as she'd said goodbye, barely a whisper.

Scratching his head, he went on his way. Never found it easy anyway trying to figure the female mind out or its workings. Something he'd said had most assuredly upset or displeased her.

Tears teased her lashes and she willed herself not to give way to the rushing current welling up inside her. Where to go to be alone stabbed at her. Not the house with its crowd of people mingling everywhere. Certainly no audience with her aunt at this moment. Slim stood between her and the barn where Prince was. So where?

Inside the iron gate she moved hovering next to the six-foot stone wall encircling the garden grounds. When she moved back where the massive oleander bushes with their thick green branches reached all the way to the ground, she sank down dejectedly and forlorn upon the carpeted ground. There she allowed the dam of tears to break. She hurt so bad and so deep—with a pain she'd never felt before in her life. There was such an overwhelming wave engulfing her; this feeling of hurt. No human being had ever inflicted this sort of blow on her. Of all the people in the world, it had to be the man she had given her heart and soul to!

She would not remember hours later how long she lay on the ground and cried, nor would she recall making the trip upstairs to her room. The rest of the day was a blank to Amanda. She did not want any part of her family that evening, or any of the gaiety that always ignited around Aunt Lisa. She wanted to be alone. So when the new servant girl came to help her dress for dinner, she was promptly dismissed.

"I'm to have a tray sent to my room, Julie, Oh, Julie, tell my mother I've a head cold so I think it best I don't pass my germs around to them and our guests. Be sure you tell my mother that at once."

"Yes, ma'am . . . right away," the girl replied backing out the door. The señorita looked all puffy-eyed like she had a good one. As soon as she was gone, Amanda buried her head in the mountain of pillows. She didn't cry though . . . not this time. This time she began to recall a million things. In recalling, she cursed herself for not listening to that annoying, infernal little voice that had tried to warn her against the too handsome drifter who had come into her life in the springtime and as suddenly left in the winter.

As she lay there she had to credit Derek Lawson for pegging him right when he'd called him a drifting gunslinger who roamed around the countryside. Dear God, she should have known there was no permanent, longlasting relationship to be had with a man like Tony Branigan. The wild excitement was there for the taking and yes, she'd taken as he had in that moment of rapture, with a passion so enflamed that all reason and sanity was swept away.

Misery faded and fury emerged. She sat up in the bed and her red-streaked eyes flashed bright. "The bastard! God, oh God, how I hate him!"

When her dinner tray was served, she gulped down the food with angry gusto. She ate every bite. When she'd finished the last crumb, she placed it at the foot of her bed.

Her door opened with cautious slowness and her mother peeked in to see if she was sleeping. Then Lisa's head appeared from behind her mother. Amanda silently resented their intrusion but smiled wanly at them.

"Bless your heart, you do look coldish," Lisa declared, coming from behind Jenny. "We missed you, chèrie."

"We certainly did, but you were wise to stay in bed tonight. Tomorrow night, we go to the Lawsons and it would be a shame if you had to miss their dinner," her mother said.

"Oh, I'm sure I'll feel up to going tomorrow night if I behave myself." Amanda had already decided there would be no more moping around over the likes of Tony Branigan or any other man as long as she lived. That was a sacred vow she'd made only moments ago.

"Ah, that's my sweet girl," Jenny declared and planted a kiss on her forehead. Lisa gave her feet a pat and suggested to her sister, "Why don't we just let her rest, eh? We'll see you in the morning, *ma petite*."

Amanda told them goodnight and heaved a deep sigh. Her long seige of crying had worked, giving her the perfect symptoms of a nasty headcold. Tomorrow, she'd have a miraculous recovery. No one would ever know about the tears she'd shed over Tony Branigan.

Mark Kane did, though, after Slim Christy told him of Amanda's strange reaction to the news of Tony's departure. Christy, fearing he'd upset her, had mentioned their encounter to Mark that evening before dinner. So when his daughter didn't appear for dinner, Mark instantly doubted whether she was truly ill.

317

Kane was guilty of devious curiosity and he could not resist sneaking a peek into the leather case Tony had given him to present to Amanda on her eighteenth birthday. It was a gold-etched locket, heart-shaped, strung on an exquisite gold chain. Tony's brief note stated, "You have mine." Mark knew he meant his heart, so it was obvious to the rancher that his beautiful daughter and his gunfighter had enjoyed more than a casual relationship. If he was any judge of jewelry, he'd wager the locket with the diamond set in the center was an old Moreno family heirloom. He'd quickly put it back in the velvet-lined case and placed it in his desk drawer.

Knowing his impetuous daughter, Mark could not help worrying. He could imagine her wounded pride at Tony's not saying goodbye—which was obvious from what Slim had said. Jesus Christ, he was placed in a hell of a dilemma, as he came to think of it! His word was his bond even though it was his own beloved daughter, and he had given the young man his word.

Come the next evening, Mark Kane was exposed to a young lady who shot his theory straight to hell. Her mercurial manner should not have surprised him, but it did. She had never looked more breathtakingly beautiful or acted gayer than she did over at the Lawsons' dinner party in honor of Mona and Jeff's approaching marriage. She mingled among the guests and flirted almost outrageously, Mark considered, with the young gents. He was especially urged to flop her bustled bottom over his lap when she carried on with Derek Lawson, who Mark sensed had drunk too much.

Armand and Lisa seemed to be having a marvelous

time among their rancher friends, and this delighted Jenny. She, in turn, was more lively and gay. In fact, Mark Kane was the only one in a sober mood, it seemed to him.

Before the evening was over, Amanda had agreed to accompany Mona on a buying spree for her bridal trousseau. The next four weeks around the Circle K and the Big D Ranch would be hectic with wedding preparations, which Amanda knew would occupy her mind and energies so she would have no time to dwell on the tormenting thought of Tony Branigan.

By the time the Kane party loaded into the two buggies to travel through the night back home, Mark couldn't shake himself free of concern about his daughter. While the others chatted away he was quiet and thoughtful. The other occupants of the buggy he drove thought he was just feeling the effects of the flowing champagne. But it wasn't that at all. In fact, he had not drunk all that much and really didn't relish the bubbling wine.

He had found himself filled with instant repulsion at Derek's fawning over Amanda during the evening. It made him choke with disgust to think that six months ago he had been literally pushing Amanda at Derek Lawson. Christ, he had to have been daft! For once, he was glad the little minx had defied him. It would serve as a lesson to be remembered in the future, he mused as the buggy traveled ever closer to home.

TWENTY-NINE

The brownish-gray stone towers of the old mission chapel told Tony his grandfather's house was near as they always did when he returned to San Antonio from his wanderings. Usually, his chest swelled with happiness to see the towering structure and the majestic palm trees. Somehow, today that exhilarating feeling was not there.

He was weary in body and spirit. The trail seemed long and monotonous and it hadn't helped his mood to have to fight off three hooligans hell bent on robbing him of his purse and sharing his grub as he'd camped the first night away from the Circle K. His grub he'd offered to share with the three, but that was all.

God knows, the last thing in the world he wanted to see when he reined Picaro up to the familar old mansion was the carriage belonging to the Gomez family. Quickly directed the stallion around to go to the back entrance so he could steal into the back hallway and wait until the carriage departed.

Tony was quite successful in entering the back of the house after tending to Picaro himself when he saw no sign of Jose in the carriage house.

He almost dropped in his track when he heard, "Senor Moreno!" He quickly turned to quiet Ignacio sitting there in the kitchen with his foot propped up on a stool.

"I don't want to make myself known, Ignacio, until Grandfather's company leaves," he told his grandfather's devoted manservant. Ignacio gave him a broad, friendly grin and nodded his head. They went through a series of sign language gestures and whispers and Ignacio explained that young Jose was filling in for him today because he had a smashed big toe.

Tony gave him a comradely pat on the shoulders and a promise of seeing him later before going on upstairs to his room. Inside his room he yanked the drapes to the side to allow the sunlight in and casually tossed his gear in the massive leather chair. As he sank down on the side of the bed he thought to himself that this room and house would be his prison for the next few weeks.

Perhaps, it was thinking of it in this way that made it seem so unlike the haven it had always been in the past when he'd spent hours within these high ceilinged walls. That old bed of fine rosewood with its headboard that reached almost to the ceiling had been his bed since he was a small tot. He remembered how he used to feel lost in its vastness. On a nightstand was his treasured miniature picture of his lovely mother. The west wall displayed his gun collection, which he had began on his tenth birthday. His books, a rock collection started in boyhood, and that old oak desk should have warmed him more than they did. But he knew what it would take to warm him, and that golden-haired girl was miles away.

He ambled around the room with lazy motions, removing his shirt and his dusty black leather boots. As he strolled by the side of his desk, he noticed the small mountain of papers, and his nose picked up a sweet fragrance, the essence of a familar aroma. He picked up the note on top and saw that it was signed by Magdalena Gomez. Tossing it aside, he took each paper in turn and saw that most were from her. Now that he was back he had to face that unpleasant situation. There was no putting it off now.

A noise below called his attention and he went to the double door leading out to the balcony just outside his bedroom. He got his first glimpse of Francisco Gomez for many months. His grandfather Esteban accompanied him as he prepared to board his carriage. The two embraced like the dear friends they were and this, Tony reminded himself, had to remain somehow . . . some way!

He watched his aristocratic-looking grandfather turn and go back inside. Esteban Moreno still cut a striking figure. There was no slump to his shoulders and he still walked straight and proud. Tony remembered how as a youth he was impressed just by the appearance of his grandfather. Even now, he felt that way.

Bare-chested and barefooted, he left the room to go greet the elderly gentleman. By the time he made it down the steps his grandfather had already been informed and was looking up toward the upstairs gallery. "Antonio?"

"Yes, Grandfather. I'm coming down." He embraced him affectionately. "Just didn't want an audience with Francisco yet. Ignacio tell you I was here?"

"No, Jose. Do you need him to go out and tend to Picaro?"

"No, sir. I've already done that. I do need a drink, though," Tony grinned. Esteban smiled, too. "Then we shall have one. Come, Antonio . . . we'll go into the library."

Tony excused himself long enough to go back to his room to get one of the fine linen shirts neatly stacked in the drawer. They'd had no wear for months now and the soft feel of one of them on his body was good after the rough material of his work garb around the Circle K. He gave a fast stroke of his hairbrush to his tousled hair and went to join his grandfather in what he suspected would be a long gab fest.

They would talk and drink and then talk and drink some more. It sounded like a darn good idea to Tony. The old gentleman had an amazing capacity for liquor.

Ignacio and Jose heard the roaring laughter coming from the library an hour later. The reveling Morenos seemed to be enjoying themselves, the two Mexicans decided. They knew it would be a late, late dinner hour around the old mansion tonight.

They went ahead and ate their *elotes*, tamales wrapped in green corn leaves. Ignacio knew that the younger Moreno's taste differed from his grandfather's, so he always had a selection on hand to please the young man.

Almost anything would have pleased Tony that evening. Most of all the liquor was a balm. But it was Esteban's surprising news that took a tremendous load off his chest.

The sly gray fox had handed him a drink and an is-

323

sue of the *San Antonio News*, a four-day-old edition. At first Tony was puzzled, searching Esteban's amused-looking face until he read suddenly of his cousin Mario's marriage to Magdalena. He read on about their extended honeymoon on the Continent. Even more interesting to note was the last paragraph about how Mario would be joining the law firm of Gomez and they would be making their home in San Antonio.

It drew a roar of deep laughter from Tony and when he could calm himself, he jested, "I think, Grandfather . . . I think we should drink a toast to the happy couple." Christ, he'd have to thank his cousin from the bottom of his heart for taking Magdalena off his hands and his conscience. He had done him a monumental favor!

"Well, Antonio I see you greet the news with joy, eh?" Esteban's dark eyes twinkled. Even knowing what Tony had told him a few weeks ago he still hadn't been sure that his grandson would welcome his cousin's stealing his girl away and marrying her. There was his male ego to consider.

"I must thank Mario when next we meet, Grandfather," Tony laughed. "And Francisco . . . how did he take it?" Tony suspected it was with a glad heart. Always, he'd had the feeling that Francisco approved more of the Moreno family in general than of him, Tony, as an individual.

"I think he is reconciled." Like an impish child, Esteban moved his chair closer to Tony and nudged him on the knee. "You will appreciate this, Antonio. Francisco came here to soothe me, not knowing that I'd already accepted the fact that there would be no marriage between you and Magdalena after what you'd told me. You should have seen him."

"I bet he was a nervous wreck. Probably hadn't slept the night before and expected that Moreno temper to flare, eh?"

"Oh, it was funny! When he took great pains to tell me quietly about the announcement in the paper of the marriage and in the most diplomatic way to excuse Mario's and Magdalena's irresponsible behavior, I must tell you I could have been an actor." With dramatic gestures, Esteban declared, "I was truly magnificent!"

"I bet you were, you old fox," Tony gave him a broad grin. "I would have been delighted to have been behind that velvet drape watching."

Ignacio had guessed right about the time they would finally decide to dine. He'd prepared a light dinner, knowing the two had indulged heavily in drinks.

After they had dined and enjoyed cheroots while still sitting at the table, Tony brought up a subject of more serious nature. "I must insist that Ignacio and Jose keep my presence here a secret. What about the women? How many are now in the house, Grandfather?"

"I find the need for only one regular woman, Antonio. I have another who comes occasionally. My social life has slackened off, especially with you gone out of town."

"The regular . . . is that still Elvira?"

"*Si*, the bossy Elvira who drives Ignacio crazy," Esteban chuckled.

"Then there is no problem. Elvira will do as I ask," Tony told his grandfather.

The hour closed in on midnight and an overwhelming relaxed feeling engulfed Tony, forcing him to bring an end to pleasant reunion with his grandfather. He rose up from the comfortable chair, said goodnight, and sought that massive bed upstairs that he would welcome getting lost in tonight. He fell immediately into a deep sleep, too tired for dreams of the golden-haired girl he'd left back in Gonzales County.

That golden-haired girl back in Gonzales County had firmly convinced herself that she hated that overbearing conceited Branigan. Once she'd ridden herself of all the tears in her body and dried her eyes the day she'd found out he was gone, she stuck her pert little nose in the air swearing never again to wear her heart on her sleeve. It wasn't worth it, and the hurt was too great!

So it was as the days passed. With company in the hacienda and the extra activities of the wedding, the hours of the day were taken up. She and Lisa had enjoyed the late night hours, much as they had when she was living in New Orleans. Perhaps it was their endless chatter coupled with a few glasses of wine that had induced her sleep to sleep every night. Whatever it was she had been sleeping.

The next two weeks were to be busy ones. There was the trip to San Antonio, which would take a few days, and shortly after their return from the shopping spree there would be the celebration of Amanda's eighteenth birthday.

Who had the time to miss the likes of Tony Branigan?

The one person who couldn't seem to let her forget

him was her Aunt Lisa. She wanted to muzzle her on occasion. Dear Lord, he'd left an impression! As quickly as Lisa would bring him up, Amanda would change the subject. With Aunt Lisa, though, it wasn't always so easy.

On more than one occasion during her aunt's visit Amanda had surprised herself with a sudden new opinion of the lady who had had her so entranced at this time last year. Was it because she was older? Was this eighteenth birthday making her leave her girlhood behind in more than one way? She was no sweet innocent, as she'd been a year ago. That was for sure, and she had Branigan to thank for it!

No, it wasn't just that, for that wasn't the only change, she had to confess to herself. Little things . . . a million little things made up the scenerio.

She did look at her vivacious aunt in a different light than when they'd last been together, and she especially saw her in a less flattering way when her mother and Lisa were together. More and more Amanda found herself admiring Jenny. Even her dark loveliness would last longer than the attractiveness of the more fashion-conscious Lisa.

Lisa's frivolous chatter didn't hold her spellbound by the hour as it had back in New Orleans. Amanda found herself moving over in the parlor at nights after they'd dined to seek her father's company as he talked with Armand, leaving Lisa and Jenny to their women's talk.

It had not gone unnoticed by Lisa and she'd quizzed her older sister about it. The truth was Lisa had intended approaching Amanda about returning to the city with them right after the Christmas holidays and

Jeff's wedding. After all, the girl would be eighteen, and Lisa thought she had found the perfect mate for her ravishingly beautiful niece.

When her sister had mentioned Amanda to Jenny, she'd smiled proudly. "Yes, Lisa . . . I think Amanda has changed. She's matured a lot, especially the last three or four months. I've noticed it too." The truth of it was Jenny Kane was more than pleased with the change. She wanted Amanda to have a more meaningful life than her party-going sister had. She feared that one day Lisa would find herself a very lonely lady.

Jenny smiled at her rather perplexed sister. "When Amanda came home it was a very hard time for her to adjust to our rather uneventful life after all the glitter and flamboyance of New Orleans. You see, Lisa, I can remember all those marvelous times. But when it's all said and done, Lisa dear, Amanda's roots are here in Texas where she was born and raised. Wander she may, but this is home."

Lisa sat silent unable to speak, for she saw all her lovely plans melting away. Her sister, she suspected, spoke the truth. Just like Jenny, when her passion for a man had whisked her away from New Orleans and brought her here to Texas, Amanda's passion for that handsome man Lisa had seen her with would keep her here in Texas.

Lisa decided then and there she'd not succeed in getting Amanda to return home with them. It made her sad. She knew it would dampen the rest of her visit at the Circle K.

Lisa could not share her feelings with her beloved Armand. She did not dare confess her excruciating hurt that Amanda was no longer an adoring audience.

The lovely Madame Vega found herself desiring to return to her familar surroundings, where the eager young dandies anxiously catered to her and gathered to sing their praises of her loveliness at the fancy soirèes. This dull Texas scene had her in a deep depression.

Mon Dieu, the last straw had broken last night when Armand bored her to tears as they lay in bed and he spoke excitedly about those horrible old longhorns. She knew she must cut this visit short before she went mad or withered away.

THIRTY

The slumped petite figure in silk and taffeta lay on the canopied bed, the vision of despair. The pelting sleet continued to remind her of the abominable weather outside that had ruined her birthday celebration. A lot of good it had done to dress up in her lovely gown of scarlet taffeta and silk and to dress her hair with bright scarlet bows pinned among the curls.

Amanda had never had such a disappointing birthday, and everyone said the eighteenth birthday was to be a most special occasion. Pooh, it wasn't, she thought dejectedly.

It had ground on her nerves that everyone had tried so hard to make up for the absence of the Alvarados and the Lawsons. By seven that evening Mark Kane came back into the hacienda and announced, "No hope of any of them getting over the roads. They'd be crazy."

Jenny had agreed and left the room to inform Consuela to carry on with the serving of dinner. There was no point in delaying any longer with false hopes. After dinner, Amanda sat with her family gathered around her as she opened her gifts. There was a grand array of lovely things from her parents and the usual lavish presents from her Aunt Lisa and Uncle Armand. She oohed and ahed over each of them as she knew she should and she tried to be gay, forcing an excitement that wasn't in her at all.

It was at the end of the evening after her mother and their guests had retired upstairs, with only Jeff and her father remaining downstairs that the surprise of the evening came for Amanda. The one bright moment of the evening, and it had to be Tony Branigan who brought it about.

Jeff's mood had been similar to hers with his fiancèe absent tonight. So he'd remained downstairs to have another glass of wine before going up to bed. Amanda had urged him to pour her one too. He smiled and went to fetch the drinks. Mark sat quietly having his nightcap of brandy and gave no protest to either his son or daughter, though he was certain both had already had enough. After all, he considered it little compensation for Amanda's disappointing night.

She had not fooled him. On that score, she was too much like him. There was no hypocrite in Amanda, and she did not wear a mask very well where her feelings were concerned. Somehow, Kane had not found the right time to carry out Tony's request. The hour had grown later and later. The time had to be now, he told himself when he saw Jeff returning with the wine.

"Well, honey . . . I'm going to take my wine and go upstairs. Happy birthday, Amanda. Wish it could have been more fun for you. Let's make up for it later, eh?" Jeff bent and gave her a brotherly kiss. Amanda smiled and gave him a nod.

Mark wasted no more time, for he'd carried the

small leather case in his pocket all evening. He'd pondered what her reaction would be, knowing what he knew about her and Tony.

"Amanda, here is one more birthday gift for you." He held out his hand with the tiny black case and she took it. As she started to protest that they had already given her enough, Mark quickly informed her, "But this is not from us, as you'll see when you open it, honey."

Tiny it might have been, but the little diamond in the center of the gold heart seemed to wink with great brilliance there in the dim light of the parlor. So exquisitely lovely it was, she saw, as with trembling fingers she held it up letting it swing on the dainty gold chain.

"It's lovely, isn't it Dad?" she mumbled in a faltering little voice. At the same time she awkwardly unfolded the note from Tony. Her hand shook and she couldn't control it.

"Very lovely, Amanda. He left it with me before he left the next morning."

Under her breath, she mumbled silently what a cowardly way he'd chosen. He could not face her. He dare not!

"He gave it to you the night before he left?" Her eyes were overbright.

"That's right, honey. Said for me to give it to you on your birthday," Mark told his daughter, wishing he could tell her more, for Mark firmly didn't believe that absence made the heart grow fonder. Quite the reverse, to his way of thinking, and he didn't like what he saw out of young Lawson. He couldn't hold a candle to Tony Moreno.

"I see." Her lovely face puzzled Mark. It was expressionless, giving him no hint of what was going on behind those lovely deep blue eyes. He could not know the hurting wound he'd just opened up again. Like a gash just starting to heal, she was bleeding again.

"Here, princess . . . let's put it around your neck and see what it looks like," Mark said.

Rather numbed, Amanda sat, holding up her long curls and allowing her father to place the dainty locket around her neck and fasten it. "Ah, that's pretty, Amanda."

She gave him a smile and willed herself to come alive if only to get from the parlor to her room. "I think so too, Dad. Even with the awful weather and everyone couldn't come I had a beautiful birthday. I thank you and Mama for everything," she told her father, even managing a light, soft laugh. Her act was good enough to please her father and convince him that her spirits were far higher than they were.

"I'm glad, honey."

"Well, do you suppose us two old night owls should go to bed?" She took his arm to go toward the stairway.

"You go ahead and I'll check all the doors," he suggested. "You know, Amanda . . . M . . . Branigan is quite a fellow." Christ, he had to practically bite his tongue to keep from saying Moreno!

By this time Amanda's back was turned and she was near the base of the steps. She dared not turn around as she replied, "Oh, yes . . . Branigan is quite a man!" To herself she lamented privately, if only he knew the whole of the man.

As she moved swiftly around the gallery, the mist of tears teased her long eyelashes and by the time her

333

bedroom door was closed a torrent of tears flowed down her cheeks. She flung herself and the many yards of taffeta across her bed. By the time she quit sobbing the only thing she was aware of was the caress of the gold heart-shaped locket. Otherwise she felt dead with numbness. The dead quiet of the night was invaded only by the sleet outside.

It seemed like Tony Branigan himself . . . this little locket. The warmth of him came to her all too vividly with the feel of it at her throat.

As she undressed she stood before the full-length mirror, her eyes going to the small gold locket. "Do I truly have your heart, Tony? If that were true how could you have left me so easily?"

But that nasty little voice that seemed to delight in showing her the other side of things and throwing a cog in the wheels prodded at her. It was, after all, a cheap fee for her whore's services to the gunfighter. Think, Amanda, it urged! Did he ever ask you to marry him? The answer was no. He'd not even had the gracious manners to tell her goodbye like a loving man would surely do. No, he had sneaked away in the dawn's early light to be gone God knows where.

When she finally finished undressing completely and slipped into her gown to crawl between the sheets, another thought insidiously crept in.

No, nothing like that had to cause her concern. Of that she was certain. She told the little voice to shut its filthy, devious mouth. She wasn't due to have her monthly flow for a day or two yet, she was sure.

She lay there listening to the sleet and it began to have a tranquilizing effect on her. Sleep came over her. But with sleep dreams came too, and they were of a tall, towering man with blue-black hair and pale silver-gray eyes whose kiss enflamed her with insatiable desire. She woke up, clammy with sweat on this chilly winter night. "Damn you, Branigan! Damn you straight to hell!" She prayed he was in as much torment as she was, but he, most likely, was lying in another woman's arms warming her with his sensuous lips and hard male body.

The sudden drop in temperatures that had brought the sleet early in the day of Amanda's birthday was reversed by the next morning. The air laden with moisture spreading over Gonzales County from the coastline moved northward, leaving the Circle K in bright sunshine. Dawn broke with the promise of a beautiful winter day.

Lisa Vega sat up in her bed with the mountain of pillows at her back as Armand tied the cord of his fancy maroon velvet robe to prepare to go downstairs to order his wife some coffee.

"You are a most handsome man, Armand. I was just thinking how very selfish I've been to wisk you away from New Orleans when so many of our friends will be having their holiday parties. Monique shall never forgive me, I know!"

"Ah, *ma petite* . . . she will. We'll stay home next year, if you wish? I would prefer it personally, and if you wish to go home early, we will. Anything you want, chèrie."

"Oh, yes, Armand . . . right after Christmas!" While Armand had to admit he'd had his fill of the "wilds" of Texas, he was rather shocked by his wife's declaration. His rump and thighs had endured enough

335

pain and he'd prefer his fancy gig to horseback any day. He was accustomed to his coffee being brought to him and didn't relish the trip now down the stairs.

Armand's handsome aquiline features were drawn in a frown as he did the finishing touches to securing his robe. "Are you saying, *ma petite*, that you wish to leave right after Christmas and not remain for Jeff's wedding a few days later?"

"Yes, *mon chèr* . . . that is what I am saying. I am so, so homesick I could cry," she dramatically remarked. Knowing her husband's generous heart and his worshipping love for her she was sure she'd not be denied.

He rushed to the bed and kissed her tenderly. "Then I will set about making our plans. I will now confess to you that I, too, am ready to get back to the comfort of our own home and the comfort of my offices instead of all this. Our ways are different, *oui?*"

"Worlds apart . . . a million worlds apart, Armand."

"Rest and we will announce our plans later. Until then it will be our little secret," Armand said, giving her a broad grin.

Almost childlike, she became very excited, her lovely face radiant and her eyes flashing. "Oh, yes, Armand. Let's don't say a word for a day or two. I don't want Jenny to nag me about staying on through the wedding."

Armand assured her he would be the one to break the news to the Kanes that they would be going home before the wedding. "I will claim that business urges me to get back. As you know, I had a letter the other day from Darias, so I can use that as our excuse for leaving a week earlier than we'd originally planned."

He turned and left a pleased Lisa sitting in bed to await his return upstairs. When Armand did return a few minutes later he was flustered and embarrassed. His was mortified to have encountered the stately, elegant Señora Alvarado in his state of attire.

"*Mon Dieu*, there is no formality in this place at all. Can you imagine, Lisa, guests coming to call at such an ungodly hour?" He gave a deep laugh," I think it is time we go home."

The two smiled at each other in complete understanding. Each hungered with deep yearning to be back where they were lavishly pampered by several house servants, along with Armand's personal valet and Lisa's French lady's maid.

Below their bedroom in the spacious parlor Jenny sat with her guest, Bianca Alvarado. "It was sweet of you, Bianca, to bring this present to Amanda, and I'm so sorry the weather didn't cooperate so you and your family could have attended."

As Consuela came into the room with a tray of coffee, Bianca greeted her in a friendly voice. "I bring greetings also to you, Consuela, from your daughter. She is doing just fine. I think she and Diego are making a good life for themselves."

"*Gracias*, Señora Alvarado," Consuela smiled, setting the tray on the table and backing away to leave the ladies to their visit.

As the two drank their coffee, Bianca discouraged Jenny's suggestion that she call for Amanda to come down. Bianca insisted that she was probably tired from all her celebrating. "You must forgive my bad manners in calling so early, but I had to go into Gonzales and I wanted to drop off this gift for her."

Jenny laughed. "It isn't too early for me at all, as you know, Bianca. I think Amanda must have stayed up much later, though. My brother-in-law and my sister are not the early risers we are here at the ranch."

"I rather gathered that from his shock at the sight of me," Bianca laughed softly. In fact, the very distinguished-looking gentleman had stared at her in the oddest way, she'd thought, as he'd almost collided with her as he whirled around the base of the stairs.

The women were in the midst of lighthearted chatter and Jenny was seeing Bianca to the door when Amanda made an appearance.

Bianca's usual poise was cracked when she noted her sister's locket on Amanda's neck. With her usual reserve and guarded emotions, she complimented Amanda about it.

"A gift from Mister Branigan," Amanda announced.

"Very pretty," Bianca coolly commented. "Well, I must be on my way, and by the way, Amanda dear, I left a little gift with your mother for your birthday." Adding her regrets that she and her family could not attend the dinner the night before, Bianca departed.

All the way into Gonzales Bianca Alvarado's thoughts were back at the Circle K Ranch. It was startling to see Theresa's locket around Amanda's throat. It brought back a flood of memories. Something else brought back a flood of memories . . . memories she had never thought to feel ever again. The brush of his hand had been slight, but the stirring within her was tremendous, for not since Miguel had a man so impressed her as he had. His eyes were as dark as hers

338

and the intensity of them had made her as giddy as a schoolgirl. For the first time since she'd fallen in love with Miguel Moreno she had seen—in Armand Vega —a man who could have stirred her interest.

All the way into Gonzales she kept envisioning the strong features of his face. He was a striking-looking gentleman!

THIRTY-ONE

A stubby black growth of beard now covered Tony's face. He knew that soon that beard would be changing his appearance drastically, especially when he donned the garb of a renegade, along with an old serape and sombrero. There would be little left to remind anyone of the clean-shaven Tony Branigan or Tony Moreno. By the time he met up with Pedro Salazar, they'd make a motley pair well befitting their assumed roles.

His patience was already wearing thin and the walls of the Moreno mansion with all its luxuries, its library of endless rows of books to read, and even Esteban's pleasant company were wearing on his nerves. He was ready for action!

Already he'd tested the garb he'd be masquerading in daily once he rode out to join Salazar at Palito Blanco. A few nightly visits to a couple of the lowly cantinas on the outskirts of San Antonio had broken up the long, lonely nights, since he could not take part in the normal activities of his life in San Antonio, or mingle with his circle of friends and business acquaintances. His one comforting refuge was the ranch, and even then he rode out and back only under the cover of darkness. At the Casa del Plata he did a lot of day-dreaming, as he was certain Mark Kane had done in his young manhood about his Circle K Ranch. It was a strange, new experience for him but he found himself fantasizing about the handsome son or the gorgeous daughter he and Amanda would have. He'd never thought of children when he'd intended to marry Magdalena.

Two would be fine, Tony daydreamed, and projecting the future. He was a selfish man where Amanda was concerned and he didn't want their whole life swallowed up by children, or her sensuous, lovely body yearly swollen with a baby. No, this was not for him!

Maybe this was a reflection back to his own childhood, for he'd never shared with a sister or brother and the truth of it was he'd never missed it. To be the center of his mother's attention and then Grandfather Moreno's had been a delight.

In the last few weeks he and Jose had become close companions and the young Mexican drove him in the buggy on his various trips around the city. Jose was known to be employed by Esteban Moreno, which provided Tony with safe passage wherever he sought to go.

This afternoon he would meet with Flanigan at the designated spot picked by the U.S. marshal. When the appointed time came, Tony went out the back of the house to the carriage house where Jose was already waiting for him.

Tony leaped up into the buggy and gave the order to go. He slumped into the position of an elderly man on the seat. "How's this, Jose?" he gave a light chuckle.

All this intrigue had greatly enhanced young Jose's daily routine and he was enjoying himself thoroughly. "Fine, Señor Moreno. You look very, very old."

"Well, now, I don't have to look all that old," Tony teased him and they both laughed as they traveled down the shaded drive ready to emerge into the street.

They went past the row of fine old homes of the city and turned to the left to go down the dirt road that led to the San Antonio River. It was there, in a small isolated shack, that Flanigan and Tony would meet.

Jose reined the bay around to the back of the shack and Tony leaped down, going on in as he recognized Flanigan's horse outside the shack.

"You are looking as mangy as old Tito, Tony," Flanigan quipped in that crackling voice of his.

"Thought that was the general idea," Tony retorted, flinging aside the battered sombrero to run his fingers through his thick hair.

"Sit down. I got a short time and lots to do. Everything seems to be hitting me from all sides this afternoon. When you get the word down from me, you're to come here, and old Tito will be waiting to take you into the camp at Palito Blanco. When we hit there and make the final roundup of the bastards, that will be the last link in the long chain. Encino and Reynosa stations will have already been hit and the outlaws arrested or killed, one or the other."

"You are convinced Tito is trustworty?" After all, his life was going to be in this dude's hands when he rode into that nest of vipers.

Chewing on the end of his cigar, Flanigan nodded his head with an assuring air.

"Then what's got you troubled, Brett?" He'd

known Flanigan for several years and the law officer had something bothering him.

"Well, Tony . . . I'm not going to lie to you. Pedro seems to be carrying off his role so I don't think there will to be any problem about you going in as his old buddy when you get to Palito Blanco. It's old Tito I'm concerned about. I've come to think a lot of that old hooligan and he's proved his weight in salt to me. But I think he's been found out, and our only ace in the hole is we've got these two dudes in jail right now. But when they were brought in I was sitting in the office there talking to Tito. One of them gave him a funny look."

"What were they jailed for?"

"Robbing and killing a rancher just outside Encino, and we're wondering if they have any connection to the Encino bunch and pulled this job on the side on their own."

"Guess we just have to play the cards as they fall, eh?"

"Guess we do, Tony. Hey, before you go let me wish you a happy holiday. I'm going home and forget all this until afterwards. Tell that old rascal Esteban hello for me? Suppose he'll even speak to me again after all this?" Flanigan laughed.

Tony got up and stretched his long legs. "I don't know whether I will, Flanigan. Haven't mentioned it before, but you've played hell with my love life."

"Can't have been that bad, Moreno, knowing you," Flanigan laughed, tossing his stub of a cigar on the dirt floor.

Tony laughed giving him a crooked grin. "Let's just say I'm going to try to start the New Year off right and make up for a lot of lost time. See you."

The rendezvous broke up and the Moreno buggy headed back toward the Moreno house and the city.

The shops were filled with shoppers and the streets were busy with the flow of buggies and horses mounted with their riders. Vendors dotted every corner. The odors of roasted peanuts and tamales permeated the air. The scents of the dyes of the peddlers' bright blankets and crafted wreaths and tied clusters of holly, pine, and cedar mingled with the many smells of the city street. Strolling musicians played their songs, taking the tokens offered them by the passing shoppers.

It was a rather festive atmosphere with the approach of Christmas that mild winter day. Tony and Jose found the street they turned on to reach the Moreno house much more crowded and busy than when they'd come the same way about an hour ago.

Jose had to bob and veer the buggy to move through the narrow street. Tony had assumed his role of the hunched old man with his wide-brimmed sombrero angled down over his face. A light, lilting laugh brought him instantly alive and the self-imposed years vanished as he sat up straight in the seat and cocked the sombrero to the side.

There, less that twenty feet away from him and Jose, in a buggy traveling parallel to them, was the golden-haired girl of his dreams. With her was Mona Lawson, and driving the buggy was the man he knew he must kill or be killed by. The score had not been settled and it must be.

The three of them were laughing and talking in the gayest manner. He watched Amanda with such a hungry yearning he felt he could choke. Those golden curls bobbed up and down her back as she chattered away, and while he couldn't see her face with her back turned to him, he could imagine its breathtaking loveliness framed in the deep green velvet bonnet. The short velvet jacket she wore outlined the curves of her tiny waist snugly. Tony stared like someone in a trance.

He didn't care that Jose was creeping along. He could now enjoy the sight he'd longed to see for so many nights now. The only thing galling him, stabbing at him like an adder shooting its venom into his flesh, was the sight of the beautiful Amanda so close to Derek. He had to remain silent and endure the agony.

Something caused Amanda to turn slightly on the seat, scanning the crowd, and in doing so, her eyes noticed the buggy riding alongside theirs. She remarked to Mona beside her, "That's a fine-looking rig for that young boy to be driving." She looked again, admiring the glossy black leather top and tufted seat. There on the side between the front and back wheels was the letter M in silver. She had no doubt it belonged to one of the most prosperous citizens of the city.

Derek's eyes darted in that direction and he barked gruffly, "That crazy Mex is about ready to get a touch of my whip if he doesn't move over."

"Oh, Derek, it's a narrow street," Mona pointed out to her short-tempered brother.

Tony heard what the overbearing, arrogant Lawson had said. A recklessness made him lean over to look at the trio. The thought that his beard was not full grown didn't stop him. The rumpled hair hanging over his forehead and his other disguises apparently were enough to fool Derek Lawson. But Amanda felt a strange magnetism in the dirty, disheveled older Mexican with his battered old brown sombrero with the golden band and his many-colored serape. Her Aunt Lisa would have termed it deja vu, but all she knew was that as he stared at her their eyes locked as if in an embrace and she could not turn away.

It was silly, or so she told herself as Derek finally had an opening in the road to pull around them. The intensity of that strange Mexican's glaring eyes remained with her long after Derek had left her and Mona off at the dressmaker's shop intending to pick them up in a hour.

Mona noted the sudden quietness of her friend who had been bubbling with vivaciousness and gaiety earlier. Amanda shook her head and candidly admitted, "I can't tell you, Mona. I truly can't. If I tried, you'd call me crazy." She gave out an uneasy laugh. "You know me and my crazy changeable moods. You know me, Mona. Lord, if anyone does, it's you."

Mona calmed her concern that Amanda had suddenly taken ill and went about the shopping for her trousseau. The list was long and the time was growing so short now that every minute in San Antonio had to count. She knew that she and Jeff were being utterly selfish in insisting that their wedding be performed immediately after the busy holiday. It was Jeff's idea and she wasn't about to suggest a delay when she could have the one thing she'd wished for all her life . . . to be Jeff's wife!

Amanda's gown was a pale blue silk, similar in style to Mona's wedding gown. The owner's assistant, a lady of Spanish descent, attended to Amanda's fitting. She brought the gown into the dressing room and helped her slip into it. As she finished fastening it, she commented, "Your proportions are close to perfection, Señorita Kane. Why, I think I could now stitch you a gown to fit without a second fitting."

"It's a beautiful gown, and I love the shade of blue," Amanda complimented the seamstress. "It looks fine to me."

"I agree. Shall we take it off?" Adele Sanchez asked. "I fear you will have a little wait for your little friend in the next room. Claudia is having to take up the bustline a half-inch on both sides, and with the lace overlay she has a tedious job with the pinning."

Adele neatly draped Amanda's gown over her arm and prepared to go through the curtained doorway. "Would it be more pleasant to sit out front? If you would like I could get you a cup of coffee or tea and you can sit on the far more comfortable settee."

"Thank you, Adele, I think I prefer that, and I will have a cup of coffee if it isn't too much trouble?"

"Not at all, Señorita Kane. My pleasure." She smiled, leaving Amanda to straightening the curls of her slightly messed-up hair.

For the first fifteen or twenty minutes Amanda enjoyed watching the stream of people passing by the dress shop and enjoyed the refreshing cup of coffee. All the time she was giving way to daydreams, thinking about all those girlish romantic dreams she'd had about a big, fancy wedding when she married. Now, she seriously thought it might be more fun and more romantic to just elope and forego all the many, many details involved with a big wedding. Sweet Jesus, poor Mona was going to be a nervous wreck by the time she and Jeff finally got to themselves.

The uniformed gentleman with the adoring young miss hanging possessively on his arm saw her sitting there, but it was too late to retreat as he would have liked to. The young local lady with him had entered the shop to get a fan she'd had Adele put back for her a few days earlier and the same young lady was the girl he'd proposed to only two weeks ago. Steve Beckenridge had carried the memories of Amanda in his heart for several weeks after she'd returned to Gonzales County and once he'd been at the point of paying a visit to the Circle K Ranch to plead his cause with her.

Steve's practical, conservative streak had won out. Happiness for them would have been an elusive thing. He was a military man, a soldier, and certainly possessed no wealth. That night outside the Armory had told him how much woman Amanda was and it frightened him, as crazy as it might seem, for he was almost twice her age.

With Prudence, it had been different. She wasn't a ravishing beauty and she'd not expect so much from a man. Everything about her would adapt to the life she'd have to live as a soldier's wife. So Steve made himself put any thoughts of Amanda behind him, as wildly exciting as she had promised to be.

He had forgotten about the trip to the Circle K, flung himself into his work back at the fort, and, a month ago, Prudence had come into his life. She was sweet and easygoing, and she had eagerly invited his attentions.

"Amanda! Amanda Kane," he greeted her with a broad smile on his face, urging Prudence a little ahead of him.

"Well, Steve Beckenridge! How nice to see you,"

348

Amanda cooed sweetly, presenting the perfect picture of the coquette with that provocative smile on her beautiful lips and those twinkling, flirting eyes.

The mere sight of Amanda intimidated the shy Prue Austin. She looked like a lovely lady in one of the women's fashion magazines. And she acted so familar with Steve.

"I'd like you to meet Prudence Austin, Amanda. Amanda Kane, Prudence . . . an old friend of mine."

"Nice to meet you, Prudence and as for you, Steve Beckenridge . . . I'm not that old!" She couldn't have looked lovelier if she'd tried. Steve couldn't control the sudden surge of desire within him any more than he could have stopped breathing.

A lump came into his throat when he tried to speak. "We're to be married in three weeks, Amanda." A feeling of contempt filled him, for the cracking of his voice was so obvious. He only hoped dear Prudence didn't sense the torment he was experiencing. That soldier part of him was trained to never show fear, but he felt so disgustingly weak it irked him.

"How marvelous! Well, I do declare this is surprising, Steve," Amanda exclaimed, letting her eyes dart from the young woman back over to the nervous Steve Beckenridge.

"Yeah, it all happened sorta' fast, didn't it, Prue?" He gave an uneasy laugh.

"I guess you could say that, dear," the young woman agreed, rather befuddled about the whole little scene unfolding before her. It was the first time she'd ever seen anything but an assured air about this captain she'd fallen so head over heels in love with.

"My, my, I would certainly say it must have been

love at first sight. You fairly swept this big fellow right off his feet, Prudence," Amanda deviously remarked, knowing Captain Beckenridge knew what she was referring to. She suddenly wished to spend no more time with the pair playing this silly game of deception she was indulging in, so without further ado, she made the excuse that she was due in the fitting room. Lifting her skirt and swishing around, she left the two standing there to go seek out Mona.

She gave a light laugh as soon as she was out of earshot. It was a laugh at herself, for she wondered how under God's good green earth she could have entertained the idea for one minute that a man like Steve Beckenridge could have filled the void Tony Branigan had left.

Bastard, he might be, but he was a man! That, Amanda, decided, put him a notch ahead of the captain. Not even in her wildest dreams could she envision Branigan quaking in his boots as she'd just seen Steve do.

Under her breath she heaved a deep sigh. Somewhere out there had to be another man like Tony. Somehow, she had to find him, or this searching heart of hers would never again know ecstasy, and would go wanting the rest of her life!

THIRTY-TWO

To have caught sight of Amanda for that all too brief moment there on the street left Tony glum and sullen for the rest of the evening. He was so ghostly silent as he sat at the long dining room table with Esteban that it bothered his grandfather.

Esteban's concern turned to anger, and the proud old gentleman, without saying a word, quietly left the table and his grandson there to brood over whatever it was bothering him. Obviously, Tony had no intentions of informing him, and Esteban would not prod it out of him.

Ignacio kept filling Tony's glass as he requested the servant to do and it was Ignacio's opinion that the younger Moreno was determined to get drunk. His assumption was correct, for Tony was like a man walking on a dry, hot desert. He ached for the golden-haired girl and the liquor was a mere substitute.

The grandfather clock struck twelve when he finally staggered away from the table and stumbled up the steps to his room. Old Ignacio stooped down to pick up the emptied glass Tony had knocked off the table but said nothing as the inebriated young señor lost his balance.

Ignacio tended to his chores before dimming the lights of the old mansion and then he went to his quarters at the back of the house. But his quarters were directly below Tony's room and he heard a sharp crash like something breaking upon impact with the floor. However, something told the Mexican servant it might be best if he ignored it.

His instincts were correct. The crash was a vase and the object of Tony's exploding Latin temper releasing its fury. The exquisite opaline vase lay in a million pieces.

The lovely Amanda was the cause of another man's fury that same night in another part of San Antonio.

Derek had had a bellyful of the fickle-minded female he was determined to have as his wife when he took over the reins and the rule of the Big D. One minute she encourages his ardor, and that he knew he was not imagining. The next moment, she was as cold as a winter's wind.

He knew that the wildest of fillies could be broken. He'd done it, and he remembered the exhilarating, lofty feeling when finally he'd subdue a highstrung horse. How much more gratifying it would be to subdue the beautiful Amanda. He'd ached to slap her face this evening.

He could still hear her voice saying to him earlier when they were along after dinner, "Derek, let's just drop the subject of marriage. What with Christmas and Mona's wedding, I think our poor families will need a rest."

"I will ask you again, Amanda." He'd given her that nice smile with the look of patience that he was so good at. Under his breath, he was telling himself that

352

he would not ask next time. He had stored in the vault of his mind a weapon he could use on Amanda, if it came to that. It would be a demand the next time and she would be forced to say yes. But that was a weapon he did not wish to use until after his sister was married to her brother. There was a perfection in his plan . . . a sequence into which each piece of his puzzle had to fit. In his crazed obsession, he would not allow anything to change his original plot.

Amanda would have shuddered with fear had she known the danger hovering so close, but Derek's madness was well hidden. The outward signs were rarely visible. Amanda just considered him a determined young man wanting his own way, as he always had.

Tony Branigan had suspected it, but Jeff Kane knew for sure Derek was a powder keg. He had treaded lightly until he could get Mona out from under the Lawson roof and away from Derek's reach. He didn't know what else he could do.

When Derek had declared his intentions of asking her again, Amanda saw no reason to have an unpleasant scene. After all, there was the long ride home the next day to be gotten through.

She shrugged her shoulders and flippantly retorted, "Well, you just ask away, Derek and who knows what the future holds. Certainly, I don't! Twenty-four hours can change one's whole life." It was Tony she saw in her thoughts as the words poured forth.

Anyway, it seemed to pacify Derek, and that was her aim.

The group gathered around the massive brownstone fireplace bedecked with garlands of greenery and a

353

huge wreath of holly hung at the center of the mantel presented the perfect family picture at the holiday season.

A massive pine, fat with green-needled branches, was decorated brightly and generously with colorful ornaments and took up the whole corner of the room with gifts spread underneath its boughs.

Consuela had served a succulent roast duck, garnishing the huge platter with her delicious baked apples sprinkled with nutmeg. There was a ham dotted with cloves for those who didn't like duck.

This evening was the time appointed for opening their gifts and was a private family affair with no guests invited. Even Jeff stayed at the Kane hearth foregoing his nightly visit to Mona.

After dinner, he singled out his sister for some reason unclear to him. Perhaps it was because when he walked into the room she was sitting alone, or maybe it was a nagging brotherly concern about his beautiful sister. Derek's constant visits to her annoyed Jeff. More and more he seemed to be the her only prospective suitor, and the long, lonely months could have a funny effect on a person.

"The eggnog is good, isn't it?" Amanda commented as he took his seat beside her. "Tell me, Jeff—are you having bridegroom jitters yet? It is countdown time now." She found it hard to put on a festive air with Jeff.

"Not really, Mandy. I guess with me and Mona it was so natural and expected. Nobody was surprised."

"That's true, isn't it? The more I think about it, I guess that's rather nice. Certainly wasn't meant to be that way with me," she said. Jeff saw the hint of sadness on her face. His sister wasn't her usual happy self.

"It wouldn't have surprised me to hear that you were leaving with Aunt Lisa and Uncle Armand," her brother confessed with a sheepish smile on his face.

"And miss the wedding? Heavens, no! In fact, that really came as a shock that they were leaving the day before. Weren't you rather taken back by their not staying for the wedding?"

"Yeah . . . in a way. But have you noticed Aunt Lisa? She'd so bored and poor Armand is so out of his element he's finding time heavy on his hands."

Amanda gave a light laugh. "You're right, Jeff. Believe me, I know that feeling, for I felt the same way those first two or three weeks after coming back."

"I got the feeling, sis, you got over that, though. Was I wrong?"

"No, Jeff you were right."

"I'm glad, Amanda. I really am." Jeff was feeling all warm with sentiment. Maybe it was the holiday season and the anticipation of his marriage to Mona. For several weeks now he had felt freed from the yoke of Derek's influence. "I missed you when you were gone those two years."

Amanda leaned over and kissed her handsome brother on the cheek. "You're sweet, Jeff, and I am truly happy about you and Mona." Any apprehensive feelings she'd had about Jeff back in the autumn months had been swept away. Even the puzzling afternoon in the old comissary had been forgotten. She just assumed that Jeff's time had been so taken up with courting Mona that he'd had little time left for Derek. It was rare that she'd seen the two of them together lately.

"Now, that's a touching scene," a voice cut into the scene of brother and sister kissing. They looked up to see their smiling aunt looking down at them.

"Aunt Lisa, I hadn't had a chance to tell you how lovely you look tonight in that gorgeous coral gown," Amanda exclaimed.

Compliments were an intoxicating ingredient as necessary to Lisa as the air she breathed and she responded with delight, "Ah, chèrie . . . thank you." She bent down to whisper in a low voice, "I am going to have to starve myself, though, when I get home. All this cooking has made every one of my gowns practically choke me. I can hardly breathe, I have to confess." She broke into that infectious laugh of hers and Amanda and Jeff joined in.

Amanda had attributed her own slightly fuller breasts and her slightly thicker waistline to less activity and fewer rides on Prince. In fact, only this afternoon she's vowed that she was going to go riding more than she had the last four weeks. She, too, could swear she'd put on three or four pounds. "You look fine, Aunt Lisa."

"No, no," Lisa disgreed with Amanda. "The French cuisine with its rich sauces is enough alone, but you mix in the Indian and the Spanish blends to make what your Consuela calls her hearty Mexican dishes and oh, la, la . . . the pounds have to come. I must say, though, I plan to serve some of her delectable dishes at my next soirée when we get home."

Amanda smiled, "You are anxious to get back to New Orleans, aren't you?" Her deep blue eyes teased her aunt.

Lisa patted her hand. "I confess I am. I could not lie to you, my little darling. We know one another too well, eh?"

Amanda nodded. Jeff excused himself and Lisa took a seat beside her niece. For a moment neither said anything as they indulged in slow sips of the eggnog and observed the others clustering at the far side of the room over by the hearth.

Lisa finally broke the moment of silence. "I don't mean to be nosy, but tell me, Amanda, are you interested in this young rancher who comes to court you so religiously . . . this Derek Lawson?"

"I don't know, Aunt Lisa." Amanda drawled her reply with a thoughtful air. "Perhaps I should be."

"*Mon Dieu*, what are you saying, chèrie? You make it sound so . . . so routine. I can't believe my ears, Amanda. Not you, of all people."

Amanda jerked around, aware that she had obviously shocked her aunt. "I only meant that we come from similar backgrounds and I guess we've rather been slotted like Jeff and Mona to be a likely pair to marry someday."

"And that is enough for you, Amanda?" A frown creased Lisa's lovely face, for this did not seem at all like the girl she knew in New Orleans with all that life and fire.

"I've begun to wonder if what you want is always right or if some unknown force keeps you from having it."

"No, no, Amanda. You wait and it will come. You are young . . . only eighteen! You wait, *ma petite!* Hear me well, Amanda. You wait!"

Her aunt's emotional outburst puzzled Amanda,

357

and it continued to do so long after all the gifts had been opened and the evening had come to an end in the early morning hours. Even after she was finally alone in her bedroom and everyone had retired for the evening, Lisa's words stuck with her.

In the next two weeks and after Lisa and Armand Vega had left the Circle K Ranch, she could not forget her aunt's advice and her serious manner. Other things began plague Amanda. Two days after the departure of the Vegas as she was dressing for her brother and Mona's wedding she was caught in a brief, but whirling feeling, and she could have sworn she was going to faint. It was Mona, not she who should be feeling giddy, she told herself.

At the wedding reception the mixture of champagne and rich cake had a most unpleasant effect on her and she was very queasy. Derek caught her out on the terrace and asked if she was ill.

"You look white as a sheet, Amanda. Here, sit down before you fall down," he insisted. She obeyed, allowing him to place her in the chair.

"Thank you, Derek. It seemed so stuffy in there suddenly."

He'd taken a seat beside her. "Christ, I don't think I'd want all that darn pomp and ceremony. I actually feel sorry for Jeff and Mona," she said.

"So do I," he wholeheartedly agreed with her. Somehow, it seemed nice to her to have his support and understanding. Derek's company was all she wanted and they continued to sit out there away from the noisy, milling crowd, and that suited Amanda just fine.

By the time it was over and the newlyweds had left

for their brief honeymoon, Amanda boarded the buggy with her parents to return to the Circle K feeling back to normal.

It had been a beautiful wedding and Mona had been a lovely bride in her snowy white gown. Amanda had never seen her look more beautiful than she had with the white veil framing her dark-complected face. How bright her black eyes gleamed! Jeff was handsome and his eyes were radiant as they adored his lovely bride. Amanda hoped with all her heart they would be happy. It seemed the two of them had waited their whole lifetimes for this very moment.

The aura of romance was overwhelming and Amanda herself a stranger in it. As she undressed, taking off the lovely pale blue gown and flinging it across the chair, she had never felt more lost and lonely. When she was completely naked, she stared at herself in the full-length mirror. Her body and every fiber of her being felt a desperate need for the fire of the tall gunfighter with his devouring eyes. Oh, how his heat could have melted the chill of the winter and satisfied the hunger gnawing so at her!

She let her hands roam across the front of her stomach and back to her waistline to rest there. There was more fullness to her figure. To ascertain it, she turned sideways.

"Hmm, I am going to have either to quit eating or exercise more," she spoke to herself and the empty room. Never had she had the slightest little hint of a tummy. Always it had been flat, even when her appetite had been ravenous and hearty. She never gained weight!

In the deepest, most secret part of her mind a

thought sparked and all the shrugging it aside did not make it go away. It had been time for her to have her woman's period and it had not happened. It was well past a few days now. To be more exact, she finally admitted as she lay awake staring at the ceiling, it was more than a few weeks.

What was it Chita had confessed to her when she'd miscarried that day after she'd married Diego? She'd been two months late when she'd married Diego. Then the miscarriage had happened a short time after the marriage.

Dear God, what would she do if it was true? So frightened was she at the possibility that she sat up in the bed in a cold, clammy sweat. She could well imagine the horrible torment Chita must have gone through for the days and nights before she'd married Diego. She was Amanda Kane, daughter of Mark Kane. The disgrace on the proud Kane name would tarnish it for years to come, and it would break her mother's heart. The impact of it all made her take a deep breath. No, it could not be!

That annoying little voice that dared to be honest when she sought to deny things as she had so often where Tony Branigan was concerned, came and pestered her there in the darkness. Remember that last night when the two of them had lain together in Tony's quarters, it prodded. Remember how he carried you to the peak of wild desire until you thought you would surely die had he not filled you with the searing liquid fire . . . his flaming body possessing you completely?

Dear God, she did remember, and nothing could make her forget it ever! If she did wed another, no man would ever do to her what Tony Branigan had. Somehow, she just knew it!

But that damn Branigan was gone, and she'd never lay eyes on him again. In the meanwhile, if what she suspected was true, she would have to do what Chita had done, as much as the whole idea was repugnant to her.

A few more weeks would give her the answer she feared to find out.

THIRTY-THREE

Two days after Christmas, Pedro Salazar rode into the roadhouse of the outlaws in Encino with his saddlebags stuffed with the so-called payoff from the operation at Reynosa. The first "domino" of Flanigan's well-paid plan had gone without a hitch. Four Anglos and one Mexican were now behind bars in Reynosa. The cattle was being held by the authorities until the tedious arrangements could be made for their return to their rightful owners. That was going to be a mammoth task with the brands altered.

Along with the five outlaws arrested in Reynosa, the two wealthy Mexican ranchers buying the stolen cattle had been detained by the authorities. Pedro Salazar rode into Encino with trepidation, not knowing what his reception would be. It could be a knife in his back or a pistol aimed at the back of his head. Hopefully, he'd be accepted still as their *compadre* and cohort.

Had he had a way to get word to Flanigan he would have suggested that Flanigan take Tito off the scene for a while. One of the outlaws had made some accusations against Tito, and Pedro feared for his life. But his hands were tied as far as sending a warning signal to Flanigan or Tito.

The cold hard fact was there was little Salazar could do about anything, really. Like this moment when he rode up to the hitching post in front of the dilapidated old shack. He would have to play the cards as they fell.

He ambled slowly to the front door and the one hombre he knew as Darto opened the door to him with an expressionless face. Only when the one sitting over in the corner called out to him with a broad grin on his ugly face did Pedro exhale a deep breath of relief and his nerves begin to calm.

"Hey, Luke, how's it been going?" Pedro swaggered over to the table. The two started exchanging news about what had been going on between the two camps. Salazar sent up prayers that the news of what had taken place down south in Reynosa had not reached their ears here. There was always that unknown possibility of something's slipping through.

That hawk face of Darto's had always made him nervous. The other one, Clem, was an idiot and had proved no threat or headache to Salazar. In a couple of days, these three would be in a jail cell, too, and it would be on to Palito Blanco. Having Moreno by his side would be a comforting feeling, he had to admit. This hideout would be the most dangerous one and certainly most the tricky of all the outlaw stations. He and Moreno had gotten out of scraps before, and Moreno was a formidable figure to have by his side at times. He'd seen men shy away from just a stare from Moreno with those ungodly gray eyes set against his dark skin. He could present a sinister image if he was riled.

Like Moreno, Salazar did not always live his life in

the role of the bandito. Like Moreno, when he was clean-shaven and well-dressed Pedro had a Latin handsomeness the attracted the pretty señoritas like bees to honey. He and Tony had shared a few cantinas and nights of revelry in the past and he hopefully anticipated that both of them would get through this to enjoy some more good times.

Many miles away to the north was a dingy cantina, with foul smoke circling toward the low ceiling and the smell of liquor, tobacco, and body sweat permeating the establishment, which was called Poncho's. The air was thick with tension and had been for over an hour. Tito sat back in the dark corner and waited for all hell to break loose, for he knew it would the minute the owner walked through the back door and saw his whore-mistress loving all over the virile young man at the bar.

She was a dancer of sorts and her dark eyes had caught sight of Tony Moreno the minute he stepped through the door. It was only by chance that Tito had happened into the place, and he'd recognized the disguised young man whose features he'd memorized long ago.

How long he'd been there he could not know, but long enough to be drunk, Tito knew. He sat close enough to know the young man was drowning his sorrows over some fair female and wanted no part of the dark-haired señorita. He'd said, "Go on, honey. Your hair's not gold." He'd rambled and mumbled something about his golden-haired darling. He'd turned his back to her in dismissal.

The woman was persistent though, urging more

drinks on him in hopes that the hombre would become colorblind. Even in that serape Moreno's handsome male figure and the rippling, muscled arms displayed enough to excite the hot-blooded *puta*.

Tony's tousled black hair fell over his forehead and his sombrero hung on his back secured with the tie at his throat. It was easy for Tito to see why Tony's good looks would attract a saucy *puta*—or a lady of any station.

Tito was pulled in two directions. He could go over and elbow his way up to Tony and try to get him to leave, or just stay put. So far, he'd considered it best he stay in the background and just observe. If necessity demanded it, he would come to the young man's aid.

Perhaps his body was showing the wear and tear of the years, but it was a huge body with a height of a little over six feet. That alone, he considered, would be some help.

The peppery Mexican woman had ignited the men standing or sitting around in pairs at the tables with her suggestive provocative dance. Except for one darting glance, Tony had gone back to his drinking.

Tonight was the occasion of old Esteban's yearly dinner at the mansion for a couple of his acquaintances and their wives. It was a traditional annual dinner, started years ago, and on a few occasions Tony had been there. His grandfather had been inclined to cancel it this year because of the circumstances with Tony, but Tony had insisted he must not do that. So he'd decided to make himself scarce.

The more he'd drunk the lonelier he'd become and the farther he'd ambled into the wrong part of the city.

He'd been at the point of taking himself a woman earlier in the evening to rid himself of this agony he felt in his loins.

Perhaps, if he'd been as drunk as he now was and the room had been a little dimmer he would now have been sleeping the night away in her bed. But in her quarters and sprawled across her bed with her pressed in his arms, he had looked down into her overpainted face, too full lips and hair as black as a raven's wings, and he had pushed her away from him.

"What the hell is the matter with you, man?" she'd shrieked as she'd jumped off the bed. "I don't have time to waste on fools like you."

"Sorry. Here," he stammered, getting up off the bed to pay the woman for her wasted time, and he removed himself from the room with the smell of her cheap perfume.

He couldn't go home though, so he trudged on down the street and across the way and down the alley he heard the music coming from the cantina called Poncho's.

It was a joint like the ones he'd frequented many times when he was down in Mexico working at his grandfather's mines and he and Pedro had caroused all night long. But this was not the type of place he usually picked here in San Antonio.

Tony usually held his liquor better than most men, but everything seemed to hit him this evening. The holidays had been something he'd just as soon forget. He hardly felt of good cheer and happy of heart. His heart ached for the woman he loved beyond all reason. Hell, there were those times he wished he'd never ridden into Gonzales County and lost his heart to that little wildcat, Amanda Kane.

By now, he realized he was drunk . . . very drunk! He felt the heat of the woman's arms around his waist and sought to rid himself of her. "Goodnight, señorita!" It should have signaled her to let go, but it didn't, so Tony exerted a strong force.

As she cussed him, it was the moment Poncho with his imposing wrestler's body happened to walk through the back door. She began a tirade directed at Tony as he continued to stagger out the door. Tito watched as she played the role for Poncho's benefit.

"Damn bitch," Tito muttered low, knowing by now what was going to happen when the burly Poncho crooked his finger toward two sleazy-looking Mexicans standing at the far end of the bar. Even the loud music didn't hinder Tito from knowing the order issued by Poncho.

He was already up and veering around the tables to leave the establishment to get outside. He moved through the wooden door, running his hand into his coat to see that he had that big knife he'd carried for a companion for years.

For all his stiff joints, he moved swiftly back into the shadowed darkness to wait for what he knew would be only a minute in coming. The two men came out. One short, little pint-size man was accompanied by a tall, reedlike dude.

Tony was stumbling along less than a hundred feet ahead and he grabbed for support as he passed by a flatbed wagon standing there. After a moment's hesitation, he went on his way. Tito knew it was now or never, for soon there would be only the open space of the street.

There would not be any extra strikes allowed, Tito knew this. Each would have to be vital and hit the target or Tony would still be in danger from the other cutthroat. He pulled himself up straight to his full six-foot-two-inches of height and his whole life swam before him before he made that giant striding step that would put him directly behind the two.

Tito's knife went in swift and deep into the back of the thin man. There was no fat or flesh to keep the blade from hitting the vital organ, and the man fell without making much of any sound of pain. Everything happened so fast as the man fell. The shorter one whirled around instantly. In his hand was the shining silver blade of a knife and he backed up a couple of steps. His short height proved an advantage to him. His knife found Tito's huge, muscled arm. The searing pain of the gash running half way up Tito's arm brought a sharp outburst from him and stopped him in his tracks.

Tony, in his drunken stupor, didn't hear the sound, nor did he know anything of the life and death struggle going on back in the distance. By now he'd turned the corner and moved along another street. The brisk winter air was clearing the fog from his brain and his steps were steady and swifter.

Back in the blackness, Tito taunted, "Come, bastard . . . let's see just how good you are." He played the little short man with no heed to the blood gushing the life out of him. He had to kill this man.

"I'll show you, hombre. I'll show you good!"

Tito found the opening he wanted and lunged in to swing the blade, but the little man leaped back to save himself from the blow. By now, Tito had the first hint of a weakness creeping into his legs, as well as his arms. Now, you fool, he silently chided himself. This one thing he must do and he could die happy, if that was the way it was written. This one thing would make up a little for all the things he'd not done in his useless life.

He made the move that must count for his whole life. The blade hit Tito's desired target and the man's anguished moan pleased him, making him relax a second too soon. In one final burst of life the little man's blade found Tito's gut as he was sinking to the ground. Tito's eyes went wide with surprised shock and he knew as he'd known all his life that folly was going to cost him dearly.

He sank to the ground beside his victim, and Tito was allowed a moment of grace to reflect and be happy that he'd done the one decent thing he wanted more than anything to do—he'd saved his fine son's life.

San Antonio knew him as the fine young grandson of the esteemed Esteban Moreno. He was Antonio Moreno, the handsome young businessman and rancher to the rest of San Antonio. Only a few years ago Tito had found out that he was his son, the son of Terrance Branigan and his lovely Theresa.

As he lay there on the ground he knew this was his last moment on earth. That Irish sixth sense had told him that in the tavern, and he'd accepted it. Perhaps, as he'd sat in the secluded corner of Poncho's as if fate had decreed he be there, he'd known. Perhaps, it had been written in the annals of his destiny long, long ago.

The sky above him was as black as his lovely Theresa's hair and the twinkling stars were blinking especially for him in this his last hour. Her dark eyes could twinkle so, he recalled. "Oh, God, sweet Theresa, never would I have thought that day I sailed away from New Orleans it would be the last sight I'd have of you." He gave a deep moan of anguish from the pain of his wound and his wasted life.

To love a woman so was almost a sin in itself, but he had wanted to give her the world or at least a little part of it. The only way he knew to provide for her and their young son was to sign on to the schooner—the *Laura Lee*—making the run to Corpus Christi.

The schooner filled with cargo had been caught in a fierce storm, tossed onto a sand bar and totally wrecked. High tides had obviously carried him away from any other surviving members of the crew and he had woken up later to the flapping wings of the sea gulls. He was alone on the sandy shores of Corpus Christi Bay and he didn't know where he was or who he was. A falling piece of the schooner's timber had blotted out his past and all memory of the woman and child he loved dearly.

He had become a beachcomber for the first few weeks, walking around in a confused daze, remembering nothing of his home many miles away in New Orleans.

Finally, he had begun working for a salvage wrecker there in the port. The tale reaching Theresa's ears back in New Orleans that had sent her searching for her husband in Corpus Christi had been true, for the sailor had, indeed, seen the robust Terrance Branigan on the docks at Corpus Christi. However, their paths had not been meant to cross, because by the time she'd arrived there, Terrance had been working with his salvage wreckers down at the south tip of Padre Island near Mexico.

Fate had played the cruelest trick on them. Desolate and broke, she'd gone on to San Antonio and her father's home by the time he returned to Corpus Christi.

With a couple of his seafaring buddies he'd been in a fight one night in one of the local taverns and a jolting blow against his skull brought back his memory. He lay in the arms of a black-haired whore calling her Theresa. His buddies were laughing about the fact that he was thinking he was in New Orleans. They had no idea the man they knew as Tito was Terrance Branigan, and he was suddenly to realize it.

He had returned to New Orleans and found Theresa and his son gone. When his foggy mind recalled Theresa's father's name and home in San Antonio, he had set out to search for her.

Never would he forget being turned away from the fine Moreno mansion by the abrupt dismissal of a cold-eyed servant. That servant was a much younger Ignacio, still deep in sorrow from the young señora's death. The servant had had no inkling this man was her husband.

He'd curtly snapped at the bearded Terrance, "The señora died three weeks ago. She cannot speak to anyone and certainly not the likes of you." The door had shut with a slam on Terrance and his heart.

He had died a little that day, and it had been years before he ever sought a glimpse of the son who'd he'd found out was now known as Antonio. From the sidelines of his own haphazard life, he'd learned things about his son through the years. He'd grown into a fine-looking young man, educated at the finest schools

371

in the country, and it was said he was wealthy, with a shrewd, intelligent mind and love from an adoring grandfather. Terrance had never dared make his presence known and spoil anything for a son who probably hated him anyway.

One rumor had always amused him, though, and he was only human enough to pridefully take the credit for it. It was said around San Antonio that, for all of the dignified, aristocratic environment Antonio had been reared in, there was a little of the rebel renegade in him . . . a reckless streak. Terrance always smiled when he heard this about his adventurous son. There was just a little of the Irish in the lad he'd named Tony Branigan. It was a solace that eased the burden in his heart.

When he finally shut his eyes for the last time, he felt at peace with himself and the world. A part of him would live within one young man, Antonio Moreno. His eyes now closed, and he willingly gave way to the tremendous weakness washing over him, so consuming, so overpowering. There was no need to fight it! Hell, he was tired of all the fighting!

So he slept.

IV

COME THE
SPRINGTIME

THIRTY-FOUR

There were no bold headlines in the *San Antonio News* about the three ruffians' deaths near the alley by the cantina the next day. Tony awoke the next morning with a terrible headache, unaware of the dramatic tragedy he'd caused. That he would have provoked any man's death would have left a sour taste in his mouth—and already had a most sour taste as he gulped down the coffee Elvira served him.

He was calling himself all kinds of fool though. Recalling where he'd wandered and the cheap whiskey he'd guzzled was bad enough, but it was rather embarrassing to have had Elvira find him asleep on the veranda. His pride was hurt for he'd always credited himself for being man enough to handle himself well. God knows, last night was the exception.

Weakness did not appeal to him in a man or a woman. It irked him to find it in himself. So he was harsh with ridicule of himself. Recklessness was one thing, but stupidity was another.

The Mexican servant, Elvira, tried to keep her face solemn and not let a smile show as she watched his bent head and slumped shoulders as he sat at the long dining table this morning. The young señor had celebrated a little too much, she concluded.

She couldn't help her heart going out to him when she'd found him early this morning. He reminded her of a little lost boy all crumpled up there on the porch. Thank goodness, it had been a mild night. There could have been a sick young man there this morning. Other than paying the price for his overindulgence, he looked fit enough.

"One more cup of coffee, eh Elvira?" He looked up at her and asked for it with a rather sheepish, wan smile on his face.

"Yes, Señor Moreno. I'll get it right away," she said, scurrying to obey his request. Once she'd served him, she left the room, having a multitude of chores to attend to after the small dinner party the elder Moreno had given the night before.

Although Tony's body tried to insist that it needed more rest, his stubborn will was not going to allow it. He'd planned to ride out of the ranch to check with Fernando on some of the changes he'd requested the overseer to see to. That ranch and his various projects out there were the calming haven for his restless soul during this time. Better to be out there feeling rotten than to be roaming around the house with nothing but idle time on his hands. He could have sworn that he'd read every book in Esteban's extensive library by now.

There was a freedom of movement for him out at the ranch that he could not have at the house in town, and living like a caged animal had frayed his nerves.

Besides, when he was out at the Casa del Plata he could dream his dreams of the future and Amanda. These were the most stimulating thoughts he could allow himself until he could once again hold his golden girl in his arms. He remembered enough about the night before to recall that even for his needs as a man not just any woman could fill the wanting or the ache.

After the feast of ecstasy he'd had with Amanda it was not in his nature to settle for crumbs that would leave him wanting and still hungry. For a man whose manner was impulsive about most things, he was patient. This, as much as anything, had come as an amazing discovery to Tony Moreno. Could a woman change him so? Obviously, she had!

In Gonzales County the winter was never a harsh one and only on rare occasions did the chilling north air drift so far south to bring snow or even the kind of sleet they'd seen the night of Amanda's birthday celebration. What few weeks of winter did linger around that far south in the state of Texas seemed to come and go quickly.

As Amanda sat atop Prince to go for a ride over the countryside she was heavy with thoughts of what the brand new year would bring in her life. This last one had been the turning point, in more ways than one. To look back was painful, and yet, it seemed she'd lived a lifetime.

Lately, she had found herself feeling ancient. Sweet Jesus, she was a far cry from the frivalous young miss who'd returned in early summer to the Circle K Ranch. Where had that girl been swept away to?

It was as if the golden palomino knew the place she sought to go and he galloped toward that particular spot along the river. Amanda allowed him to have his way.

Her head felt like it could explode from the frantic pressure and worry engulfing her. If she'd been as certain then as she was now, she would have accepted her aunt's invitation to return to New Orleans. Maybe, she could have figured out something . . . some way out of this dilemma. At least, she would not be here at the Circle K flaunting her shame at her parents and their lifelong friends. Oh, God, how she hated Tony Branigan! How she ever could have been so stupid irritated her even more. Oh, the price she was paying for that folly!

For over a week now she had not slept and the constant question prodded at her. What are you going to do, Amanda? It was with her day and night, and the answer was always the same. She didn't know.

Her little spot of paradise didn't even seem as serene as it once had. Never had she felt so alone as she did sitting there on the ground after she'd secured Prince to the trunk of a nearby sapling. Not caring if she ruined her new maroon riding ensemble she lay back on the ground and cried, hoping to empty all the agony tearing her apart.

Soon the springtime would be coming and with it the seed of her wanton folly with Branigan would blossom. Nothing could stop it! Neither her wealthy rancher father nor his power could not cure this ill. It was not fair. Branigan was as guilty as she, but he walked away with no price to pay. No, it was damn unfair!

The white Arabian stood with his arrogant head held high. Its rider stared down below, and had it not been for the deep, rich maroon color he would never have given the area a second glance. With a start, he

378

reined the Arabian down the knoll, because by then he'd noticed the mass of fanned-out golden hair. Christ, was she hurt, he wondered? It was certainly unlikely Prince had thrown her, for Amanda was too good a horsewoman for that.

Sobbing so, she didn't hear him come down the sloping ground or leap off his horse until he called out her name. "Amanda? Are . . . are you . . . . good Lord, Amanda . . ." He rushed to get to her and comfort her, a million wild thoughts rushing through his mind at seeing her tear-stained face looking up at him. If someone had laid a hand on her he vowed to kill him.

"Honey, what is it? Tell me," Derek urged and patted her to soothe whatever pain was stirring such a flood of tears.

"I just want to cry, Derek. Please just hold me and let me get it all out," she pleaded, relishing the comfort of his arms. They felt good, and at that moment they represented the safe feeling she needed so much.

"Ah, darling go ahead." He positioned himself to take her in his arms and up on his lap and there they sat for a few minutes. Derek rained light kisses on her cheeks and forehead with the kind of tenderness that sometimes endeared him to her. She let herself completely drown in his arms.

Whatever had brought all this about Derek didn't know nor did he care. All he knew was that it played into his plans perfectly. The house was without the presence of Mona now, and soon David Lawson would be forever removed, so it was time for Amanda to share it with him now.

"Amanda, you feeling better now? I wish you'd al-

379

ways let me comfort you this way. You know I want to . . . always have," he murmured softly in her ear. She turned slowly to gaze into his eyes, as though she was searching them.

Had her father been right months ago when he'd pointed out the admirable qualities of Derek? She'd come to realize he'd been right about many other things.

Her deep blue eyes staring up at him like that and those soft half-parted lips so temptingly close urged him to bend slightly and kiss her. She gave herself up to him, responding to his lips and letting his hand pleasantly caress her. More than ever she realized how hungry she was for the touch of a man.

When he released her, he was pleased to see the flush of passion on her lovely face. This was the moment and he dared not let slip away. "Marry me, Amanda. It could be good with us if only you'd give us a chance."

He took her lips again, finding it hard to keep the control he felt he must. Again, she responded to his long, lingering kiss. Derek's spirits soared as he felt her body pressing against him. But he held her from him to pull from her the answer he wanted. "Amanda, say you'll marry me. Say it!"

Why not, she thought? Why not, indeed! What was love anyway? Look what a mess she'd gotten herself into by giving what she'd have sworn was complete love to a man who'd professed to love her. So what, indeed, was Love?

"All right, Derek! Let's get married just as soon as we can,' she replied with a firm set to her jaw, almost like she was making a business deal. Yet her eagerness stunned Derek, and he soared to the blue sky with delight at her quick response. He'd finally won! So, filled with elation over his victory, he took her into his arms again to assure himself it was true. He felt intoxicated as he held her and let his flashing blue eyes scan the countryside and dreamed again those grandiose plans for their life about the empire they'd rule like a king and queen.

When he finally released her, he searched her lovely, tear-stained face. "Were you serious about not wanting a grand wedding once when we were talking, Amanda?"

"I was," she answered. More than ever she would not want an ordeal like the one Mona and Jeff had just punished themselves going through.

"All right . . . you just leave everything to me." Things couldn't be falling more perfectly into place, Jeff mused.

"I'll be most happy to leave everything in your capable hands, Derek," she said with a hint of a smile on her face.

His ego was exalted and his spirits soared to lofty heights. He knew he would be pinching himself to be sure all this had happened this afternoon. This had all gone beyond his wildest hopes with the unexpected turn of events this winter afternoon.

He rose up from the ground extending his hand to Amanda, and she took it. It all seemed very strange and she moved almost as if she was dazed at the swift turn of events in her life. This was the last thing in the world she'd imagined coming about and it only went to prove the suddenness with which changes in life could occur.

Had she not sworn to her father that never would she marry Derek Lawson? Now she had accepted his offer of marriage without any prodding or urging on Mark Kane's part.

Now here they were walking arm in arm like lovers and he spoke to her about his plans to be away for a few days on a brief business trip. "As soon as I return we'll be married, honey. Hell, the whole idea of eloping makes it a little daring, don't you think? Let's face it, Amanda, neither of us are exactly like the rest of our families."

"I guess you're right, Derek. We've always been the rebels, so to speak," she agreed. Derek found himself wondering whether he liked this sweet-natured Amanda as well as the haughty little firebrand he usually encountered. Actually, her new mood was to his advantage, and so he wouldn't fault it.

Only one thing did prick him sorely. When they prepared to mount up on their horses he took her into the circle of his arms and she had about as much life in her as a rag doll. He told himself that she was a little numbed by the afternoon. So absorbed was he in his fantasy, which was so close now to being consummated, that he gave no serious thought to nor did he put any significance on Amanda's unexpected acceptance of his proposal.

They rode toward the Circle K, both consumed by their private thoughts. The Alvarado buggy came into sight. As it pulled up to them, Señora Alvarado greeted the two young people with her usual gracious manner. Except for her driver, she traveled alone.

"Nice to see you, Señora Alvarado," Amanda greeted her.

Bianca gave her a smile, noting something she couldn't quite put her finger on—but there was something different reflected in the lovely girl's face. Young Lawson looked and acted unusually warm, which Bianca found a marked contrast to his cool contempt. More than once she'd been thankful he'd never chosen to visit the Rancho Rio too often. Usually when she looked at that clean-cut face of his she found it expressionless, as though there was no feeling or heart within him.

"And your parents . . . are they well, Amanda?"

"Yes, ma'am, they are fine. Mother is ready for a few weeks of quiet and peace with the holidays over and our company gone."

Bianca laughed. "I'm sure she is, especially with that lovely, lovely wedding following so closely afterwards. Your sister is a beautiful girl, Derek. I've never seen a more beautiful bride." Her cunning eyes measured him as he made his reply. That young man didn't like her, she mused. It wasn't her imagination, she was certain.

"Thank you, Señora Alvarado." He gave way to the sudden impulse to add, "Soon there will be another wedding, I'm happy to say. Just this afternoon Amanda did me the great honor of accepting my proposal."

His declaration took Amanda completely by surprise and she could have throttled him there on the spot. How dare he announce their plans when she had not had a chance to even tell her parents? She was completely appalled by his act.

Bianca quickly sensed Amanda's displeasure for her eyes turned the deepest amethyst shade and her long eyelashes batted as she looked first at Derek and then back to Bianca. "Please let me set the record straight, Señora Alvarado I've not had the opportunity to inform my parents yet. So it isn't official. Derek, dear, you impatience amazes me." She almost gave a hissing sound to her voice and the smile she gave him was forced.

It was, indeed, a curious scene unfolding in front of Bianca and she found it interesting and disturbing at the same time. Being a gracious person, she extended them her congratulations and urged the driver to be on his way.

The minute the wheels of the buggy started to roll, leaving a cloud of dust rising on the dirt road, Amanda jerked Prince's reins around, glaring at the man she'd just promised to marry. The old Amanda had returned with all the fury of the spitfire he knew so well.

"You . . . you had no business doing that, Derek. I don't see why you thought it so necessary to tell the Señora Alvarado this afternoon."

"I'm . . . I'm just so happy, honey," he mumbled, trying to soothe her ruffled feathers. The innocent look he tried to get onto his face was really far from innocent. He had very definite reasons for his announcement. The whole of the afternoon had been sheer perfection in his scheme of things. Lady Luck was riding on his shoulder.

They parted, but not like lovers. Amanda questioned whether pride and honor were worth it. All the way home it was not Derek Lawson she cursed but the scoundrel, Branigan.

Flaunting his marriage to Amanda in the Señora Alvarado's face had added to the pleasure of the afternoon for Derek Lawson. He roared with laughter as he got out of sight of her and rode toward the Big D Ranch.

THIRTY-FIVE

Señora Alvarado made her trip into Gonzales and back to the Rancho Rio. During that time her thoughts kept straying back to her encounter with Amanda Kane and Derek Lawson. That couple were not meant for one another and her woman's instincts were convinced of it. She had felt no resentment at seeing her dead sister's locket around the pretty Amanda's neck earlier, but now indignation sprang up like a trenchant thorn.

That locket had no place with Amanda Kane if she became the bride of Derek Lawson. That night in the comfort of the Rancho Rio Bianca determined to say something to her father when she got to San Antonio. But what could she say? It *was* Tony's gift to give, but it should have been given to the girl who would be his wife. It should have been a treasured, cherished object, since it had belonged to his mother. Bianca felt very strongly about that.

She could not excuse Tony for being this thoughtless and irresponsible. The truth was it filled her with disappointment, leaving her disillusioned.

However, Tony had left the Circle K Ranch without

so much as a trip to the Rancho Rio to say goodbye. When she'd inquired of Mark Kane about her nephew he had had no answer for her as to where he'd gone.

If she had to honest about it, she was more than delighted about her own son's marriage into the Gomez family and his plans to join Francisco. Mario seemed to have his future laid out very well. Miguel was taking over for his older brother with an enthusiastic zest that had amazed Bianca. He was doing a superb job. She had no qualms at all about leaving the ranch in his hands when she went into the city to see her father.

The little locket causing so much furor with Bianca seemed to be having as disturbing effect on Amanda that night as she lay trying to get off to sleep. She had been tempted to remove the damnable thing from her neck and her fingers had gone to the clasp a dozen times to do just that. Something always seemed to urge her to leave it be. At times like this, she honestly wondered if there was such a thing as being bewitched by someone—as she had obviously been where Tony Branigan was concerned.

She got up from the bed and went to the window to look out into the night. Was it always more desolate and lonely in the middle of the night? Somehow, at dawn things never seemed as hopeless.

After she'd left Derek to come on into the grounds of the ranch, she regretted her promise to marry him. But as her fury at him had subsided, she realized his proposal had been a godsend. It was even more perfect that he wished them not to have a large wedding and to elope.

She chided herself harshly. After all, she couldn't have it both ways. That devious little voice always nagging her so much of late took a delight in reminding her that she needed a husband in the worst way if she was to save herself and her family from disgrace and shame.

There was no backing out now and she had to accept the dirty trick fate had played on her. She would marry Derek and the child she carried would be his for all practical purposes. God knows, his real father would probably never come this way again.

If she ever laid eyes on Tony Branigan, she swore to kill him. Without one qualm, she could aim a gun and pull the trigger putting a bullet in his wicked heart.

It was the hour just before daybreak when Amanda's eyes finally shut in sleep and she'd come to terms with herself and her future. All the arguments were over and she decided to quit fighting with herself over something as futile as the situation she was in.

The next morning, she was resigned to her fate as she went downstairs. She felt an amazing calm as she greeted her father and mother at the breakfast table.

Jenny noted the glowing radiance on her daughter's face and mentioned it. Mark was quick to declare it was the healthy country air. "I noticed right away that Lisa doesn't have the pretty glow to her cheeks that you and Amanda do. She has to paint it on."

His comment caused Jenny to laugh. "Oh, Mark!"

"But it's true, and poor Armand can't do a darn thing without huffing and puffing. That city living makes a man as soft as a woman."

"Armand was out of his element, Mark, just as you would be if you were in New Orleans. You'd not know what to do with yourself." Jenny glanced at Amanda, winking her eye.

"You're darn right I'd know what to do. I'd hightail it back to Texas just as fast as I could," he declared assuredly.

After they finished eating and Consuela had cleaned away the table of the dishes, leaving only the coffee cups, Amanda decided it was a proper time for her to tell her parents about her plans to marry Derek. Lord, after his abrupt announcement to Bianca Alvarado she hardly knew what to expect. It should come from her, not from someone else.

She wasted no time embroidering or building up to it, but came straight to the point. "Papa, I have something to say to you and Mama this morning." Her eyes danced nervously from one parent to the other, causing them to become nervous.

Her manner was so cool and serene that Jenny felt no apprehension that it was bad news. Mark Kane knew without one shred of doubt she'd announce her plans to go to New Orleans soon. With Lisa's recent visit so fresh, Mark was certain she'd tried to sell his daughter on the idea. With Amanda's eighteenth birthday past, he was prepared that she'd use that as her bargaining tool to get her way. Well, this time he wasn't going to be so agreeable about it.

He leaned back in the chair, prepared to hear the news. "Let's have it, honey! What do you want to tell your mother and me?"

That moment before she opened her mouth to speak, she silently thought that her father would be pleased. He'd won! "I've accepted Derek's proposal of marriage." Quickly, she looked over at her mother and added, "Don't faint, Mama. Plans don't have to start for a while."

389

Mark was struck blind and he couldn't speak, for his throat was as dry as the desert. As she had so often in the past, she completely surprised him. Always, she would be his child of wonder, he guessed. A child she wasn't, though.

With Jeff, Mark could usually anticipate his actions and his thoughts. Amanda had really thrown him this time, as sure as if he'd been atop one of the wild mustangs. He felt as breathless sitting there.

"Honey, I have to admit this takes me by surprise. I had no idea you and Derek had gotten so serious," Jenny stammered. Her fingers worked nervously with her skirt, which was a habit when she was upset. Even as a child she had twisted her gown as a nervous habit and Lisa would fidget with her hair. She gave no hint of this upset to Mark or Amanda, but she could have sworn her daughter and that likable Tony Branigan had felt an attraction for each other.

"I guess it was inevitable. Papa, remember? When I came home in the early summer and you brought up the subject of Derek and me?" What was it with them, she wondered?

Mark Kane cursed silently to himself. Dear God, he wished she'd hadn't reminded him of that. For many weeks now he'd regretted that move on his part and it was coming back to haunt him now. "I remember, honey. But are you sure about this, Amanda? After all, you aren't exactly an old maid . . . just now eighteen."

He certainly wasn't overwhelmed with joy, and she was stunned by her father's reaction. She'd have thought he'd welcome the news. Instead, he acted very subdued, almost displeased.

"You say . . . you say, no immediate plans are in the making, Amanda?" he prodded at her, hoping he'd heard her right, for he'd been rather stunned while she was talking a few moments ago.

"Yes, Papa." She gave a smile at her mother. "I wouldn't put such a huge task on mother so soon after the holidays, Aunt Lisa's visit and Jeff's wedding. She needs a few weeks of rest."

Mark heartily agreed. "That's sure the truth. Mama is a little weary. That's most considerate of you, honey." More important, Kane mused, something could prevent the marriage from taking place. Just maybe, Branigan would return. Kane always prided himself as a man of his word but he'd be hard pressed to keep that vow if it came down to it. Time . . . he'd play for precious time!

He found it just a little hard to convince himself that his daughter was in love with Derek Lawson when she wore that little locket constantly around her neck. Damned if he'd noticed it off from the night he'd given it to her. Now, that Kane found a little hard to figure. Women had never been the easiest thing in the world for him to figure, though, and he'd be the first to admit to that.

The strange atmosphere of the dining room left Amanda confused and when they went their separate ways she was still somewhat bewildered by the whole episode. As the day went on the surer she became that her parents were not elated over her news as they had been when Jeff had made his announcement about his plans to marry Mona.

In the next few days it seemed to Amanda that they acted as if she'd said nothing to them. Even Consuela said nothing. Strange!

When Derek came to dinner she wondered if he detected the coolness in Mark Kane. Oh, it was obvious to her. Derek apparently paid no attention and directed his conversation to her and occasionally to Jenny. Actually, he acted as aloof toward Mark Kane as the rancher did toward him.

Amanda felt a tenseness sitting there with the two of them. At the end of the meal, it seemed to Amanda, it was an arrogant act on Derek's part when he boldly inquired of her father, "I hope we have your approval, Mr. Kane. I know Amanda has told you of our plans." Amanda noted the Derek's blue eyes locked into her father's. Kane's face showed no expression or emotion when he replied to young Lawson. His comment was most diplomatic, but noncommittal.

"The Lawson family has always been held in high esteem by the Kanes, Derek." Without saying more, Mark took a sip of his red wine.

It was not what he wanted to hear and Derek had to restrain the resentment he felt from showing on his face. The old bastard would live to regret it, he promised himself. Wait until he married his precious daughter and he ruled her like he'd rule the Big D. Oh, yes, he'd make the arrogant old rascal eat crow.

"The feeling is mutual, Mr. Kane," he smiled, exhibiting a gracious warmth that was obviously false.

The tense air in the room suddenly made Amanda feel faint and she yearned to get away from the table quickly. Her lovely lavender gown pinched at her waist and she felt like her breasts were going to spill out over the low-cut neckline. The temptingly, sensuous sight of her made Derek all that much more eager

392

to finish up his pending business so he could carry her away with him. Once they returned no one could do a thing. It would be done, and, for sure, the marriage would be consummated.

When Jenny and Mark excused themselves to leave the young couple to themselves, Mark felt repulsed at the possessive way Derek's hands touched his daughter. Inside, his gut turned and twisted. He had noted the cold stare of Derek's blue eyes, and Kane had a premonition that there was more behind that quiet, straitlaced young rancher than he'd realized. Maybe he was being the typical critical father trying to find something wrong with the young man taking his daughter away from him. Fathers were supposed to feel this way, so he'd always heard. For Amanda's sake, he prayed that was all it was. Deep in his heart he hoped the marriage would never take place.

Later when Amanda walked to the gate with her fiance, Derek snaked his arm around her waist pulling her close to him. Although she didn't move away, something about his new boldness repulsed her. There was no pleasant feel to it as on the day he'd proposed and comforted her.

"After tonight I'd say we'd make the right decision to elope. Guess I should have known your father would never find any man quite up to his standard to marry his daughter," he contemptuously smirked.

Amanda tried to shrug it off by replying, "You know how fathers are about their only daughter, Derek."

"Yes . . . suppose so," he muttered, letting his hand move up to cup her breast boldly. His touch was rough, so much so that she jerked away to stare at him. His eyes devoured her salaciously and he had a grin on his face that she felt like slapping away. "Do you mind, Derek!"

He gave a light chuckle. "Sorry, honey . . . you drive me a little wild and I get carried away." How full and marvelous that lovely mound was to his touch! His body fired and his pants bulged with his desire to take that supple body of hers.

"Try not to get that carried away. Bruises don't exactly excite me, Derek Lawson." It was not the time to think of Tony Branigan but she did in the most painful way, comparing his caress, which always ignited such desire in her, to this crude fondling of Derek's. It chilled her, and she wanted to be rid of him. And this was the man she was going to marry! Dear God, was there no other way out of this?

She went through the motions of a goodnight kiss and allowed the straying hands to go over her breasts with a more gentle touch. Even this tender touch had no effect on her as she stood like a statue, unmoved and unaffected.

Later, she lay alone across her bed with the silver rays of the moonlight darting in and out of her window, making varied shadows reflect against the walls from the swaying branches of the tall trees just outside.

What options did she have? Only two, it would seem. She could marry Derek to give this child a name and save herself from disgrace. Otherwise, the fine name of Kane would be tarnished. She could not think of anything worse happening to her proud father. He did not deserve to pay for her stupid mistakes or suffer her heartaches.

The rebel in her still blazed, though. Nothing decreed she'd have to remain with Derek Lawson the rest of her life. She and the child could leave then without dishonor and humiliation befalling her family.

No man would ever humble her again. Once was enough. Let Derek think what he wanted to think as long as it suited her purpose. Love? Dear Lord, she realized tonight that she didn't even like Derek Lawson.

THIRTY-SIX

Bianca Alvarado's unexpected arrival at the Moreno house set into motion a flurry of activity, with the younger servant girl accompanying Elvira upstairs to ready the guest room for the señor's daughter. Jose struggled with her luggage and Ignacio hurried into the kitchen to prepare fresh coffee as Esteban had ordered while he and Bianca retired to his study.

"Why didn't you let me know you were coming, Bianca dear?" The elderly gentleman was in a quandary as to what to do in regard to his grandson's presence.

Bianca gave a lighthearted laugh. "Because I didn't know myself, until two days ago, Father. I got two letters that made up my mind for me. Mario and Magdalena are to arrive back here any time now. Naturally you can imagine I am most eager to see my son and my new daughter-in-law after so many weeks. The other reason is Elena's invitation to her party. You remember Elena Allende?"

"Ah, yes. I know Elena's husband, Alfredo, very well. Fine man." He fidgeted in his seat to find an excuse to make himself absent for a moment to warn Antonio of his daughter's arrival at the house.

As Ignacio entered carrying the tray and prepared to serve them the coffee, Esteban told his daughter he would be back in a minute. "Go ahead and refresh yourself Bianca. Ignacio still makes the best coffee in the world."

"I know." She smiled up at the servant. "I still say you should come with me to the Rancho Rio, but if you did my father would disown me."

Old Ignacio knew she was only teasing and gave her a broad smile. "Señora Alvarado is, as always, most kind. Nice to have you here again, señora." Before he turned to leave he inquired if there was anything else she wished. He knew exactly where Señor Esteban had rushed to.

Bianca dismissed him and took a sip of the steaming black brew and found it amazing that she didn't feel the least bit weary from the long journey. It could be the excitement about seeing Mario soon. By the time her father returned to join her, she had drunk half the cup of coffee and eaten one of the delicious little spice cakes.

By the time she'd had a second cup she was suddenly hit with a tired feeling and asked to be shown to her room. By the dinner hour she seemed refreshed and descended the stairs to join her father in her usual elegant black gown with her glorious blue-black hair in double coils adorned by the high Spanish-style comb tucked at the back of her hair.

When the news of her arrival circulated the social circle of the Moreno family, the invitations flooded the house. Bianca was always a popular guest when she arrived in San Antonio and she knew many people among the leading citizens of the city. So Tony did not have to be as cautious as he'd prepared himself to be.

The first two days of her visit went by without any incidents. It was merely a matter of being confined upstairs when Bianca was between social engagements. Far more disturbing to him was the news from Flanigan that his guide, Tito, had met an untimely death in a dark alley and he would now be forced to go alone to the rendezvous spot. There would be no guide to take him on the back trail to the spot set up months ago.

When they'd sat in Flanigan's office discussing this, Tony could tell the U.S. marshall was disturbed. "Don't like this, Tony. It was meant to go like clockwork. Now it's going to be a tricky operation. You and Pedro could miss each other. I've drawn a map here for you to study and we'll go over the landmarks for you to look for." He shook his head, dejected and low in spirits. "Hell, a mere half-mile off could mess you up!"

"I'll just have to take my chances, Brett. Scout around if I don't come on Pedro. With this map here I'll have no trouble finding the shack in the woods if I don't meet Pedro. I'll just have to ride on into their camp on my own and play a hell of a bluff job."

"That could be dangerous, Tony."

"The whole thing is going to be dangerous anyway. If Pedro is there everything will go smooth as silk. If he happens not to be around, I'll just have to convince them I'm his old buddy. When do I leave?"

"No later than Saturday night. You've got about a six-hour ride. You are supposed to meet up with Pedro in the early morning hours at that point right there." He pointed the X marked there on the piece of paper.

Tony pushed back from the old oak desk, stretching out his long legs before standing up. He took the paper and folded it, tucking it in his pocket. "Guess this it it, Brett," he declared, giving that crooked smile of his to the gray-haired lawman sitting there so stern and serious with his many grave misgivings. The young man standing before him had been very dear to his heart since their first encounter, and he'd appointed himself Tony's protector on that occasion. He'd watched him grow as a man and felt a certain kind of pride. Now as they parted he felt a tinge of regret that he'd asked this favor of Tony Moreno.

The dice were tossed though and there was no taking them back now. It was in the hands of fate.

It was twilight time when Tony mounted up on the feisty Arabian he'd named Sultan to ride back home. Like Brett, he had a few misgivings. That was the trouble when you had to depend on some old drunk like Tito to do your dirty work, he thought to himself. You could never depend on them when the time came. If it was to be a matter of leaving in the night Saturday, he'd have to ride out to the ranch sometime tomorrow and get Picaro. He'd left him out there the other day and ridden Sultan back into San Antonio.

As he turned the corner of the street where the old stone mansion stood in the center of the street, he reined Sultan to go to the back entrance. This was a spirited guy, he thought about the Arabian, and his selection had been a wise one. Between him and the fine mare, Shalimar, there would be some fine foals.

He gave young Jose a friendly greeting as he rushed through the back door and toward the back stairs. The voices of his aunt and Esteban resounded down the long hall. He picked up bits and pieces of their light-hearted conversation. But for the sudden urge to go back down the steps and get himself a drink from the liquor chest there in the spacious dining room he wouldn't have heard the remarks that shattered his sanity. He'd slipped through the room and got his drink as quiet as a ghost. He passed Jose and the grinning Ignacio, knowing what the young señor was up to. All the secret goings on reminded Ignacio of Antonio's prankish boyhood days. Time had passed all too fast, Ignacio lamented thoughtfully.

As Tony's strode back through Ignacio's kitchen with a glass generously filled with liquor the latter noticed an odd look on the young man's face. When he requested that Jose be sent to his room immediately Ignacio knew something was definitely wrong. The broad grin on his face had vanished and a frown etched his brow. An impatient, enraged manner reflected itself in the young señor who just moments ago had been in a fine mood.

Tony marched on upstairs with his booted heels making sharp, heavy thuds on the wooden steps and Ignacio knew there was a fury blazing in the young man. He prodded young Jose into swift action.

When Jose entered the room he was reminded of the most fierce warrior he'd ever imagined. It seemed anything in his way was getting tossed aside. The menacing look on his black-bearded face as he bellowed out instructions to the young Mexican made Jose tremble in fear of not absorbing all the many tasks he was assigning for him to do.

It riled Tony all the more to know he'd have no time to get Picaro and would have to settle for Sultan for his trip into Gonzales County.

Jose stood, watching Tony calm his frenzy long enough to sit down at his desk and scribble two hasty notes. He finished one and looked up at the wide-eyed Jose. "This one you will give to my grandfather—only when he is alone. Tonight after I leave—you understand?"

"*Si, si* I will, Señor Moreno," Jose stammered, shifting his body from one foot to the other.

"This one is to be delivered to Father Tomas at once. It is most important. As soon as you prepare my horse and put this stuff over here in my saddlebag, you ride for the Mission Concepcion. Only Father Tomas gets this. You tell him Antonio says it must be done as soon as I arrive, Jose"

Jose nodded his head. "I tell Father Tomas you say it must be done as soon as you arrive. Should I prepare the horse now?"

"Yes—and Jose, tell Ignacio to give you two flasks of my brandy to put in the saddlebag," Tony barked, raising up from the chair. The white shirt he wore was being hastily taken off and flung on the bed and being replace by the black one.

As he sat on the edge of the bed he put his muscled legs out of the pants he was wearing and switched to the black ones, he fumed and cussed this new turn of events which he needed like a hole in the head.

He felt like he was walking through a damned nightmare and had been since the minute Bianca's clear voice had cut through that dining room as he was pouring the whiskey into his glass.

Actually, it was Esteban's comment that had first caught his ear when he'd heard his grandfather say,

"Ah, yes—the Kane family. I never met Señor Mark Kane, but naturally I've heard of the fine Circle K Ranch. Perhaps, too, I've heard you talk of them over the years, Bianca."

Tony had lingered there to hear what Bianca was going to say next. She said some other things that held no importance to Tony but then she made such a casual remark about another wedding to take place soon in Gonzales. "Our children are all getting married, it would seem, Father. My Mario started it all, and the Kanes' son, Jeff, married the Lawson girl. You've probably heard me speak about the Lawsons who own the Big D Ranch?"

"I think so, Bianca."

By now, Tony found himself straining to eavesdrop on their conversation. Who was there to be married next that she was preparing to reveal?

"Well, I have to confess, Father, that I would not have been surprised if Mario had tried to woo Amanda, and he did sort of flirt around with the idea, I know, but I guess when Magdalena came into his life Mario lost his heart completely. So now the Kanes' daughter, Amanda, is to marry Derek Lawson. *Dios*, that will make three weddings in our countryside in the last three months!"

Amanda to marry Derek Lawson? No—never! He could not let her do it. If he had to hogtie her and keep her captive until she came to her senses, he could not let that happen. The crazy little wildcat could not so soon have forgotten all those nights they'd shared. Hell, it was all he thought about in his empty bed at night. What had it been now—six or eight weeks? He'd lost count, but the heat of her remained with him, searing and burning him with an ache. Had it not meant that much to her? He could not believe that. If she had forgotten so quickly the ecstasy of his arms then he'd brand it deeper this time. All he knew was he was going to Gonzales County and carry her away to where Derek Lawson couldn't touch her or claim her until he, Tony, had a chance to convince her all over again. He'd tamed her once and he'd do it again.

With his determined mind made up and his plans set in motion, his cool, calm manner returned. At first when he'd heard Bianca's words he'd thought his head would explode with the crazed fury churning there. Now, he was a man hell bent to carry out the mission of rescuing the woman he loved better than life itself. The risk of endangering himself at this moment didn't enter his mind, for the only thought possessing him was that he must get his golden-haired Amanda here before he took off to Palito Blanco to do the job for Brett Flanigan.

From the minute he'd seen the satiny golden body with that glorious hair of spun gold cascading down her naked back in the little cove of the Guadalupe River the first day he rode into Gonzales County, he had known he'd found the girl his reckless heart had always yearned for. He would not allow anyone or anything to steal that dream from him.

Slipping quietly out of the house as he'd slipped in only an hour ago, he took his leave. Esteban and Bianca were still engaged in their lighthearted chatter, unaware of the furor that had been going on within the walls of the mansion during the last hour.

Tony mounted up on Sultan, giving one final order to Jose before he reined the horse to go. "Be on your way to Father Tomas, Jose. *Adios, amigo,*" he called back to the young Mexican with a sight mellowing to his voice.

Jose knew not what mission Tony went on, but he knew no one should try to stop him, for he would conquer and be the victor. Like a knight in shining armor, he rode off to do battle—or so it looked to the admiring young Jose.

THIRTY-SEVEN

Mark Kane's wedding gift to his son and new bride was to be their own home built there on the Circle K, and by the time they returned from their honeymoon the construction had already began. Come the springtime, it should be ready for them to move in. Until then, Jenny had made the bedroom next to Jeff's room into a cozy, comfortable sitting room. Young people needed that special privacy when they were first married and adjusting themselves to each other, the wise Jenny Kane realized.

She was more than pleased to see the radiant glow in both their faces when they returned from their trip. It was Amanda about whom she was concerned. Something troubled her daughter, yet Jenny hesitated to say anything to Mark. Perhaps Mona's presence in the hacienda now would help lift Amanda's spirits.

With Derek away the last two days on his business trip, Jenny had noticed Amanda just moping around the house, and she felt sorry for her. Even her beau wasn't there to come by in the evening. She didn't seem to be going on rides or enjoying Prince as she used to either.

Jenny thought surely Amanda would accompany Mona in the buggy that afternoon to pay a visit to her father, but Amanda had politely refused with some lame excuse.

Mona didn't question it for a minute and went on her way. Such a dear, sweet girl, Jenny thought. Just to look at Mona was to see a kind, gentle soul and she had a rare loveliness that Jenny felt Mona never gave any thought to. Jeff could pat himself on the back that he'd picked the very best for his wife. His mother just prayed he would always cherish such a gift.

After Mona left the Circle K Amanda sat in her room attending to a chore that was becoming more and more frequent. She sat in the chair by the window tediously taking the tuck out of her twill riding skirt. She cursed and fumed for her skill as a seamstress had never been as good as Mona's. Coolly and calmly, Mona would have had the minor sewing repair done in ten minutes.

Amanda had been sequestered for over thirty minutes now to release that extra little inch that would give her so much comfort. When she'd accomplished the task she chose the pretty bright scarlet loose tunic and instead of tucking it inside the divided skirt she fastened the tooled silver belt Juan Santos had made for her for Christmas around her waist. Looking in the mirror, she chided herself for being so sensitive. No one can tell, she reprimanded herself. That annoying voice taunted her, though, and pointed out that it was her own guilty conscience that plagued her.

Haughtily, she shrugged her shoulders and turned from the full-length mirror. As she placed the flat-crowned hat to the side of her head, she had to confess that the voice could be right. It was merely her own imagination, and there were going to be no obvious signs for a few more weeks, and by that time she'd be married to Derek. In the meanwhile, she'd starve herself. Lately, she'd been famished and had had no will power to resist Consuela's delights. That would have to change.

It was at Prince's stall that Jeff ambled in to find his sister. He'd been under tremendous pressure since his and his wife's return to keep his mouth shut. Now, as he saw her standing there he was tempted to turn around and go back out the barn door.

When he and Mona had lain in the bed the night before and his sweet wife was so elated about the announcement that her brother and Amanda were to be married, he had tried to pretend a pleasure he was hardly feeling.

Yet, if he told Amanda what he knew about Derek he wasn't sure of her reaction. He couldn't chance it! Christ, it was a hell of a predicament to be caught in!

"Jeff," she called to him. Her lovely face broke into a smile.

"Amanda, are you goin' for a ride?" he asked, striding up to her. Funny, he thought to himself, that she'd not wished to accompany Mona over to the Big D this morning. He knew his wife had asked her.

"I was thinking about it," she replied with an off-hand air. Suddenly, she turned to look up at him with a dejected expression in her eyes. "Haven't seen much of you lately. Want to ride with me, big brother?"

He gave her a broad smile. "I just might do that, sis. Yeah, I will." Perhaps, it might be a very good idea, and it could give him an opportunity to talk to her about this thing about marrying Derek. He didn't want this for Amanda and it was like a knife turning in his gut every time he thought about it.

"I'm so happy for you and Mona, Jeff," she remarked as she busied herself preparing Prince for their ride.

"Thanks, sis and . . . and I want you to be happy, too," he confessed. He could not resist adding, "Are you sure that Derek is the man for you, sis?"

She tossed her golden tresses back and gave a shrug of her shoulders as she flippantly answered him. "Who can say, Jeff? Guess it's a gamble."

A frown creased her brother's face. She seemed so casual about it. Entirely too casual! She certainly didn't sound like a young girl in love, but then, there had been a change in Amanda since way back. An older brother could sense that about his own sister.

Sister or not, she exuded a sexual sensuousness that only women who'd been with a man seemed to reflect. It showed in those periwinkle blue eyes, and in her walk, or in the way those rosebud lips lifted into a knowing grin. Hell, he couldn't pinpoint it, but he knew. Somehow, he didn't feel that it was Derek. Mario, perhaps? Another possibility could have been Tony Branigan.

"I have to agree with you, Amanda, about that. You were always different. I guess I just never figured on you and Derek."

Under her breath she told herself neither had she. God forbid, neither had she!

Before she could reply, a buggy came up the drive with a rolling cloud of dust rising up behind it and they both stood watching. It was hardly like Mona to be so reckless or daring. They both realized that something must be wrong over at the Big D for her to be driving so erratically. Jeff rushed forward and Amanda followed.

When Mona pulled up on the reins of the buggy, they could see the tears in her eyes. She leaped into Jeff's anxious, waiting arms and sobbed.

Perplexed, Jeff quizzed her about what was wrong. She kept shaking her head and sobbing. Amanda had never seen such a pathetic, lost-looking child as Mona seemed encircled there in Jeff's arms. When she was finally calmed enough to speak, she stammered, "That's just it, Jeff. I don't know—really. It just wasn't like Father. He was so cold and remote, as though I was a stranger. It was as if he didn't want to touch me, Jeff."

She broke into a new round of tears and Jeff held her close in his arms, looking over at Amanda with a quizzical look on his face. Amanda stared back at him with her fine brow raised, finding it impossible to believe David Lawson could be anything but adoring with his daughter.

"Was he ill, Mona?" Amanda asked her. Mona shook her head and told her he seemed fine. "In fact, I'd swear he'd put on some weight." She said she had tried to ask about the ranch and her brother, but all she got were short, snapping answers. "I could tell I just wasn't wanted around."

"Let's just drop it for the time being, all right? I may just drive over there tomorrow and see what this is all about, Mona. There has to be some reason for your father to act this way. I've known David Lawson too long, and there has to be some logical explanation for this." Jeff masterfully led Mona toward the hacienda and Amanda walked slowly and thoughtfully back to the barn.

While he had said nothing to her, Jeff was certain that Derek was at the botton of it. Today, he'd put it aside, but come tomorrow he was going to visit his father-in-law.

There could not have been a happier or a more pleased man than David Lawson when his son told him that Amanda Kane had agreed to be his wife. It was a marvelous thing in life for a parent to see his children marry so well. To David, it was like an extra blessing or bonus in life. His only regret was that darling wife wasn't there to share this time with him.

Soon his little Mona would be returning to Gonzales County to start her new life as Jeff's wife. Their union did not deprive him of a daughter but added to his life a son. In that moment, he was a man enjoying complete happiness.

So he had descended the stairway that late winter morning feeling as chipper as a man far younger than forty-six, greeting his housekeeper with an exuberance that surprised her. With Derek gone the last two days she had only him to care for, and he suggested she declare this day a holiday after breakfast was served.

Perhaps the house being so empty of people would have normally been lonely if he hadn't felt so complete with happiness. So the morning passed at a lazy pace as he took an extra cup of coffee and went into his study. Actually that big old desk of his had been used far more by his son than by him lately. The idea seized him to take a more careful look at the books he'd left

410

to Derek. Of course, his son had kept him informed, but he had the time today to study the figures. He should get more active than he'd been.

Derek had been accommodating by leaving the drawer unlocked where the ledgers were kept. He smiled, thinking to himself that it had always been the rule to keep that drawer locked. Anyway, as it happened, David was glad Derek had been remiss.

He took the next forty-five minutes going over the entries and all seemed very much in order. He'd have to congratulate Derek when he returned. He opened the drawer to replace the ledger and noticed something foreign lying there. A worn leather-bound book or journal. He knew instantly it should not have been there, nor had it been there about a week or so ago when he'd looked in the drawer. Why would it be there with the ledgers? The answer had to be that Derek had put it there. No one else could have.

Something drew him like a magnet to pick it up and something mysterious and strange engulfed him as he handled it and flipped open the cover. He knew why as he gazed on his wife's handwriting. He sat there with time stopping around him like a man in a trance. By the time he'd finished reading the entries in the journal he was a man despoiled, robbed of everything treasured and dear to his heart.

Before putting the journal back in the drawer he knew his son had purposely planted it there and left the drawer unlocked. Derek wanted him to read it and know about Mona. The boy was a demon, David sadly realized.

It was at this moment the daughter he'd loved so much had rushed through the archway. He looked at her and saw the truth with his own eyes. Dear God, she could have been little Maria Alvarado's older sister, which, in truth, she was. In that moment, he hated her, and the adultery that had created her.

He wished to hurt her as he was hurting. When she turned and left, he knew he had. For that, he hated himself. To undo the wrong, he removed the journal from the drawer and flung it and all its evil into the blazing fireplace. Watching how easily the fire destroyed the journal, he knew what he must do. This home he'd had such pride in and the love he'd felt within its walls had all been a sham and false. No longer was it Mona's home. She was now a part of the Circle K and that was how it should be.

He roamed the rooms taking one last look and he sat down for a while and poured himself glass after glass of the fine Madeira. He lost track of the time as the afternoon faded and dusk settled over the countryside.

The wine had its effect on him and he felt as weary as though he'd gone forever over the hills and valleys of the countryside on a long trail ride.

He gathered together the items he would need to accomplish what he would do before this night ended. Before him as he went about the house, as if to taunt and haunt him, was that clean-cut, ordinary face of his son. It was a ordinary face, just like his. Clear blue eyes and the mop of sandy brown hair with a straight narrow bridge of a nose. Dear Lord, who would have guess the vileness behind that facade!

Son of his loins! He wanted to retch and not have to admit it. But then he'd always been a rather plain, ordinary man himself, without the glamor and striking good looks of a Miguel Alvarado or the impressive,

412

powerful presence of a Mark Kane.

He had not the power to destroy the land but his fine two story house, which had housed this devil's spawn, would forever be destroyed along with the journal, already ashes in the fireplace. Derek would never live here.

The study was an inferno as David climbed the stairs, and he laughed, thinking about the wealth he'd piled on the floor by the opened safe. Like a raging wildfire the flames trailed down the hallway and into the parlor. Had anyone been near a moment later he would have heard one sharp, defined blast of an explosion came from above. Dame Destiny had joined David Lawson in laughter, for Derek had most certainly outsmarted himself. His bounty was but a pile of ashes, and the fine home he'd anticipated bringing Amanda to as his bride was a devastated hull of charred, scorched timbers.

Across the way, on the other side of the dense pine wood, a lone rider galloped through the night's darkness. Except for the eerie hooting of a night owl the countryside seemed ghostly quiet. Tony had a feeling about the hooting of a owl, but this night he paid no attention to it, reining the Arabian on toward his destination.

Neither could he take the time to be delayed in getting to the Circle K Ranch and Amanda. However, he kept thinking he smelled the burning embers of lumber or wood. But then his angry gray eyes were directed straight ahead.

THIRTY-EIGHT

All the Kane family had retired for the night, except Jeff. Excusing himself to take a stroll in the garden and have a smoke, he told Mona to go on up and he'd join her shortly. This thing with Mona and her father bothered him more than he dared let his wife know. It was just too out of character for the man.

He ambled unhurried around the grounds and puffed on the cheroot. Toward the north he caught the flashing reddish-gold glow light up the sky for a brief moment, but in his preoccupation he shrugged it off as distant lightning.

He found himself at the back wall of the courtyard garden and had turned to amble back toward the patio when a deep male voice spoke barely about a whisper. *"Amigo?"* Jeff turned to see an imposing figure, almost sinister looking, all in black. In the dark, Jeff couldn't tell much about the man's face covered in a heavy black beard.

"Who the hell are you, and what are you doing back here sneaking about?" Jeff demanded to know of the intruder.

The man moved away from the bushes to stand in

414

front of Jeff. "You don't know me, *amigo*?" The voice was laced with a heavy accent, as he gave out a laugh.

Jeff strained to see the face staring at him. "I never saw you before." The man's long hair reached the collar of his shirt with the sombrero resting on his back and unruly dark hair fell over one side of his forehead.

Tony gave a deep throaty laugh. "Jeff, it's Tony. Tony Branigan."

Jeff gave a laugh and shook his head. "Sweet Jesus, you could have fooled me. What the hell are . . ."

"I'm going to tell you if we can go over there by that bench and sit down to talk." Jeff's reaction was as he'd hoped. If he'd fooled him then he could fool just about anyone. It gave him a shot of confidence for the job ahead.

They sat on the bench and he told Jeff the whole story as he'd told it to Mark many weeks ago. "I'm trusting you, Jeff. I guess you realize that?"

"Yeah, I know. Always knew there was something about you. Just couldn't quite put my finger on it."

"Now you know, and now I've got to take a chance on asking you something you may not like. Just how much and how bad are you involved, Jeff? I want to spare you if I can—you understand?"

"I'll level with you, Branigan. More than I liked but not as bad as I could have been. The night Derek and I had a fight over a personal matter—well, hell, I'll tell you. It was something he said about Mona. That night I washed my hands of Derek, 'cause I knew then that guy was crazy."

"I'm glad to hear that, Jeff." He offered Jeff a drink from the flask he had with him.

"Weeks before that I was so sick at my stomach I

415

drank myself silly. I was always used to Derek leading me around by the nose but this was too deep for me and I knew it. I never killed anyone and I never stole from anyone but my father, but damn it, I knew! I knew what that crazy bastard was doing."

Tony heaved a heavy sigh of relief, for he had every intention of protecting Jeff's involvement if it wasn't too serious.

"The cattle I took from Father's herd was almost like some boyish prank, or so I thought at the time, and it paid off all those darn IOU tabs I signed for Derek's buddy at the Red Garter. Hell, it wasn't long before I knew which way the wind was blowing. Derek is a bloodsucker." Jeff's head bowed with his shame.

"And that was all you ever did personally other than know?" Tony anxiously inquired.

"That's it. Oh, now wait a minute—there was one other thing. I kept some gold for Derek. He flung this pouch at me as we were riding home and told me to keep it safe for him. Well, I did for a couple of days, and then one day when Amanda and I were checking the sacks of grain she almost found it. Boy, I'll tell you it scared the hell out of me. I am not cut out for that kind of stuff, Tony. So I busted my butt riding over to the Big D and gave it to Derek. That sonofabitch laughed at me." Jeff found Tony easy to talk to and he felt cleansed as he talked.

Tony believed every word Amanda's brother was telling him. Basically, he was a nice guy. His trouble was being overwhelmed by the strong-willed Lawson. He was too easily influenced. He decided that their would be no mention to Flanigan about anything where Jeff Kane was concerned.

"How's Amanda?" Tony knew he must have Jeff's help to whisk her away from that house and out of Gonzales County.

"All right, I guess. She's planning on marrying Derek and that's tearing the hell out of me, Branigan."

"Not if you'll help me, Jeff." Tony declared with a sharpness in his voice and a firm set to his jaw.

"What do you mean?"

"I'm kidnapping her tonight!"

"You . . . you're what?"

"I'm taking your sister captive tonight, taking her to San Antonio where my grandfather lives and keeping her there until I get this job behind me. After we leave you can tell your father and mother. Your father knows and has for a long time that my intentions are honorable. But the little idiot will not marry Lawson. She can't love that bastard."

"On that I agree. She's too moody and gloomy to be in love. Heck, I talked to her this afternoon and she acts like it's some damn business deal instead of a wedding." Jeff's words were honey to Tony's ears. Who was to say what sort of trickery or blackmail Lawson might be using on her, he decided.

The two put their head heads together to plot the strategy of how best to do the deed. "You'll never get that spitfire out of the house without waking up everyone, Tony. My idea would be best, I'm telling you."

Tony gave an uneasy laugh. "But it's just one more thing she's going to hold against me when she finds out."

"You want her, don't you? You want her out of here

417

tonight?" Jeff's direct, positive approach gave Tony a new feeling about the young man. "Hey, I'll even help you. Besides, it could be more convincing with the two of us. I'll stay back in the shadows."

After they'd run through the details once more of the plan for Amanda's abduction, they gave each other a comradely handshake and Jeff left him there in the shadows.

Tony waited, tensed and nervous for Jeff's sign that it was time for him to enter the unlocked back entrance of the hacienda. Jeff was to gather a packet of grub for them and check the upstairs to see that all was quiet and all the occupants were asleep. When Jeff came out of the house to go to the barn and ready Amanda's palomino for the long night ride, only then was Tony to slip up the backstairs to Amanda's room.

Dear God, he didn't like the idea of bringing her out of the house at gunpoint and the threat of harm to her father and mother, but except to gag and hogtie her he'd never manage it, as Jeff had pointed out to him.

The means didn't matter at this moment. Only the result was his concern. Later, he'd take the utmost pleasure in soothing her ruffled feathers. It wasn't a matter of masculine conceit but more the certain feeling that this love that beat so strong in him was as forceful in Amanda. He knew it, and nothing could have changed his mind.

Jeff came down the flagstone path toward the gate with the packet in his hand. He went through the iron gate and toward the barn. Tony delayed for the amount of time he figured it would take him to have Prince saddled up when he left the garden to enter the house.

He was cautious to step softly for he had no desire to stare down the barrel of Kane's six shooter and have the ungodly task of trying to explain this nocturnal escapade as though he was a thief invading Mark's house.

As he entered her room noiselessly and stared down at the sleeping beauty lying there with that mass of golden hair fanned out so attractively on the pillows, he felt like a fool drawing the pistol from his holster.

Sitting down on the edge of the bed he clasped his strong hand down over her mouth as he bent down to caution her not to make a sound or he'd kill her. God, he could hardly bring himself to say that.

Amanda's body jerked instinctively and then tensed. She made muffled sounds of protest. The intruder's fuzzy face was so close to hers she could feel the featherlike touches of the dark beard. A mean-looking brute, he was.

When he softened his deep voice to give her his command, he spoke in a very thick accented tone. "You will get up, señorita and dress. If you don't wish harm coming to your parents from my *compadre* then you will not make a sound to alert the brother across the hall. Comprehend?"

She nodded her head and those lovely eyes of hers were wide with shock and anger. In the dimly lit room he could envision them flashing with fire. To restrain himself from capturing those luscious lips was almost more than he could endure. Leaning over her soft, satiny body to whisper in her ear caused a liquid fire to flood him.

The rounded mounds of her breasts tormented him, so sensuously displayed in the sheer gown and partially bared. Instinctively, his hand almost reached to caress them, but he denied himself the pleasure.

Was this devil one of the outlaws roaming the countryside raining havoc, Amanda wondered? Was he going to take her to ransom her back to her wealthy family? She could not chance harm coming to her mother or father and so she complied with his orders to get up and dress.

She couldn't help her spitfire tongue lashing out at him, though. "Can you at least turn your head, you . . . you . . ."

"Watch your tongue, señorita," Tony quieted, her keeping his own voice lowered. Sensuous splendor, she was!

She jerked something from her armoire and with agitated motions she slipped into the blouse and the brown riding skirt. Perhaps, a jacket would be in order too, she thought, not knowing what this animal had in mind or where he would take her. Tony stood in the shadows of the dark bedroom, grinning with amusement and sneaking a peek a couple of times.

When she had her boots on she stood up, her head held high in defiance. "What now, *señor?*" she smirked in the most distasteful tone.

"Come here," he ordered. She came slowly toward him, feeling helpless but determined not to let him know it. When she stood before him, he secured her wrists, making certain the bonds were not too tight. "Now, we go, señorita—very quickly but quietly down the stairs. The back stairs."

It amazed her that he knew the layout of the hacienda so well. It must have been up the back stairs he'd come up to her room.

420

Had she not had her parents' welfare to think about she could have tried something . . . anything to throw a stumbling block into his plans. Her only hope, and that was a slim one, was that one of Kane's men might be around the grounds as she was being gently shoved on through the back door and out into the night. He ordered her to the barn, making her walk in front of him.

When they entered Tony saw the palomino was outside the stall readied for their ride and knew somewhere back in a stall somewhere in the huge barn Jeff stood, observing them.

"Allow me, señorita." He hoisted her up on the animal and felt her body flinch at his touch. He would make that change, he promised himself. He then turned to mount up on his own horse, reining the Arabian over to take charge of her reins and lead her mount out of the barn. He had to forego any farewell to Jeff, but he was sure he'd understand.

They rode through the barn door and out into the dark countryside toward the pine woods. Amanda swayed in her saddle, not knowing what fate awaited her at the hands of this Mexican desperado. He looked a fierce sight with his villain's face, and he was so menacingly tall.

They rode for over an hour before he finally allowed them to stop by a small creek and water the horses. She was of the opinion from the lay of the terrain that this little stream must branch off the Guadalupe River and empty into the San Antonio River. She felt certain they'd traveled westward from the Circle K.

She grasped for something to delay them and pleaded, "Can't we rest a moment more?"

421

"Later, we'll rest," Tony told her. He was glad it was dark, for a grin came to his face. The little minx! He knew exactly what she was trying to pull.

Without further delay, he hoisted her back up on Prince and they went on their way. Amanda realized escape was almost hopeless and she also realized her captor was staying on the back roads.

Tony was feeling weariness gnawing at him and was anticipating getting to Father Tomas' mission so he could grab a couple of hours of rest before putting in the long ride south after he had Amanda deposited with his grandfather. Once they arrived at the mission he had one more hour to travel before arriving at the Moreno estate.

He saw Amanda's slumped shoulders and more than ever he welcomed the distant sight of the lofty gray stone towers of the mission. The new Arabian had proven himself well in endurance.

As the first rays of dawn were breaking Amanda found herself being ushered into a strange place by an elderly gent who had to be eighty if he was a day. He had to be some type of servant, she assumed, in his loose baggy pants and tunic, for he was not wearing the garb of a priest. Yet, she also assumed it to be a mission from the austere look of the front chamber she walked through. It was obvious the bent-over old man knew her captor. This seemed peculiar to her.

It also increased her interest in the man striding beside her with the battered sombrero shadowing his face. His dark skin and his accent left no doubt that he was Mexican. There wasn't much left for her to see on his swarthy face so abundantly furred with blue-black whiskers. But he was a husky one, and

422

extremely tall.

She was ushered into a small cubicle of a room, sparsely furnished and drab. It had a musty smell, but Amanda could not have cared less when she spied the narrow bed with fresh linens. She was so tired that her brain seemed not to be functioning. She didn't turn around to observe the two men or the door shutting, but made her way to the bed to lie down.

Had she stood by the door and listened she would have heard the old gentleman clad in the light-colored loose pants and tunic admonish her captor in the strongest terms. "If I did not believe you to be an honorable man, Antonio, and if I did not feel the deepest regard for Esteban, I would have no part in this."

Tony took his arm and reassured him as they walked down the tiled hall, "I assure you this woman is loved and respected. She will be my wife. I would die before bringing harm or shame to her, Father Tomas."

"Then I must believe you, Antonio. Perhaps, I can perform that wedding service for you, eh?"

"No one else could," Tony laughed. "Now, where can I rest for a few hours?"

"This way, Antonio. I will wake you at what time?"

Tony told him, but Father Tomas had seen the weariness on both his and the young woman's face. A few more hours, should they sleep over just a little, would not matter, he privately decided as he left Tony in his quarters.

As the noon hour came Father Tomas, now in his traditional priest's garb, checked on the two young people. His gentle heart and compassion went out to them and he couldn't force himself to rouse them. Besides, one more hour would see them to the Moreno mansion. He let them sleep. He had no knowledge that Tony had yet another rendezvous to keep.

THIRTY-NINE

Some fourteen hours had passed since the time Tony and Amanda had entered the mission grounds and were shown to their separate quarters. The effect of so much sleep left Tony feeling dulled, like he'd been drugged heavily, as he sat up on the cot. For a few minutes he sat there, trying to get his bearings and rubbing his eyes. Brushing his long fingers through his lion's mane of hair he realized how exhausted he must have been.

As he stood up on his long legs he felt unsteady so he took a seat back on the cot. It was at this moment that Father Tomas trailed by a Mexican servant came to stand at the door. "I thought you and the señorita might use this before coming on up to my quarters for a good meal, eh?" He handed an oversized cup filled with steaming black coffee to Tony, making certain he had a firm hold on it before releasing it.

"Take this one to the señorita, Lucinda. I'm sure she will welcome it, too," Father Tomas remarked, turning back to Tony greedily gulping from his cup. "I would say you were a very weary traveler, my son."

"More than I realized, Father," Tony smiled, looking up at the diminished little priest he'd known forever it seemed. It was he who had given Tony such comfort at the time of his mother's death.

"Then I will go on and allow you to finish your coffee. You know the way to my rooms, so bring the young lady when you are ready and have a good meal before you're on your way on into the city, eh?"

"Yes, Father—we'll be there shortly. I thank you so much for all you've done."

Father Tomas smiled warmly at the young man sitting there on the cot. Those gray eyes of his were still, at times, the eyes of that lost little boy of so long ago. As impressing a figure of a man as Antonio had become, Father Tomas still saw the boy in him.

"No need for thanks, Antonio." He took his leave to see that the meal was ready to be served to the young couple he'd sheltered.

Tony mistook the daylight fading outside the high windows for the dawning of a new day. It was only after he and Amanda had eaten the meal that he was shocked to learn the truth. He would have exploded with rage if it had been anyone else's handiwork except Father Tomas's. That gentle soul's intentions had been for the best, but the good father could not know what his act of compassion would cause in delays.

For the first time Amanda heard the priest address this bearded desperado as Antonio. Last night she'd questioned nothing. Refreshed by a long spell of sleep her mind was alert. She suddenly realized as she sat at the table eating that the bent-over little man in the baggy white pants who'd greeted them in the early morning hour was the man now garbed in the priest's robe. Why would a man of the cloth be in league with a captor of women as this man had to be? He had taken her from her home and she was beginning to suspect now he had acted alone. Had she thought that last night she would have given him more opposition.

As they rode off into the twilight, she was a different woman from the sleepy-eyed, addled one he'd taken so easily from her bedroom chamber, and Tony was very much aware of it. Alive and vital, her eyes were flashing bright.

"Who the devil are you, señor? This whole thing does not make any sense!"

"Ah, it makes very much sense, señorita! As you heard Father Tomas say, I am Antonio," Tony said with a thick accent to his words. Had the sombrero not been jauntily cocked over the front of his face she could have seen an amused, devious gleam in his eyes.

Ah, the little wildcat was there for him to see now.

"Well, Señor Antonio—I fear your little deed last night will cost you dearly." She held her head with her pert little nose stuck up in the air.

The rest of his life, he mused. Aloud, he replied, "But for a beauty such as you, the price is nothing."

Her head darted around and she glared at him. The fury was there for him to see in those gorgeous amethyst eyes. Now, just what was he hinting at, she wondered?

"My beauty, as you call it, will never give you any reward or pleasure, señor!"

He laughed deep and loud. "Don't count on that, *chiquita*. Don't count on that at all!"

Her body tensed and Tony knew his words had made an impact. Dear Lord, her beauty overwhelmed

427

him so much he wanted to halt up the horses and take her there on the ground. But he satisfied himself with the thought that having her there waiting at the mansion would urge him to finish the mess at Palito Blanco all the sooner to get back to San Antonio to her.

Amanda decided his sudden quiet mood was not good for he might just be anticipating raping her. Best that she try to keep him talking about something . . . anything.

She chattered away on nothing in particular, but all the time her mind was racing crazily about something the man had said. What was it?

The concealing darkness was closing in on them all too quickly to please Amanda and anxiety sprang up in her. Just as quickly it subsided, as she saw over in the distance the signs of a town, or ranch, perhaps. She asked the desperado, "Where are you taking me? Over there . . . where I see the lights?"

"That is right, señorita." Tony offered her no more information than that. He knew he had neither the time nor the patience to deal with Amanda tonight. To tame her after what he'd done would prove tedious and he dared not try to fool himself on that score.

Best she knew as little about all this as possible until his return, and then he planned to devote leisurely hours to her taming, if it proved to be that difficult.

As they got to the outskirts of the city she suddenly realized that it was San Antonio they were riding into. He had taken the back trails and paths or she'd have realized it sooner. She smiled, feeling a surge of hope. At least, it was a city where she was familiar with the surroundings and some of the citizens. So should she get the chance to escape this hairy animal holding her she could seek refuge with the Beckenridges. A spirited bravado churned within her, and she turned to the rider with that familiar haughty, smug air of hers and smirked, "I know where you're taking me, señor."

He could sense the cold aloofness in the way she drawled out the "señor," and he smiled. "And where is that, beautiful lady?"

"San Antonio!"

"Ah, smart as well! You have been here before?" He played his mysterious role to the limit.

"I have, and I have friends here."

"If you are a good girl and behave yourself then you might live to see them again."

"Oh, you! You bas . . ."

Tony interrupted her. "No, no señorita! Do not call me foul names, for that is not being a good girl."

"Oh, shut up! How would the likes of you know what is good?"

He adored her, with all that fire in her eyes and her face and her head lifted in defiance. She was a seductive sorceress, bedeviling him beyond all will power.

Some force made Amanda aware of the searing, lusty eyes devouring her intensely, and she boldly returned his stare. The brilliance of the moonlight focused on his face as they came out of the wooded area into the clearing. She was flooded with the eeriest feeling. She found herself held in a trance. Except for the distraction of his leading her through a wide entrance to go up a long, winding drive, she would not have turned her eyes from him. The sight greeting her eyes was a shock. They'd entered some fine estate, and

429

she saw a massive, sprawling stone house set among tall palm trees. This was no mission. This was someone's grand, stately home.

She gave a quick glance behind her and saw some youth hastily closing the wide iron gate they'd just passed through. The property was enclosed by a five-foot stone fence.

She was struck dumb at this strange, unexpected turn of events. It was to some squalid shanty in the bad part of the city she'd have suspected this bandit would take her—not this.

Tony smiled as they rode on, for he could almost read the thoughts roaming through that pretty head of hers. He said not a word as he reined up on Sultan and Jose came running out. He gave the boy the sign to say nothing and Jose complied, merely greeting them with a "Good evening" as he took Sultan's reins. Tony lifted Amanda out of the saddle and down to the ground to stand by his side. Her sudden quietness could have pleased him if it hadn't been so unlike her. That perplexed him as he urged her to the back entrance.

Amanda sat quietly where he'd ordered her while he spoke in a lowered voice to a man she assumed to be a servant in the grand old house. The man gave her a fast, quick glare and turned his attentions back to the young bearded man who had brought her there. In lowered voices the two exchanged words.

The next several minutes happened so fast she was like a person carried down the currents of a swift-moving stream of water. A middle-aged Mexican woman guided her to a suite of lavishly furnished rooms that consisted of a bedroom and a beautifully decorated sitting room. She informed Amanda that her name was Elvira and anything she'd need she had only to request.

It was only as she was left alone in the room to wander around in her strange, new surroundings that Amanda came to the conclusion it had all been expertly prepared and timed. It was true insanity! What was it all about?

She was brought a chilled bottle of white wine and glasses and a perfumed bath was prepared for her enjoyment. A most luxurious robe of deep purple satin was laid out on the bed, along with a diaphanous nightgown of pale lavender. It was so lovely that Amanda had to sigh as she picked it up to examine it.

When she requested that she be left to bathe in privacy Elvira quickly exited the room without a fuss. A prisoner she might be, but anyone would have thought she was a visiting princess.

While some young ladies might have been frantic at the dilemma Amanda found herself in, she wasn't. The cool white wine had relaxed her before she stepped into the tub of perfumed warm water. She lathered herself with lazy motions, enjoying the sweet odor of the soap. When she had rinsed herself free of the suds she lay back languorously to gaze around the room and admire the loveliness of her prison surroundings. Even the colors were her favorites. Pale blue dominated the room, with touches of violet and purple in the silk and velvet pillows. There was a exquisite, dainty lady's desk with a chair cushioned in purple velvet. A magnificent dressing table and stool stood against one wall and on top of it were cut crystal miniature bottles of perfume and a fine silver brush and comb set with its matching hand mirror. Some pampered lady had surely occupied this room, it was obvious. The fine Turkish rug had to be very expensive.

How could some renegade have access to such a fine home? This question nagged at her as she lay back against the back of the tub.

Downstairs Tony took a light supper with his grandfather before going out into the night again. Esteban protested to his grandson that he should get a good night's sleep, but Tony quieted Esteban's concern. "Father Tomas saw to that by allowing me plenty of sleep, Grandfather. Besides, I'm already twelve hours overdue to meet Salazar. That isn't exactly in my favor." He cursed himself the minute he saw the look of concern on the elderly man's face. He quickly sought to remedy his mistake by breaking into a broad grin and jesting, "But with her waiting here with you I can assure you I will be hurrying to get back." He winked at his grandfather.

"You must prize this young lady very highly, Antonio. She must be very rare for you to put so much worth on her that you endanger your own life. I'm most eager to meet her," Esteban remarked, a serious tone in his voice and much concern engulfing him for his grandson's venture down south.

"I do, and now I must be on my way. I want to look in on her for a minute before I leave. Guard her until I can return, and only then will I tell her who I really am and why all this has been necessary. Remember, she is a sly little fox, and she'll try to pry it out of you."

"You just take care of yourself, and I will do my

432

part," Esteban assured him as they locked in a warm embrace. Tony left the room to rush upstairs.

When Amanda hear the door open she assumed it to be the servant Elvira bringing her the supper tray, but as she turned around in the tub she saw it was the black-bearded man standing there ogling her there naked in the tub. He was a most awesome sight. In the dimly lit room his pale eyes stood out like beacons of silver fire.

She sank lower into the tub and tried to find her voice after they had locked stares for a second. "You have a nerve, señor!" She tried to pose a bold indignation she wasn't exactly feeling. She told herself that now she knew what this was all about. She was like the harem girl being bathed and perfumed for the sheik for his pleasure and taking. Well, maybe he would have her, for all she had to do was look at his huge body to know she couldn't win the battle against him. But she was going to fight him all the way.

He took a striding step closer, letting his eyes devour all that loveliness, so lush and tempting. Tony told himself to stay a distance away or the fire of her would surely consume him. God, he'd never hungered so for a woman!

He took one more step toward the tub, his body swelling with desire. His ghostly silence made Amanda more nervous than if he had said something. Everywhere those unusual eyes slowly went over her seemed to leave a searing trail. She twisted in the tub of water, still staring up at him. "I hope you are getting your eyeful," she snapped at him.

"Oh, I am, my beauty. I most certainly am."

Amanda felt like a poor helpless rabbit about to be

pounced upon by a hunting dog. She turned from the sight of him. Something about this man was compelling in a mysterious, strange way. As she'd locked her eyes with his a force so strong had shot through her it frightened her and made her question her sanity.

In that next moment everything happened so fast she found it all hard to put in order later. He was there bent down by the tub and his huge tanned hand had turned her face toward him. The touch was tender gentleness, though, and his lips were on hers, strong and demanding. One big hand cradled the back of her head just as he wanted it and the other went to cover her breast, caressing it with lazy, featherlike touches. It was a divine sensation!

Amanda was not aware of her soft moan of pleasure, but Tony was. He whispered words of love against her ear in a lusty, husky voice. Christ, he cussed this whole damned mess with Flanigan!

He was fast reaching a point where he knew he had to tear himself away from this wildfire woman or he'd never leave this room tonight. He'd lift her satiny damp body from that tub and carry her to the bed and make love to her as he yearned to do, all night long.

When he forced himself away from her, he saw her eyes closed with delight and pleasure and he whispered farewell to her and raised up hastily to leave the room. His overwhelming flame remained with her long after the door had slammed. She was shaken to the core of her being. That strange feeling of déjá vu was with her again.

No man had stirred such wild, savage sensations in her since . . . oh God, she didn't even want to think his name, much less say it. Tony Branigan! Why did she seemed only to be aroused to these lofty heights by men of such caliber. Was there something cheap about her? Was she not like a proper young lady was expected to be?

Once before her body had felt that ecstasy, she recalled as she dried herself with the large towel. She'd never been the same since where another man was concerned. Not with Derek Lawson or Steve Beckenridge! Only now had her senses been stirred to that point of anticipated rapture. She dropped the towel with a suddenness as she recalled his words of love. *Amanda mia*, he's whispered in her ear.

There was something else about that bearded one that reminded her of Tony Branigan, but her mind was too muddled right now to sort it out.

FORTY

The night Jeff Kane watched Tony Moreno spirit away his sister he could not help thinking how he should have suspected something was going on between them. No ordinary people were those two! How natural it was that they should have attracted each other. The intrigue of it all would appeal to Amanda's daring nature.

Later, as he lay by the side of his own sweet Mona with sleep impossible, he could never imagine her dealing with such a happening. He reminded himself that he must get to his father the first thing in the morning to explain the strange events of the night before, before his mother came down for breakfast. As it had been around the Circle K Ranch all his life, Jeff knew his father was always the first to descend the stairs, at least a full half-hour before Jenny Kane came down for breakfast.

When the clock struck six the next morning, Jeff laboriously made himself get up and dress. Slipping silently out the bedroom door so as to not rouse his wife, Jeff went downstairs to encounter Mark Kane.

At his place at the head of the long dining room

table, Mark Kane sat, accepting the first cup of coffee Consuela was pouring; the first cup was always the very best one, Mark swore.

He looked up to see his son coming into the room, and it was a pleasant surprise. Mark had found the changes in Jeff since his marriage to Mona a pleasing improvement. "Mornin', son."

"Father." Jeff ambled on in, taking a seat next to him. Mark's deep, demanding voice called out for Consuela and she came scurrying through the door again.

When she had filled Jeff's cup and returned to her kitchen, Jeff wasted no time in fear that his mother would appear. "Father, I've got something to tell you before Mama comes down. We had a visitor last night. Tony Moreno came back."

"Hell, he did?" Kane frowned. "How'd you know about the Moreno bit, I mean?" That had been told to him as a confidence so how did Jeff get wind of it?

"He confided in me. He had to so I could help him take Amanda away."

Kane reared up in the chair. Anger etched his face and he looked like a bull ready to charge. "Make sense Jeff! Just what the hell is all this nonsense about? Where did he take my girl?"

"He took her to his grandfather's house in San Antonio . . . a Señor Esteban Moreno. He swore to me that you knew of his intentions toward Amanda and that I was to tell you so you and Mama wouldn't be concerned. Said he'd be damned if he'd let her go through with this marriage to Derek."

Mark Kane eased slowly back down into his seat and said nothing. A slow smile came to his weathered

437

face. He could envision himself pulling just such a trick had some bastard tried to beat his time with his sweet Jenny. A sudden explosive raucous laugh broke from Kane.

"Dad? Dad, wha . . ." Jeff sat staring at his father's reaction, unable to finish what he was about to ask.

"I *like* that man!" Mark still shook with laughter. "Yes sir, by God, that's the kind of man she needs. One like him takes the bull by the horns and goes." He leaned over to his son and confessed confidentially, "Tell the truth, Jeff, I wasn't too damned happy about that marriage she was planning with Derek. No, sir!"

"I wasn't either, Dad," Jeff admitted.

"You weren't, Jeff? Glad to hear you say that, son." Mark Kane was about to say more to his son, and his tribute of pride would have pleased Jeff, but a sharp rap on the front door interrupted their conversation and brought Consuela rushing out of the kitchen.

Even without the words being spoken by his father, Jeff felt a new confidence in himself and sensed a new camaraderie they shared lately. While he'd not had a chance to put his feeling into words, Tony Moreno's faith and trust had boosted his morale. He realized now that it was himself and not other people he should have blamed for his weaknesses in life. Only he was the one at fault. Blaming the others was a flimsy, childish excuse.

The trio ushered into the dining room by Consuela were a grim-faced bunch, Kane noted. All three men were known to him and Jeff. The two younger men were Sheriff McCurly's deputies, and Clay McCurly had been around Gonzales County about as long as Mark. They were about the same age.

"Clay, I got the feeling there's bad news from the look on your face," Mark said after greeting the three.

"Sure is, Mark. I don't know when I had a blow like this. Jeff, son . . . I've really got a whopper to throw at you seein' as how you and Miss Mona just married."

Mark barked a loud, impatient demand for Consuela to bring three more cups of coffee before turning his attention back to Clay McCurly. "What's happened, Clay?"

"Well, Mark . . . don't rightly know other than the Big D was hit by one hell of a fire last night and that nice old house is just lyin' in a big pile of ashes. Went too fast to just be an accident. Someone done set that fire, Mark. Worse part—and it seems, Mark, it was self-inflicted—David Lawson shot himself."

"What? Ah, now Clay." Mark shook his head with disbelief, not accepting the sheriff's theory.

"Nope, Mark . . . swear to God. There was a bullet in his head. That, in itself, was a miracle, Mark considering the way that damn house was a mountain of ashes."

"If the house was like that then maybe David was put there after the fire to make it look like he shot himself, Clay. That don't make sense to me."

There are various reactions a man can have when a dear, lifelong friend dies. Kane had experienced the feeling of being hit hard in the gut, and now he felt numb talking with his other old friend, the sheriff.

Jeff was still there, feeling stunned all the time they were talking. Finally, he stammered, "I . . . I guess

I'd better go up and tell Mona." His face was ashen as he walked slowly from the room dreading to break the wretched news to his wife. It seemed more like a nightmare you prayed to wake up from to find it wasn't true.

Clay McCurly dismissed his two young deputies to head back into town. His motive was a private talk with Mark about something that had been gnawing at him ever since he'd ridden to the Circle K to dispatch the news to Kane.

"Can we walk a bit, Mark?"

"Sure," Mark said, pulling up out of the chair and walking around the long table to join the sheriff.

The two went out the door and down the stone path and on through the iron gate. Only then did Clay bring up the subject on his mind. "There was no sign of that young hellion, Derek, Mark. Seemed funny to me. What do you think?"

"I understand he was supposed to have gone somewhere on some business for the ranch. You know David had been giving him more rein for over a year now?"

"Yeah, I knew that, and I've wondered just how wise that was in the first place. There's been a few rumors floating around Gonzales for months on that boy."

"Anything bad, Clay?" Mark quizzed the sheriff.

"Oh, I guess the truth of it is, Mark, I always pegged him as a worrisome lot to David. Now, that boy of yours did his mischief, too, but that Derek . . . hell, I can't pinpoint it." Clay added that he'd sent a couple of men to do some checking around the countryside.

"Maybe I'm wrong, Mark, and God knows, I hope I am, but I got a real bad feeling about this . . . a real bad feeling."

Mark gave a nod of his head, for he had a feeling the sheriff was right. Poor David had paid the supreme price. Why would he want to take his own life?

When Clay left the Circle K Mark turned his thoughts and efforts to the job at hand. There were things to attend to and Mona was going to need all the help he and his family could give her.

His wrath was something he'd have to forget about for the time being, but vengeance would be carried out. He made a solemn vow to himself as he walked back into the garden courtyard. That, Kane vowed to himself, included Derek.

Many miles away in the outskirts of San Antonio, a more humble dwelling was a charred rubble. No one gave it any consideration except U.S. Marshal Flanigan. He suspected that a drifter had probably taken up residence there and set the shack on fire in a drunken stupor. It really didn't matter, Flanigan mused, for old Tito was already buried in the cemetery. Flanigan had seen to that, for he owed Tito that much.

The old hooligan had always fascinated Flanigan, and he could never figure it out. He'd spent an hour going over the remains of that old shack, which had yielded up nothing to clear up the mystery of the old man. Any keepsakes Terrance Branigan had on his person had been washed out to sea when he was shipwrecked years ago off Corpus Christi Bay. When his memory was restored and he had labeled himself Tito, he had nothing left from his past but one thing . . . a son.

That son would never know it was his father who'd saved his life. Fate and Terrance Branigan had decreed it that way.

The air had just enough chill to it to keep him alert as Tony left the lights of San Antonio far behind him. While Sultan had more than proved himself a fine horse on the swift trip to Gonzales County, he felt more at home in the saddle atop Picaro. He had to remember to reward young Jose for carrying out all his instructions to the letter.

With the long hours of sleep back at Father Tomas' mission and a good meal shared with Esteban, he felt in top shape. His spirits were at a peak with Amanda in safekeeping and her beauty had his blood running hot and churning. Every fiber of his being was alive and he had everything a man needed to want to stay alive. This night Tony Moreno owned the world!

It didn't worry him that he was arriving some fourteen hours past the time he was to meet with his old *compadre* Pedro. He'd carry off his role to perfection, he told himself, feeling an abundance of assurance.

Picaro's strong long legs carried him swiftly, following the banks of the San Antonio River southeastward. The moon was high in the dark sky now and he'd pushed himself and Picaro hard for almost an hour. The terrain was now changing into the flatland country. When he came to the place where the Frio River met with San Miguel Creek he stopped by a grove of mesquite trees to give himself and his horse a rest.

Lighting up a cheroot and taking a swig from his

canteen, he pulled out the map Flanigan had drawn for him. If he kept up the pace he'd set for himself he'd arrive well before daybreak and that would be in his favor.

The thought of seeing Pedro again was pleasant. He and Salazar had shared some good times in the past and there was no one he'd rather have fighting beside him than Pedro in a tight spot. When this damn mess was behind the two of them, perhaps they'd ride back to San Antonio together. In a more lighthearted vein, he pondered whether he should chance introducing that good-looking devil to Amanda. He had been quite the gent with the ladies, for as long as Tony had known him.

Pedro Salazar was an enigma and while Tony guessed he knew him as well as anyone around San Antonio, he really knew nothing of him past six years ago, nor had Salazar sought to enlighten him.

Before starting out again he took a generous slug of the brandy in his flask. There were a few miles more to go and time wasn't going to stand still.

When he reached the point Flanigan had labeled Three Rivers, he halted Picaro to survey the area. There were three trails, and he veered to the right as the marshal had told him to do. If he was lucky, he would find Pedro waiting there. So he slowed Picaro's pace as he wove through the trees and up the trail with his eyes devouring all sides of the narrow path.

He spotted the shack of sorts Flanigan had said would be at the spot. It was more like a shed than a shack, Tony considered as he came upon it and saw there was no horse standing by the side of it.

Like a stalking cat, he came slowly down out of his

saddle and walked as softly as he could to check out the shed. There was no one there.

But the sensitive Picaro's instincts told him there was someone around and he gave out a whinny causing Tony to react like the gunfighter he was. His hand clutched the silver-plated pistol. The deep bass laughter Tony heard could only belong to Pedro. "Hey, *amigo!*"

As dramatic as an actor coming on stage, he sauntered cockily from behind the trees smiling that broad smile of his. "What did you do, amigo . . . oversleep?"

"Pedro!" Christ, you're a sight for sore eyes!" The two grabbed each other in a comradely embrace. Releasing each other, they broke into a round of roughhousing.

Finally, both were ready to call it quits and Tony pulled out his flask to offer Pedro a drink of brandy. As they both took a seat on the ground and leaned up against the thick trunk of a tree, Tony asked him about the latest developments among the outlaws at the shack they'd soon be going to.

"I made contact with Jack here in the woods a couple of days ago, and all had gone well in Encino. And as you know just coming from San Antonio the Reynosa raid went smooth as silk. This is it, *amigo* . . . tomorrow night. The gringo boss comes tomorrow night and the five up there in the shack are a restless, nervous lot . . . waiting for their cut of the loot."

"Five, eh?" Tony took another gulp from the flask.

"*Si* and a woman. You're my old sidekick from up Kansas way and you've come to join up with me so when I get my cut we will ride for New Mexico together . . . right?"

"That's right. Tell me, Pedro have you flung my name at them yet?"

"Only said a dude by the name of Tony." Pedro smiled a broad, pearly grin at him.

"Perfect. Glad you didn't mention a last name." All through his night ride to meet Salazar he had given a lot of thought to that one particular item. It was always the little things that could foul something up. If Pedro had flung the name of Branigan it could have blown the whole operation to the sky. Salazar's curious nature had to know why, though.

"It depends on who this 'gringo boss' turns out to be. If it's Sid Thomas, the name Branigan won't mean anything. If it's Derek Lawson, then I'm going to have to hope he doesn't recognize me when we come face to face. You'll just have to let me take the reins on this one, Pedro," Tony told him. He knew his personal vendetta with Lawson would come sooner or later, and he knew beyond any doubt that Derek's guilt was a certainty. What Tony was not sure about was whether it was Sid Thomas who had recruited Lawson into the rustling operation or the other way around.

He was soon to find out, for Pedro had raised himself up from the ground and suggested, "Time to get this show started, *amigo*. I'm more than ready to be through with it and get to the city and a beautiful señorita who's pining away for old Pedro." He gave Tony a playful nudge in the side and winked one of his dark eyes.

"My feelings exactly, Pedro," Tony agreed, checking his matching silver-plated pistols to see that they hung on his trim hips at just the right angle. Satisfied he sauntered over to where Picaro was tied to a sapling while Pedro ambled back into the wood to get his horse.

Remembering the tantalizing sight of Amanda in the tub and the bewitching beauty of her face, he was fired for action.

FORTY-ONE

Esteban sat there in the small room where he usually did when he dined alone. Elvira, his devoted servant, knew he preferred the bright, cheery room instead of the spacious formality of the dining room. But this morning there was nothing bright or cheery about Señor Esteban's mood.

He was the personification of gracious dignity but those black eyes were brooding when she served him. As dark as that dressing jacket he had on, she thought to herself. She didn't like to see him in this mood.

Rarely had he been at odds with his grandson as he was this morning, and what riled him more was the fact that he was could not explode at Tony about it. Esteban was never a man to be pushed into a corner he didn't wish to be in. Tony had inherited that trait from him, he guessed.

This act was too rash and too reckless even for the doting Esteban, who had refused his grandson very little since he'd become a man. Keeping a beautiful young lady in his home against her wishes did not have a pleasant taste to it. He would not go that far, even for Tony.

He would place a servant to watch the entrances and lie, if he must, to her, but he could not bring himself to keep the young lady a prisoner up in that room. That seemed too cruel, although he could appreciate Tony's concern that she remain here until his return. He concluded impulsively that he would send Elvira up to her and insist she join him for breakfast this morning.

"Elvira!"

"*Si*, señor?" Elvira came trotting into the room.

"Ask the señorita to join me here as soon as she is dressed."

Elvira hesitated for a minute until Señor Esteban gave her a harsh look. "I know! I know, but I'm changing those orders, Elvira. This is my house . . . not Antonio's!"

"*Si*, señor . . . right away!" She rushed out of the room and up the steps directly to the room Amanda had occupied since the evening before.

"Señorita? It is Elvira."

"Come in," Amanda called, grateful to know the footsteps she'd heard padding down the hallway weren't those of the man whose face had haunted her sleep last night until total exhaustion had overtaken her.

Entering the room and seeing the girl with the long golden hair falling in lovely cascading waves over her shoulders and down her back in her frilly underthings, Elvira could understand why the young señor was hell bent on keeping her under lock and key if necessary. Her figure was in the full bloom of feminine perfection and her eyes were the most beautiful shade of blue, like cornflowers and blue bonnets.

"The señor requests your company to join him in breakfast, señorita."

"Well, Elvira you go tell your señor I don't care to dine with him."

Elvira stood for a minute not knowing what to do. Amanda turned back from the mirror where she sat at the dressing table combing her hair. "Well? Did you not hear what I said? If he thinks he's going to make me jump to his demands he's crazy and you can also tell him if he dares to come to this room and enter without knocking like he did last night he can expect a . . . a vase smashed over his head."

Elvira had to restrain a smile coming to her face, for she knew Señor Esteban would never do something like that. She was talking about Antonio. "Please, señorita . . . please forgive me but Señor Esteban . . ."

"So that is his name, eh? Señor Esteban!"

"No, señorita. Señor Esteban is the one who wishes you to dine with him. Perhaps I should tell you he is an elderly gentleman, and not the one you speak of."

"Then who is the one I speak of?"

"Please, señorita. You must speak to the señor about that. I am only a servant. May I assist you in dressing?"

"I . . . I guess so," Amanda stammered. Why not? It could be the first step to getting out of this place by getting outside this room. Last night after the visit from that strange man she'd checked the door to find herself locked in. This morning it was still locked.

Elvira took a gown from the large armoire and held it out for Amanda's inspection and approval. "Would this be all right?"

Amanda admired the cut and color of the gown. It was simple and unadorned except for an edging of narrow lace around the sleeves and a squared neckline in a lovely shade of deep, rich blue. Elvira pulled out a pair of slippers almost the same shade of blue and expressed a hope that they would fit.

The gown was a little snug and the slippers were a little large but Elvira took a small piece of cloth and tucked it in the toe of the slipper making it an almost perfect fit.

"*Gracias*, Elvira." Amanda gave her a soft laugh and the servant laughed with her, taking a sudden liking to Antonio's ladylove.

"Ah, you are most beautiful!" She had to bite her tongue to keep from adding that she could see why Antonio's great infatuation with her had been so overwhelming. After all it had been only a brief time ago that he'd been engaged to marry Magdalena Gomez, and now she'd married another man.

The two descended the stairs and Elvira guided her to the room where Esteban sat reading his paper and sipping from his cup. When he looked up to see the young woman coming into the room in his wife's gown filling it out so magnificently he could more than understand his grandson's obsession about keeping her. She was a winsome miss! Utterly breathtakingly beautiful!

She walked right up to him boldly with those dainty shoulders flung back proudly and those blue eyes framed with thick dark lashes locked right into his.

He rose from his chair and pulled one out for her. "Good morning, señorita. May I present myself and say how delighted I am to have you join me. I am

450

Esteban Moreno, and this is my home."

If Amanda had meant to be haughty or waspish, this elegant old gentleman quickly swept such thoughts away. She was instantly impressed by his looks and his manner and she took the seat he offered. "My name is Amanda Kane, if you've not already been informed, Señor Moreno."

"Yes, I know your name, señorita but it is a pleasure to meet you. Please, what may Elvira bring you . . . coffee?"

Amanda ate a light breakfast that was as delicious as any Consuela could have prepared and took an extra cup of coffee. She found the old gentleman easy to talk with and an interesting conversationalist. He was sharp and witty, bringing forth a burst of laughter from her by the time they left the table. He'd captivated her with that debonair manner of his in the last hour.

"Señorita, could an old gentleman impose on you to take a stroll with him in his garden?" Esteban asked, finding her company a pleasure. Amanda could not suppress a smile as she noted the twinkle in his dark eyes. He was a charmer and the longer than she'd been around him the more she could imagine what a figure he'd been as a young man.

"If you'd like, Señor Esteban," she replied. So they left the house, going out the side door from the dining room across the terrace. As Esteban was privately scrutinizing her, she was doing the same to him. When she felt the moment was right and they'd walked the length of the manicured grounds of the fine old estate, she turned her gaze on him to inquire, "Why was I brought here, Señor Esteban? I find a man of your stature a most unlikely cohort of the brute who brought me here."

Esteban bristled instantly. "Brute? Did he harm you, señorita?"

"Well, he kidnapped me from my home! I hardly call that an act of a gentleman!"

Esteban breathed a little easier and he admired the spirit in that young, beautiful face as she denounced Antonio's method of keeping what he considered was his . . . his lady. He appreciated her ire and understood it. She was no simple-minded woman, but one with a stubborn will. Exactly the kind of woman to hold and keep Antonio's attention.

"Have you not had gracious treatment since you've arrived her, señorita?" He sought to avoid her direct question.

"I have."

"And so you shall continue to have. I promise you this. I can only tell you that my part in this is an obligation. You will be the final judge about all of it, señorita."

Amanda shook her head, preplexed. "I fear none of it makes any sense to me. Am I being held for ransom?" It was the only possibility she could come up with, since it was a well-known fact that Mark Kane was a very wealthy rancher.

Esteban laughed. "Please forgive me, señorita, but no. Absolutely not . . . it is not for ransom!"

In spite of herself, she could not be irritated by the elderly gentleman's refusal to tell her why she was being kept there and why she had been taken from the Circle K.

The day passed into evening and they dined together and talked. She played the guitar for his enjoyment and they played dominoes until almost midnight. When she finally went up to her room she was pleasantly tired but relaxed.

Another day passed in much the same way. Esteban found Amanda charming and entertaining. Antonio had picked himself the perfect mate, his grandfather decided. For that reason, Señor Moreno wanted this to work out for his grandson.

On the second evening in the old mansion, Esteban urged Amanda to play chess with him. Intending to have some of his favorite brandy as he did each evening, he offered her some. As he did he almost made a slip of the tongue when he commented, "This is also Ant . . . my sister's favorite brandy." As he turned his back to her, he grimaced. He must watch himself, he reprimanded himself silently. But he could now easily see why Antonio had no chance against all this bewitching charm.

"Does your sister live in San Antonio, Señor Esteban?"

Esteban turned to answer her. "No, not now." He quickly changed the subject. Amazingly, he realized, this beautiful girl had no concept of her devastating effect on men. He'd wager on that. However, Esteban could not know what was going on within that pretty head of hers at that very moment.

She used her womanly wiles during the next hour to entice the gentleman to drink more brandy, and she joined him in another glass. If he drank enough, she considered, she could get him to reveal something about this strange state of affairs she found herself in. However, she was soon to realize that it was her head that was whirling and feeling giddy.

It was the gallant Esteban who escorted her upstairs to be sure she didn't tumble down the steps. Even after he'd seen her to her room and said goodnight, sleep didn't come to her. Through all the fog and maze her thoughts were clear enough to accept the fact that she was going to have to be smarter.

More shocking to admit to herself, she realized she'd not sought any way to escape from this place. It was as though she'd accepted her fate—and this was not her nature. The old man had charmed her so that, crazy as it might seem, she had enjoyed the last two days.

Tomorrow, she vowed to check out the huge house, for he'd placed no restrictions on her movements inside. She was being treated more like royalty than a prisoner. From Elvira, she'd learned that the fine gowns she'd been wearing had belonged to Señor Esteban's dead wife.

Something about the señor's face puzzled her. That sly old fox had an amused look when she'd looked up without warning at times, and she wondered just what he was thinking. Oh, how she'd like to pry out the secrets he harbored inside that snow-white head of his.

Tomorrow, she would try her hand at outsmarting him. He was clever and as sharp as a tack, but she could be too. It was time she played a more clever game if she was going to outfox Señor Esteban.

Tony followed Pedro into the cabin with every nerve taut, prepared that he might come face to face with Derek Lawson. Four of the mangy lot sat at the table playing cards. They were a typical mixture of outlaws,

454

all unshaven and wearing clothes unchanged for days. The room was smoke-filled, and coming in out of the fresh, brisk outdoors Tony was aware of the body odor, dirty dishes, and spilled liquor around the room.

Pedro made the introductions and Tony was accepted as they greeted him in an offhand manner. Squeaking noises pulled Tony's eyes to a room off the main one and he saw a man and woman rise up off the bed. Pedro hastily bent down to whisper to Tony that the woman was Luke's whore. "They don't call him loco for nothing, *amigo*. That *puta* is just as crazy. Watch both of them."

Tony didn't allow his eyes to linger in their direction any longer and turned his back on them. It took only two minutes for a dame like that to stir up a fight, and he knew this for sure.

Nita had seen enough to whet her appetite through the doorway. When Luke made a move to leave the bed, she moved over to the edge to get up too. She pulled her drawstring blouse up to cover the exposed voluptuous breasts Luke had been fondling and stood up, giving her broad, fleshy hips a wiggle as she reached up under her skirt to pull the tunic down, making sure she flaunted the deep cleavage of her bosom to tempt the stranger.

While Luke ambled on in to meet the new man, Nita ran her fingers through her long dark hair, pulling it back behind her ears and away from her face. Her tequila-soaked brain told her that she had retained the exotic beauty of her youth. But that had faded long ago. No longer was the skin like soft satin or the eyes bright and twinkling. There had been a time when her sensuous body would have tempted many men who would now find her repulsive. Only the likes of Luke, with the need of a vessel to relieve his physical need, had any use for her body.

Her musky body odor greeted Tony even before he saw her standing there by him. He gave her a half-hearted grin and turned back to make conversation with Pedro.

A hand nudged his arm. Her foul tequila breath floated up to his nose. "Your name, hombre? What is your name? I'm Nita."

Tony gave her a mumble of sorts. "Tony," he told her, and again he quickly let his eyes dart back to Pedro and the big dude named Luke, who looked like a mountain man, so tremendous was he. The smell of tequila was on his breath. Quicker than a whip his arm lashed out and yanked Nita to his side. The slam of her body against his was so hard she grimaced. "Behave yourself, bitch! Your head is hard, I think. Can't you see our new guest ain't the least bit interested in your wares?"

She gave him a hiss like a snake showing no awe for his size or his temper.

FORTY-TWO

The afternoon had moved at a snail's pace. The liquor consumed by the group was having a mixture of effects. A couple of the men were slumped in drunken stupor and the card game had broken up. One left the cabin to go outside. The one named Jack Dawes fidgeted nervously. Tony didn't like the way he kept eyeing him. Pedro had tried to urge Nita to stir up some grub, which she prepared to do reluctantly.

A burly character they called Pecos was getting jumpy and impatient to be on his way back to the Big Bend country where he'd drifted in from several weeks ago. He and Dawes were getting like too sore-tailed cats. Dawes didn't care for the Mexican's snide remark when he asked, "Hey, Dawes, when is this gringo boss of yours going to get here?"

Dawes didn't care for Mexicans to begin with, but at least, Salazar was a quiet one. This Pecos was a loudmouth and a despicable individual. He'd snapped back at him, "He'll he here by nightfall."

When Pedro motioned Tony over to share some of his food, he reluctantly tried some of it. The very appearance of the woman dulled his appetite, but Pedro

457

pointed out that it was the only chance they were going to have until they left this place behind. "Grit your teeth and close your eyes, *amigo*," Pedro laughed, showing those pearly white teeth of his with a broad smile.

Tony gave it a try but it was bland and tasteless. After three bites he shook his head at a grinning Pedro and remembered that he'd had Jose put two filled flasks in his saddlebag of good whiskey. "Be back in a minute." He went out the door.

He stood by the side of Picaro, pulling out the flask when a voice called to him by the name he'd introduced himself. So certain was he that it would be Lawson that he had made the quick decision to call himself Tony Romero.

For a moment, he didn't turn in response to Dawes' beckoning him. "Hey, Romero!"

"Yeah?" Tony turned swiftly with the flask in his hand. Dawes walked up to him. "I've been trying to figure out where we've met."

"Don't think we have. I can't recall any meeting."

"Damn, I got this feeling we have. Fine-looking horse you've got there." He rubbed Picaro's silky mane. "Ever hear of Clay Allison, Romero?"

"Sure . . . hasn't everyone?" Tony got the feeling he was getting ready to make some point, and he didn't have to wait long. As if Jack Dawes was proudly displaying a medal, he boasted cockily, "I rode with him for a while. Anyone ever tell you that you look like him?"

"Can't say anyone has," Tony answered him warily.

"Maybe that's what it is," Dawes said, turning on

458

his booted heels to amble on back to the cabin.

The red-gold skies had turned to a bluish purple as Tony walked back toward the cabin. He was in no hurry to go back inside, as the freshness of the air was a far more pleasing than atmosphere in the shack. The deep purple twilight turned his thoughts to Amanda and made him more anxious to be away from this place. Her eyes were that same shade of deep purple when she was warm with passion, he thought.

He took a hefty swig from the flask. A sound came to his ears that sounded like hoofbeats. His whole being tensed as he listened. It was rather like the anticipation when he was a child at Christmas tearing away the wrappings from a present to see what was inside.

He moved to some thick cover of underbrush as the hoofbeats echoed louder. The realization had hit him hard in the face when Dawes had made a comment about his horse that the minute Lawson rode up he'd recognize Picaro. He should have brought Sultan, he chided himself. There has to be some little flaw to the most carefully laid plans, he thought standing there, listening and watching.

He quickly plotted out in his mind how many were in the cabin and outside. There were those two over in the corner, helpless in their drunken stupor—so they posed no threat. One roamed the woods out here somewhere, and that left Pecos and Dawes in the cabin with the woman.

He wanted his enemy having no advantage by recognizing Picaro on sight. It was a slim possibility that the fast descending darkness would favor him. He stood frozen to the spot, every nerve in his body taut, his silver-gray eyes piercing the distance between the underbrush and the edge of the woods where the rider would emerge.

The nerve in his strong jaw twitched and he clenched his teeth sharply as that unmistakable white Arabian suddenly appeared in the lane. Tony had never waited this long to seek his revenge before, and he churned with voracious pleasure at the thought of giving Lawson his due.

He watched him ride up to the hitching post and dismount. Tony stood silently watching him walk up the two wooden steps to the cabin and enter the door. He was just preparing to move out of his hiding place when he heard a crackling branch echoing behind him. He halted to wait and listen. Nothing could alert the occupants in that cabin now. Tony squatted down in the underbrush cautiously.

He saw the figure almost parallel and the outlaw's cheroot guided Tony's eyes as he went sauntering on toward the cabin. Tony let him move slightly ahead of him before he made his move, his hand tightening its hold on the handle of the razor-sharp knife. It had to be a swift, sure, and soundless kill, or Pedro could be in for trouble.

Like a predatory cat, he moved for a few seconds before making the strong stroke that would plunge the knife into the outlaw's back. Except for one final gasp of life, the man never knew what happened. Like a black panther, Tony had moved up behind him.

Tony's long absence was making Salazar nervous and edgy, especially now that the gringo boss had appeared. He was not at all what Salazar had imagined. He was the image of the upstanding, law-abiding rancher of the countryside. But perhaps there lay the irony of all this.

Pedro noted his disdain as his cold eyes scanned the room and spied him, the woman, and Pecos sitting at the table. The young rancher had no great love for Mexicans, he surmised instantly. His thin lips seemed to snarl until he turned his attention back to Dawes.

"Let's get this business over with . . . quick!" Derek motioned Jack into the back room. While he was bone-tired, Derek had no intentions of lingering overnight in this squalor. He would ride back to the little hamlet he'd passed a few miles back and stay there before riding home to the Big D the next day.

Tony watched outside through the window as Dawes took the stack of bills from his saddlebag and piled them on the rumpled bed. The blood money . . . there it lay!

Tony could not hear what was being said by the two men, but he watched as Dawes was sent to the next room and Derek made use of the time he was absent to greedily tuck the loot into his own saddlebag.

Dawes returned bringing two glasses of liquor, but his expression quickly changed when he looked down on the bed and saw the diminished stack remaining there. Tony grinned, watching the two. That Dawes could be a mean sonofabitch, Tony suspected, and Derek might just have overplayed his hand on this one.

Something told Tony there was no love lost between those two, either. He saw from Derek's manner and his upraised hand that he was trying to quiet the irate Dawes. They sat on the bed together. Four piles of money were placed there. Tony watched as Derek brought forth an additional amount and placed it in Dawes' outstretched hand.

It was done. The payoff was made, and it was all he needed to arrest Derek Lawson. He moved around the shack to join Pedro inside once the two men had risen from the bed and moved toward the door to join the others.

With his gun drawn and ready he turned the corner of the shack and leaped up on the porch to lunge through the door. Knowing Salazar would take his cue, he bolted into the room. "Drop your gun, Jack!" Tony demanded, taking a quick, brief glance to assure himself that Pedro Salazar had Pecos and the woman covered. With all the ease in the world his Mexican cohort sat, grinning across the table at the speechless Pecos and the cussing Nita.

"*Caramba*, what is this?" Pecos questioned.

"I'll tell you what it is, *amigo*. We got two yellowed-bellied bastards here," Jack snarled.

Gunbelts dropped to the floor as Tony and Pedro moved to secure the lot. Tony held them as Pedro moved to shackle the woman and the man, Pecos together. Then he placed handcuffs on both of the two drunks, who mumbled something only to close their eyes again. They were both too dazed with liquor to care.

"There's one bastard missing, *amigo*," Salazar pointed out to Tony. But Tony hastily corrected him. "No, there's two, but I took care of one before coming in. Think you can handle this here? Cause I'm going after the one who got away. That's the one I want the most."

Tony had not counted on Derek's going through the

back door. He'd assumed he'd walk on back into the front room as he'd started to do. Obviously, he had turned back and left through the rear as Tony had rushed through the front door.

"Go after him, Moreno. I can handle it here," Salazar urged, his eyes burrowing in on Dawes.

It couldn't have pleased Jack Dawes more to hear that. While he'd dropped his holster and guns like the rest, he had a tiny concealed Derringer and should the opportunity come, he'd use it. It looked like that moment might be in the offing. With Salazar's formidable friend gone, he'd stand a good chance of making his getaway, he considered. The new hombre had made him nervous since he'd first set eyes on him earlier today.

As if reading Dawes's mind, Tony halted for a split second at the threshold to caution Pedro. "Don't give that bastard an inch, *amigo*. He's the kind who'd take a mile."

Pedro flashed a pearly smile. "Go, amigo. I'll take care of him. You just get the other one, eh?"

Tony rushed out and leaped on Picaro, spurring him into a swift gallop to make up for the ten minutes or so headstart Derek Lawson had on him.

The moon was up and the land lay flat. Tony felt certain Derek would take the trail northward to go directly to Gonzales County. He had been on the trail for a few minutes when he began to question his theory, for he saw no signs of the white Arabian up ahead. The moon shining so brightly across the countryside should have made them show up easily, he reasoned.

He halted Picaro. Could he have figured all wrong?

Disgruntled that he probably had taken the wrong trail, Tony suddenly caught the sight of the white Arabian moving to enter a wooded area toward the river winding beyond. He spurred Picaro into swift action. He could not lose sight of him again or he'd never pick up his trail in those woods.

Once he reined the horse to the edge of the woods, Tony moved more slowly and with more caution. His alert ears could hear the currents of the river below and he decided to stay on the rise and search below. That white animal was going to be his ace in the hole, standing out like a lit torch in the night's darkness.

To push on through the heavy growth of bushes would make too much noise and alert Derek if he was below so Tony dismounted from Picaro and tied him to a sapling.

Luck was with him, for he'd gone only a hundred feet or so before he spotted Derek's horse. There was no sign of Lawson. Tony moved down the slope of ground closer to the pebbled bank of the river wondering where the Arabian's rider was and a couple of times he checked behind him as he came to a halt by an oak tree.

Then he saw the despicable bastard emerging from the woods as he fingered the front of his pants. Obviously, he'd gone to relieve himself. Such boiling hate churned in Tony at the sight of him . . . hate he'd never known before in his whole life.

Tony charged out on the bank with his guns drawn and aimed. His voice was menacing and demanding. "Hold it, Lawson!"

The moonlight focused down on Derek and Tony could see his hand's reaction and he warned, "Don't do it, Lawson!" He took two steps toward Derek, stopping short when Derek broke into an unexpected laugh. "Fancy meeting you like this, Branigan."

"Yeah, real funny, Derek, and long overdue. I take great pleasure in finally settling a long overdue score with you. You think I haven't had your number for a long time?"

Another shrill burst of laughter broke through the night. "It would appear you had a devil of a long time getting around to settling the score. For a hired gun you don't seem to have a hankering to use that gun of yours, Branigan." Derek taunted him.

"Oh, I could have taken you at will, Lawson. There were higher stakes involved. We wanted them all and we've got them now, with you included."

"What the hell you mean by 'we'?" Derek's voice took on a more high-pitched tone and he shifted back and forth from one booted heel to the other. "You talking about old man Kane? I know he wasn't too pleased about me and his precious daughter going to be married."

"That isn't going to happen either, you crazy bastard. I've seen to that."

Derek forgot about the two matched pistols aimed straight at him as he surged forward. "What are you trying to say, Branigan?"

"Stay right where you are, Lawson!" Tony warned him with his finger positioned on the trigger and an itch to pull it. He had the sadistic desire to let Derek know he'd taken back what was his. "I have Amanda. She was never yours, Lawson."

"You . . . you have her?" Derek's voice was shrill, cracking with panic. There was no cool arrogance left

465

and he came at Tony like a wild Comanche, giving a savage scream. Tony waited no longer to restrain the itch of his trigger finger. His moment of revenge was at hand.

The riverbank echoed with the exposion and then a second one. Yet there was a third shot, and it took a minute for the impact and for Tony's reflexes to react as he stumbled back on the sand and pebbles. With an animal instinct he hugged the ground low, trying to ignore the burning, searing pain in his upper thigh and trained his pistol toward the trees where he thought the shot had come from. It wasn't from Lawson's gun. Lawson lay by the river's edge with his face down in the water and the air was filled with acrid smoke as Tony held still, moving not a muscle.

Hunched and almost crawling near the edge of the woods was a figure. Tony knew he had to make good on that first shot or he'd give his position away and the cover of the trees was too far away. His fingertips had felt the warm liquid of his own blood as it made a steady stream down to his knee and foot. He knew it was flowing with gusto.

If the moon came out from behind the cover of clouds he was going to be a prime target on the open space of the bank. Whoever it was over there was playing it cool and cautious, moving at a snail's pace. Tony was getting impatient and the darkness was protecting the stalker.

He was amazed when the tall, lean figure stood up to his full height to move toward the fallen figure of Derek. Tony took aim, pulling all his strength together for the feat and aiming for a vital spot.

He pulled the trigger for the second time and the

stalker fell on top of Derek there by the river. Both were stilled in death and their blood mingled in the waters of the Nueces River.

Tony lay back on the ground with his blood draining out on the sand and he sighed with exhaustion. His hand limply released his pistol as he gave way to weariness.

Salazar had ridden wild as the wind on his roan to catch up with Dawes after he came out of the stunned daze caused by a rap on his skull by Dawes. The shots had directed him to the spot where the three men lay. At first he thought Tony was dead too but, he discovered that his heart was beating regularly and steadily.

He had to get that blood staunched or Tony wouldn't be alive long, Pedro realized. Tying their two kerchiefs together and using a part of a branch, he made a tourniquet of sorts.

Tony roused to see his Mexican friend's pearly smile greeting him. "*Amigo*, you got yourself in a hell of a mess, I think. I got to get you to a doctor. Can you ride if I get you up on the horse?"

"I can ride, but get me home, Pedro."

"But *amigo*, I don't know about that. Maybe we can find a doctor nearer."

Tony stubbornly shook his head and said no. Golden hair and cornflower-blue eyes urgently beckoned to him. He wanted to go home to Amanda.

"You hold on, *amigo*. Pedro will get you home. You can bet on it," Salazar swore to his friend. By heaven or hell, he would!

FORTY-THREE

Pedro Salazar was not afraid of the devil himself and he'd led a reckless, wild life, but as he traveled along the banks of the San Antonio River that late night, he was afraid for his friend. The damned stubborn fool was going to bleed to death on him. The bandage he'd made from his extra shirt in his saddlebag was oozing with the red stains of Tony's blood.

When he knew he was entering the outskirts of the city and the small adobe houses stood closer together, he began to breathe easier. If Tony could just hang on a little while longer he'd be at the Moreno estate and Señor Esteban could send for the family doctor. Salazar felt certain the bullet was still lodged in Tony's thigh from the look of the wound.

By the time they turned down the street where the two story big stone and stucco house was situated, Pedro spurred up his gait and yanked on Picaro's reins. Although the upper part of the house was dark there was some light downstairs. Those lights came from Esteban's study, where he sat, deep in thought about the beautiful young lady he'd just shared such a delightful evening with. He was feeling like a cur after she'd left him.

The last few days he'd come to know her better. Her company had been a joy. She had a genuine warmth. She could be sweet—but not syrupy sweet. Esteban smiled and took a sip of brandy remembering her volcanic explosion of temper when he had stubbornly defied her. Determined to stand staunch about not revealing the truth to her about Antonio, he had witnessed the fire in her, which was wild and savage. He admired that quality, too.

Nevertheless, each day she was becoming harder to deal with because of his genuine liking for the girl. He would play no more games like this one, even for Antonio's sake.

Upstairs in her darkened bedroom, Amanda could not sleep, even though she'd taken off the lovely robin's-egg-blue gown trimmed with black lace she'd been wearing and slipped into a nightgown. She sat on the edge of the bed fingering the beautiful black jeweled comb she'd worn in the back of her hair which Señor Esteban had told her was hers to keep. Staring out the window watching the magestic palm tree branches sway back and forth, she tried to fit the strange pieces of this puzzle together.

There had to be a reason. Logic told her that. Things like this just didn't happen in this day and age. Perhaps in New Orleans, where ships came in and out the harbor, lovely girls were whisked from the city and countryside and carried to strange lands and sold into slavery or to wealthy sheiks, as her Aunt Lisa had once told her. But here in San Antonio or Gonzales County, it just didn't seem possible.

There were moments when she felt like the holiday

469

turkey being fattened up for the kill and the dinnertable. That fine gentleman seemed nice enough, but his dark eyes ogled her with scrutiny when he thought she wasn't looking. He was almost too gracious and too generous. What in hades was it all about? Darn it, there had to be an answer! It was driving her a little crazy. She'd always credited herself with being clever, but this one was beyond her.

She glanced at the ormolu clock ticking away and saw it was almost midnight. But what did it really matter, since she had the privilege to sleep as late as she wished? She listened, thinking she heard a noise outside.

A sudden rushing of heavy footsteps and a mingled chorus of voices invading the night's quiet brought Amanda off the bed and out the door of her room. She rushed to the railing to peer down below to see Señor Esteban talking very animatedly and excitedly to Ignacio and Jose along with a tough-looking man carrying another of the same appearance.

"What in the world . . ." She started to bolt down the stairs, stopping short when she remembered she had on only the very sheer nightgown. So she rushed back to her room to get the silk robe and dashed out of the room. But by the time she tripped hastily down the steps the gathering had dissolved and only the elderly Ignacio was scurrying back to the kitchen.

"What is going on in this place tonight, Ignacio?"

He was getting water heated and took no time to answer her.

"Well? I asked you a question, Ignacio!" She tapped her foot impatiently and placed her hands firmly on her hips. The servant moved around her and went into a small closet to get cloths. Concern for the young señor and anxiety to have everything ready when Jose returned with the doctor made him speak in a way he would never ordinarily dare do. He turned with his dark eyes sparking and snapped, "I have no time now, señorita. It would be best if you just go back to your room."

"Oh! Well, I'll swear I never!" She bounced out of the kitchen realizing the futility of trying to pry anything out of Ignacio.

She ambled around the long hallway, but it was quiet and there wasn't anyone to be found there or in the parlor. She even peeked into the darkened study but found no sign of Señor Esteban.

Giving a shrug of her shoulders and dejectedly sighing, she went up the steps to her room. She certainly intended to have a word with Señor Moreno about all this, she promised herself.

She took off her robe and flung it across the chair. Like a discontent cat she paced the length of the bedroom back and forth. Something was sorely amiss in this house tonight—or was it morning by now? As she reached the length of the room for the fourth or fifth time and started to turn to pace back the other way something pressed her to glance out the window. A figure on a horse rode back down the drive. It looked like it was the same rough-looking man she'd seen about an hour ago down in the hallway carrying the injured one in his arms.

When she made herself lie down on the bed she knew it would be forever before she went to sleep. Her insatiable curiosity would be prodding at her for the longest time. Remaining shadows of the night lingered.

She knew one thing for certain—whoever that injured man was, it gravely concerned Señor Esteban Moreno. He had had a terrible look of pain on his face.

Pedro Salazar knew it too as he took his leave of the Moreno house, but he'd gotten Tony home where he'd wanted so badly to be and the doctor had arrived, so there was nothing left for Pedro to do now. Like Señor Moreno, he'd do some praying. As he made his way to see Flanigan he emptied the last sip of liquor from Tony's flask that he'd forgotten to leave behind. A lot of loose ends remained to be cleared away back there in the distance. Two dead men lay on the bank of the Nueces River and back in that cabin in the woods three men and a woman were shackled. It had not gone exactly the way it was planned, but they had broken up one of the most lucrative cattle-rustling operations in Gonzales County and the surrounding countryside. If all went well with Tony Moreno, they'd celebrate that success when he was up to it.

As soon as he reported all this to Flanigan, Salazar was going to hibernate for at least a week with his beautiful black-eyed señorita, Carmelita.

When Elvira came to her room with a breakfast tray Amanda was taken by surprise and indignantly questioned the Mexican servant. "I was planning on dining downstairs, Elvira!"

"Well, señorita . . . Señor Esteban sends his regrets that he was unable to join you this morning. He suggested that I bring you a tray," Elvira tactfully remarked.

So sly all the occupants of this house had suddenly become, Amanda thought to herself. She accepted the tray after she propped herself up against the pillows putting on a sweet angelic expression and saying nothing. But the wheels of her mind were turning. She would show them all that she was no dummy. She'd eat her breakfast and after she was dressed, she was going to explore this spacious house on her own. It was no ghost she'd seen last night.

When Elvira came back to pick up the tray and she curtly dismissed her, the Mexican woman could not be annoyed with the pretty miss. Amanda sounded like a spoiled child when she inquired, "Then would I be permitted to go to the library, Elvira?"

"Why, of course, señorita," she smiled, her eyes mellow and warm.

"Well, I thought I should ask," Amanda said walking over to the armoire to pull out a very tailored white blouse and a soft, flowing maroon taffeta skirt splattered with tiny white rosebud figures.

It took her a short time to dress and run the brush through her hair. The soft waves fell over her face until she took a long satin ribbon to secure it back behind her ears in a very casual style.

In the next half-hour she checked out each and every room of the upper level before going downstairs. Once she almost collided with Elvira in the hallway and darted hastily into one of the unoccupied bedrooms down the hall from her.

Downstairs, she moved with more care. She could hear Ignacio and Jose talking in the huge kitchen but the parlor and formal dining room were quiet and unoccupied. When she checked the library and the study she found no one in there, either. She concluded when she found that injured man that that was where she'd also find Señor Esteban.

She roamed into areas of the sprawling old house she'd never been in before and there were many little crannies and nooks than she'd imagined. She had to stop short to keep from running into Elvira as she hastily darted from one of the little rooms past the kitchen area to the back of the house.

She gave a deep moan of relief as she leaned against the door. "Mmmmm, that was close." She was not to catch her breath though before she was startled to hear an answering moan. It was then she realized this was a small sleeping room of sorts. Looking across the room she saw on the bed the object of her searching. The injured man had obviously given out the moan and she walked slowly over to the side of the bed.

Such a mass of black hair, all rumpled and matted reached to the tip of his bare tanned shoulders. The blanket rested around his waist and with his back turned toward her she got the full impact of the width of his shoulders and torso from the waist up.

She stood for a minute before reaching out to touch his back with a featherlike touch. It was like touching a hot stove. He was burning with fever. Her cool touch made the man move slightly and she saw his broad chest sprinkled with black curly wisps that matched the hair on his head.

She drew back with a grimace as if the full impact of his bearded face caused her a moment of pain. This man was the one who'd taken her from the Circle K. She stared down at that face for the longest time as if she was in a trance. Strange sensations shot through

474

her and she shook her head, trying to tell herself no.

Was she losing her sanity? Was that devil's spawn casting one of his spells on her? She found herself wanting to linger and keep looking at him. It was as if her slippered feet were frozen to the spot there by the bed. She told herself over and over that this bearded man could not be Tony Branigan. He simply could not be the man who was without rival where her wild reckless heart was concerned. It had to be insane folly and madness.

She watched as his black lashes gave a flutter. They were long for a man's lashes, she noted, when they stilled and rested against the man's tanned skin. She saw that the magnificent male body she beheld didn't seem marred in any way.

Tony's eyes opened but for a brief moment and closed again. Amanda gasped, her hands grabbing at her stomach. "Dear God, it . . . it is him! But how . . ." She found herself sinking to the floor for there was no chair close enough for the support she needed there and then. "Oh, my God . . . Branigan!" she moaned in agony.

Those eyes! They could belong to no other. How those cold silver-gray eyes had haunted her night after night! Try as she might she'd never been able to forget in the rapture of their love how his eyes had made love to her with as much passion as his lips, those hands, and his body.

Tony Branigan and Esteban Moreno! Where was the connecting link? There had to be such a link, and Señor Esteban Moreno was going to tell her, she furiously determined as she struggled up off the floor. Fighting the weakness engulfing her she left the room and marched with firm determination in her step to seek out the señor and demand that he tell her the truth.

As it happened Elvira was sauntering down the hall with her arms piled with fresh linens. "Can you tell me where Señor Moreno is, Elvira?"

"*Sí*, señorita. He strolls in the garden."

"*Gracias*, Elvira." Amanda swished past her to head for the grounds of the estate. She spotted him easily sitting over by the fountain looking as stiff and still as the statues there in his garden. Such a woeful look was etched on that impressive face of his that she felt a moment of compassion for the gentleman who'd been so nice to her. Nevertheless, she intended to register a vehement protest about being kept in the dark any longer. Enough was enough!

"Señor?" She walked on up to him and stood in front of him. Dear Lord, how drawn his face was and ashen. His dark eyes were red-streaked and it was obvious he'd slept little.

"Yes . . . what is it?"

"I want the plain, unvarnished truth, señor. I demand to know just what is going on here? Why I was brought here . . . by that man in there who's hurt? I happen to know that man as Tony Branigan." She stood poised with those deep blue eyes glaring at him with the violence of a turbulent storm.

"Sit down, señorita," he insisted. He felt very old this morning, far too old to do battle with a spirited miss like Amanda Kane. Tony lay in there with a raging fever, so neither could he fight for himself. So he decided upon a plan to keep her here until his grandson was up to holding this young woman he so obviously loved with all his heart.

"So you know this young man, eh?"

"Of course, I do. What he is to you I don't know, but I know him. His name is Tony Branigan and he was my father's hired gun for many weeks at the Circle K Ranch, from where, I might add—this man abducted me to bring me here." She shook her head dejectedly and added, "For the life of me I can't figure a fine, genteel gentleman like you in league with the likes of him!"

Esteban's tired face broke into a wan smile. She was adorable in all her fury. "Dear little Amanda, it is a matter of blood."

"I fail to understand you, Señor Esteban."

He reached over to pat her hand and his dark eyes looked directly into hers as he said. "I cannot tell you the whole story, for you see that is not within my power or my right. This I can tell you, and so I will. The man you call Tony Branigan is my grandson and his name is Antonio Moreno. I can also tell you he is seriously ill and could die. Most important, I know he loves you beyond all reason or common sense. The rest is Antonio's story to tell you himself.

Amanda's head was swimming and now it was her face that was ashen and pale. She tried to listen to the señor's next words but she felt like she was walking through a thick, foggy maze. "I will not hold you here any longer if it is your wish to return to your home. In fact, I will send my carriage and you to the Circle K Ranch this afternoon. I might add, though, I would desire you stay. I've become very close to you, Amanda. I could use your strength at this time. You are a lady I've come to admire a lot, señorita. You have a

477

strength I feel rather drained of this morning." Mist teased at his eyes and Amanda put her arm around his shoulders. A feeling of compassion consumed her.

"I will stay a day or two more, Señor Esteban," Amanda told him, reaching over to plant a kiss on his cheek. More than ever Esteban knew why Antonio loved this golden-haired girl so devotedly. He, Esteban, loved her too!

He merely gave her an understanding nod of his snow-white head coupled with a grateful smile. They sat for a long time there in the garden, holding hands without a need to talk. Their silence was their bond of understanding.

FORTY-FOUR

A dark shroud of gloom hung heavy over the Moreno household. It was reflected even in the servants' faces and Amanda wondered whether it was concern over the man she now knew was Antonio Moreno or the elder señor's well-being. He was spending virtually all his time by his grandson's bedside.

When the young Dr. Martinez came by to check in on his patient that evening, he saw immediately what Esteban's long vigil was doing to him and turned to Amanda to say, "Señorita, I'm going to ask for your help in seeing that my orders are carried out. Señor Moreno, you must go to bed tonight and get a good night's rest."

Amanda spoke up, letting her eyes admonish Esteban. "He will, Dr. Martinez, and I will sit with Tony. I promise you this even if I have to drug him."

Dr. Martinez was the son of Esteban's old friend, and to hear the young lady being so bossy with Señor Moreno, whom he'd known all his life, amused him, and pleased him, as well. He'd have to tell his father about this later when he dined with him that evening.

"The next two days could be rough ones for Antonio," he told them. The wound was deep, since the bullet had deflected when it hit bone, he told them. The high fever was due to infection. "Antonio is as strong as a bull, señor, and that is in his favor. It is true his condition is unstable right now, but we'll just keep doing what we're doing. Keep his body cooled, señorita, with damp clothes, and try to get as much liquid down him as possible. Pay no heed to the talk he's doing. It is delirium caused by the high fever. He could even hallucinate, but don't get unduly concerned."

Having informed them about what they could expect and promised them to check in on Tony again the first thing in the morning, the doctor bid them good evening and left.

Playing mother hen to Esteban, Amanda insisted they were going into the dining room to eat the hearty dinner Elvira had prepared, and then Esteban was going to retire to his room to rest. "I shall relieve Ignacio for the next few hours and then Jose can take a turn. You, my dear Señor Moreno, are going to rest for eight hours."

As they dined Esteban suddenly realized how easily she'd taken on the role of mistress and he'd allowed it. Well, why not? It seemed rather nice to envision her in that role and looking across the table now at her sitting there in the candlelight he thought she made a breathtakingly beautiful hostess at his table.

In the next few hours, Amanda witnessed all the symptoms the doctor had described. Once she thought she was going to have to call for help as Tony lunged up with an inhuman strength, raving and ranting out of his head. His body seemed so hot pressed against her as she held him down. He'd quieted just as suddenly but the foul odor of the fever seemed to linger there on the front of her bodice where he'd touched her.

She took the cool cloths and laid one on his forehead and took another to lay across the front of his chest. They seemed to soothe him, because he gave a soft moan.

She pulled back the sheet covering his long naked body. She knew so well that marvelous male body, and nothing marred the perfection. She placed another damp cloth across his lower torso with care not to disturb the fresh bandaging the doctor had just put on his upper thigh.

Feeling extremely weary after the wrestling match a moment ago, she sat down to stare out the window. Even seriously ill and lying there so still, he was more man than any she'd ever known, she thought to herself. Whatever he called himself . . . be it Tony Branigan or Antonio Moreno . . . he'd left her without so much as a goodbye, and that hardly seemed to her like a man in love. She didn't care what Esteban said. Not one tiny letter had he taken the time to write.

If she owed Tony Moreno nothing, she felt she owed Esteban a few hours of rest. She leaned her head back and closed her eyes. While the damp cloths quieted and eased the heat of Tony's body, she rested and drowsed.

How long she slept she didn't know but it was the calling of her name that roused her. It took a moment for her to grasp that it was Tony mumbling her name over and over. His deep voice sounded just as it had in the heat of their passion as he murmured, "Amanda *mia.* Oh, Amanda, I want you."

She was suddenly overcome hearing him in his fevered state calling out to her and tears slowly crept down her cheeks. "Oh, damn you, Tony! Damn you! Don't you know how you hurt me so?" she moaned in her own agony and pain.

She knew he didn't hear her for his body was as hot as a branding iron again. She went through the ritual of wetting the cloths and applying them back on the same parts of his body. She lifted up his head and held a glass of water to his lips long enough for a drop or two to enter his mouth. Still holding his head, she took her other hand away to push back an unruly wave away from his forehead. Again, she put the glass to his dry mouth and managed to get about a spoonful of water down him without gagging or choking him. When she released his head back onto the pillow, she dampened the last cloth to place it on his head. He started to mumble again with disjointed words but suddenly Amanda put them together and understood the puzzle of her having been brought here to his grandfather's home.

She could hear the grinding of his teeth as he spoke with venom and hate. "Can't let . . . no, that bastard will not have her. Amanda . . . mine. Derek . . . madman . . . crazy. Safe with Grandfather."

She mellowed with love then for the man lying there, and she could not fool herself anymore as to why she'd stayed. As it had been since their eyes had first met, a strange magic pulled her to him. A force so strong she was powerless to resist him. Yes, damn it . . . she loved him as she would never love any other man, but that didn't solve her dilemma about being pregnant. Did he wish to marry her? He had never offered that nor would she want him to just because of the child. After all, she had pride.

A man considered his mistress his, but that didn't mean he wanted to marry her. That was all Tony Branigan had ever said to her, she recalled, sitting there looking at him there in the bed. Oh, yes, he'd said he wanted her, or that she was his and no one else's. He might have called her beautiful or lovely but that's not a man saying he wants you as his wife, she told herself. He'd not promised to love her forever and ever.

Ignacio came to the room, insisting that Jose could take over for the next few hours. "You are tired, señorita. Now, please . . . come along."

She gave him a nod of her head, turning back to see that Tony seemed to be resting well. Ignacio watched as she moved down the hallway slowly, only confirming his opinion that she was worn and weary.

Ignacio checked the young man, taking note of the drapes of wet cloths she'd applied. No false modesty had kept her from seeing to Antonio's needs. He admired that in the young lady. It appeared from the missing water of the pitcher that she'd persistently urged the liquid down her patient. A rare jewel in one so young.

It was three in the morning when Amanda went to her room and she slept deep and long. Señor Moreno gave orders to Elvira not to disturb her regardless of the hour. "When she's had all the rest she needs, she will wake up," he declared. Even when the noonday passed and midafternoon came, Amanda still slept.

She knew nothing of the changes going on within

483

the walls of the old mansion. While Tony's fever was still with him, the doctor had agreed with Esteban that he could be moved to his bedroom where it was more comfortable and certainly more pleasant than the small cubicle he'd been quartered in since the night he had been placed on the narrow bed bleeding like a stuck hog.

All this was accomplished while Amanda slept. The faces of all around the house had taken on a cheerier, brighter look. The young señor was much better.

Amanda finally woke up, amazed when the smiling Elvira told her how long she'd slept and announced the encouraging news about Señor Antonio's improved condition. "Señor Esteban requests you join him for dinner."

Later, as she sat across the table from Esteban, she was pleased to see that he looked a little better. Esteban extended her his thanks for helping him tend to Tony. "Your touch must have helped. I swear it seemed Antonio made an improvement during the night while I slept. I do thank you, Amanda." He seemed unaware that he had dropped his formal air of addressing her and now it was just Amanda when he spoke to her.

"I heard from Elvira that they've moved him upstairs. Is he taking nourishment now?"

"Not much . . . just sleeping, mainly. But the fever is much less." Esteban told her. He had done the right thing by urging her to stay on a few days. She cared for his grandson, he knew that now, whatever their differences were—and with such people as his Antonio and the lovely Amanda, he could imagine some very explosive scenes. He knew his grandson to be a hot-blooded oung man, and she was a woman of fire and passion. Once Antonio was himself Esteban had confidence he could take over the reins of this situation.

"We will let him sleep tonight, eh?" Esteban suggested. Amanda agreed that rest was the best tonic for him.

Once she retired back to her room after the dinner and a spell of conversation with Señor Moreno, Esteban stole silently up the steps to look in on Tony before he retired. When he leaned over to lay his hand on Tony's head, he found it cool. His grandfather's touch made him open his eyes. "Grandfather?"

The elderly man felt the tremendous weight of the past few days hastily lifted and he leaned down to kiss his grandson's cheek. "Oh, Antonio! Antonio! Those words sound so good coming from you. I didn't know if they ever would." He cared not that tears were visible in his eyes. His prayers had been answered and he needed no doctor to tell him that Antonio was going to be just fine.

"It was that bad, eh?" Tony asked with a flippant, lighthearted air that pleased Esteban even more.

"Si, my son it was that bad. You are going to be fine now."

Tony declared himself famished and erased any remaining doubts Señor Moreno could possibly have had. He went at once to order Ignacio to prepare some broth and tea, which Tony gobbled down like a starved wolf. He insisted on something more substantial and tastier, but Esteban promised that for breakfast.

"We must talk, my son. Something very important to you, I think. Now that you are yourself back in this world, I want you to have the strength you might need when you face the little lady."

"Amanda?"

"Amanda. She is still here, but I offered her the chance to return home after you arrived wounded."

"You what, Grandfather?"

Esteban quickly raised a protesting hand. "She didn't go. She is here . . . right down the hall, Antonio. But I'm going to keep her away from you for another day, until you are stronger. She's a prideful miss, Antonio, and stubborn as the burro. You aren't going to have her falling into your arms after all that's happened."

Tony gave out his first broad smile. "I see you've come to know a little bit about my beautiful Amanda."

"*Si*, I have and I like what I see, but I also see a woman too proud to humble herself even to the man she loves."

"She does love me, Grandfather. She could fight me the rest of her life, but she does love me."

Esteban reached over and patted Tony's arm. "I think so too, and I'll tell you something else, Antonio, I think she has that lovely glow of a woman expecting a baby . . . your baby, Antonio?"

An amazing surge of strength shot through Tony and he reared up to a sitting position. "A baby? Amanda?" It was very possible. He smiled, remembering.

Esteban gave a soft chuckle. "I'm certain, knowing you, the possibility exists. Yes, Antonio, I think the young lady is expecting."

Tony became a stammering idiot and the amused Esteban decided he must give him some sage advice

"It is my opinion you should ask her to marry you fast and most certainly before she confesses this to you. She must not know that you know she's expecting when you ask her to marry you. Her pride would not allow that. You see what I mean?"

It was Tony's turn to pat his grandfather's arm. "What would I do without your priceless wisdom, you sly old fox?"

The two said goodnight, with their plans firmly laid out for the next day. Tony would play the invalid a little longer. But the truth was the broth had given him some energy and the broken fever had unclouded his mind. He tried, once alone, to sit on the side of the bed before rising up to stand for a minute on the carpeted floor.

As it was plotted between Esteban and Tony, Amanda had to be kept from his bedside. With the utmost discretion and clever maneuvering by Esteban at keeping Amanda entertained and occupied, Tony indulged himself in the trays of food being brought to his room. For the first time in days, Tony sat on a stool, and with Jose's help enjoyed bathing himself for a change. He dressed himself in a pair of silk pajamas, feeling that he'd finally returned to the man he preferred to be . . . Tony Moreno. The role of Tony Branigan was no more, and only one good thing had come out of it all. He'd met Amanda Kane. It was an even score now with U.S. Marshal Flanigan.

He felt as if this day he was starting a new life, free to pursue the dream he'd had since childhood—running his ranch outside San Antonio and raising his fine Thoroughbred horses that would be sold and prized all over the world. He'd never been a man to dwell in fantasy, nor had he ever envisioned himself a father. He was amazingly pleased at the prospect. He surprised himself also that it wouldn't have to be a son to please him. A little golden-haired angel would be as treasured as a fine, husky son.

With all this on his mind, he summoned Jose and wrote a message to Father Tomas. He told Jose to leave pronto!

When Esteban and Amanda returned to the house from an afternoon jaunt in his buggy, the elderly gentleman found the need for a nap and excused himself. The day of conspiracy between him and Antonio had been hard on his nervous system, he concluded. There was a time when the intrigue of it all would have exhilarated him, but age seemed to be forcing him toward a more peaceful pastimes. Well, so be it!

On the stairway, Amanda met Elvira coming down the steps. "How is the señor, Elvira?"

"He sleeps so peacefully, señorita," Elvira was quick to inform her.

"I see." She tried not to let Elvira see her disappointment, for it had been her intention to peek in on him. Instead, she went on to her room to refresh herself after the ride around the city. The city could use a rain, for the dust had swirled as the wheels of the buggy had rolled along. It had been obvious that the springtime was coming from the verdant hues everywhere they drove.

It was blessed comfort to rid herself of the snugfitting gown and lie across the bed for a while in her undergarments. She knew already which of the gowns she was going to wear down to dinner. It would be the lavender one, from which she'd remove a rather large tuck in the bodice.

Later when she stood before the full-length mirror to observe herself there was no denying the flatness of her belly was gone and there was, indeed, a rounding there. Damned if I'll tell you though, Tony Branigan or Tony Moreno, she silently mused. Having to humble herself so would be more than she could endure. To trick Derek Lawson was another matter.

Perhaps Tony wasn't the gentleman his grandfather was. Perhaps he wasn't a marrying man. She turned from the mirror, giving a shrug of her shoulders and consoling herself that there was still a little time before her condition would be obvious to all.

Esteban had refreshed and rested himself before the dinner hour and she was such a glorious sight sitting there in the cnadlelight across the table from him that he found it hard to play his role of the weary old man. Play it, he did though, and so well that Amanda played right into his hands.

"You retire early, Señor Moreno and I'll go up and sit with Tony for a while."

Esteban was generous with the fine Madeira wine during the evening. Amanda's guilelessness never suspected the dignified gentleman's motives. Actually, it was only after she'd slipped through the door of Tony's bedroom and taken a seat in the overstuffed chair by his bed that the impact of the wine hit her. Giddiness washed over her so that she slipped out of the chair and sought the empty space Tony wasn't using there on the massive bed.

Dear Lord, the softness felt so good that she let herself give way to the sinking feeling. It still had not dawned on her how many times Esteban had poured

489

wine from the crystal decanter sitting there on the table.

Silvery moonbeams streamed through the windows of the room. Tony had not drawn the drapes before he'd lain back down on the bed after one of his several jaunts around his room during the afternoon hours. Each time he'd paced around the room it seemed his muscled legs were a little stronger, and the rubbery, jellylike feeling was less noticeable. He'd welcomed the less bulky bandaging Doctor Martinez had put on his thigh when he'd changed the dressing that morning.

With his walking cane he would have attempted going downstairs with no hesitation, but that could mess up his scheme. His meals had been solid, hefty food, and he'd smoked his cheroots. Indulging himself with the luxury of his favorite Napoleon Brandy, life had taken on a brighter glow.

He had not really intended to nap, but it had just happened as he'd sat on the bed reading. Something made him rouse and at first he just lay there until he knew what it was wafting to his nose. Suddenly he realized who that sweet, intoxicating fragrance belonged to, and he turned from his side to lie on his back. When he touched the softness of her body and knew she was there on the bed beside him in sweet repose, there was an instant response in his body. There was nothing ailing him too much now, he gratefully realized.

He raised himself up on one elbow so he could get the full impact of her glorious golden hair fanned out there on the pillow and those long lashes curled slightly resting against her cheek. Her gown was

490

tucked in such a way as to show off the roundness of her belly, and he swelled with love for her and their unborn child resting within her. God, he yearned to place his hand there in a gesture of tenderness to express his love of it. Esteban had definitely been right, for Tony clearly remembered the flatness of her petite figure.

Leisurely, he examined every divine curve and endured the tantalizing torment of her overflowing, full breasts exposed in the low-cut gown as she lay on her side.

"Amanda *mia. Mi vida,*" he murmured softly as he bent to take her half-parted lips in a kiss, for he could not resist the sweet nectar of her any longer. His strong arms encased her like a vise, for he was determined to subdue her if she tried to resist him, which he anticipated she would do.

Those amethyst eyes opened wide, flashing with that wonderful fire and fury as he held her to his bare chest.

She could not move nor could she scream, but she kicked and fought like a wildcat with her legs and arms. Trying to protect his injured thigh, Tony flung his good leg over her hips and his huge hands took her flying hands and held them upward as he pressed himself over the front of her.

"No, *querida.* Don't fight me . . . not anymore. I love you. I've always loved you and wanted you for my wife," he murmured in her ear, remembering his grandfather's advice. But she still fought furiously. His romantic assault had come with such unexpected suddenness that she was reminded of one Tony Branigan who took what he wanted. He would not do that

491

again. She'd paid her price for hurt and pain.

"No, Tony Branigan or Tony Moreno! No, I'm no a toy you take out to play with like a little boy with hi yoyo. No, damn you!"

Her leg brushed against his wound just enough t make him gasp with pain. "Damn little hellcat! Sto it and shut up! I love you! Hear me! I love you."

His lips covered hers, daring her to try to speak o protest. His hand moved from her arm to caress th jutting breast pressed against his bare chest. *"Que rida, quiero hacer el amor contigo."*

She knew not what he said but his deep voic pleaded with such warmth and passion that her body didn't wait for her voice to answer. He felt her plian body yielding with the same yearning as his and h gave a soft chuckle. "Ah, Amanda *mia,* you do wan me to make love to you. Has it not always been so?"

It was useless to fight it. Amanda knew this. Thi man had branded her deeply and so completely long ago. "Yes, Tony, you unscrupulous devil! It has al ways been so." Her arms snaked up around his neck.

He felt the sweet undulating body beneath him and delighted that the same creeping wildfire spreading over him flamed and burned in her.

But as they fused together, Amanda froze suddenly. "Tony, maybe we shouldn't . . . your wound?" He quickly quieted her fears with an eager husky declaration. "I'm burning with fever, *querida,* and only you can put this fire out."

Amanda knew that to deny him would be denying herself and she wanted him so much every fiber in her being cried out for his love. This madness between them was like a Texas wildfire spreading and burning and only he, Tony, could put it out.

Her half-parted lips beckoned him to take them, and her flushed body pressed against his, demanding to be satisfied. Her hands encircled his neck, her fingers playing lovingly with his hair.

"It's been so long, Tony. Show me . . . make me your woman again," she purred softly in his ear.

"With pleasure, *chiquita*. With the greatest of pleasure!" He cupped her fuller breast in his hand and bent down to kiss it. His other hand trailed gently over her rounded belly where their child nestled and the very thought made him swell with love for her. Now was the moment he must carry out Esteban's sage suggestion. He must erase any doubts or pride she was harboring.

Burrowed between her thighs, he raised up slightly to gaze upon her impassioned face. The love was there to see in her eyes and his gray eyes let her see the depth of his adoring love for her when he vowed, *"Mi vida, Amanda mia!* More than my woman, Amanda *mia.* My wife!"* He kissed her letting his lips linger. Then he added, "A baby . . . a child, Amanda, of this great love we know! I want that so much. Say you want my baby."

"Oh, yes Tony! I want your baby!" She pressed against him, for now he'd spoken the words she wanted to hear him say. He thrust open the floodgates, all powerful and forceful. She moved with him in that river of rapture, whirling with wild, savage currents. They were one, body and soul!

Tony was a greedy lover and his masterful lovemaking made Amanda greedy too. He left no part of her silken flesh untouched as their torrid tempo built and

493

mounted that lofty summit to the heavens above where only true lovers ascend and linger. The treasure found there is beyond words, but lovers know it. Amanda and Tony reached that glorious height and lingered there for some precious golden moments.

Her lilting laughter and her soft moan of pleasure was all the eavesdropping Esteban had to hear outside the bedroom door to urge him to move on down the dark hallway. A broad smile gleamed on his face. It had all worked out the way he'd so cleverly planned and prayed it would. Sleep was sweet that night for Señor Esteban Moreno.

Long after they'd drifted back down from that special peak of paradise, Tony still held her close in his arms kissing her moist cheek with soft tender kisses. When he thought about how close he'd come to losing her to Derek Lawson he pressed her closer to his chest, for she seemed all the more precious to him. Tomorrow he would tell her about everything that had happened, but not tonight. This night was theirs and theirs alone.

Feeling her body so close to him and feeling the flush of the passion from their torrid lovemaking still with her, he was fired anew. He wanted to taste the sweet nectar again, for he still hungered.

He nuzzled her ear. *"Quiero hacer el amor contigo."*

The tenderness in his voice was all she had to hear to answer him. "Yes, *querido*. Yes!" The flames of his fire were already rekindling her desire. She, too, hungered!

For one fleeting moment she noticed the millions of twinkling stars firing so bright in the Texas sky. She remembered the night she had cried out to them asking why she couldn't sweep this man out of her life. Now, she knew why it was impossible. It had been written in the heavens long ago that she belonged to Tony Moreno forever and ever!